The Infernal Riddle of Thomas Peach

Jas Treadwell

HODDER &
STOUGHTON

First published in Great Britain in 2021 by Hodder & Stoughton
An Hachette UK company

1

A CIP catalogue record for this title is available from the British Library

Hardback ISBN 978 1 529 34732 6
Trade Paperback ISBN 978 1 529 34733 3
eBook ISBN 978 1 529 34734 0

Typeset in Sabon MT by Hewer Text UK Ltd, Edinburgh
Printed and bound in Great Britain by Clays Ltd, Elcograf S.p.A.

Hodder & Stoughton policy is to use papers that are natural, renewable
and recyclable products and made from wood grown in sustainable
forests. The logging and manufacturing processes are expected to
conform to the environmental regulations of the country of origin.

Hodder & Stoughton Ltd
Carmelite House
50 Victoria Embankment
London EC4Y 0DZ

www.hodder.co.uk

THE INFERNAL RIDDLE *of*

THOMAS
PEACH,

Gentleman, of C___ton B___, Somerset-shire;

With an *authentic account* of certain

NOTORIOUS
EVENTS

occurring in that county

anno *Domini* 1785

Containing also some *metaphysical* discoveries,
of a very remarkable nature

CHAPTER ONE

READER! — Good-day to you!

And good-morrow, too! for our acquaintance is destined to be long. We are sure of it. We see it in your eye — There is something about it, which bespeaks a mind out of the common sort. The gleam of curiosity — A philosophic cast —

We flatter ourselves, we are never mistaken in these matters.

It is curious – significant, we think — That you join us in contemplating that most interesting of objects, to all whose habits of thought run in deep secret courses, unfathomed by the busy majority of our fellow-mortals — a TOMB.

Will you step but a little further into the church-yard? — We have a stone to shew you, which will repay your attention. —

You do not hesitate. We have not erred in our estimate of you. — You are one of those who understand, by rare instinct, that no quarter-hour is better spent, than in such a place. — Among the tranquil society of the dead.

For what truly meditative soul can fail to wonder at the multitude of histories here closed and laid to rest? — and reflect, like Shakespear's melancholy jesting prince, that all our wit and ambition — all the griefs which afflict, and the joys which delight us — the fretting circumstance and earnest design, between which we steer the tempestuous course of our being — All this, is at last to be sealed in a plot of earth a stride across. — Left with not a word to say for itself, beyond *Here lies* — a name — and perhaps a pious encomium, scarce different from the lines scratched out on our neighbour stones, which time and slow ruin have already begun to cancel?

We begin, you see, as we mean to continue, in *fine stile*. — Be assured, this is no common tale.

We are heartily glad our paths have coincided here, at the gate of St. _____ in the town of ____-upon-Thames, where that famous river escapes the mud and mire of the city, and turns its silver back on all that lies below. What business has hurried you out of London, or what reluctance detains you in this charming spot, we do not presume to speculate. Only permit us — A step or two this way, if you please —

Here — Observe this memorial, modest, yet dignified — Erected to the memory of one THO.S PEACH.

Consider it well! for we will venture, that your boots have never pressed the earth of a soil more pregnant with remarkable secrets, nor your eye passed as lightly over a name more deserving of its attention.

Perchance, in your years of adventure, you once conveyed yourself to the remotest island of the world, there to contemplate those handfuls of earth where *Buonaparte* lies at rest, though he once made toys of kingdoms. Or, perhaps, you have stood at the grave of Alexander — we know not, we confess, precisely where it lies — Or of any great potentate, whose word once brought down the walls of cities. What is there to detain you in the name of *Tho.s Peach*? A man, you may think, who lived, and died; merely one among his fellows in the church-yard, come to dust.

Yet if that dust could speak! —

Why, that is our endeavour, in a nut-shell.

In the antient days of these islands, the druidic priests would gather in circles of stone, to commune with the souls of their ancestors, and receive from them prophetic wisdom. We are no oracle; nor do we pretend ourselves apprentice to any magic, save that common to all who dip their pen into the well from which a *Milton* or a *Landon* conjured marvels the whole world must wonder at, until the day it ends in fire and darkness — We mean, *the English tongue.* — Yet we intend nevertheless, to RAISE THE DEAD.

Come forth from this your place of rest, *Thomas Peach*! — Walk and breathe again! — for one has come, who has in their eye that particular mark, by which we know them worthy to hear your tale!

Our summons is heard. —

Courteous reader — You shall not regret our encounter. This we declare, in the most sober truth; that no druidical prophecy ever struck its half-savage hearers with greater amazement, than this history of ours must impress upon all who attend to it; even in these modern days, when marvels arrive at our imperial shore on every rising tide, and miracles are monthly reported in the proceeding of the learned societies.

Without further preamble, then! we transport you to the year seventeen eighty-five, when *Buonaparte* terrified only his play-mates, and the comet of *Landon*'s poetic genius had not yet entered the earthly sphere. — And, to the county of Somerset-shire — whose steep-sided hills were then but newly cut by the canals, and whose burgeoning port* thrived on the whip-scarred back and manacled limb of a licensed traffic in human flesh!

In that time and place we shall find our hero. — Tho.s Peach, Esq.

To all eyes but ours, he appears an unremarkable man. He is no longer in the prime of his strength, nor yet quite entered upon his middle years; he is perhaps five-and-thirty. He could not tell you the precise day of his birth, being of somewhat uncertain parentage. In the matter of the location he is more determinate, yet his answer leaves so much unsaid, as to be almost no answer at all.

— I was born, madam, at London.

— London! A great many are born there, I suppose.

— I suppose so.

---

* We see by your look that you are perhaps unacquainted with the county. Let us speak without epithet: we allude to *Bristol*, in those days among the first cities of the kingdom, after the monstrous and all-consuming capital.

If you yourself, reader, were the lady interrogatrix in this exchange, and possessed of sufficient curiosity to press your enquiry, despite the evident diffidence of the gentleman, you would doubtless proceed to ask, *which parish* of the city had the honour of his baptism. But we must inform you, that Mr Peach resides in an unfashionable old house, with but a single parlour, which stands alone on the side of one of the low steep valleys in which the present corner of Somerset-shire abounds, a morning's ride from the nearest town worthy of the name. From this you may gather, that his neighbours are what we may call good honest country folk. — To whom the name of *London*, signifies a single chimaerical monster, one part king and lords and commons, another part — dressed in silks and calicoes — incomprehensible fashions, and a third — the hind-quarters, we suppose — rotten with every kind of vice, and wallowing in the skirts of Mother Gin; and the whole no more to be imagined as an assemblage of distinct boroughs and parishes, than Pandemonium itself.

— You have preferred the country for the air, I suppose?

— The air is indeed very pleasant hereabouts.

— They say there is nothing like it for the constitution. We have the waters at Bath, too, you know. All the quality are to be found there.

— Those waters have been famed since the time of Julius Caesar.

— La, sir! — you are an educated man, I see.

Mr Peach only inclines a little, and shakes his head even less, as though at once to acknowledge, and throw off, the compliment — Leaving poor madam little the wiser.

— A London man, and educated! I wonder you haven't mistaken your way, sir. For you know, we have already a parson. Aha, ha, ha.

— If I have strayed, madam, then it was a fortunate error, to have led me to so charming a spot.

From which you may further deduce, that Mr Peach is adept in evading the curiosity of those, among whom he has, for no reason they are able to extract from him, come to live.

Indeed, there is much about Mr Peach that baffles enquiry.

It is plain enough that he is *a gentleman*. But to which species of gentleman he belongs, is as mysterious as the headwaters of the Nile. Is he a *sporting* gentleman? — He has sat several hands at loo together, and swung a willow among the less drunken sort of cricketers, though Farmer Bowler, who is the first *bat* among the neighbouring villages, finds him excessively watchful, and less lusty in his application than befits a man of spirit. The younger Miss Furzedown swears, she once saw three partridges hanging by their necks outside his door. — But — which settles the matter — He does not ride at hounds.

Well, then! — is he an *enthusiastic* gentleman?

Such was the general opinion on his first arrival in the country, prompted by his plain neat habits, and the curious air of solemnity which attends him, as though he has been transplanted to the woods and fields, from some antique temple of dust and hiero-glyphs. He is often to be encountered walking in the roads, unac-companied, with the exact gait and pace of one who walks for the sake of it, and not — as good stout fellows ought — for the purpose of conveying themselves from one spot to another. In those days, a man of sober dress and serious mien, found strolling at all hours in the open air, might very well be suspected of Methodistical leanings. Within a month of Mr Peach's appearance it was universally agreed, that his perambulations had no design beyond searching for a field to set up a-preaching in, and he would soon be tormenting the farmers and yeomen with sermons.

— I'll *sermon* him, says Farmer Townsman, turning a cudgel in his one hand, while the other holds fast to a pot of cider. It is Farmer Townsman's immovable faith that the agents of corrup-tion are ever ready to steal the pot of cider from his rightful grasp, should his vigilance waver for an instant; the excise men, or the scientific improvers, or, in his darkest dreams, the French.

— If he sermonize a word in my hearing, I'll *sermon* him, sir, and I'll sermon him back where he came from, be he never *sir* or *man*, and d___n me if I don't.

5

But the general opinion proves itself mistaken. — At the discovery of which error, it forgets itself, and pretends never to have thought any thing of the kind. For in all his ramblings, Mr Peach is not heard to trouble his neighbours, nor his neighbours' neighbours, with more than a polite *Good-morrow*, and perhaps an unexceptionable remark on the pleasing spectacle of their kitchen-garden, or the prospects of wet weather.

Is he, then, a *gentleman of trade*?

If so, it must be such a business as can be conducted invisibly. Papers come and go, it is true. Dick the inn-keeper's lad brings parcels wrapped in foolscap, and inked on the outsides, which smell to him of learning. Mr Peach sends him back on his mule with a penny for his trouble, and as often as not with letters for the stage-coach, though for the stile or smell of these he cares not a whit, having new coin of the realm to engage his interest in their place. Such exchanges of letters, perhaps hint at a species of commerce — But, even in this nook of Somerset-shire, bounded to the west by the sea, and to the north by the estuary, devoted time out of mind to the breeding of sheep and the gathering of wool — Even here, the means and manners of trade are not altogether unknown. For the increase and general circulation of trade — we need hardly remind you — has been the most remarkable, the most universal, the most irreversible change in the constitution of the nation, these past three score years and ten. Thus our good honest country folk, though they toil at the scythe and the spinning-wheel, know so much at least, that trade is sharp-eyed and nosy — keen, and interfering — Ever talking itself up, and worming its way about. Mr Carter the button-maker must always be prating of the price of shell, and the iniquity of cheese-paring tailors. Mr Smith the wainwright goes knocking at every door, offering his repairs, and never waits to be asked. — Yet here is Mr Peach, busy with nothing of the sort. He is never known to *button-hole* a man; he keeps himself to himself; and is, by every outward mark, a quiet solitary fellow.

Is he a gentleman of *fashion*? To this enquiry a word will suffice — He is not.

Is he a gentleman scholar? But what is a gentleman scholar, if not another name for a man of the cloth? — and Mr Peach is never seen at church.

Is he, then, a gentleman *free-thinker*? Such men, as all the world knows, are troublemakers, seducers of dairy-maids, and engines of every sort of wickedness. Yet though there are many, who wish Mr Peach were a more convivial fellow — And a few, who cannot be persuaded otherwise, than that a man of whom so little can be determined, must be *up to no good* — Nevertheless, at the time our history begins, when Mr Peach has been in the country for nigh two years, it is conceded every-where that he is an harmless sort of gentleman — Whatever other sort he may be.

It is sometimes murmured, that a man so mysterious, must be endowed with secrets. — That his obscure habits, indicate one who does not wish to be discovered. — In short, that he is a man, *with a past.* — But what that past may hide, is a matter of mere conjecture. Mr Peach appears to have no connexions — no prior acquaintance — no history, of any sort.

Who are his people? No one can say. — You, reader, will presently find yourself at an advantage in this matter. Be so good as to endure your share of the general ignorance a page or two longer, for, you understand, we prepare our portrait as might a *Reynolds* or a *Romilly*, drawing our hero in mere outline, without distinct face or form — So that you may wonder, as the country people do, WHO IS THOMAS PEACH? — Are the Peaches some body, or no body? Do they — as the rustic wits have it — grow on every tree? Or are they only to be found in well-tended soil, in the warm confines of a garden? None can recall hearing the name abroad, except two or three who have taken their wives and daughters to town to see the play. — They themselves can tell you nothing of it, for they fell asleep at the raising of the curtain, and were woken only by the concluding marks of approbation or displeasure. — But they recall the womenfolk, all their way home, sighing at the adventures of poor pretty Polly PEACHUM.*

Is he a Church and King man? The parson has sat at cards with him, but cannot vouch for it, though he won't say a word against the fellow neither. — Parson Taverner is not known to be much exercised over matters of religion.

Is he for the ministers, or against them? Is he 'in' or 'out'? He will drink the king's health beside the next man, when loyal cups are raised — But, as he says, who would not? — for he wishes ill-health to no creature alive.

— Why, d___n me, sir, not even a Frenchman?

— I am sure the people of that country suffer the pains of tooth-ache and ague as miserably as we.

— A Frenchman? A d___d, popish, foppish, poxy Frenchman?

— Poor fellow, says Mr Peach, mildly. — If the pox have him, you and I need hardly drink to his distemper.

By which answers, a proud and proper Englishman — and in this vicinity, there dwells no other kind, by their own careful estimation — Such a man, we say, might wonder, whether this Mr Peach be truly their fellow or not. — Yet he drinks his majesty's health, as you see, and adds his not unpleasant barytone to the chorus of Rule, Britannia.

Is he a man of feeling, or of reason? Is he in jest or earnest?

Is he an *addition to society*?

No one is certain — or if one is, another is equally certain on the other side.

Is he *rich*, or *poor*? — those two fixed and absolute states of being, ordained by God for the benefit of all, according to those whom wise Providence has seen fit to place among the ranks of

---

* The Beggar's Opera is half a century and more old, at the time of our history, yet its fair heroine Polly may still be admired on every provincial stage, five nights in seven. — We should suspect her of having drunk from the fabled spring of eternal youth, had she not fallen at last into age and obscurity, in the decades subsequent.

the former? *This* question, surely, admits of easy answer, for any vacillation on the matter seems to speak of some doubt in God's own mind, which is untenable in any theology.

Let us be certain, then. — He is not poor. The poor labour and suffer, and are drunk. Tho.s Peach walks, and sends and receives letters, and raises neither voice nor hand to any man. He has the tenancy of a solid house of good old timbers and thatch, though low, and in an obscure situation, and on the damper side of the valley. There are three servants; Jem, the boy, and Anny, the maid, who *live in*, as the saying is, the one above the stable, and the other next-door the larder; and also Mrs Shin, who thanks God she has never been in service since she entered the married state, and goes to her own home and husband every night, but is nevertheless in receipt of wages from Mr Peach for the express purpose of managing his household and supplying his table, and is therefore *a fortiori** his house-keeper, will she or no.

These are not the visitations of poverty. — But, neither are they the appurtenances of riches.

A quibble! — you say. A false paradox! Our hero — we suppose you to continue — Is evidently — a man of THE MIDDLING SORT.

We admit the justice of your riposte. But, consider — Why, if this is so, is Tho.s Peach to be found in rustic retirement? and not in town, where the people of the middling sort go, to swell their ever-increasing numbers? Where is his shop? — Where his practice? — his means, of *getting on*? Why seeks he not to raise his station, nor seems to fear a descent?

Reader — We know you to be a person of attentive and discriminating observation. We have said it already — We see it in your

---

* Our reader may perhaps be a student of logic or the law, and object, that we misuse the Latin term. We make no apology. — The art of the *necromantic historian* — for such we stile ourselves, raising as we do our hero from the obscurity of his tomb — is neither logical, nor, in strict consideration, lawful.

look. Else we would have let you pass the church-gate, with no more than a nod, and never begun to expound these great mysteries, among whose small beginnings we now occupy you. We guess, therefore, that you have already divined the sure way to resolve this question. You do not need us to remind you, that no store of knowledge about a man is more richly and readily mined, than the gossip of his domestic servants.

— His board is plain enough, says Mrs Shin.

— That's well.

— Plain mutton, and a piece of cheese with his bread.

— Aye?

— And good beer. Nor he never stints on the house-keeping neither. Not like some of the gentlemen. Nor counts every penny in and out. A mean thing, I call that. A shabby practice. I could never abide an household as pinches every penny.

By which it appears that Mr Peach is at once frugal and liberal; and so, we are none the wiser.

Let us enquire of the younger folk instead.

— Why, 'tis all books! — says Anny, the maid, to whomever will listen — You never saw such a quantity of books. There can't be so many words in all the world. He cares for *them* like any thing, though he drink from the same dull old pot every day, and only three pairs of breeches, and them all the same one as the other, and three kerchiefs without a bit of stitching on them! I says to him, Lor, sir, don't you want to send to Mr Farmer, the tailor? For surely he could, if he had a mind to. But he won't think of that, or of new china, or any thing new or nice, but only his books. And so dark every thing is! There's a chest at the bottom of the stair, which I'm sure it must be full of bones, it's so black and old. Though what do you think he says it is instead? — Anny does not wait for your answer — More books! Lor, sir, I says to him, won't you take them out, for what use is it them all shut away and they can't even be read? For so I was thinking to catch him out, and have him open the chest, and so we'll see what there may be inside it, really! But he won't, and he says, Let them lie in peace Anny. — Like he was talking of a dead thing! I'm sure there's a key. It must be in his pocket always, for I've never found it, unless he keeps it up-stairs, where I'm not to think of going —

Well, you say, with pardonable impatience. — And what says the stable-boy, Jem?

— He's a good master.

No more than that?

— He gave us a shilling at Christmas-tide.

Jem looks at the ground, and blushes. He is sixteen, a thin lad, with a catch or stammer upon his tongue. From Anny you may learn more than you asked. — From Jem, you will discover barely any thing. — Though he will offer you this:

— The master bears up under his sorrow.

And thus poor tongue-tied Jem brings us, by an indirect road, to the last and greatest question, touching the mystery of Tho.s Peach — The question of infinite portent. — IS HE A BACHELOR?

Now, reader, you may be minded to protest, that notwithstanding every subtlety of philosophy, it cannot in the least degree be a matter of doubt, whether a man have a wife or no. There may be, you will allow, certain circumstances, which might accommodate some uncertainty. To take the example nearest at hand — We cannot say whether you, reader, are sworn *to have and to hold*, &c. — Nor can *you* determine the same of *us*.* Nevertheless, it must be agreed, that in cases of personal acquaintance, such uncertainty is utterly forbidden. To speak without ornament, all who know Tho.s Peach, must be perfectly apprised of the matter. It cannot be otherwise.

Let us be plain, then. — He is NOT a bachelor.

For it is widely known, that Mr Peach *has* a wife. — This, despite the curious circumstance, that no body has ever seen her.

---

* Though we rejoice to inform you that we are not; and, moreover, we earnestly recommend the single state, to all who have yet a choice in the matter, be they man, woman, child, widow or widower.

Poor lady! — she is very ill — And must keep to the low room above-stairs, under the roof of the house, in her bed — All the day, and all the night as well — And only Mr Peach himself, is permitted to attend to her.

— Poor Mrs Peach! — is it for her health you are come to the country?

— Alas, madam. I fear even the famed waters at Bath cannot improve her.

— Her condition is so very bad?

— It is.

— Good lady! Yet I hope, it may not be — I hardly know if I ought to ask.

Mr Peach allows madam several moments uninterrupted, for the purpose of resolving her doubts.

— I hope, there is not much danger?

— You are good to enquire, madam. We do not fear overmuch, provided only that Mrs Peach be not disturbed in the smallest degree.

— Oh, you need never trouble yourself on that score! The situation here is peace itself! I am vastly relieved. We have none of your London noise and pother hereabouts.

Mr Peach and his visitor together survey the prospect from his door-step.

— You know, I'm sure, there is Doctor Law in town.

— I have heard of the gentleman.

— They do say he does marvels. He was brought in to see the daughter of the Duke of _____.

— That lady, I regret to say, I am not familiar with.

— Familiar! Ha, ha. Oh! — Madam covers her mouth. — Do excuse me. I ought to mind the poor lady up-stairs.

— Your solicitude does you credit, madam.

We here omit some pleasantries, conducted, in truth, more in accord with the visitor's inclination than the host's.

— I am sure Doctor Law would ride this way, if sent for. He was not too proud to visit my old uncle. In Weston.

— There is nothing to be done with the doctors.

— Nothing at all? Can it be so certain?

— Quite certain.

— Mercy! Poor lady.

— You have a good heart, madam. Be assured, Mrs Peach will not worsen for lack of bleeding and patent powders.

— Well! I hope so. But must she be confined always?

— It is the only safe way.

— Alas, what troubles visit us, in this vale of tears.

Mr Peach sighs. — It is possible he has found in madam's sentiment, a significance she did not intend to put there.

— Well, sir, we are good people hereabouts, though we have no London airs, and we shall bring you and your lady such comfort as we can, I dare say.

Some further pleasantries are again omitted.

— The want of company must be very trying for her.

— It is a burden Mrs Peach bears with patience.

— Does she so, does she so! good lady. Yet it must be a trial. For I always say, in good company every thing becomes tolerable. The pleasure of society is free to all, is it not?

— I have always found it a coinage circulated every where, and estimated its value accordingly.

— Precisely so! We are of a mind, I see.

Mr Peach bows.

— Perhaps —

Mr Peach waits.

— I might bring a bowl of my broth? Depend upon it, there is nothing like it, in any ailment. It is simply the bones of the beef, boiled, with the peelings, and a drop of sugar. A dish of broth will do Mrs Peach all the good in the world, I'm sure.

— You are very kind.

— Then it is settled! Might I present it to Mrs Peach to-morrow? We shall have beef for supper.

— Alas, madam, I fear you have misunderstood. Mrs Peach's state does not allow the least disturbance.

— Well, you may rest easy! and easy as any thing, for I shan't disturb her a bit. Only a moment to take the broth up and present my compliments, and set down the jug where ever the lady pleases.

— The thing is quite impossible, madam.

— Do you say so?

— Quite impossible.

— Is Mrs Peach then so very weak, that a mere friendly word puts her in danger?

— In the most extreme danger.

— Good heavens! Oh! I must not exclaim so. I must speak low.

At which madam leans somewhat in at the door, and raises her voice.

— Do — forgive — me — Mrs Peach! I meant not — to trouble — you!

Madam retreats again, adopting a loud whisper.

— Poor, poor lady! You will present my excuses, I hope?

Mr Peach will do so.

— It quite grieves me, to think of the loneliness of her confinement. There must be some thing to be done to relieve it.

— Nothing at all.

— She need not receive company like a fine lady. We have none of those airs hereabouts, you know, sir.

— Nevertheless, madam. Nevertheless.

— Well! it is a very grievous thing.

— It is our lot to take the world as we find it, and not otherwise.

Madam is saved from the difficulty of appreciating this *Stoical* opinion, by the diverting of her attention to the upper windows of the house, which protrude in rustic fashion from the angle of the thatch.

— Is it not a rather low room?

— I have seen higher.

— A low room, they say, is not good for the animal spirits.

— I am pleased to say Mrs Peach's animal spirits suffer no ill effects from it.

— I wonder that she will have the shutters kept close!

14

— It is to prevent the obtrusion of light and sound.

— Yet she must have air, surely?

— Air, madam, like the pleasure of society, is both free and ubiquitous.

— Indeed, sir. All must agree with you, I hope! I do myself, that's certain. — Might Mrs Peach venture to sit in the window, I wonder? For taking the sun and the good fresh air. I might wave, like so — Madam greets the casement with a refined flutter — And present my compliments. There could be no harm in it.

— I regret to say you are mistaken. Nothing is so expressly forbidden to Mrs Peach in her condition than sitting at the window. A window is indeed of all things most to be feared. It has been my constant care these two years of my dear wife's indisposition to guard her from such dreadful apertures. You would tremble, madam, to hear of the narrow escapes we have had, when a moment's inattention has brought the lady too much in the proximity of that fiendish device of the architect's science, a WINDOW!

That evening, over her supper of beef, madam gives it as her determined opinion that Thomas Peach is a monstrous tyrant, whose design is to bring his poor wife to her grave, by denying her air, light, Doctor Law, and female visitors; most likely, in order to get his grasping hands on an inheritance.

The hypothesis is taken up in certain households, and, like the old physician's doctrine of the yellow bile and the black, has its day. It accords with that taste for the *Gothick*, which our older readers may remember, was fashionable among novelists and other tittle-tattlers, in the years to which we have translated you. But, as the bubble of fashion swells, only to burst — And, as the advancement of science casts what was once fixed and acknowledged doctrine, into the fire, along with the rest of the outworn rubbish of the past — we are generous with simile, and like the overstocked merchant offer you two, when one might have served your purpose — The theory is overtaken by its more modish cousin, introduced in that part of Somerset-shire by none other than loquacious Anny, of whom we have already had the pleasure.

One day, in conversation with Mrs Cooke, she pronounces the fateful words: —

— I don't believe there's any body up there at all.

Mrs Cooke, who takes in the more genteel sort of washing, is so astounded at this Copernican revolution in the universe of her thought — which consists exclusively in the orbits, the zeniths and nadirs, and the retrograde motions, of those of her neighbours she deems worthy of attention — That she places her hands on her hips, to maintain balance.

— I do swear it, says Anny. — I never heard a single sound. Not so much as the creak of a board or the scratch of a mouse. Not for all my months in service. Only last week I lost a button, and climbed the stair to see if it fell off on the landing, him being out a-walking, for he says we mustn't go up the stair, you know, but I couldn't see the harm in it, and I went ever so quiet. And then I had to go on my knees crawling to look all about, for it's dark as pitch on the landing, for he won't have the window open, except at night. And my ear comes to the door, as it must, you know, from me looking in all the corners, and just at that very moment I fancied there's the button, all stuck down in a little hole between the boards, so what was I to do but stay as quiet as ever I could, while my finger and thumb tried to pull it up? I'm sure I was kneeling there three minute together, and not so much as drawing a breath, and my ear as close by the door as this — Miss holds up the said finger and thumb — So what can I do but listen, though I never meant to? And what do you think I heard all that time?

Mrs Cooke will not hazard a guess.

— Not one thing.

Mrs Cooke waggles her head, and says, Don't mistress Peach sleep a-days?

— Sleep, without tossing and turning! without breathing! I hardly call that sleeping. It was all quiet as the tomb. — I'd swear it in any court in the land, my hand on the Bible. I'd swear it before the king himself. There's no such body as Mrs Peach, and I'll never say a word different, and you may bring me up before the justice and I'll still maintain it. Who can say there is, tell me that? Who's seen Mrs Peach, or heard a word of her? I'll tell you who. Not a soul, that's who.

— The gentleman do.

— He may very well say he do! And I may say, I go to my little room behind the parlour and see the Pope of Rome, and who's to deny it then, for it's only my word that says so.

— That were very pert. And like as not thee'd be d____d for it.

— Don't teaze, and be stupid! I don't say I *do* any such thing — Only I *might* say it, and who's to say I don't?

— Why, Anny, the parson would tell thee not to. — The Pope of Rome!

Anny begins to tire of this exchange — And fears, she has cast her seed on stony ground. But Mrs Cooke, though slow, runs deep, after a fashion; and having once effaced from her brain the picture of little Anny Pertwee playing the harlot with the bishop of idolaters and Frenchmen, she begins to see the justice — And, which is more significant — The *interest* — in this new hypothesis.

Before the week is out she is relaying it, to all who will listen — Which is to say, every body.

— Little Anny do say, there be no Mrs Peach at all.

Nothing can be more gratifying than the sensation produced by this intelligence. Society is transformed. Conversation, which hitherto ambled circuitously around the same antient parish paths — ever turning at the old familiar cross-roads and stiles — Now discovers a broad new turnpike, driven straight across the land — And disdains to go by any other way. Anny Pertwee, until that moment in the general estimation a gad-about girl, her tongue forever running on this or that, becomes a person of celebrity among her own sex. Thus it is, that by the turn of the year in which our story begins, when barren fields and bitter winds mean there is little work or pleasure to be had out-of-doors, you may hear by every fire-side and in every tavern the thousand-tongued rumour, whispering — Thomas Peach *is*, after all, a bachelor!

Reader, you are — as we are ourselves — a person of discernment. You smile at our little canvas of country gossips, and take no notice of opinions thus promulgated. — Much as a judge disdains evidence merely circumstantial, or given as hearsay. But be pleased to consider the case, under the more austere and searching light of EXPERIMENT.

Experiment! — That touchstone, of a truly scientific understanding — Nursemaid of reason!

Anny Pertwee, we admit, says much. — It may please you to know, that we intend to abridge her contributions to our history, wherever possible, in future pages; and have indeed made our best endeavours in that direction, during those scenes, where strict historical necessity has already compelled us to introduce her. — Yet in among all she says, we confess we find a seam of true metal. For, though she be entirely ignorant of the science of old *Bacon*, or the Frenchman *Descartes*, or even the good British commonsense of *Locke* and *Hume*, she has by mere accident fallen upon a test of — the *experimental method*.

She says to herself — we may suppose — Very well; here is a man, master of the house in which I serve, who declares, *My wife is confined to the bed-room up-stairs, and is never to be disturbed, and the door never to be opened nor so much as knocked at.* — Now — When I subject his assertion to the trial of EXPERIMENT, what do I find? — Why, by your leave, sir, I find not a single confirmation of it. And therefore, I have leave to doubt it — And — which is, we confess, less the index of a temperament truly *scientific* — I shall tell every body so.

Thus, reader, having assured you of the mere impossibility of any doubt upon the question — having, indeed, determined it ourselves, with an unwisely* categorical answer — We have perhaps brought you to a state of some perplexity.

---

* It is our practice on occasion, to take up our pen after dinner, and thereby permit the attendants of *Bacchus* a degree of admittance, into the company of *Clio*. We have reached that stage in life where habits are, alas, not to be remedied.

Let us, then, lay out the facts, as we have them.

Here is Mr Tho.s Peach, outwardly a man of education and good sense, who has taken a moderately comfortable, though very far from fashionable house, in a retired situation; and in the upper floor of that house he has installed his ailing wife, behind a door he keeps always locked, and windows he will only open a little at night-time; because her health is of such extreme delicacy, that he will admit no one but himself into her presence, nor risk any contagion from beyond the room where she is confined. — And here is Anny, engaged in the household in the capacity of maid, unable by any means to discover for herself, who or what occupies the up-stairs portion of the house; nor ever seeing or hearing the least sign of the supposed Mrs Peach.

On this presentation, we think it safe to say, that the facts are conformable to our prior declaration.* For the case of Anny, strictly considered, does not contradict the case of Mr Peach, because, to have *no evidence* of a thing's existence, is not to have *evidence of its non-existence*; and if, as Mr Peach maintains, the condition of Mrs Peach is such that she must pass all her days in perfect stillness and silence, then it is no wonder to find poor Anny unable to satisfy her tormenting curiosity — No matter how frequently she will take advantage of Mr Peach's fondness for walking in the country, by ascending the stairs, and listening at the door — Or how often she will go in the room at the end of the house, where she is not required to go, and cast an eye over Mr Peach's papers. — The which breaches of the trust Mr Peach implicitly places in her, we are compelled to admit, she indulges in, more regularly than she would wish it known.

— Begging your pardon, sir.

Mr Peach lowers an octavo volume of sermons to his lap, and looks to the door of the end-room.

— Granted, Anny, with pleasure.

— Sir?

* That 'Mr Peach is NOT a bachelor' — *vide supra*.

— No matter, no matter. What is it you wish to say?

— Only, sir, and I know it's not my place to ask, but I wonder about the mistress. Mrs Peach, sir. Her name.

— Her name, Mr Peach answers with a sigh, is Eliza.

— Only it's an hard thing, sir, to be in service to my mistress, and not even rightly know her name.

— Is that so very hard a thing?

— It is, sir.

— Then I am pleased to have lightened the burden.

— Begging your pardon, sir, nor her face neither. People do say, What sort of lady is your mistress? But I can't say whether she's dark or fair, or great or small, or her nature, though I am sure she's very good, nor I wouldn't have you think I'd breathe a word different. I wonder sometimes whether she even knows there's such a creature in the world as I, and me her own maid, for if I'm the maid in this house, then amn't I her maid too?

— She knows you quite well, Anny, and is grateful for all you do, and says you're a good girl.

— Does she so? I'm glad to hear it.

— Then I have soothed your troubles twice over. We must count this a lucky day.

— You do talk with her of me, then?

— A man and his wife may talk, I suppose?

— Beg pardon, sir, humbly. I remember my place.

— I trust you do.

— Only, I never see — But, I ought not to speak of it, sir, I know.

— You know you ought not, says Mr Peach, mildly, And yet you do.

— Oh, sir! don't be hard. — Will you turn me out?

— Heavens, child! — Come, approach.

— Ah! I couldn't.

— Well, stay at the door if you like, but I would speak gently, and it might suit your hearing better if you would consent to stand there, by the fire-iron. That way, you see, we shall neither of us need to raise our voices.

— It's only I'm not used to the room, sir, for I never like to go among your books and letters.

— That is very praiseworthy. Rest assured, I shall not request that you open a book, or pick up a letter. See, I put my own aside. — The octavo sermons are moved to a trestle of oak. — Now, come.

— Very well, sir.

— So, Anny, tell me. Are you content with your station?

— Sir?

— Your situation in this house. Do you find your duties tolerably agreeable, and your wages not insufficient? You may speak with candour, for, look, here we are by the fire together.

— I hardly know how to say, sir. You don't chaff me, nor mean to turn me out?

— Because you ask with what name my wife was baptized, and wonder how she looks? I would be a cruel master indeed.

— I know you aren't any such, sir. You are very fair.

— I think I am, Anny. There are those, you know, who will say my dear Eliza has neither name nor face at all.

— I don't take your meaning, sir.

— It is rumoured there is no such lady as Mrs Peach.

— God forgive us! What a thing to say! I can scarce believe it. Will folks say such wicked things?

— Whether it be wicked, we must leave a greater judge to decide, should He chuse to concern Himself with it. But, you see, your questions must appear altogether innocent in the comparison.

Anny is not altogether certain of Mr Peach's meaning — Though her interest in the conversation has fastened on another point.

— I hate to think people will say such things. I'm sure I never heard it myself.

— Well, never mind that, Anny, but tell me, are you content in your situation?

— Most surely, sir, and I don't complain of any thing, nor speak out of turn on any matter. There are many who will gossip, though I don't name names, for that wouldn't be right, but I know how to behave, I dare say.

— I am heartily glad of it, child. — Look, then; you say you are content with us, and we say we are content with you. And so we shall have no more talk of turning away nor chaffing. And here's tuppence for you.

Were this tale of ours a *moral fable*, set down for the instruction of mankind, we might tell you that the receipt of this small token hung as heavy on miss's conscience, as did the thirty pieces of silver, in the pocket of him to whom they were paid. — We must inform you instead, that no sooner has the coin vanished into Anny's fair hand, than she begins to picture, not a noose around her neck, but a new bit of ribbon in her apron.

— But, says she, her natural pertness restored by the evidence of her master's good-humour, Does my mistress speak of me indeed?

— I make a good report of you.

— You converse at night, then, sir? For the lady is not to be disturbed during the day. I never hear so much as a word.

— Alas, Anny, I fear I may not discuss with you the *nocturnal conversations* between man and wife. You are but fourteen, are you not?

— Fifteen come Michaelmas.

— Go along now. I do think you're a good girl, Anny. But go quietly! — this is a well-made house, and a slight thing like you won't make it rattle, but we must always have Mrs Peach's rest in mind.

You may well imagine, how Anny exercises her hearing that night, and every night after, as she lies in her little room beside the larder. — How she creeps from her bed, and holds her breath, and lets her door fall open, though not so much as might make the hinges cry out — And listens — As hard as ever she can. The house is indeed of stout construction — Thick-boned and thick-walled as those Somerset yeomen, who once made it their home, before its plot of wooded land flattered the greedy eye of a greater man. We suspect, now we have cause to consider the matter, that Mr Peach had these virtues in mind, when he chose to take it. — Anny's ears have the keenness — and, we dare say, the shapeliness — of youth; yet no whisper of *nocturnal conversation* penetrates through the lath and the great old beams to where she stands.

Only, one night in twenty — And that so faint, it could almost be a dream — She fancies, she can discern the murmur of Mr Thomas Peach, scarcely more distinct than the sound of air in the woods above the house. — But of an answering voice, there comes no hint at all.

CHAPTER TWO

It is the historian's task —

We beg your indulgence — From time to time, the progress of our narrative must pause, to allow for reflexions of a *critical* nature.

These reflexions, we must advise you, are no mere diversions, or ornaments — But necessary, to your proper apprehension of our purpose. Our method being as far from the common manner of your every-day scribblers, as our subject is from their matter, we do not scruple to explain ourselves, when the occasion requires it. We would not hazard the risk of a misunderstanding between us — A thing most fatal to the maintenance of wholesome society — Most of all, when our acquaintance is but newly begun! And so —

It is, we say again, the historian's task, not to set down every minute circumstance, but rather with a single all-encompassing eye to view the *whole*, and by the exercise of judgment select those distinct *parts*, which are necessary to record; exactly after the practice of the cartographer, who marks on a single sheet of paper the length and breadth of a whole nation — an expanse otherwise impossible to be comprehended in one view — and records the principal towns, rivers, harbours, roads, regions of waste land, &c., never thinking to make note of each stream or hillock or hamlet.

Thus in the course of our first chapter, we have, reader, apprized you of the *essentials* of the case of Tho.s Peach, as it stood in the month of May in the year 'eighty-five. An hundred other puzzles have been posed, and an hundred other smaller rumours risen, and swollen, and burst, and not one person in the country is any the wiser for any of them. It might fairly be said, that there are as many questions touching the nature of the gentleman, his business, his history, and his domestic arrangements, as there are brains to ponder them, for there is not a neighbour of his, high or low, for miles about, but has vexed themself with some doubt or other, only to give it up at last, with an *Hem!* or *Well, it's all one*. But with this mass of lesser mysteries, we need not trouble you. — For, behold! we have arrived at our second chapter, and shall dismiss the prologue, raise the curtain, and, May being of all the months of the year most apt for beginnings, commence our history proper.

Our scene is that same end-room, where we observed Mr Peach in conversation with Anny the maid. The room has been appended to the body of the house, in some distant former year, with little regard for elegance and proportion, but it exhibits nonetheless the chief virtue of rustic architecture, that is, a great determination to keep the rain and rats outside, and the warmth within. This nook of eccentric angles and rough-hewn beams is illuminated to-day by the brilliance of a fine after-noon, entering through two windows, beside the larger of which — for they do not match — our hero stands, holding a letter to the light.

He lets the pages fall a little, and turns to notice the prospect beyond the glass — By which we may understand, that we have arrived just as Mr Peach finishes perusing the contents.

We will not expend either our ink or your patience, in describing the shadow that seems to fall over him, despite the brightness of the season. His reflexions you may imagine for yourself, once you have read the letter, which we hasten to transcribe:

DEAR NEPHEW, for by that name I will one last time be
pleased to acknowledge you, for the sake of the memory of a
BROTHER so dearly loved and so much regretted.
    That I once entertained great hopes of you, cannot be
denied. Despite the circumstances of your birth, there were

*always such marks of talent in you, that gave your father to
think, in words often expressed to me, who you may well
believe cannot lose the remembrance of such sentiments
pronounced in those dear accents I never shall hear more, that
you would in due time attain such a station in life and such
repute in the world as would heap honours upon the name of
PEACH. Nor could these effusions be dismissed as the natural
fondness of so good a father, when in every early trial of
temperament and education you shewed such promise that all
who knew of it, remarked on it. You were indulged equally
with your sister, and moreover given all those advantages not
suited to a daughter, though she the acknowledged child of
the family. On that day of sorrowful remembrance, when our
heavenly Judge took to Himself my brother and your
father — a soul too full of goodness for the world! — I knew
it for my duty to continue in the same path, and do all in my
power to secure for you the enjoyment of the same advantages, though my own position was then attended with much
trouble and difficulty. It was my duty, and my pleasure too; for
you were the only copy, however imperfect, of that stamp of
masculine virtue then for ever broken.*

*By your evident signs of decency, honesty, and a blameless
and upright temper, I thought you the son of such a father. By
the good learning you were already possessed of, and the
knowledge of true religion without which all learning is folly
and vanity, I knew you for a man worthy of admiration, seemingly destined to advance to a place where all the world would
acclaim your worth.*

Alas! That SEEMING!

*I will not pain my remembrance by recalling all that has
passed. I do not admonish you with the promises unfulfilled,
the hopes dashed, the time wasted, the duties neglected; the
good living rejected on a whim of what you were pleased to
call conscience, though a truly dutiful conscience would have
acknowledged the great expence laid out by a loving UNCLE,*

for the purpose of securing you so notable an opportunity of preferment; the marital union most imprudently entered into, and most unfortunately and miserably concluded.

I repeat, I do not dwell on these. Were it possible you should feel shame in the recitation, I would spare no detail, and fill these pages with just complaints of your YEARS of unprofitable idleness and distraction, with no other aim than the most benevolent one, of bringing you to an acknowledgment of your faults, and so offering some prospect of FUTURE AMENDMENT.

What, Thomas, have you done, since the tragic events, which brought that span of years to so unhappy a conclusion, but spurned your own family, and all other decent society besides? I need not inform you, how you have been enquired after. I need not say, with what anxiety, a loving sister, and a concerned uncle, have hoped to hear news of you, month upon month, with all too fruitless an hope. You were pleased to vanish from my view, and from the view of all the world, so that it was not to be determined whether you were alive or dead, or gone to sea, or I know not what.

Are these, sir — I do not, I cannot call you NEPHEW now — the actions of a PEACH? Is this the fruit of the hopes placed in you? Is this the way towards obtaining even that decent sufficiency, which the misfortune of your birth might have set as the summit of your worldly ambitions, though the encouragement of those who were pleased to call you their FAMILY once opened the prospects of something far above? To remove yourself from London! Without any prior justification, or any explanation subsequent! I have had no account of your behaviour from your own hand, sir. ONE LINE from your pen might have excused it. That you did not deem us worth that solitary line, is enough to confirm beyond any proof that no complaint of mine can touch you, nor any reproach move you. That you have NO REGARD for your sister, or for the memory of your devoted father, or for me!

27

I put aside the lamenting pen. All regrets are finished. It only remains for me to inform you, sir, of what receipt of this letter makes plain, that I have at last received report of you. I learn that you are retired to the country, in a situation the meanest imaginable, far removed from the society of men of taste and learning. You reside, I discover, in an HOVEL, at a distance from every place of note. You pursue no favour, nor are engaged in any useful occupation, but live in PERFECT IDLENESS.

I must further report, that you are lately sought by certain countrymen of your late father-in-law, who have so far pursued their unwelcome inquiries, as to accost me at my own door. The attentions of such men cannot but be excessively distasteful, to any person of good reputation. Yet it is not so painful to endure their presence, as it is to discover, that you retain an association with these, while entirely disavowing those, whose claim on your duty and your affections ought to be, though it is not, sanctified by the bonds of kinship!

In short, sir, I consider you lost to me, to your own name and honour, and to your father, whose untimely death spared him the knowledge of your shameful decline.

I must therefore inform you that the annuity of which you have been in receipt from my hands; the sum I have not stinted these many years, for the sake of the unshakeable regard in which I hold the memory of the best of brothers, though year by year I have watched as hope withered to disappointment, and early promise surrendered to idle whim and dissipation! that sum shall cease to be forthcoming, from this day.

I add furthermore that from this same day I consider you expunged from the honourable record of the family, and desire that you make no further use of a name, to which only the generosity of a man of every social and civil virtue gave you any degree of entitlement.

Lastly and irrevocably, and with the most awful solemnity, I declare, that you will NEVER SEE ME AGAIN.

Do not think to write with your apology, nor any other
application. None will be received.
  In sorrow I sign myself for the last time,
Yours, &c.,
AUGUSTUS PEACH, Esq.

Mr Thomas Peach preserves his pose for several seconds, the papers grasped lightly in a drooping hand, his head turned to the light. — An interval, which had afforded us the opportunity to paint his features for you, were it extended but a little longer, for he stands as still as though before an easel. We rather fancy the portrait might have done for that famous prince of Denmark, to whom we have already alluded, had the royal gentleman escaped his fate, and lived on into the beginning of his middle years, when we suppose the excess of his youthful passions to have decayed to a more settled and comfortable gloom, and those tormenting reflexions on the vicissitudes of mortal existence, to have become as it were the familiar companions of his thoughts, their sting drawn by long acquaintance — Nay, indeed, perhaps become almost welcome, as any thing may become, no matter how griev-ous or irksome, if by its constant presence before us we grow into the habit.* But the world will not have this masterpiece, to rival the productions of *Zoffany*! — for who should pass by the window upon which Mr Peach gazes, but Anny, fetching water.

The sudden view of the fair and loquacious maid prompts Mr Peach to recollect that defect of *curiosity*, which afflicts her no more nor less, than it afflicts every person employed in domestic service in every household in Britain, and, we do not doubt, in the houses of all the other nations of the earth. — He lifts the letter again, and considers the matter of its disposal.

— What are we to do with you, uncle? It's too warm for a fire.
He considers the privy.

---

* A curious phaenomenon, which must explain, for nothing else can, the long endurance of certain marital conjunctions.

— No, he says. I'll not soil my a__e with you.*

He folds the sheets of the letter as small as the paper allows, and places them in the pocket of his breeches.

That evening, after supper has been taken, and Mrs Shin dismissed, Mr Peach has assumed his nightcap and taken to his bed, with his wife.

— I have received to-day a letter from Augustus, he says.

— That is unexpected, I think, dear?

— And unwelcome.

— How is he?

— He is magnificent. He is pompous as a patriarch.

— And Sophy? Is there news of her?

— I am afraid to say, my dear, he does not write with news.

— Will you read me the letter?

— Forgive me if I don't. I am endeavouring to put it out of my mind.

— An unkind letter, then.

— I shouldn't have cared a jot for unkindness. But alas, my dear, he has done us palpable harm.

— I think no further harm can come to me, Tom.

— Dearest Liza. I hope it may be so. Yet you would not wish us to be moved from here, I think.

---

* To such of our readers as may object to the recording of coarse terms, we make triple rejoinder. First, we remind you that we are a *necromantic historian*, restoring to life the body as well as the soul. Second, we beg you to make allowance for the age in which our history passes, when the general manners of the nation had not yet been elevated to that pitch of delicacy where they stand to-day. And third, we must inform you, that the future course of our narrative will positively compel us to bring before you conversations and incidents, from which strict decency must recoil. We therefore expose you to this solitary *a__e*, as a species of inoculation, against the more virulent plague to come. If the present dose make you unwell, we advise you to pause a while, and then administer it again, thus — A__E —; and continue to repeat the procedure, until you are able to proceed in comfort.

— No indeed! But can a letter from your uncle displace us? Has he turned bailiff now? You told me this house is on another man's land. It is in the country, is it not?

— I hoped I had put us beyond the reach of his interference, or any body's. But I learned to-day of my error. He writes to say he will cut off the hundred a year.

— From your papa?

— Yes.

— Oh, Tom. How can that be? It was settled on you by your papa's will. You must go to law.

— And be ruined, Liza. We cannot afford the law.

— But is the will to be disregarded?

— I have been reflecting on it. There are several indications in the letter, to suggest that uncle Gus will swear Papa was not my father after all.

— But that is a lie. Can a body swear to a lie, and go unpunished?

— A body can, my dear, and does, every day. I believe Augustus is confident of casting doubt on the terms of the settlement.

— I know you had no love for him, and he not much for you. But I can scarcely believe he would write to you so.

— Oh, no, my dear. No, his language is all wounded honour and sorrowful disappointment. It would make you laugh, except his design is no matter for amusement. He calls my father the best of men, and pretends to revere his memory, and says I shame it. He paints me the profligate heir. He won't write his true purpose until the last page, but it's plain to see for all that. He hints I have no right to the family name. For which I care not a fart, but the right to the annuity is a different thing. Depend upon it, something has come to light, and if I go to law, which at any event I cannot do, he will bring forth his new document or witness or what-have-you, and the will would be challenged.

— Perhaps we ought to rejoice, that you may not after all be related in blood to such a man.

— Very true, my dear. Though I might rather endure the odious consanguinity, with a roof over us, than rejoice alone in a ditch.

— Odious consanguinity! — indignation has made you splendid, Tom. — But surely he can't have us put out of the house.

— He cannot. But, equally, the rent must be paid.

— Then there is nothing put by?

— Alas, my dear, I fear there is not. I have been eagerly awaiting the annuity for some weeks now.

— Might you apply to Sophy?

— My sister has not much love for me.

— You are too hard, Tom. She was always kind to me.

— She wished to seem kind, so people would praise her for her condescension. But she had no affection for you.

— You judge every body by your own temper, dear.

— As do you. But whichever of us has the right of it, I think I cannot appeal to Sophonisba. She and I have not seen each other these two years, since we removed from London. I can hardly now come to her cap in hand, and expect a very friendly answer.

Mrs Peach is silent a while. Mr Peach is accustomed to these *lacunae* in her conversation, and waits.

Below, at the door of the room beside the larder, Anny stops her breath and strains her hearing. It is a still night, with no noise of wind to interfere with her exertions.

— If you were compelled to leave the house, Tom, would I be able to go with you?

— Believe me, it is all I have thought of, since I read the letter.

— Perhaps it is best that you let me go.

— Never.

Thomas Peach speaks the word with more vehemence than he intends, with the result that Anny's ears catch the hint of an impassioned murmur. — They are talking — they are talking! she thinks. — Or perhaps they are doing — another thing —

— You have such trouble for my sake.

— It is because I am the pattern of husbands.

32

— Is it? I think it must be. Leave me, then, so you may be perfection to another woman.

— If you can find me one whose company I can bear, I will consider it.

— Are you teazing, now, Tom? I can't be certain. You were so serious before.

— I am indeed, Liza. I wish for no other companion, and if at last we are to part from one another, I will be content for ever with your image in my remembrance. There is the truth, in sober terms.

— I think you are quite foolish, to be so determined about what is yet to come.

— I was always determined.

— You was.

— Bull-headed, you always say.

— Do I talk so? Poor Tom. You have wed yourself to a shrew.

— Yet uncle Gus upbraids me for my dearth of ambition. Because I decline to dance attendance upon persons of fashion, and would not take holy orders.

— You said, my dear, you would put his letter out of your mind.

— So I did. — Wise Lizzy. Well. I must consider what's to be done.

— Might you apply to your friends in town, the philanthropic gentlemen?

— I believe I shall. Mr Farthingay must be persuaded to extend credit in the matter of the rent.* — That's the first I must do. I think it will not be impossible. Farthingay seems a good-natured man, though he talks of virtue a good deal, which may be a mark in his disfavour. — The Society is appointed to gather on Thursday. I shall attend, in hopes of seeing him there. It will require me to be absent a night.

---

* This Mr Farthingay, you will understand, is master of the land, on which Mr Peach's house sits, and the man to whom his tenancy is owed. — You are to become acquainted with the gentleman, in our next.

— Will that be soon? I cannot tell one day from another.

— Forgive me, dear. It is not to-morrow, nor the next day, but the one following. To-day is Monday.

— The time is all so alike to me.

— I know.

— I recall how I used to fret about to-morrow. It seems a strange thing now.

— You may leave the fretting to my part.

— You know, Tom, I think an odd thing sometimes. I think, if you could be as easy in your mind as I am, how pleasant that would be.

Mr Peach appears much affected by this sentiment of Mrs Peach's, and makes no answer.

— Are you still by? says she. — Have you fallen asleep?

— Not yet.

— You are tired, dear.

— It is very trying, having one's head filled with another's unpleasant words.

— Then I shall think of some other thing, to put in your head.

Mr Peach understands the turn his wife intends to give the conversation. He adjusts his recumbent posture accordingly. — And here we let the curtain fall on our second chapter; for we have now supplied you with a view of the stile of *nocturnal conversation* enjoyed by the couple, and think it only just that they be allowed to indulge the remainder, without our notice.

CHAPTER THREE

Sound, trumpets! — Strike, cymbals! — We put aside our warbling wood-pipe, to whose sylvan notes we sang these rustic diversions, and with loud fanfare instead proclaim our scene — the TOWN.

That so complete an alteration can occur, between one page and the next, you will think less surprizing, when we inform you also, that a period of nigh three entire days has passed. — Thus it is, reader, that the turning of the page — an interval you might have thought of no longer duration than the tick-tock of your pocket-watch, or the drawing in of a breath — has allowed us ample time, to transform the place of our action. — We thumb our nose at those *unities* proclaimed by old Aristotle, for any law of art held in disdain by the GENIUS OF SHAKESPEAR, compels no obedience of ours. Look about you. — You no longer find us in the pleasant vale where dwells Tho.s Peach, at least for so long as he is able to afford the tenancy. Here, instead, is the smoke — the brick — The carriage-wheels and curses — hawker's cries and drunkard's howls — The glass shop-fronts, and painted signs, and fresh-inked bills, of *Bristol.*

We have conveyed you to the very evening of that Thursday, the mention of which produced some uncertainty in Mrs Peach.

Mr Peach has that morning called for his horse, and sent Jem and Anny home to their own amusements for the day, and locked up the house — which, thinks Anny, he would not do if his wife were really above-stairs, for what if there's a fire? — And then ridden the several miles separating him from the town, stopping only to enjoy a pic-nic of cold pork and mustard at a cross-roads under a blooming hawthorn tree; and, in that same spot, to dig a small hole, eight inches deep in the earth, in which he buries the folded pages comprising the letter from his uncle. For, he reasons, as those convicted of the wickedest crimes, were hung from a gibbet where two roads met, in order that their unquiet spirits would not know which way to proceed, and be thereby prevented from haunting the blameless living, so the malignity of Augustus Peach may likewise be left bewildered in its grave, until the paper rot altogether.

We note this curious action of Mr Peach's in passing. It seems a thing of no importance — An harmless superstition, or comical eccentricity. — Nevertheless, reader — We must advise you, to take note of it. There may be cause to recall the circumstance, in a future chapter.

The evening finds him afoot, among a thousand others; nay, tens of thousands! — men, women, children, of every station, speaking twenty different tongues, hurrying or sauntering, observed or ignored, in pursuit of gain or fleeing it. He has left the horse at an inn, where he will stay that night. The appointment he keeps is expected to occupy him until a very late hour; and though he knows many worse ways to spend a fine spring night, than riding fifteen or twenty miles of road under the stars, he will on this particular occasion decline the opportunity of a nocturnal homeward journey; for — we are frank with you, reader — he suspects he will by the middle of the night be extremely drunk.

Through the Babel of the burgeoning town he passes, until, by dint of ascending the slopes which overlook the windings of sweet *Avon*, he comes to a quarter of fashionable houses, newly laid out in elegant parades and terraces. At the corner of a square is a particularly fine mansion, protected from the risk of public indignity by iron railings, and displaying behind its acreage of sash-windows an expenditure in candles, which would not dishonour the light-house of *Eddystone*.

In front of this temple of urban splendour, Mr Peach stops. — Here is his destination — Here, the Ithaca of his day's

36

Odyssey — Here, the appointed meeting-place, on the second Thursday in every month, of the ANTI-LAPSARIAN SOCIETY.

Nothing, reader! is so entirely characteristic of the age to which we have translated you — those most opportune years of a century of seemingly perpetual improvement, between the end of the war with the colonies, and the commencement of the struggle against insurgent France — Than such gatherings of inquisitive amateurs. If we were to picture the Spirit of the Age, we would make him one of these gentlemen, wearing a black frock-coat and a pair of spectacles, resting one arm on the *Encyclopaedia* of Diderot, or the latest proceedings of the Royal Society, and gesturing with his other hand towards a model of a steam-engine — With an halo above his head, signifying the light of *Reason*, and — no whit less respected or necessary, despite its inferior place in our composition — a sack of promissory notes at his feet, to represent the foundation of all his science and philosophy, in the accumulating profits of commerce. On this same evening, if we were able to cast our eye over the comfortable new houses in the rising towns all over the kingdom, we would see countless such societies preparing to gather, for the convivial exchange of knowledge. — Societies for the Improvement of Agriculture — for the Advancement of Chemistry — for the Perfection of the Art of Mining — the Rational Dissemination of the Principles of Mechanics. — Societies for the Destruction of Superstition, for the Refinement of Public Morals, for the Abolition of Discontent; for every thing and any thing you may think of, so long as it tend to the amelioration of some thing, or of all things! — and so long as the means to that happy improvement, be understood to consist in the endeavours of British gentlemen, of no rank but not inconsiderable means, in whose wise and benevolent hands the whole future of the earth undoubtedly rests.

— Good-evening, sir, and welcome.

— Good-evening, Jonathan. I trust you are well?

— Very well, sir, thank you. You have not your Newton medallion, I see.

— I have mislaid it again.

— Think nothing of it, sir. I will have one fetched for you directly.

— Thank you, Jonathan. — Mr Peach passes the man an emolument, which he knows will be welcome, though it is not considered necessary. — May I ask whether Mr Farthingay attends this evening?

— He does, sir. With a guest. They alighted not ten minutes past. There is his carriage.

Mr Peach's sensations are mixed. He is relieved to hear, that the chief aim of his lengthy excursion — that is, the opportunity for discussions of a delicate nature with his landlord, Mr Farthingay — lies within his compass. He is doubtful, however, regarding the *guest*, who may be expected to occupy the gentleman's attentions, and thus perhaps render the prospect of private conference more remote.

It is not usual for guests to be admitted to gatherings of the Society. It is, in fact, a thing Mr Peach cannot recall in a single instance. — It may be, that the charter of the Society debars non-members from attendance. The charter is somewhat profuse in clauses. — Mr Peach believes he was present at the majority of the gatherings, in which its terms were established, but he cannot pretend to have them all by heart.

Jonathan looks to the left and right, and then leans towards Mr Peach, though in a stile perfectly dignified.

— A female guest.

By a motion of his brows, Mr Peach silently expresses his appreciation of this intelligence.

No where in the charter of the Society is the company of females forbidden. His recollection on this particular point is quite certain, the matter having been subject to warm, if always suitably convivial, debate. But he is equally certain, that there never *has* been a woman present at any assemblage of the Society, in the twelvemonth of its active existence. Mr Davis, at the gates of whose house we are standing, goes so far as to remove his female servants on the evenings appointed. — The better, so he says, to promote that spirit of free and manly fellowship, in which the business of the Society is exclusively to be conducted — According to Clause the fourth, of its charter.

But — we hear you expostulate — What can be the nature of its business? — The Improvement of Agriculture, you have heard of — The Refinement of Public Morals, you can understand, God knows! — but what in Heaven or on earth, is an ANTI-LAPSARIAN SOCIETY?

Why, reader, it is no more nor less than what the name plainly indicates, which is to say, a voluntary association of philanthropic gentlemen, created to oppose, or perhaps to reverse — the prefix admits of either interpretation — the FALL OF MAN.*

If this explanation leave you none the wiser — or, which we think the more likely, for we doubt neither your sagacity nor your Latin — If you wonder how the gentlemen propose to atchieve such a purpose, by assembling every month, to consume beef and punch — We can only invite you to attend to our narrative, for we will have occasion to report matters, which may perhaps shed some light on this admittedly intricate puzzle.

A small ray of illumination appears, in the form of the brass medallion, which is pressed into Mr Peach's hand as the door of the house is opened to him, and which he fixes to his coat as he steps within, to encourage the general impression, that he has worn it all day. This oval of metal is stamped with the head of *Newton*, in three-quarter profile, wearing a long nose, and a longer wig. We add, that on the large table occupying the centre of the room into which Mr Peach is shewn, among the dishes of

---

* It is a source of perpetual amusement to the members, that the Society, when referred to in conversation, is — by a confusion of the prefix *anti-* with its homophone, *ante-* — very often mistakenly thought, by the uninitiated, to be devoted to investigating the state PRIOR TO the Fall of Man; which, they do not need to add, would be entirely ridiculous, ha, ha!

elegant viands and sweetmeats, is a bust of that same famous man, crowned for the occasion with an hoop of bay. By which signs you will gather, that the gentlemen of the Society have cast Sir Isaac Newton in the role of honorary President, or guiding spirit. — An harmless imposition — the great man being long dead, and so unable to take that offence, which biography informs us he was, alas, ever ready to assume — But one, which we may briefly explain, hoping thereby to cast a glimmer of light on the Society's founding principles. For the genius of Newton was — we need hardly tell you — to expose, and demonstrate, the fixed mathematical laws, by which the phaenomena of the world, nay, of worlds beyond the world — of the *entire universe* — are necessarily governed. Sir Isaac as it were deciphered the hiero-glyphs, in which the great Volume of Creation is written, and translated its elements, and wrote down its Grammar. He may be said to have made plain the very *language of the Creator*, in its ineffable order and perfection. — For the present purpose let us only add, that the gentlemen of the Society believe Newton to have revealed an universe in its essential nature UNFALLEN; perfect, lawful, and amenable to reason; and they agree, that there must therefore be some flaw in the arrangement of the world, accounting for the evidently IMPERFECT state of earthly existence; and, furthermore, that this flaw, being not *essential* — for Sir Isaac has demonstrated that Creation is *essentially* flawless — must be *correctible*; and so they have resolved to discover the said flaw, and correct it, and thereby restore all things to their state of original perfection.

Reader, we beg you to dwell neither on the *philosophy*, nor the *theology*, of the Society's ambition. Our history, we most assuredly promise you, will give you cause to exercise your wits on matters more profound. We advise you with all earnestness not to exhaust them in this, merely our third chapter! Resume instead with us our interrupted narrative. — For our hero is now equipped with a glass of strong punch, and has acquired a companion likewise accoutred.

— Your health, Thomas!

— And yours, Selby.

— What cheer, then, you old dog? D___n me, if every time I see you, you don't look a full year closer to your grave. Come, man! Drink! How go your spirits?

— Tolerably well, I hope.

— Tolerably well. Ha, ha, ha. Tolerably well, says he. I don't mean, *How d'ye do.* Your spirits! Your ghosts, and remnants, and what have you! Have you any thing to report?

— I beg your pardon, Selby. No. Nothing to-night. I have been much oppressed with other matters, and neglectful of my duty to the Society.

— Never you mind, Thomas. If you ask me, you chase the wild goose, sir. You pursue the phoenix. The chimaera. You would get with child a mandrake root, as in the verse of old Dean Donne. I mean, you attempt the thing impossible.

— Do you think so.

— Indeed I do. Though I think none the worse of you for it, man, and I'll knock the nose of any that does. But, d'ye hear, I'll wager an hundred pounds you'll find no ghosts, nor mesmeric flim-flam, nor what-have-ye, though ye spend all the year hunting after 'em, view halloo! Five hundred pounds.

— I have not the sum to hazard.

— Fifty, then.

— Nor that much.

— Thomas! Are you fallen upon hard times? — The gentleman claps Mr Peach on the arm, dislodging a drop or two of punch. — Come, eat, drink! You are too lean, man. It will never do.

There are some dozen men in the company to-night — we do not count the servants — And each appears more delighted than the last, at Mr Peach's arrival, and indeed at the house, and the victuals — At each other — and themselves. The usual enquiries are made after the health of Mrs Peach — Much the same, I thank you, Mr Higgins; no decline, though no improvement — And upon other matters domestic and local. *Unusual* enquiries are also made, continuing the theme touched on *supra* — That is, whether Mr Peach has made any discovery of spiritual or otherwise incorporeal beings; which might, in other company, be deemed a subject not fitted to promote good conversation, but appears to give neither our hero nor his interlocutors the least surprize or qualm.

Indeed, much of the talk we overhear, as we follow him about the room, runs in courses not often charted among polite *salons*, or at the tables of the great. — There is Mr O'Sullivan, a gentleman of Ireland, descanting upon the mathematical symmetries of fruits, vegetables, nuts, and leaves. Here is Mr Hendry, explaining the distribution of metals in the earth, according to the theory that the 'great globe itself' is created in a series of concentric layers, like a spherical trifle-pudding. Our host, Mr Davis, stands tall and severe by the fire-place, while one Doctor Thorburn, a new addition to the Society, addresses him, with great animation, and at no little length, upon the perfection of Political Science shortly to be attained by the Confederated Congress in the former colonies of America. — Doctor Thorburn, we may add, is himself an American gentleman, or *man* as he prefers to stile himself — For — he says, waving an expostulatory digit — For, Friend, your old ranks and stations of men are not compatible with the *true freedom* of an *uncorrupted society* where all are *equals and brothers*.

— And where is Mr Farthingay?

— Farthingay! Is he expected?

— He is already arrived. His carriage is in the street.

— Look about the room, Thomas. I see no Farthingay. Nor any man in masquerade, who might be he. We'd know him by his belly at thirty yards.

— Has he been called away already? asks Mr Peach, with a sinking heart.

This exchange happens to occur near the fire-place, and is overheard by Mr Davis, despite the efforts of Doctor Thorburn — Who believes that the incomparable virtue of the system of government being established by the Confederated Congress, is best proclaimed in a clarion voice, the readier to assist its inevitable diffusion throughout the world. With the appropriate excuses, Mr Davis begs to draw Mr Peach aside for a word.

— Mr Farthingay is within, sir. He will join the company presently. I understand he seeks your private opinion on a matter of discretion. I have arranged the use of a room up-stairs for the purpose. — Mr Davis, who is a tall man with an upright bearing, inclines at the waist. — Mr Farthingay also requests that the matter not be generally alluded to. I shall, of course, oblige him in that request myself.

— As will I, says Mr Peach. — But what can he want, I wonder?

Mr Davis gives Mr Peach a significant look, and taps his nose, and straightens, and is absorbed once again into the circulations of the company at large.

— It concerns the mysterious *female guest*, thinks Mr Peach, ten to one. — Which we do not offer as any great proof of his perspicacity, for we would wager double the odds that you, reader, have arrived at the very same conclusion, and in as short time.

— Do you hear the prating of our whiskery friend, Thomas, says that same gentleman, who a moment ago pressed the punch into our hero's grasp, and now comes murmuring beside him again. He is a Mr Selby White; and his particular efforts, on behalf of the grand purpose of the Society, at present comprise certain experiments in the varieties of intoxication, to which the human frame is susceptible. — For he hopes to account for the action of *material* substances, on the *intellectual* faculties; and thus, to discover the fundamental unity of *reason* with *nature*. — He indicates Doctor Thorburn, the colonial gentleman, with a discreet motion of his head.

— I can hardly fail to hear him, says Mr Peach.

— Ha! well said! if the Doctor's present enterprizes fail, he might set himself up as the town crier. But, Thomas, what d'ye think I mean, by his *present enterprize* — hey? I will wager five pounds, you shan't guess it.

— I must decline your wager again, Selby. I have not spoken to the gentleman. — Has he not only lately joined our number?

— His ship sailed in but a month or two ago. But, shall I tell you? — all the time since, I hear, he goes about the city, talking of his New Republic across the water; and it is whispered, that he is sent to see its flag planted, upon our British shores. — Mr Selby White accompanies this intelligence, with several winks, and an intimate and confidential look.

— He is an ambassador from the American Congress?

— No, no, Thomas, no. Nothing of the sort — Nothing so formal. — Ask him, and he'll deny it — Deny he is any thing, but plain Doctor Thorburn. But there are murmurs nevertheless — That he sounds out the waters — Examines the ground, to see whether it may be ready for planting — You understand, hey? I have it from more mouths than one, that the Doctor is come to investigate whether what was done *there* — May be done *here* — And the ship that brought him, was laden with some good American silver, to help his enquiries. — With this hint Mr Selby White appears to content himself, for he taps his nose, and nods wisely. — Come, Thomas, he says, I'll introduce you, and you may take his measure for yourself. — Doctor Thorburn! may I?

Mr Peach is presented to the American gentleman, who is delighted to make the acquaintance of another member of the Society — Declares, that he welcomes the friendship of every man, who concerns himself with the progress of mankind, towards the state of universal perfection — Will not offer a bow, for he disdains all such servile ceremony, but shakes our hero by the hand, with tremendous vigour — And asks, what is Mr Peach's particular contribution, to the noble aim pursued by the company?

— An insignificant one, I fear, says Mr Peach. — I add little to the Society at present, beyond a willing ear for the work of others. My wife is unfortunately very ill —

— Pish, man, cries Mr Selby White, clapping Mr Peach on the arm. — You have no need to hide your light under all this modest *bushel-ing*, in this company! — Mr Peach is a scholar of spiritual researches, sir, he says, turning to Doctor Thorburn. — He is our professor of phantoms. — Our doctor, of the dead — D___n me — I can't think of a title, to go with *ghosts* — But whatever you call him, he is your man for all such matters — Ha! *immaterial* matters —

— My dear Selby — begins Mr Peach, hoping to quell the eloquence of his friend. But it is too late. — The attention of the Doctor is engaged.

— That is very remarkable, says Doctor Thorburn. — I confess myself much surprized to hear such things spoken of, in this society. I wonder, my friend, what practical advantages can derive from investigations of that sort? — for, as the example of America demonstrates for all the world to see, it is incontrovertibly evident, that the lot of mankind may only be improved, by the atchievement of *true* liberty, sustained by the *practical* implementation of perfected government.

Mr Peach demurs. — Has no great hopes for his enquiries — Murmurs, that they represent no more than a curiosity of his — Mildly reproves Mr Selby White, for presuming to mention them, in such company —

— Nay, Thomas, nay, exclaims Mr Selby White, clapping him now upon the other arm, You shall not escape your catechism. — Doctor Thorburn ought to hear you. I think there must be ghosts in America too — Unless General Washington's declaration frighted them all back under the ground?

The Doctor reddens. — In his opinion, the famous *Declaration* of the year 'seventy-six is too solemn a subject for raillery. He appears to be preparing a somewhat warm answer. — Mr Davis intervenes.

— Mr Peach, he says, will not object, if I say that his enquiries have an unusual character. The same might be said of many other occupations pursued by our brethren of the Society. No great discovery was ever made, by following the well-worn tracks of lesser men. — An *American* must agree, must he not?

Mr Davis's manner is complaisant. Doctor Thorburn inter-prets the remark, as a compliment upon his nation. — Is molli-fied — And shakes Mr Selby White by the hand, and Mr Peach also.

— Mr Peach, continues Mr Davis, is too modest to stand as his own apologist. But I hope he will permit me to observe, that his pursuits are entirely worthy of the grand aims of our Society. From the most antient times recorded in history, to our own days, there is no period of the world, in which supernatural apparitions have not been popularly reported. If it were ever possible to produce evidence that such reports were credible, would that not be a signal atchievement, in the advancement of human knowl-edge? — A *confirmed* observation, concerning the future state of our existence, would certainly be of the greatest practical conse-quences to our conduct in this life.

Mr Peach bows to Mr Davis, but suggests, that the gentleman does him too much honour.

— That is very well, says Doctor Thorburn. — I shall not dispute it. It will never be said, that an American withholds his respect from any endeavour, which tends to the improvement of mankind! I shall be the first to congratulate you, brother Peach, when you are able to make a *confirmed* report of the fate of any human soul, beyond the grave. But I declare, it can never come about. The great Author of creation has undoubt-edly so determined our mortal existence, that it is divided by an impassable gulf from the realms beyond. It is for that very reason, that the American Republic deems matters of religion to be no part of the science of government. — This wise policy of ours may very justly be named among the greatest advances in the history of human society; for what miseries have not been inflicted upon the peoples of the earth, by endless wars of religion!

— What d'ye think of that, Thomas? says Mr Selby. — Our good brother Doctor Thorburn here declares, you shall never find a ghost. You may as well give up the chase.

— I have found one, says Mr Peach, and shall therefore continue to search for others, when leisure permits; though the unfortunate indisposition of my wife —

— Have you found one? cries Doctor Thorburn.

— I have, sir, says Mr Peach, with all his habitual mildness.

— That is scarcely credible. — A confirmed ghost?

— I should not call it a *ghost*, says Mr Peach. — The terminology must be uncertain.

— I marvel at your declaration! — I wonder how you assert it so positively!

— As do I, sir, says Mr Peach, with a small inclination of his head. — It is for that very reason I hope to enquire after other reports. It is a principle in many branches of knowledge, that a single instance carries little authority.

— The *hapax legomenon* of the philologists, says Mr Selby White. — You understand, Doctor Thorburn, he adds. — Perhaps the addition is a little mischievous, for it is clear enough from the Doctor's look, that he does not recognize Mr Selby White's somewhat school-masterly allusion.

Before Mr Peach must decide, how to remove himself from this conversation, which he finds not at all to his taste, he is saved from any decision — For here now comes Mr Farthingay among the company, to our hero's equal relief and satisfaction — And to general cheers, huzza's, &c.

As befits a man of wealth, and some note in the world, Mr Farthingay occupies a larger portion of it than others do. — It may be said, in accordance with the Newtonian system, that he exerts a great *attraction* upon the adjacent bodies, due to his superior *mass.** Therefore — or perhaps for another reason — he is crowded, and huzza'ed, and clapped about the shoulders, and shaken by the hand.

---

* If those of our readers better acquainted with the system are able to correct any error in this sentence, we shall be grateful; or at least, we shall pretend to be; for, in truth, our concern is rather with our *metaphor*, than our *mathematics*.

Mr Farthingay is, it transpires, in a manner of speaking the *guest of honour*. —

The Anti-Lapsarian Society observes no gradations of degree — Has neither president, nor officers, nor members merely probationary — No masters, journeymen, or apprentices. Doctor Thorburn grumbles at this — For, says he, the Confederated Congress has proved beyond the necessity of further demonstration, that *true freedom, equality* and *brotherhood* are only attained, when men of superior talents are raised to a representative position — But this is by the by. The assembled gentlemen are, by the Society's lights, equal in station. Nevertheless, it is the custom of the gathering — forgive us, we should say, its *law*, for the procedure is established in the fourteenth, fifteenth and sixteenth Clauses of the charter — That at each meeting, either one or two of the members shall make report to the others, of their progress in their chosen fields of enquiry, tending always towards the grand object of the Society as a whole.

On this night Mr Farthingay is the sole gentleman appointed. — The floor will be his — Though not, by order of Clause the twenty-ninth, until after dinner.

Seats are taken. China is brought in. The delicacies laid out by way of *ouverture* are removed, and the body of the feast is presented. — We pass over the greater part of this meal without further note, except to assure you that Mr Davis has stinted nothing, and most particularly so, with regard to his cellar. All is wine, song, and the highest pitch of good cheer, until! —

We trust you attend to us, reader, and have not been lulled into a stupor by all this meat and drink! — UNTIL, we say, the unmistakable sound of a FEMALE voice, raised in furious protest, penetrates into the room, from some higher place in the house.

Mr Davis rises, and with whispered instructions dispatches a brace of servants. Eyes and questions follow them. Only Tho.s Peach directs his look towards Mr Farthingay — On whom has fallen, a look of the most despairing mortification.

The commotion above becomes more pronounced. There is trampling up and down the stair — Back and forth, across the boards of a room overhead — while the female tones increase in violence — and also, which is unfortunate, in distinctness, so that a few words become audible, and they none of the politest. There are oaths, and other coarse expressions, and threats barely to be distinguished from curses. — In short, it cannot now be doubted by any member of the Society, that there is taking place, under the very roof where they have gathered in a spirit of philanthropic complacency, a most bitter contest — Between numbers of their host's domestics, and some fearsome harpy, who might by the sound of her be that very *Eris*, or Discord, that spoiled the feasting of the Olympian gods, and set in motion ten years of most un-philanthropic slaughter.*

At this unpleasant interruption, a species of impalpable fog settles over the company. Each gentleman turns and murmurs to his neighbour, and is unsure in what direction to look.

— God's blood, says Mr Selby White to Mr Peach. — Does Mr Davis keep an whore? Are we never to be free of women? — Mr Selby White is by this hour greatly drunk.

The harpy's screams are on a sudden muffled. A servant enters, red-faced from exertion, and also from a wound above his eye, of a width and depth corresponding to the trajectory of a fingernail administered in intemperate fury. This poor fellow mutters a word to Mr Davis, whose naturally sallow complexion has paled to something resembling cold ashes. The latter nods, and whispers in turn to Mr Farthingay. — Who now rises, with every mark of reluctance and heaviness of spirit.

— Gentlemen, he says. Gentlemen.

He gestures for all to resume their seats. Some others had begun to rise. — This is, after all, a *philanthropic* assembly. — There are many present, who feel that *something must be done* — Even when they cannot, in the precise instant, be certain what the thing may be.

* The Trojan War.

— Gentlemen, says Mr Farthingay, a third time. — The noise you have heard, I grieve to confess, is the sound of my DEFEAT.

Solemn looks are exchanged, among the seated members.

Mr Farthingay continues — I am much saddened that the failure, which belongs to me, and to me alone, has broken the merriment of our Society, which ought to be our triumph and our pride.

— The Society! shouts an enthusiastic gentleman, overcome by emotion, and raises a glass. The toast is echoed and approved of. The impalpable fog dissolves somewhat. Above-stairs, the battle appears to be concluded, though an occasional heavy blow is heard, akin to the spasms which are said to attend the subsiding of the earth-quake.

— I had intended, continues Mr Farthingay, to give a full account of the experiment to which I have devoted all the meagre hours of my leisure, after dinner. But I find I must make my miserable confession without delay. I am obliged to apologize — To you, Mr Davis, whose good hospitality has been so rudely treated, and to you all, my fellow *Anti-Lapsarians*, who expected this night to enjoy without restraint the felicity of our Society!

— The Society! – Huzza's, further toasts, sounds of approbation, &c.

— There is, Mr Farthingay resumes, an awful solemnity settling upon him — There is at this present moment secreted in a room above, with the prior knowledge and consent of the estimable Mr Davis, a young woman, until recently of my household.

This intelligence immediately procures for Mr Farthingay the entire attention of his audience.

— This person — Mr Farthingay draws a kerchief from his pocket — Forgive me that I cannot bring myself to name her — This creature came to my attention many years past, at that time when my endeavours in the world had been blessed with such success as permitted the acquisition of Grandison Hall. With the purchase of the estate came the necessity of engaging a number of servants. Through what negligence I know not, there arrived among them a particular scullery wench, who in short time proved herself to be carrying a bastard.

Mr Farthingay pauses to survey the assembly, with all the gravity of a bewigged dean, examining his congregation, to assure himself that his sermon is properly attended.

— I knew, he continues, as you know, the unhappy fate awaiting girls who fall into such imprudence. The future, to which the silly wench had condemned herself, I could do nothing to avert. But in the eager warmth of my youth I resolved that the poor infant, the innocent fruit of a liaison in whose wanton folly it bore no part at all, should not suffer with the guilty mother. When the girl came to her time, I gave order that the child be taken from her if it lived, and brought to the household, and raised in Grandison Hall. So it was that seventeen years ago I stood by the font as god-father, and gave a poor spotless babe the name which — Here Mr Farthingay dabs at his eyes with the kerchief — Which I can no longer bear to speak!

Mr Selby White is moved to search out his pocket-kerchief also.

— You will understand, brothers of the Society —

— The Society! cries a too enthusiastic member, raising a glass — Upon which he observes, that neither his cry nor his gesture now meets with the approval of the company, and bows his head.

— You will understand, proceeds Mr Farthingay, with an awful look at the abashed member, That the young woman, whose intemperate raging just now abused the hospitality of this evening, is that very same child, offspring of lust and drunken shame, whose taint could not be expunged from her blood, no, not though infinite, nay, I believe *unprecedented* pains were taken over her education and care! For it was not merely my intention that the infant be cloathed, and housed, and provided with the minimum of those comforts which it must have been denied, had it been compelled to share the fate of its unhappy mother. No! I had conceived a project in every way more ambitious, more noble, I dare say, and more in accord with the spirit of scientific benevolence which animates all of us, my brethren and fellows. I must enlarge for some moments on the nature of my purpose. It alone can excuse what has been done to-night.

Mr Selby White decides he had better replenish his glass.

— You are all familiar, says Mr Farthingay, with the Émile of Rousseau.*

An indistinct murmur passes around the table, whether expressive of assent or doubt, we cannot be certain.

— Though the philosophy of Rousseau is necessarily vicious, being formed by a Frenchman, and in consequence naturally deficient in both common-sense and sound moral feeling, it must nevertheless be universally admitted that the project of the Émile is a worthy one. To raise a child free of all malign influence; exposed from the day of its birth only to correct models and exemplary behaviour; to teach only the best, and absolutely to exclude the worst, of human nature; in brief, to raise an human being as close to perfection of outward manner and inward sensibility as is possible, by a perpetually diligent attention to every moment of those years in which knowledge is imparted, social habits are learned, and character is formed! — who would not deem *this* a worthy enterprize? This, gentlemen of the Society — *This* was my resolution, in the case of the unfortunate infant delivered into my care. My purpose was to oversee in all points the education of the child, so that by the age of its majority I would have created a person entirely wise and virtuous, possessed of every finer feeling, and utterly incapable of, because ignorant of, any ignoble thought. I do not need to ask you, my brothers in philanthropy, whether this was a worthy ideal. I do not enquire of you, whether the ardent benevolence of my youth had taken aim at a glorious target, or whether its atchievement would justify the care and expenditure

---

* For the benefit of our readers unacquainted with the literature of France, or with that portion of it produced by the extraordinary Rousseau, we will add, that the work alluded to is a species of didactic romance, in which is presented an ideal method of educating the young.

lavished on the pursuit, or represent a notable triumph in the annals of philosophy and science!

At this climax of rhetoric there is a species of subdued roar, as though the company would once more break out into huzza's and draughts of celebration, were they not conscious of respecting the tragical manner Mr Farthingay has assumed.

— Possessed by this, I flatter myself, not altogether unworthy ambition —

— Entirely worthy! interjects Mr Selby White, striking the table with his palm, in the vigour of his emotion. — Worthy of — Allworthy!*

One or two of the members are heard to hiss. Mr Farthingay favours Mr Selby White with a look of Olympian solemnity.

— Possessed by this ambition, he continues, when all is silent attention again, And discovering the infant to be female, I resolved that she be reared in imitation of the most exquisite pattern of feminine virtue which history, philosophy, or literature affords. I refer, of course — I refer to —

Mr Farthingay is for several moments overcome by an excess of sentiment, and has recourse again to his kerchief.

— I refer — to — the divine — the incomparable — MISS HARLOWE.

— Miss Harlowe! goes the whisper around the table. — Ah! Poor Miss Harlowe! — Many pockets are reached for, and not a few tears are gently wiped away.

You, reader — for we see you are a person of feeling — You may yourself require an interval, in which to heave a sigh, in remembrance of Clarissa Harlowe, the tragical heroine of Richardson. — We afford you the opportunity, by taking a moment to observe, that Tho.s Peach is not seen to be moved at the mention of that name, sacred to all refined and delicate sensibilities! — a thing perhaps very shocking to you. We hasten to inform you, that our hero is not so utterly deficient in taste and

* *vide* Justice Fielding's History of Tom Jones.

education, as to be unacquainted with the lamentable history of Miss Harlowe. We can only conclude, that Mr Peach declines, for reasons of his own, to share the general sentiment roused by Mr Farthingay's confession. — With this brief interval of speculation we must be content — For your own sigh of sympathy is come and gone, and we, like Mr Farthingay, must continue.

— I shall not, gentlemen, recount the whole course of the child's education. It has been a labour of seventeen years. Seventeen years of unfailing diligence; of patient care; of, I think I may say, the exercise of a sustained benevolence, not often to be met with in the annals of charity; and all, alas, alas! wasted. I need only say that from her earliest days, the child was taught only those habits, and exposed only to those influences, as might form a MISS HARLOWE! No sooner was she capable of reason and sympathy, than I myself began to introduce her to the very thoughts and feelings of that matchless creature, as recorded in her own words.* Year by year, we read together the effusions of that virtuous pen, from which pour the most perfect sentiments of obedience, humility, honesty, judgment, and every feminine grace. As we read, we reflected, so that every lesson might not

---

* The vagaries of taste are without rhyme or reason. We fear, that this work of remarkable genius has fallen somewhat out of fashion. — An hundred years since, matchless *Shakespear* was thought inelegant, and in need of improvement. — What are we to do, but throw up our arms in despair at the world's follies, and set as little store as we may, by the fickle judgments of modish taste? — But what are we about? — We meant only to remind you, in case it be necessary to do so, that Richardson's Clarissa is among those numerous novels of the preceding century, which are conducted entirely in *letters*. His heroine is a prodigious penwoman. — Hence Mr Farthingay's allusion. — And now, observe — To any, who complain at the length of our history, we make this reply: here is a not insubstantial foot-note, which we have been compelled to include, merely to account for one single phrase, in the midst of an extended oration! — All because we cannot be certain, whether our reader be acquainted with one of the most celebrated monuments of modern literature. The moral is — If you would have our book shorter — *Look to your own education.*

only be fixed in the reasoning capacity, but sink deep into the heart. I pride myself, brothers in philanthropy, that for sixteen years my project was attended with every mark of success. Had any of you been introduced to the young lady a twelvemonth past, and obtained but five minutes conversation with her, you would have gone away dazzled. You would have declared her a paragon. Kept from all inferior company, acquainted daily with every thing which inclines the mind to taste and the soul to virtue, she was on her sixteenth birth-day a lady, who would have graced a palace — nay — a throne! You would have said, as I did — As I often did — ah! how! the recollection grieves me — That here, in flesh and blood, in the happy bloom of youth, is the living image of — Clarissa Harlowe herself!

Our chapter, we see, threatens to swell as substantial as Mr Farthingay's sorrow. — There is no remedy but to abridge his further expostulations, on the subject of hopes dashed and noble intentions defeated, for it is his favourite theme, and he rhapsodises upon it with powers of invention and variation, that would not shame a *Beethoven*.*

Of the material part of his address before the Society you are now sufficiently apprised. We pass over some further lamentations, and summarise what remains. In rhetoric distinctly less effusive — as though Mr Farthingay has, like Icarus, allowed the wings of passion to carry him too high, and finds himself plummeting earthwards willy-nilly — He explains, that the young lady on whom his scientific experiment had for sixteen years been conducted to his complete satisfaction, became in her seventeenth, surly, coarse, and unmanageable; though with no alteration in the method of education, or the management of daily

---

* The name is perhaps not universally known in these islands. Allow us to inform you, should it be necessary, that Herr Louis v. Beethoven was a musician of Vienna, a place noted for its *cognoscenti* in that art; among whom his compositions have gained much notoriety, for force and ingenuity, if not for strict correctness and elegance.

intercourse, which until that period had proved so conducive to the formation of a character free from such defects. He is unwilling to dwell on a subject so evidently painful. He confesses only that the flaws suddenly apparent, have, like cankers, grown greater and blacker as the year proceeded, despite his strenuous yet tender efforts at correction; and that he has at last been compelled to renounce the project entirely, the young woman having in recent months sunk so low, as to be fit only for an *asylum*; to which unhappy refuge he is presently conveying her, diverting from that journey only this one night, for a purpose he begs the gathered gentlemen to allow him to keep private, though it requires the particular assistance of *one* of their number. — Here his look falls for a moment upon — Mr Thomas Peach.

Mr Farthingay resumes his seat, without adding *coda* or *envoi* to his lengthy oration, and stares in the bottom of his glass. The figurative fog, or metaphorical mist, to which we alluded earlier, descends once more over the feast-table of the Anti-Lapsarians. Neighbour shuns the eye of neighbour — Colleague knows not what to speak unto colleague. Mr Davis whispers to a servant, who whispers to Mr Farthingay, who withdraws from the room — to uncertain applause from an handful of the members — Sympathetic in character, we suppose.

Mr Davis invites the company to join him at pipes, cards, and brandy, in another room. One and all are eager to leave the table, upon which that poetical pall has so immovably settled.

— Devil of a business, Thomas, murmurs Mr Selby White.

Mr Peach wishes only for his few minutes of conference with Mr Farthingay. — Although, as you may well imagine, he is doubtful how to broach the matter of his rent, after the scene just described.

But Mr Farthingay is not in the withdrawing-room.

To every body else, his absence is welcome. Relieved of the need for discretion, they fall to discussing what they have heard, and in moments the Society's conversation has resumed its habitual vigour, if not altogether its good spirits. Mr Peach, however, is anxious lest the whole purpose of his long ride be frustrated. He is on the point of absenting himself from the room and going in search of Mr Farthingay — a body too prominent to elude a determined quest — When his elbow is caught.

— Up-stairs, Thomas, says Mr Davis, in a discreet tone. — You are expected.

A cluster of candles illuminates the landing. A great sash-window of twenty-four panes gives onto mere darkness, and is set a-murmuring by rain. Despite that unseasonal noise, and the more cheery sound of mingled conversation carried up from the withdrawing-room, the house appears to Mr Peach suddenly quiet — As any place must, if one is removed abruptly from the company of a dozen men, to the solitude of one. The servants are not to be seen.

At the summit of the stair Mr Farthingay waits in a settee. Its legs, unlike his, are in the classical stile, and seem about to suffer by the comparison — But are relieved of the risk, by his rising.

— Mr Peach, he says, taking our hero by the hand. — I am inexpressibly grateful.

— The obligation is all mine, sir. I had hoped above all for the honour of a brief interview.

— Dreadful circumstances, Mr Peach.

— I wish it were otherwise.

— More dreadful than you know.

— I am heartily sorry to hear it. The more so, since my own circumstances are become a matter of concern.

— I must ask for your absolute discretion.

— You may depend upon it. In every matter.

— Mr Davis assures me you are entirely to be trusted in that regard.

— I hope I may. Indeed, I hope I have your confidence entirely, for, as you know, you are so good as to allow me the tenancy of a portion of your estate. Concerning which —

— Mr Davis has, I trust, prepared you for the possibility that I might beg a request of you?

— He has. And it will be my honour to comply to whatever extent may be possible, the more so because I beg to be permitted to make a request in my turn.

— Will it, sir, will it! — Mr Farthingay shakes Mr Peach by the hand again. — I am inexpressibly obliged.

— As to any obligation, sir, that may be discharged at once, if you will be good enough; for —

— You must wonder for what purpose I wish to consult you.

Our hero has a certain familiarity, with the frailties of men — and, alas! of women — Perhaps as a consequence of a life richly endowed with disappointment. At the present moment, he recognizes in Mr Farthingay that particular frailty — particular, we say, but *universal* also — which causes a man to attend to nothing, except whatever subject is of interest to himself. The gentleman's eye wanders anxiously and restlessly, and there is a pallor in his complexion, as though his flesh had been manufactured in painted wax, like the ghastly simulacra of Mme *Tussaud*.

Nevertheless, Mr Peach's cause is of a nature too urgent to be surrendered without a contest.

— I would so wonder, he says, had I leisure to; but permit me to mention, Mr Farthingay, that the matter I must bring to your notice is of such pressing concern to me, as quite to forbid such leisure. Although I believe you might resolve it in the time it takes to say ten words, if you would but be so infinitely good as to pronounce them.

Mr Farthingay blinks once — twice — A third time.

— Well, he says. — I shall explain my purpose, then.

Mr Peach maintains a deportment entirely upright, manly, and polite, but in his soul he heaves a tremendous sigh.

— And again I beg you, continues Mr Farthingay. — No word of this to be repeated.

— I shall say nothing to any man living, and only a little to the most discreet of the dead.

Mr Farthingay stares but a moment — then continues — Thereby concluding a small experiment conducted by Mr Peach, who has silently proposed to himself the hypothesis, that he might say almost any thing at all, without its diverting the gentleman from his intended course —

— I understand you interest yourself in the nature of incorporeal beings. Spirits and the like. Existences not earthly.

The gentle despair, which had begun to insinuate itself within Mr Peach, gives a little way.

— I hesitate to speak of it, Mr Farthingay continues, patting his pockets in abstract confusion. — Before this year of grace I had never thought of such things. I might have smiled at the mere mention.

— You could not be blamed for it.

— But is it so? Have you expertise in things of the sort?

— You heard it, I suppose, from Mr Davis, or another of our brethren in the Society, whose word is not to be doubted, I hope.

Mr Farthingay gathers his resolution, by linking his hands behind his back. — An effort which, due to the particularities of his anatomy, causes his back to bend to a degree near painful, thereby bringing his head excessively upright — The whole posture resulting, expressive of solemn dignity.

— Will you, sir, at my personal entreaty, consent to enter the attic-room, where that fiend in human form is presently constrained, and examine her? I would have your opinion, whether it is possible she is *possessed.*

Mr Peach's astonishment is not to be described.

— There is no danger, Mr Farthingay continues. — She has been bound. The force of her violence is scarcely to be credited for one so young, and wearing a woman's form, but, I thank Heaven, she cannot escape her fetters. There are nevertheless two stout fellows at the door, who may assist in an instant.

— Mr Farthingay, says Mr Peach. — Forgive me — I must be clear in my own mind. Do you believe the young lady to be under some malign and unearthly influence?

— I know not what I believe. My wits are confounded. The sum of what I know is that the gentlest, the wisest, the best of children, is become — A thing —

Mr Farthingay is briefly at a loss.

— I shall not prejudice your examination, sir, he says, with an unhappy shake of the head. — If, that is, you consent to make it. I beg you, sir. — He would, we think, fall to the ground and clasp Mr Peach behind the knee, in that posture of supplication attributed by Homer to the defeated warriors of Troy — Except that his person is not that of an *Hector*.

Mr Peach is in a curious difficulty. The unexpected event has presented an opportunity. — He is sensible that he might easily say, Well, sir, I do consent indeed, provided only that you also consent to relieve me of the requirement of my rent, at least until the quarter-day following. — A more delicate form of words also occurs to him, we hasten to add — Although he guesses, that Mr Farthingay, in his present state of mind, is unlikely to feel any but the most direct blow. Nonetheless, he thinks it would hardly be a noble thing, to press home the advantage.

— If I oblige you in this matter, he says, where might I find you afterwards, to give an opinion?

— Then you do consent! I am inexpressibly — I cannot say how deeply I feel —

— Excuse me, sir. It is my pleasure to perform any thing which will oblige you; but I must be sure of having conference with you immediately after the interview with the young lady.

— Of course, Mr Peach. — Do not doubt it.

— If I might suggest that I attend you at your carriage, which I understand waits outside? You might retire there in the interval, and thus avoid the risk of society, which at this moment you have no wish to encounter, I think.

It is agreed as proposed. Mr Peach is directed above-stairs. — He is on the point of beginning the ascent, when Mr Farthingay takes his elbow.

— Mr Peach, he says, in a strange whisper. — *Look in her mouth.*

Mr Peach is once more overcome with surprize.

— You will have to unbind her. She may commence cursing, and emitting every foulness. But do not fail to look. It is the very point — It is the heart —

Mr Farthingay turns away, with every sign of the most extreme mortification, as though he cannot bear whatever thought he was about to voice.

He descends, towards the lively sound of conversation. — Mr Peach, after a moment's reflexion, from which no enlightenment, nor any other benefit whatsoever, is forthcoming — Proceeds in the opposite direction.

A pair of Mr Davis's men stand outside a low door, under the angle of the roof. One has a blackened eye.

— Safely trussed, sir, says the unwounded servant, nodding at the door. — Won't give trouble. Call out at once, sir, if there's the need.

The other man presents Mr Peach with a lighted candle.

— Is no one else within?

— Stay in the room with that! Beg pardon, sir. No. We keep a good bit of oak between us and the devil, if you please, that's what we'll do. — The man makes a gesture somewhat akin to crossing himself, though he appears unpractised in it.

Mr Peach considers whether to interrogate the fellows further, and decides against it.

— These, he thinks, are doubtless ignorant and superstitious men. Whatever there may be to see within, I shall attempt to view it through unclouded eyes. It is scarcely surprising, that a girl of seventeen, brought up from birth in a species of confinement, and under a discipline at once so eccentric and so rigorous, might turn resentful in the extreme. — And, he continues — for Mr Peach's thoughts proceed in leisurely manner — he is a *tortoise* of philosophy, and not an *hare* — What human creature would not resist with every possible exertion, and with all the violence they could muster, the prospect of confinement in an asylum?

Reader, we have made you thus privy to the inward discourse of our hero, only because it is necessary for our narrative that you should be. — We think it likely nevertheless, that on hearing Mr Peach thus reason with himself, in sentiments so temperate and humane, you ask yourself, Can this truly be a man of *fantastical* leanings? — Is it possible, that a mind capable of these just and reasonable reflexions, should in any degree occupy itself, with such barbaric remnants, and such children's prattle, as this nonsense of spirits, and possession, and incorporeal beings, which Mr Peach's acquaintances appear to think are matters of particular interest to him?

Will this man assert, as he seemed to assert in the presence of Doctor Thorburn, the actual existence, of a *ghost*?

We told you, did we not, reader, in our very first chapter, that Tho.s Peach is a *man of mystery*. —

Perhaps you doubted us. You may have suspected, that like a travelling mountebank we thought to *bamboozle* you, with exaggerations and speculations, merely for the purpose of engaging your interest in the dull ordinary wares we had prepared for your perusal.

We forgive you your doubts. — The world, we know, abounds in histories more or less tedious and insignificant, yet advertised with the most egregious pomp.* Be assured, discriminating reader, that we are guilty of no PUFFERY.

But here is our hero now — The candle in one hand, the other upon the latch — The door open — The plain room beyond. — It is, in the ordinary course of things, given over to the use of Mr Davis's valet.

Behold, the chair drawn to the centre of the room, away from window and fire-place, both of which are equally black and cold —

And, in the chair —

We must open a new chapter.

---

* Parturient montes, nascetur ridiculus mus. — Horace.

CHAPTER FOUR

In the chair is a monstrous thing.

The only illumination is that which our hero has introduced to the room, for Mr Peach has closed the door at his back, to the great relief of the men standing without.

In that barely sufficient light, it is impossible at first to know, whether the occupant of the chair be human creature — beast — Or some mannequin, assembled by a lunatic dress-maker, according to the whim of her diseased phantasy.

Its lower portion corresponds, at least in some degree, to the description suggested by Mr Farthingay, *videlicet*, a young woman; for there are skirts, and feet beneath them, shod in plain muslin.

Above that, the horrors commence.

The figure appears to have no arms. Its body is wrapped in some object which might be a leather waistcoat, fashioned to the design of *Torquemada*, if we imagine that Popish fanatick turned tailor. — The garment is all buckles, and straps, and ties, and studs like the heads of nails, which at the entrance of the candle shine with an evil radiance.

Higher still, is the approximation of an human head, with a length of black hair unbound. The flesh of the lower half of this head has been obliterated. In its place is only a muzzle of shadow.

Tho.s Peach is a man of ordinary bravery. — Which is to say, he is capable of ordinary terror, when faced with a vision so dreadful. He is rooted at the door, and cannot approach.

The head of the ghastly mannequin raises itself, as though

pulled up by its invisible strings, and he finds himself under the gaze of a pair of black eyes. —

The eyes, our poets are fond of saying, are the seat of the soul. Certain it is, that nothing is so immediately expressive of the presence of a fellow human creature, as the direct communication of a look. Feeling himself watched, Mr Peach in turn observes the hideous representation in the chair, for what it is — No *night-mare* after all, but a young person. — Her legs are fastened by ropes to the legs of the furniture — Her upper body bound, in a strait-waistcoat, which restrains her arms at her back — And, most cruel of all, her mouth stopped, by a stiff mask, placed tightly over cheeks and jaw, and fixed with a strap behind her head.

— And has she been thus constrained all this while, thinks Mr Peach, without even the comfort of a candle? Miserable creature! — He spies a lamp upon the night-table, and by the application of his taper sets it a-glow.

At this gesture, the imprisoned woman turns aside, for which Mr Peach is grateful. — The gaze of an apparition so grotesque, like that of the Gorgon, is not long to be endured.

He brings the lamp closer. On his approach the woman attempts a convulsion, rattling the chair. Her breath — forced through the nose — turns rapid. Whether these symptoms arise from rage or fear, he cannot determine.

— But, he thinks, it behoves me to mollify the former as much as the latter, for what harm may this poor thing do me, no matter how furious, strapped and swaddled as she is?

Mr Peach makes a grave and respectful address, and speaks thus —

— Permit me to assure you, madam, that I intend no harm, nor am I come to add to those indignities which I regret to see you suffering.

He is gratified to observe that the convulsion ceases.

— The light is painful to your eye. I shall set it down while you accustom yourself. I hope you will not be offended if I draw up a chair?

There is another such object in the room, with a seat of

horsehair. He places it at a distance neither presumptuously close, not coldly distant, and seats himself.

— My name, madam, is Thomas Peach.

The young woman raises her head once more.

His first terror subsided, Mr Peach is able to meet her look with some equanimity. The eyes are not those of a mad dog in a muzzle — But nor do they appear altogether calm and reasoning.

— My purpose extends no further than a few minutes in your company. Though I am sensible that your liberty has been taken from you, I cannot think it right to impose on you in such a situation without regard to your wishes. If you object to my presence, you need only signal as much, and I will leave you at once. I shall not extinguish the lamp.

The woman continues to regard him, with a frank, forthright, and steady gaze.

— Do you so object?

Mr Peach cannot decide whether the motion of the head, which follows after a considerable interval of silence, be intended for denial or affirmation, or indeed for any purpose at all. He is conscious that his situation threatens to become ridiculous, as though he were attempting conversation with a caged bear. Regarding the particular subject on which Mr Farthingay seeks his opinion, he can as yet see no evidence one way or the other. No smell of sulfur or brimstone lingers about the room, and the extremities lashed to the legs of the chair are human feet, and not cloven hooves, to judge by the shoes in which they are contained.

As to the eyes — Or rather the soul, onto which, according to the poetical figure just mentioned, those twin orbs give a view — Tho.s Peach rather suspects the poets must be in error, or that he has found that famous *exception*, which is commonly, though nonsensically, said to *prove the rule*. — For the gaze of the young person is not at all like the window in the figure, transparent, and disclosing what lies within — But resembles rather the covering of ice on a black mountain tarn, in the month of February, under a storm-laden sky.

— Do you understand me, madam? he says, and when there comes no response, — I regret, he continues, that I have not the authority to relieve the circumstances, which painful as they are to observe, must be a thousand times more painful to endure. Nevertheless, I am requested to give an opinion on your unfortunate state, which, if I am able to do so, may be of some small advantage to you, in perhaps lessening the harshness of this treatment. I cannot give that opinion, without determining whether you are capable of rational conversation. May I once more enquire, whether you hear and understand me, and request, that you signify as much, perhaps by a distinct nod, thus? — He demonstrates in dumb-shew, and is greatly relieved to see that the demonstration is copied, though he fancies he observes also a sudden spark of passion in the person's eye, which he does not much like.

— I am obliged, madam. I repeat, that if in the present distressing circumstances you resent this intrusion, I shall leave you at once, upon receipt of the same signal, thus.

The gesture is not this time repeated.

— Well, says Mr Peach, emboldened by these successes, We shall go along then, since you raise no objection. Though I think we should do better if the hindrance was removed from your mouth. We shan't get far by nodding and winking.

From behind the mask comes an human gargle. The young woman has attempted to speak.

— You understand me perfectly, I see. — Mr Peach leans forward a little, though not overmuch — He desires that his manner convey as much ease as is possible. — Then you will also understand, he says, that if I relieve you of the noxious restraint, you would do well not to give cause for it to be reimposed. There are two men waiting at the door, who I fear have strict orders to intervene in the case of any disturbance.

She nods, as though to signify, — *I do indeed understand, and acknowledge the wisdom of the suggestion.*

— I must tell you, madam, I have been in the house all evening, and could not help but overhear expressions of great agitation and violence. However pardonable they may have been — If the performance were to be repeated —

She shakes her head, with energy.

Mr Peach is by now satisfied that whatever the poor creature's afflictions may be, her rational understanding is unimpaired. He stands.

— Permit me to approach, then, and I shall remove the unpleasant garment. And let us both be as quiet as we may, lest any other party be tempted to replace it.

The mask is strapped with two buckles. Mr Peach has to disarrange the young woman's hair in order to reach them — An interference she bears with patience. He wonders now that he ever took her for any thing but a slight young person, most barbarously disfigured by the trappings of her incarceration. He releases the muzzle.

All at once the illusion of a ghastly mannequin is entirely dispelled — And in its place, a most pitiful sight — Merely a girl of seventeen, twisted and tied like a goose for the oven. She spits and coughs and gasps.

— I might call, Mr Peach begins, for a glass of —

— Pray, sir. Pray, good Mr Peach. Do not move from where you stand.

— Why, child, begins that gentleman again, surprized beyond measure at these sudden accents, so passionate with grief, and yet tuned with such modest sweetness; and he takes a step around the chair.

Forgive us, reader, if we seem pedantic — It is of great importance that you understand the position of the parties relative to each other. — Our hero is presently situated *behind* the chair, the buckles of the odious mask being of course fastened at the back of the lady's head. He takes a step, we say — Or the beginning of a step. At this small motion, she turns her neck to conceal her face, and writhes against her confinement in the most pitiful agitation, and again cries, — Step back, sir, I beg you! if the plea of a poor unhappy woman have any power to move you, and she one most cruelly used, as never frail woman has been used!

A knock at the door rouses Mr Peach from his astonishment. One of the servants calls — Shall we enter, sir? Is she escaped?

— No, calls Mr Peach. Do not open the door. Disturb me no further, on any account.

— Oh, sir, says the prisoner, in a murmur, her head still turned aside — You are too good — Only step back again — I cannot bear —

— Be easy, madam, Mr Peach says, likewise keeping his voice *piano* or *pianissimo*, and he withdraws himself a little behind the chair again. — Do not distress yourself.

— I thank you, sir — I shall endeavour not to — Though I can hardly add, with my own feeble powers, to the great weight of distresses others have heaped upon me — Oh! —

These sighs, and others we do not trouble to record — for they would delay our narrative through *repetition*, which ought rather to proceed by *accumulation* — Are pronounced so gently, and with such a becoming delicacy of regret, that it is scarcely credible to think the same tongue should have uttered them, which earlier in the evening was heard to howl and rail in the most profane terms, and that loud enough to penetrate through an intervening floor of the house, and to disturb the mingled conviviality of some dozen gentlemen. Yet credit it Mr Peach must! for the evidence of his own ears is not to be gainsaid.

He again enquires, whether a glass of water might be acceptable. The suggestion is declined, with expressions of humble, though not servile, gratitude. He offers to move the lamp, that the lady might receive a greater portion of its light — But at his first motion towards the night-table, she reiterates, in the most piteous tones, her plea that he remain where he is.

— Must I then converse exclusively with the back of your head?

— Forgive me — It is the shame I endure — The thought of the spectacle I must present is insupportable to my feelings — To see it reflected in the eyes of another — The pity and horror — Oh!

Indulge me in this, sir, if you do not hate me!

— Well, well. I shall dispose myself on the side of the bed.

You will have learned before now, we hope, that Tho.s Peach is not above the ordinary a vain man. — We dare say, his share of that vice is indeed some distance short of the common distribution. He is quite content to seat himself in a valet's bed — Though we doubt his uncle Augustus would take so light a view of the matter.

— I would not scruple so, she says, with less of passion in the words, Were my humiliation not so complete — I should not otherwise embarrass you.

— There is no embarrassment, madam.

— If — Perhaps — My arms might be loosened but a little —
Mr Peach hesitates.

He is touched to the heart by the lamentable treatment the girl is put to. Yet he does not forget the crashing and cursing in the house, and the scar received by one of the servants, and the black eye sported by another.

He reasons with himself in the following manner —

— What was the first object I proposed to myself upon undertaking this strange interview? It was to determine whether the person be rational creature or no.

— It may now be established that she *is* rational; for all her sentiments and ideas conform to reason, and testify to an unclouded comprehension of the actual state of things; the occasional vehemence and disorder of her language being easily accounted for, as the natural effusions of one oppressed by such extreme treatment.

— Supposing, then, her reason quite unimpaired, what must be its governing purpose, in the current circumstances? — Surely, the hope of escape. For no person in their right mind could submit to such usage, or face without resistance the threat of confinement in an asylum for the insane.

— If, therefore, she attempt to persuade me to unbind her, it is to be considered neither devious, nor in any way vicious, and still less diabolical.

— Nevertheless, though her desire for liberty be altogether

natural, it does not follow that I must conspire to assist it. For though I myself see not the smallest evidence that she be any thing other than a girl tyrannized by an hare-brained scheme of education, and now most cruelly treated, yet I am not appointed judge or jury in the case.

— I fear, he says, after the lengthy interval required by the deliberations just transcribed, That I have no authority to ease your discomfort beyond what is done already. I am commissioned to speak with you, which I could not do without unbinding your mouth. I am glad to have done so. Further than that I must not go.

— Then am I friendless, and without hope in all the world, says the lady, weeping a little, though quietly.

— I am very sorry for it.

— Are you the doctor?

— The doctor! no, child, I am not.

— Are you the priest?

— Indeed not. I am still less learned in the care of your soul, than of your person.

— You mock me, sir.

— Believe me, I do not.

— I think you do. All the men make me their sport. I am to be carried up and down, and fastened to chairs, and made an exhibition, for the amusement of such as you. Is this the house where I am to be kept?

— I assure you, this interview is not in the least part amusing to me. The house belongs to a gentleman of the town.

— A gentleman! well may he call himself a gentleman! though I do not call it genteel, to make one's home a dungeon, and a place of torture, and give it over to the ruin of an helpless woman!

Mr Peach is not sure whether the sentiment be entirely just, but he is compelled to admit that the lady's indignation is excusable.

— I hope, madam, that no further injury will be done to you here. I have some acquaintance with the house, and with the gentleman. Whatever may be done to assist in restoring you to a more comfortable situation elsewhere, I shall undertake to do.

— Elsewhere! then this is not yet the dreadful place, to which I am condemned! This is but a fore-taste, of the trial awaiting me!

— Madam, I must ask you a question. I beg you to hear me with patience.

— Sir, I am deprived the free use of my limbs, and am in agonies of misery and despair, yet I will summon what patience I can.

Mr Peach silently acknowledges the justice of the rebuke. He thinks — Miss Clarissa Harlowe might have answered thus.

— I would know, he says, what account you can give of how you came to be confined in this regrettable fashion. You were not restrained, I understand, when you first entered the house; but since that time, I think you have not always conducted yourself as you do now.

The young woman raises her head from its deep bow. Thomas Peach still has no view of her face — Do not, reader, forget the disposition of the parties! — Yet he feels an alteration in her manner.

— So this is the nature of your commission, she says.

— I ask for my own satisfaction merely.

— You said you were no priest.

— Nor am I.

— But you would have me confess.

— Madam, I would hear you recount the evening's events in your own words.

— You wish me to say, I am a wicked vicious girl. You wish me to own all my faults, so you may tell me I deserve every cruelty laid on me. You would call me harridan — Ungrateful child — Cursed baggage —

— Patience, madam.

— *Patience*, you say! It is always *patience*, and *Calm yourself*, and *Remember who you are, Miss Riddle!* I am always to be meek, and endure every thing!

— Do not be angry. Or we may rouse the servants.

— I will answer your question, she says, keeping her voice low, yet all the sweetness of manner is gone from it. — I came here because I was compelled to come. As I am compelled in every thing. I have every day been in ropes and straps and muzzles, though sometimes they are invisible, for they are made only of words. I was to be examined. I was to be presented to the curiosity of some gentlemen, like a dog that will sit up at a command, or a toy to amuse a child. I cannot endure — This treatment — I cannot! — and will not! — But I am made to endure it, by violent hands. As I am made to endure your interview.

Mr Peach rises from his place at the side of the bed.

— I am very sorry to have offended, he says. I will impose no further.

— Oh, she says, in a voice changed again, Do not leave me, I beg you.

— I must. My commission is discharged.

— I am intemperate — I shall be patient — Only stay a little.

— I shall make what representation I can on your behalf.

— No — Speeches cannot help me now — One moment, I beg you!

Mr Peach has begun to think of his bed at the inn. He wishes for nothing so much as to put this whole business from his head, which threatens an ache. He draws himself up with a sigh, and says, — A moment only.

— To-morrow, she says, I must be given over to doctors and priests. I shall be shut away for ever. This night is my last hope — You, sir, are my last hope of happiness in this world. In the name of a just and merciful God, I beg you, release me — I beg you!

Mr Peach sighs once more.

— I fear, says he, we can none of us expect either the justice or the mercy of God. I cannot do as you ask.

— Do not say so — You can, sir — It is a matter of moments to loosen these knots — I ask no more than that.

— It is not in my power.

— I will permit you the enjoyment of my person.

Mr Peach's senses are dulled by the lateness of the hour, and the

72

quantities of punch he has enjoyed, and above all by the eccentric character of the conversation he has been put to — So that he stands for several seconds, unsure of the young person's meaning.

— The full enjoyment, she continues. — I am *virgo intacta*, a state pleasing to all gentlemen. Only release these bonds, and I will open all this unploughed field for your planting. Or if you prefer I will attend to your pleasure with fingers and tongue. Or you may have my a__e. Or each of these delights in succession, as you please. On that very bed. You might forbid the servants entrance if you are heard. Would that not be a fine pleasure, sir, to deny the lackeys ingress, in the very moment you are admitted to the inward chambers of my virgin flesh? Or else we shall force silence and discretion upon ourselves, and seal each other's mouths with ardent kisses even in the height of enjoyment. Release me, good Mr Peach, and in moments I am your slave — To do with as you wish — I will demur from nothing — Nay — I will be eager — I will —

This extraordinary peroration is only brought to a stop when the young woman — *lady* we ought not to name her at present, we think — finds Mr Peach no longer behind her, but at her side, staring in the utmost amazement. With a cry she turns her face away. —

But he has had a glimpse, and in that glimpse, an hint of a thing so far beyond his powers to comprehend, that it has obliterated even the effect of the person's language — which effect, you may well imagine, is not inconsiderable.

Reader, you will recall Mr Farthingay's whispered instruction, to *look in her mouth*. —

Mr Peach steps in front of the chair and looks again.

At this, the woman sets to tossing her head from side to side and shrieking — Which in turn brings the rough fellows at the door to hammering, and calling out, whether their services are required. Amid this sudden bedlam, the woman commences the most violent efforts to throw herself out of her confinement — out of the chair — out of her own mortal case, it would seem, from the mere fury of the exertions. Yet she is cruelly and securely fixed, and cannot prevent Mr Peach from seizing her head in one hand and her jaw in the other. With an effort of strength, and of no small courage either, for the howls of the imprisoned creature would drive off a pack of wolves, and there is every risk of receiving a bite, he holds her mouth open — Stares — Only a moment or two, yet long enough to confirm the hideous impression received at his first glimpse.

The interior of the mouth — tongue, teeth, and every part — and the inside of the lips — Is all — BLACK — black as night — as pitch!

It appears the woman has expended all her efforts, in the attempt to prevent Mr Peach discovering this ghastly sight, for now they have proved vain, she gives them up. She discontinues her shrieking, and twisting, and rattling.

Mr Peach releases his hold, and calls to the men at the door that they must not enter. He meets the young person's eyes again.

Be pleased to remind yourself, reader, that for the duration of the conversation, which we have just now recorded, Mr Peach sat at her back, and therefore had not those orbs in view. — Now he studies them again, he wonders he could ever have thought the girl sweet-natured and delicate in temperament. — For, there is in them *something* — He knows not what it is — He cannot, in the present agitation of his thoughts, describe it — Only he is sure, that he has never seen the like, and hopes he never will.

On the point of leaving the room, he turns again.

— Pray, he says, very low — Remain quiet. I think they will leave you be, so long as you are quiet. I would not have you muzzled again.

He tells the servants they must not go in — And then makes his way down-stairs.

The Society has recovered its jovial spirits, on the evidence of the sounds which emanate from the elegant part of the house, but Mr Peach has not the least desire to rejoin it. He walks out unnoticed by all save Jonathan, to whom he returns the borrowed medallion, not wishing to be responsible for the loss of yet another, which would be the fourth such item he has mislaid, in the period of his membership of the Anti-Lapsarian Society.

Mr Farthingay's carriage waits in the street — And Mr Farthingay waits in the carriage — Within which comfortable and modish conveyance Mr Peach is invited to join him, by urgent gesture.

No sooner is the door pulled to than Mr Farthingay raps on the roof to signal the *Drive on*, with no thought for the fate of the other gentleman; who thereby discovers, that to the series of surprizing adventures he has met with this night, is now added — Abduction.

— Well, sir — Well — What is your opinion of the case?

— Mr Farthingay, says Mr Peach, his patience stretched beyond endurance, I will deliver my opinion, after you have consented to hear me on another matter.

— Another matter?

— I am in difficulties, sir. An unfortunate family dispute has left me in this moment, and for the near future, close to destitution, to which state I must infallibly be reduced, unless relieved of the most pressing demands, by the extension of credit.

Mr Farthingay appears no whit less bewildered, than if this sentence had been pronounced in the language of the Hindoos.

— I am sorry for it, he says, at last, in the manner of one whose sympathy has not been in the slightest engaged. — But what of the young person — the creature?

Mr Peach leans forward, and places an hand upon the ample knee of his interlocutor.

— I cannot pay my rent, sir, he says, pronouncing each word between the first and the last, with school-masterly emphasis. For good measure he repeats them — Cannot — Pay — My Rent.

— Most — Mr Farthingay blinks in his confusion — Most regrettable — Unfortunate — But how am I — Do I understand that you apply for charity?

— Sir. You are the landlord.

Mr Farthingay is thunder-struck. — I?

— You, sir. I occupy the cottage at Widdershins Bank. The land belongs to your estate. It is in your power, Mr Farthingay, and yours alone, to decide whether Mrs Peach and myself shall be turned out, and go I know not where. My wife, you may be pleased to recall, is very ill. And now I must beg you to halt the carriage, for it has turned out of my way.

— But — Dear Mr Peach —

The gentleman so named pulls down the window and shouts for the horses to be stopped. He places an hand on the door.

— Nay, cries Mr Farthingay — Do not alight. I must have your opinion. Upon the other matter — Come and see me — We will resolve — Come to Grandison Hall, at your earliest convenience.

— I thank you, sir, says Mr Peach, counting this poor triumph the best he is likely to obtain, Mr Farthingay being so evidently distracted out of all reason. — Shall I attend upon you to-morrow, before dinner?

— Yes — To-morrow. But now —

Mr Peach opens the door.

— Now, says our hero, it remains for me to inform you, that after examining the unhappy creature, I am unable to discover in her any sign of evil influence, beyond that which must naturally be ascribed, first, to the condition in which I found her, and second, to the disadvantages peculiar to that system of education, which was to-night so eloquently described to the members of the Society. Good-night, Mr Farthingay.

— But, exclaims Mr Farthingay, though in a whisper — as though he fears to be overheard, by the surrounding darkness — The *mouth*!

— Excuse me, Mr Peach says, stepping down to the street. — I have now some distance to walk to the inn. My opinion remains as I have stated it. I shall attend you at Grandison Hall, before dinner to-morrow, with the greatest pleasure.

And so, repeating his *good-night*, he takes his leave. — One gentleman proceeds a lengthy journey home by carriage, while the other goes to his place of rest in his own shoes. And if, like our fellow-historian *Plutarch*, we were to conduct an exercise *comparative*, and attempt to say which of the two went on their way the least contented, we should swell this fourth chapter of ours to double its dimensions, without arriving at a definite conclusion — For each seems as dissatisfied and uncertain, as the other. — Instead of which *Sisyphean* labour, we shall without another word hasten both of them to their beds, and ourselves too — Where, we devoutly hope, the visions we have raised in these pages will not trouble our dreams. For, as glaziers are in the nature of their trade often afflicted by the poisoning of the blood, and mill-workers in theirs by distempers of the lungs, so we who practice the art of *necromantic history* are condemned to suffer the visitations of the galloping *night-mare*.

CHAPTER FIVE

The daubers and gravers of old Italy —

— Pray — Reader — Do not start so — We know what we are about —

The painters of Italy, we say again, knew an art, called in the language of those countries *chiar-oscuro*, which signifies *light-dark*. — A term which good British tongues may hesitate to pronounce, for fear that by asserting the conjunction of opposites, they might be speaking mere nonsense — As who should say in a single word, *east-west*, or *yea-nay*, or *soup-mutton*.

But, fear not — The ingenious Italians intended no such paradox — nor, indeed, meant to approximate the sublime phrase, in which Milton envisions the throne of the Almighty, in the third book of the Paradise Lost* — But only described a particular skill, whereby they coloured some parts of their canvases nearly black, and other adjoining parts nearly white — And by the contrast, atchieved some thing or other, which the connoisseurs of our Royal Society may explain to you, if you desire to be *enlightened* further.

This trick of Latin oils and easels we hereby appropriate, for the higher purposes of *British history*. — For, after the Stygian horrors of our preceding — The nocturnal room, with its dreadful prisoner — Behold us now all at once in the open air, under a cloudless evening sky! and before that prospect, of all things most pleasing to the eye and heart — An ENGLISH COUNTRY SEAT.

* 'Dark with excessive bright.'

78

We need not tell you, reader, that the fine old house before you, which like the more elegant sort of dowager, retains enough of visible antiquity to convey a stately and reverent charm, while correcting the unpleasant remainder with tasteful improvement, is — Grandison Hall.

In vain will you search for the name, among the records and memorials of Somerset-shire. Though the foundation dates to the time of the first James, and the family, which for successive generations occupied and enlarged the house, is a tolerably antient one, the old name they knew it by was surrendered, along with the estate, when it was sold to Mr Farthingay.* Nor will you find report of Grandison Hall in the news-papers or gazettes of to-day, for a reason which it will be part of our business to supply in its proper time, and which we therefore decline to give at present. Mr Farthingay chose the name himself, upon acquiring the property.

That the ordinary people of the county, whose fathers and forefathers lived and died, as secure in the certainty that the great folk dwelt in ____ Hall, as that the sun dwelt in the heavens, were not much pleased with the alteration, you may well imagine. — And this is the cause whereby Tho.s Peach appears on our scene somewhat later than the hour expected, and more than a little discomposed by his hurry. For the place lies to the south and east of Bristol — in which city, you will recall, he has passed the night preceding — Whereas his home at Widdershins Bank is to the south and west; and, therefore, he is not well acquainted with the road he must take to Mr Farthingay's house; but, each time he has halted at the door of cottage or farm, to ask the woman at the wheel, or the boy throwing sticks at the cat, whether he be on the right road to *Grandison Hall*, the enquiry has as often as not been

---

* The history of their decline is not without interest. — It touches upon an ill-fated expedition in search of the fabled *Abominable Snow-Man* of the Himalaya, and a consequent entanglement, with an high-born female impersonator of the *Mooghal* lands. — We regret we have not leisure to unfold it.

met with surliness or silence. — For the people still resent the name, and will not acknowledge it.

Mr Peach had indeed despaired of the journey altogether, were he not impelled to proceed, by the absolute necessity of his interview with the master of the house. Nor might necessity itself have been sufficient, to overcome the equally implacable refusal of the country to admit the existence of any such place — for, when God created Whitchurch, and Marksbury, and Compton Dando, He most certainly did not ordain a *Grandison Hall* — Had it not been for a remarkable encounter; which we must briefly relate.

Mr Peach had been riding up hill and down dale, as uncertain in his course as the ever-descending sun was fixed and straight, when he came upon an hill topped by a coppice, commanding a picturesque prospect westward; the which *vista* was being studied, with the most earnest attention, by a lady, seated upon a stile, and wearing on her head an extraordinary wide conical hat, in observance of no fashion our hero had ever made acquaintance with. At the margin of the road two horses cropped the grass, while a negro in breeches and a white shirt lay upon his back, holding over his breast an octavo note-book bound in green leather. This latter gentleman was the only one of the party to acknowledge the rider's approach, by raising his head for a moment from its recumbent position. — Upon which he nodded, then placed his finger across his lips, to indicate, Mr Peach supposed, that the lady's contemplations were not to be interrupted — All with an air of easy familiarity, which Mr Peach should certainly have thought insolent, had he been the sort of man who must always insist on the respect he feels is owed to him. — Which sort of man, he is not.

Though the significance of the gesture was plain, its explanation remained mysterious — For Mr Peach could see no pressing need for silence — No business being transacted, which must not be interrupted — No shy creature being observed, that might take flight at any noise.

Nevertheless, we think he would have touched his hat and ridden on in peace, had it not been for his increasingly desperate state, for he observed the angle of the sun, and knew the hour of his appointment already passed, and still with no secure notion of where the object of his journey lay. He drew up his gelding, who was glad of the rest — The animal being almost as tired of the journey, as its rider. — And thus Mr Peach began —

— Good-evening, sir —

Upon which unexceptionable pronouncement, the lady seated upon the stile emitted a great sigh of exasperation, and threw her hands into the air.

— Great Heavens! she cried, while the man stared at Mr Peach with a rueful look.

— If I have offended, said the rider, a little perplexed, I must beg pardon. I am expected at Grandison Hall, and fear I am out of my way. I hoped you might have the kindness to direct me. Indeed, the sooner you do so, the sooner I will remove myself.

At this the lady turned to examine him. She appeared to Mr Peach a spirited and well-favoured person of perhaps four- or five-and-twenty, with a somewhat haughty look, which might have been quite disdainful and proud, had it not been for the ridiculous effect produced by her mode of dress, in particular the hat.

— Oblige the gentleman, please, Caspar, she said, resuming her study of the landskip. At which the man rose to his feet, pointed along the road, and began describing the way Mr Peach was to follow; but he had proceeded only as far as the leftward path at the bridge beyond the church, when the lady raised an abrupt hand.

— No, she said. — I shall do it myself, as an exercise, and I shall extemporize in blank verse.

Caspar reached for the note-book, which had fallen in the grass, and extracted a lead-pencil from a pocket of his breeches.

— No copy will be necessary, added the lady — Upon which, Caspar replaced the pencil, closed the note-book, clasped his hands at his back, and stood in a posture of attention.

After an interval sufficiently long, to produce in Mr Peach some intimations of embarrassment, the lady stretched out a declamatory arm, and spoke, thus —

This mazy road the wanderer pursues
Until it meets its twin; where th'occident orb
He sets before him, 'til the tower he spies
Of Dunstan's fane. There downward course he takes,
Until the rushy murmur of the stream
Delight his aural sense. Anon he rides,
Pursuant with the flood, 'til at the bridge
He sinister proceed, and cross the wave.
Thence climbs he from the moistened vale, and on,
Diverted not by sideward-tending roads,
Until, where grove of oaks their umbrage lend,
He at his left hand spies the longed-for roof
Where fumous Farthingay his dwelling makes.

Her verses of instruction concluded, the lady then added — You are not puzzled by the epithets, I may presume? *Roof* for *house* is synecdoche. The signifying of the *whole*, by reference to the *part*.

— An admirable figure, madam, said Mr Peach, touching his hat. — Your verse fulfils the highest aim of poetry, by being both delightful and useful.

The lady inspected Mr Peach with renewed interest.

— You allude to the *qui miscuit utile dulci* of Horace. I myself think it is no high aim at all, but a mean and plodding one. — To brew up poetry like a druggist's concoction, one part usefulness to two parts delightfulness, taken by a spoonful before dressing in the morning. If poetry reach no higher than that, we may as well leave it to spiders, and crabs, and every crawling thing.

In his hurry to keep his appointment, Mr Peach had not the least desire to dispute the point, and so, having offered his thanks, he rode on, though in a much better humour than five minutes before. For not only was he pleased at the information obtained, but much amused, at the quaint manner of obtaining it. He smiled often at the thought of the poetical lady, and her curious hat, and her patient amanuensis, and repeated her verses to himself as he went along, past the tower of the village church of St Dunstan, and down to the little river, and over the bridge, and so forth, all in accordance with the lines — only the last of them giving him pause.

— *Fumous*, he said, is not good. Nor can I conceive what the doubtful epithet may signify, applied to Mr Farthingay.

But the only ears able to hear his complaint belonged to his gelding, on whom, we fear, his exercise of judgment was entirely wasted.

So now — our diversion into *belles-lettres* completed — Reader, we return to our *present* narrative — Our hero at last approaches Grandison Hall, along a brief avenue of lime-trees, whose young leaves are in their May transparency, and catch the gold of the evening like so many nets. The sight pleases him less than its beauty deserves, for the evident marks of the declining day cannot but remind him that he has many miles to ride home, and must now certainly travel a good number of them in darkness.

Nevertheless, he endeavours to assume a sociable countenance, the better, he hopes, to ease Mr Farthingay into compliance — *fumous* Farthingay, he thinks, wishing he could banish the alliteration from his brain, where it has taken root like the most truculent of weeds. — For he is above every other thing determined, that a journey so tiresomely prolonged, shall not prove to have been in vain.

He is admitted — Is announced — He is conscious of his tardy arrival, and prepares his apology —

He might have saved himself the labour — for — He is not expected at all.

After the usual delays, and passings of messages, and sitting in the hall listening only to the disapproving tut-tut of the clock, he is shewn in to fumous — we beg pardon, to *Mister* Farthingay. — Whereupon it is soon evident, that the gentleman has entirely forgot the invitation issued the night previous.

Explanations — Excuses — Reminders — all follow, which do little to keep either man in a good temper. The greater embarrassment being on Mr Farthingay's part, it necessarily falls to Mr Peach to assume the more soothing manner, in contradiction to his inward impatience, and so to the further detriment of his spirits. — For to be obliging is, we think, no great hardship, in general — But to be *obliged to be obliging*, is another matter, and chafes on any nature, but the most servile or cunning.

In defence of Mr Peach, we must lay the blame for the following exchange, to the aukwardness in which Mr Farthingay's lapse of memory has placed him. It occurs after the explanations are concluded, and the latter gentleman has sent for his steward.

— And have you, Mr Peach, considered further your view on — The other matter?

— The young lady?

Though Mr Farthingay is under his own roof, he looks about, as though fearing to be heard. — Yes. Understand, I would not speak of this before anyone. I have forbidden mention of the topic.

— I would be glad not to return to it myself.

— But did you not — Could you think it — entirely *natural*? Her *mouth*, Mr Peach! — Mr Farthingay lifts his fingers to that part of himself, as though the meaning of the word were not plain. — So — Deformed!

— I observed no deformity, sir, says Mr Peach.

Mr Farthingay is amazed. — You did not?

— None at all.

— But did you have light, in the room?

— Indeed. I lit the lamp.

— Then you did not see — Her mouth — the tongue — All —

Mr Peach awaits the next word quite calmly. He amuses himself, with the thought that it might be — *fumous*.

— You saw, says Mr Farthingay, unable, we suppose, to pronounce the epithet — Nothing untoward in those parts?

— Nothing.

— But did you not speak with her? Did she not say vile things? Indecencies? Did she not use language — I would not ask you to repeat it —

Impatience is now burning within Mr Peach, and, we must think, scours away the bitterness of falsehood from his tongue, for he answers with perfect grave simplicity. — Our conversation, says he, was not long, but for its whole duration the lady expressed herself only in the most suitable terms. Though she was moved to regret her situation in passionate language.

— I can hardly credit it.

— That is unfortunate, Mr Farthingay, for credit is the very thing I most earnestly hope you will extend me this evening.

— Yes — Indeed — Your pardon, sir — I do not doubt, &c.

In this manner is checked every effort of Mr Farthingay to engage Mr Peach upon the subject of his ward and god-child; and we suppose this to be our hero's intention, for he answers all further enquiries in as few words as he may, with the sturdy brevity of a Quaker, though, alas, without the scrupulous regard for truth to accompany it. — The consequence being, that both parties have succumbed to a gloomy silence, by the time the steward is announced.

We shall not linger over what follows. Though it be the prime object of Mr Peach's visit, it strikes at a *tangent* — if a geometric metaphor may be permitted — to our interest in the scene. In summary; the steward, whose name is Stewart, opens the estate books, and shews Mr Farthingay the parcel of wooded land, upon which is found the house of Widdershins Bank; which, though situated miles distant from Grandison Hall, belongs to the manor, as a result of transactions in former generations, whose intricacies Mr Stewart sees fit to explain at length, conscious as he is of the dignity of his office.

Mr Farthingay being persuaded that he is indeed Mr Peach's landlord, there follows an uneasy conversation. The master wishes to do any thing he may — The steward, mindful of his duty, suggests — with many a doleful cough — That there is nothing to be done.

Mr Peach will not plead like a beggar. It is not, as is commonly said in such circumstances, that he is too proud. Rather we would say, that he is not fitted for it. It is out of his nature. — He lacks effusiveness.

— And have you indeed not twenty pounds in the world? says Mr Farthingay.

— I have not ten, replies Mr Peach.

Mr Farthingay sighs in wonder and sorrow.

— And what prospects have you of obtaining funds, were we to agree a quarter's remission?

Mr Peach has spent the former part of the day revolving this very question in his own mind, and has not yet satisfied himself as to the answer. — Nevertheless, he seizes upon the hint, following the adage that the iron must be struck before it begins to cool.

— Every prospect, sir, I assure you.

The steward, who is heard to tut beneath his breath, humbly suggests that Mr Peach might be somewhat more definitive, concerning the precise nature of the said prospects. Mr Peach's powers of invention do not rise to this challenge with much magnificence. Nevertheless, after some vague talk of London, and relations, and preferment, and a vacant living in an obscure parish of the county, and after various further mollifications and assurances — A quarter's further grace is agreed, and shaken on, and sealed with a glass of brandy.

Mr Peach is more relieved than joyed, at his victory. He cannot fail to think that the danger is merely delayed, and not averted. But he expresses himself infinitely obliged, &c. — And so the business is concluded.

He is pressed to stay for dinner, though Mrs Farthingay is not at home, being presently with her relations in Bath, and there will be little ceremony about the meal. With difficulty, he declines. His purpose atchieved, all his efforts are now bent towards beginning the long ride homewards — Though he cannot but fear giving the impression of ingratitude, which would in the circumstances be as *impolitic* as *impolite*. — In short, the gentlemen are still in conversation, and the hour growing ever later, when there is an interruption heard in the hall — Doors clattering — Voices raised.

— Ah, cries Mr Farthingay, now we shall persuade you to stay — Come, sir — Allow me the honour of introducing Miss Farthingay.

In the hall, stamping earth from her boots and issuing instructions to servants, is the poetical lady, whom our hero encountered by chance upon the road. The curious hat has been discarded, and her hair is adorned instead with a number of those floating seeds, which blow about the country at this time of year. She is occupied in removing them, and does not at first observe the gentlemen approach.

— Arabella — my dear —

— Good-evening, Papa.

— I had not looked to find you in such a state.

— In a state? We have only been out riding.

— Arabella — Pray, attend — I would introduce you to a gentleman.

At which the lady becomes aware of the visitor, and smiles, in a manner which suggests she finds the renewed acquaintance most amusing.

— I have had the pleasure, says Mr Peach, and bows, more according to the usual manner of such introductions.

— The gentleman passed us in the road, says Miss Arabella Farthingay, for so we may now name her. — I think he might be riding it still, had the fates not thrown our paths into conjunction.

— Miss Farthingay was so good as to direct me.

— Well! exclaims Mr Farthingay. — This is splendid! You are met already! You must now consent to dine with us, Mr Peach. — My dear — Permit me to introduce — My friend, a gentleman of the country, Mr Thomas Peach. Mr Peach, Miss Arabella Farthingay, my only child, and all the joy of my advancing years.

— I suppose I am, now, says the lady.

— You might address yourself with a degree more of politeness, says Mr Farthingay, in an indulgent tone. —And dress yourself likewise, indeed, ha! ha!

— Forgive me, Mr Peach, for presenting myself thus before
you, says the lady, continuing to pluck at her hair, and so disar-
ranging it further. — Though, says she, the second impression
being identical to the first, I expect you are not greatly surprised.
I shall appear more *a la mode* at dinner, but the cause may be lost
by then. Earliest impressions strike deepest, it is said.

— Can ye never be content with *How do you do*, Bella? says
Mr Farthingay, with no less of happy complacency, than was
evident in the previous admonishment. — My daughter, he adds,
fancies herself a poet.

— A poet must be rich in fancies, Papa.

— Indeed, says Mr Peach. — It is Horace who tells us so, I
think.

Miss Farthingay favours Mr Peach with another look of
amusement.

— And how, says Mr Farthingay, proceeds Clorinda to-day?
My daughter is assembling sonnets, you know, on the loves of
Clorinda. They are to be printed by Mr Browne at Bristol.

— Clorinda had intended to muse upon a distant landskip, and
compare her waning prospects of happiness with the scene at
sun-set, but she was unfortunately interrupted by a fellow passing on some less elevated business.

— You must add your name to the subscribers, Mr Peach!
Indeed you must.*

---

* The method of publication by subscription, in those days common, is
now, we think, all but forgotten. Reader — we should not like to guess at
your age — Yet we fancy we see the freshness of youth in your countenance.
Let us inform you, then, that according to this now *antique* method, a
certain number of persons promised in advance to purchase the volume,
thereby greatly reducing the risk of the venture to the printer. You may
still chance upon volumes from those years, with the names of the
subscribers printed within.

Mr Peach is already under an obligation to Mr Farthingay, yet continues to decline the repeated invitation to share his table. It is therefore impossible for him to resist this further demand, particularly in the presence of the lady authoress. — He is urged to add a second subscription, in the name of Mrs Peach, for, as Mr Farthingay insists, the Loves of Clorinda will be eminently suited to the enjoyment of ladies, being the effusions of a *female pen*; but is able, though with difficulty, and at the expenditure of more time, which at present he is almost as unwilling to part with as guineas, to persuade the gentleman, that the frailty of his wife's health forbids the proper appreciation of elevated literature.

— Then we must not be importunate, Papa, says Miss Farthingay, linking her arm in his. — For in such cases there is no remedy. I fear Mama has a touch of the same condition. She takes the waters at Bath, you know, sir, but comes home no more sensible of the beauties of poetry than when she left.

— Don't teaze so, Arabella. You ought to be more mindful of the commandment. Honour thy father and mother.

— And so I do. A poet does honour by speaking truth. Do you not agree, Mr Peach?

Mr Peach begs their pardons, but must be away. After further pleasantries, not worthy of record, he escapes the house, and goes in search of his gelding in the stable, where that animal has enjoyed an hour's respite.

He is mounted, and about to ride, when Miss Farthingay comes running from the door, lifting her skirts like a child, calling, — Mr Peach! a moment! —

— I must ask your forgiveness, she says, a little out of breath. — I did not mean to make light of Mrs Peach's illness. It was not well said.

— Think nothing of it, madam.

— Alas, I cannot, even if you will. I am ashamed. Papa says your wife is very ill.

— It is an affliction she has learned to bear, and I also, though my share of it be the lighter.

— The illness is long standing?

— Some years.

— I am truly sorry for it.

Mr Peach touches his hat.

— You must take no mind of the subscription. Papa will always press people so. I wish he wouldn't, but I fear my verses are become his new hobby-horse.

— To judge by your lines *extempore*, it will be an honour to be named in the end-papers of your sonnets.

— You are gracious, Mr Peach, where I was not. That was mere doggerel, composed in jest, and in no good humour. I have forgot the lines, and hope you will do the same.

— On the contrary, madam, I must remember them in reverse, to find my way home.

Miss Farthingay, whose remorse, though expressed in language rather too familiar, is unfeigned, requires several moments before she is able to smile at this sally.

— Though, Mr Peach adds, I must in that case begin at *fumous Farthingay*, which I confess —

— Do not repeat it! cries Miss Farthingay. — A vile epithet. I shall read ten odes of Horace before I sleep, as penance. But I see you are not offended, sir, and so I am content again, and will not detain you. Unless you consent to dine with us after all, at my own particular request.

— I must return to my wife, madam.

— Certainly you must. A good journey to you, then. I think we have no highwaymen hereabouts, nor unquiet ghosts. The worst you may meet upon the roads in this country is ill-tempered poets, who may be readier to exercise their wits than their discretions.

— It has been a pleasure to become acquainted, Miss Farthingay.

— One thing further, sir.

Mr Peach sees the lady is in earnest, and suppresses his impatient sigh.

— If by chance you happen upon my father's *former* hobby-horse on your way home, will you treat the poor creature kindly, and spare a shilling or two? It is a thing that wanders upon two legs, having now no home to go to, and it will not ask for your charity, though in great need of it. In greater need than my book of sonnets, certainly, and more deserving.

Miss Farthingay lowers her voice.

— To speak plainly, sir, there is a poor girl not three days past turned away from Grandison Hall, and where she is gone no one can say. We are forbidden to speak of it. You would not tell Papa, would you? I will add only, that I think she was not well used.

Mr Peach is much surprized at the receipt of this confidence. He has nevertheless the presence of mind to assure the lady, that he will neither repeat their conversation, nor pass the girl without notice, should he happen across her in the road. — Although he knows, as you do, reader, that the event is impossible, for the unfortunate object of Miss Farthingay's good-hearted concern, is undoubtedly the same person whom we encountered in our previous chapter, not wandering vagrant, but about to be committed to an institution of supposedly benevolent confinement. — The which curious puzzle we shall leave our hero revolving, as he 'homeward wends his weary way,'* and draw the curtain across our scene.

* The Elegy of Tho.s Gray.

CHAPTER SIX

We, too, must now return to Mr Peach's sturdy cottage beneath the wood, though neither the length of the journey nor the lateness of the hour, inconveniences *us* — For, reader, our conveyance is no surly plodding beast, but a *necromantic pen*, which transports us across the intervening miles with such remarkable rapidity, that lo! we have arrived BEFORE we departed! — A thing which every philosopher in the alphabetical gamut from Anaximander to Zeno declares to be quite impossible, though we have atchieved it with no more than an handful of words.

We assure you, we intend in the course of this our narrative to subject the accumulated wisdom of these philosophical carpers and croakers, to several further indignities, with as little ado.

It is, now, the AFTER-NOON of that same day, which was seen to be drawing to ITS CLOSE at the conclusion of our last. Do you doubt us? — Observe the angle of the sun. See the various members of the household of Mr Peach, wondering in their several fashions where their master may be. For, you will understand, he is expected some time ago, having informed Mrs Shin and the rest, that his visit to Bristol would occupy him but a single night — the lengthy diversion to Grandison Hall coming about quite by chance. Yet the house is all shut up — And, should any body spare a few minutes to bide and listen, entirely still.

Mrs Shin is not inclined to give herself the trouble of waiting any minutes at all. She is of the opinion that she has enough to do, with fetching provision for Mr Peach's table, and carrying it along the road, on a warm day, only to find the door closed against her, and no answer to her knocking. She leaves a basket at the door, and, having an house of her own to go to, where, she hopes to God, a poor honest hard-working woman would never receive such treatment, goes home.

Jem has returned to the stable earlier in the day, having passed an unwilling night by his native hearth, under Rowberrow Hill, two or three mile distant. His family do not rejoice at his visits, unless he brings his wages. — He finds equally little delight in their company, preferring that of Mr Peach's horse, who can be relied upon neither to complain of his ingratitude, nor beat him. On this day, as we know, the beast is absent, along with its master. — Accordingly, once Jem has discharged various duties of his own devising, and then passed an hour or two humming a tune, and carving indecipherable figures into the manger, he goes wandering in the fields — To muse upon fickle fortune, cruel fate, and other subjects suitable to his years and cast of mind.

Who, then, gives a thought for Mrs Peach? — unattended and helpless, in the sealed house?

Who, but Anny, the inquisitive maid? — The which young person, we are in justice obliged to record, preoccupies herself with the unhappy condition of her mistress, less from an excess of sympathetic feeling, than because she has for several days and nights been able to think of nothing else.

— 'Tis all quiet as the grave, she says to Mrs Shin, for the two of them have happened upon the locked door at the same hour, though coming from opposite directions.

— I would it were as cold, says that lady. — Walking such a great way under this sun, and only to find no body home!

— No body? says Anny. — Only the mistress, if it please you, for she's at home, so he says. All alone up-stairs, never making a sound. So he *says*.

— You may put your nose in where you oughtn't, Anny Pertwee. I'll not be so foolish.

— I don't call it foolish, to wonder at a wife closed up in the house night and day. I don't call it a bit foolish. Suppose there was a fire? or villains come to do robbery? We ought to call up to her, Mrs Shin. — We should inform you, reader, that this colloquy is conducted in near *whispers*.

— We're not to disturb her, and you know it as well as I.

— That's all very well, Mrs Shin, but then what's to become of the mistress, in an empty house?

— I'll not stay to hear you prattle on. I've more to be doing than sitting on door-steps a-prattling.

— He tells us we're not to disturb her — Not to set a foot on the stair — Never to clap eyes on her — Not even to whisper an *how d'ye do* at the door. But now he's gone away who knows where, and left not a soul to care for any body, nor no provision for our poor lady's meat or drink, if she wanted any, which she don't, for there's certainly no such lady at all. I shan't believe it. There's no body home at all, or I'll never say another word!

Mrs Shin does not condescend to give her opinion on the subject — Though it has become a matter of great and general interest in the country, and you may be sure her mind is often sought, she being as it were in a position of acknowledged expertise. Privately, she may admit to a modicum of curiosity, not to say uncertainty, concerning the actual existence of the supposed Mrs Eliza Peach. But, among her neighbours — and most especially, before a pert inquisitive thing like little Anny — She considers it more dignified, to stand aloof from the vulgar gossip; and has been much gratified to discover that by this means, a certain tincture of the mystery of the household in which she is employed, attaches itself to her own person, to the considerable increase of her standing among the circle of her society. — Though in truth the currency of reputation is of less concern to Mrs Shin, than the more tangible *specie*, which so long as she receive weekly from Mr Peach, she does not greatly care what else may happen in the house, up-stairs or down.

Thus in due time, as the day reaches its after-noon, Anny is left alone at the door, listening and waiting still, and conducting inward disputes with herself, thus. —

— I'll call up.

— I mustn't call up.

— But I shall, for what can be the harm in it? I shall say, Mrs Peach, Mrs Peach, are you well, Do you need any thing?

— I am forbidden it. I'll be turned out.

— But the lady is all alone and has no body to look in on her, and there's no knowing how long the master may be away. It's my duty to call up. I shall stand directly beneath the window and use a gentle voice. I can't be blamed for it.

— And there is no such lady, so what have I to fear? Sure there can't be.

— Then WHO DOES HE SPEAK WITH AT NIGHT?

In such litanies of self-examination — from which she gains precisely the same spiritual benefit, as all the rest of those who profess the discipline, such as the Calvinists, Jesuits, &c., which is to say, none at all — The fair maid loses much of the day, until the demands of curiosity surrender to those of hunger, and she repairs to the village.

It is, we remind you, reader, the month of May. — May, the crown of sweet spring — When every man who can drive the plough, or swing the hoe, from the proudest yeoman to the meanest hired hand, must be at his labour from dawn to dusk, for the earth readies itself to put forth her abundance of fruits, and the young lambs skip in the fields, &c. &c. — we ourselves have but scant familiarity with the rustic life, and have opened our *Georgics* in search of exempla. The men, we say — and Vergil says the same — Must be at their tasks and their tools. — In spite of which, in this particular village, as in others up and down the island, the men give not two figs for Vergil, and are instead exercising the right of free-born Britons, to occupy themselves as they please, chiefly in playing cricket, and being drunk.

It pleases fate to ordain, that among the good fellows to-day honouring those two antient sports, is one Ned Lumm — A lad as remarkable, for his excess of *height* and *breadth*, as he is for his deficiency in *depth*.

Ned Lumm has passed every day of his sixteen years, unnoticed by the eye of history. We would have allowed him to continue so for all the remainder, until he come to rest at last in his plot in the village church-yard, were it not for the interesting fact, that he has for some months looked on Anny Pertwee with a fond eye. We would go so far as to say, that her image has become deep fixed in his heart — Or, at least, in some sensitive and palpitating part of his constitution — We cannot say with confidence, which organ it be. What is certain, is that the part in question is aroused on the instant, and fills with inward warmth, when its beloved passes by the cricket field, a pretty colour in her cheek after walking two or three mile in an indifferent humour.

All the world knows, or ought to know, that the chief virtue of the sport of cricket consists in a man's being able to cease playing, or resume, much as he pleases, without any alteration to the progress of the contest — Or, indeed, without his fellow-players being much the wiser. Our Ned avails himself of this time-honoured rule, and abandons the yard of grass and dandelion where he has stood, for the most part immobile, playing the game, in order to engage in the altogether more earnest pursuit of the object of his affections.

A word, reader. —

There are, among lovers of literature, some, who take particular delight in the *pastoral romance*. Should you count yourself among them — We must not permit your hopes to be raised.

We do not object in the least to sighing swains and blushing shepherdesses — Indeed, we read with pleasure the Arcadia of Sir Philip Sidney, in our younger days — though we think our days were a great deal younger at the commencement of the venture, than at its conclusion. — But, alas! this tale of Anny and her Ned promises no such enjoyment. In plain words, Jill cares little for Jack. She is not lacking in admirers, in every village hereabouts, and finds no cause to favour this Ned above the others, or indeed to bestow especial marks of kindness on any of them at all; having discovered, that it is a great deal more delightful to be admired, than to admire; and having by the exercise of her own wits concluded, that to encourage *one* would be to discourage *all the others*, which would, according to simple mathematics, much diminish the sum of her delight.

Yet though her heart, or whichever organ be adapted to the pleasure, rejoices not in the unexpected approach of Neddy Lumm, it is altogether otherwise with her intellectual faculties.

Perhaps she has been meditating further on the mystery of Mrs Peach, as she walks — Or perhaps the inspiration is an heaven-sent thing, no more to be accounted for than the meteor of a summer night. — However it may be, at a stroke Miss Anny conceives — a STRATAGEM.

We need not tell you, reader, that among the many blessings and marvels of young love, is that curious property, whereby the enamoured may be persuaded to almost any act, no matter how contrary to reason, morality, and good sense, if there appears the smallest likelihood that its execution will win them the favour of their chosen fair. Anny has learned this lesson long since, and made good use of it. Hitherto she has found its virtue mainly to consist in procuring sweet morsels at another's cost, or ridding herself of the tedium of some small obligation of time or labour, by inviting some besotted lad to undertake it instead. Now, though! — now a project infinitely grander unveils itself to her conception.

— There, she thinks, is the house at Widdershins Bank, all closed up, and Mrs Eliza Peach supposedly a-bed within — Leaving the poor helpless lady prey to any accident or disaster, as fire, house-breakers, &c. — What, then, if there were to be a robbery in earnest? Who could blame the lady's maid, if, in such an extremity, concerned only for the welfare of her mistress, she were to *put aside the strict instruction never to disturb the up-stairs room*?

Now, Anny is as good a Christian as any of her acquaintance, according to her own opinion, and indeed better than most, and would not wish the violence of robbery upon any house at all, to say nothing of the one where she is herself employed. But — and here is the touch of genius, in her stratagem! — Would not the *appearance* of a robbery have all the virtue of the notion, with none of the harm? Would it not equally well give her cause to rush to the rescue of her mistress — Fear not, good lady — I, your maid, am here, and will see no harm done! — And this, without any *real and present* danger at all?

And might not some such *appearance* be contrived — With the unwitting assistance, of a vigorous accomplice? — Such a person as, for example — Ned Lumm?

Infinitely contented with these reflexions, she is livelier than usual. Her elevated spirits shew well in her, to the helpless detriment of poor Neddy. Because she is pleased with herself, Anny will be pleasant with him. — She smiles, and prates, and consents to share his simple meal, and laughs off the rude sallies of those who observe them sitting down together. So the day wears on to evening, while her doting swain, who until the present occasion has never enjoyed more than ten minutes in the fair damsel's company, before being dismissed with a toss of her head, and a pretty *Hum! I don't care*, falls deeper and deeper into the snare. — Though dreaming all the while that he is coming nearer and nearer to the highest bliss his heart, or whichever organ it may be, can conceive.

— I'll go home now, Neddy, says Anny, when the first star is out.

— I'll walk with ye, Anny.

— Will you? I'll chuse if you'll walk with me, or don't, I think.

— Chuse that I do, then. For I do love ye so.

Anny laughs prettily, and says, Foolish Neddy, You know you don't, and things of that nature, which we need not record — But she is nevertheless certain to ensure that the boy accompanies her, as she sets out towards the scene of her anticipated triumph.

It is ever the way with the most brilliant stratagems, that the possible objections to their success, which seem but mere cavilling trifles when the plan is conceived, grow more pressing, in proportion as the time of execution draws nearer. — As a distant mountain peak appears no bigger than a thumb-print upon the far horizon, yet rears up ever taller at the traveller's approach, its dreadful precipices clearer to the sight with each turn of the road, until he comes under its shadow, and sees the blasted trees clinging fearfully to its slopes, and, far above them, the eagle circling the snows of the peak — So Anny's expectations are step by step overwhelmed, by a dreadful thought — That Mr Peach may ALREADY HAVE COME HOME! — to the utter destruction of her plans.*

Fear not! — we hear you say — Fear not, fair damsel! — I have read the chapter preceding, and know the gentleman is not expected for several hours yet! — But, Anny cannot hear your reassurances. She must go on her way in agonies of doubt, much to the displeasure of her paramour, who had hoped that her heretofore complaisant manner, allied with the gathering dimness of the trysting hour, might encourage in her the admission of certain liberties, which a man of gallantry must seek every opportunity to obtain. — Instead of which, Anny grows impatient and cross, and will not hear of it.

So the youthful pair proceed, each of them increasingly out of temper, until the valley of Widdershins Bank is reached.

There sits the house — Difficult to be seen in the shadow of the wood above — All is silent, dark, and deserted.

Mr Peach has *not* returned — The plan is *not* ruined! — With a skip of her foot Anny points and cries — Oh! there's no body at home! — And in the sudden excess of her reviving spirits she takes her swain by the arm, and presses herself against that very substantial limb, and says again, — Look, Ned, 'tis all dark in the house.

— What shall we do, Anny? says Ned, which is little to the purpose — The lad being near robbed of his faculties, of which

* We have in this sentence included an *Homeric simile* — At no extra cost.

he had not a very great store before the assault, by the impression of his lady's bosom upon his elbow.

Now — It is an element of Anny's grand conception, that she will pretend to be disappointed at the locking of the house. — For this imposture will allow her to suggest to Ned the particular course of action, on which her whole design of *feigned robbery* depends. — She recalls this feature of the design several seconds too late. — Her joy and relief, at discovering the house empty, and Mr Peach not yet returned, have already been expressed in those happy exclamations, just recorded. — But her natural confidence in her own cleverness overcomes this small error. Without hesitation, she releases her hold upon Ned Lumm, and makes a perfect alteration in her manner, pouting and crossing her arms.

— How vexing! says she, with a mighty sigh. There's no body at home!

To hear the very same words spoken in such doleful accents, which but a moment ago had been pronounced with eager joy, might bewilder even a man of philosophy; and Ned Lumm is no such man. He is also ignorant of the poets — And thus has no proverbs of the fickleness of woman, to console him.

— The gentlefolks is away, mebbe, he says.

— How shall I get in? cries Anny, warming to her task. — Oh! 'tis most vexing, indeed!

— Nay, be not vexed, says Ned, reaching to her with that suddenly cold and comfortless arm, which but a moment before enjoyed the warmth of Anny's bosom. — She evades its grasp, with a pronounced shrug.

— I shall be vexed! For it's my own little bed, and all my poor things are by it, my cap and brush, and I don't have any key! Nothing can be so tiresome. I am the unluckiest girl alive, to be shut out from my own room, and here's night coming. Oh, what am I to do, &c. — And she continues to lament in this vein, harping on her grief like the psalmist — Until, by cunning degrees, she comes round to the great cap-stone or crux of her stratagem, thus —

— You might break down the larder door, Neddy.

Ned's surprize at this remarkable suggestion is much softened, by the return of the bosom against his side.

Anny adopts a melting tone. — 'Tis but a flimsy thing of a door. And you're a great boy, Ned. They say you're strong as a bullock.

Ned's passions have been raised — thrown down — raised again — again destroyed — And are now in a trice lifted to a surpassing height. At these rapid turnings of Fortuna's wheel he is become dizzy, and scarcely sensible what he says or does. Thus afflicted, he is no more capable of resisting flatteries and blandishments, than — Any other man, who receives a compliment from a pretty woman.

— I'm the strongest in the village, he says. — I broke Dick Gurney's head at a cuff.

— Oh, Neddy, says Anny, I do love to hear you talk so. Won't you shew me how strong you are, by breaking in the door?

— I might do it easy.

— I know you might, she says, with another press on his arm, and so they go down to the side of the house, the fair maid repeating her encouragements all the while, until they stand before the larder door, which gives on to a dark and dripping inclosure, under the steepest part of the hill, shrouded with ivy.

— There, says Anny. — It's such a little door. Look, Neddy, here's a stone you may use.

Now, reader! we need hardly remind you, that it is one thing to boast, but altogether another to perform the deed boasted of.

Faced with the door itself — The dark — The stillness of the old house, recumbent like a sleeping beast, and of the hill, and the wood above — Under this assembled battery of influence, the natural obduracy of Ned Lumm's intellectual powers gives way a little, and some small notion of what is proposed, steals into the inward region of the soul.

— Nay, Anny, he says. — But 'twould be house-breaking.

— House-breaking, do you call it? rejoins Anny, flying into a passion. — When it's my own little room within? I never heard a thing so dull, as to call going into a body's own home house-breaking.

— But, nay. 'Tis the gentlefolks' house.

— And isn't it mine just as well? For where else is my home, if not my little room next the larder? Come, Ned — says she — restraining her impatience — resuming her sweetest manner — the bosom is pressed again into service — Come, let's not lose time talking. Here's the stone, I'm sure it will do.

— But would ye have me break the door?

— Not break it, Neddy! Only move it just a little, that I can slip in, and then I'll be safe and home inside, and ever so grateful. Take the stone now. — With a great effort she lifts the said object into her own grasp. It is a broken corner of the old mill-stone, which has stood outside the larder door since time immemorial, for the convenience of generations who wished to scrape their boots before entering. — She cannot sustain it long — And drops it, into the capacious arms of her paramour.

By this deed, she intends to hasten the execution of her strata-gem — But, the effect is the opposite one. For now that the instru-ment of the proposed crime lies palpable and weighty in his grasp, the imagination of Ned Lumm — a power not easily roused, without external aid — Presents him, with a vivid picture of what might follow upon the deed.

— I'll be had before the constable.

— Pish! Where's the constable? I don't see any constables.

— 'Tis agin the laws. 'Tis house-breaking.

— There you are again with your house-breaking, and laws, and constables! When all you must do, is help a poor girl to her bed.

— I'll be put in chains, and sent to the colonies.

— You never will. Don't be such a stupid thing.

— Grandfather Lumm were sent to the colonies, and never heard of again.

— And haven't you heard, there's no more transportation now, for the war is lost, and the colonies have made their own king?

— What'll I do, if I go before the justice?

Anny's patience, which runs not much deeper than Ned's imagination, is now exhausted. In common with every other person, who ever delighted themselves with the crafting of stratagems, she has been found utterly unprepared for the resistance of actual events, to the visionary prospects of her conception. — All she knows, is that Ned Lumm must break the larder door, because she wishes it. — The possibility that he may not do so, is not to be admitted.

— If ye break the door, I'll shew you my f___y, she says.

This intelligence causes Ned to drop the broken corner of the mill-stone, which falls some fortunate inches apart from his shoe.

— Will ye, then?

— I will.

— Ye must swear it.

— Do ye call me a liar now? cries Anny, in a rage. — You have me walk all this long way, and you won't help me to my bed, and now you say I'm a liar. I wonder I ever thought of you to accompany me. I ought to have walked straight past, and never heard a word from you, and gone to Dick Gurney, for I think he'd have been a proper man for me, and he always wishes to do me kindness, and counts it a pleasure to do any thing I ask.

— Nay, don't fret, don't fret. But ye must swear to it.

— Well, if I must, you horrid beast, I swear it.

— Swear to shew your f___y.

— I do, I do! Now be at the door!

— And then give me a kiss.

HOLD! — you cry, rising from your chair at the fire-side, where, we see, it is your customary pleasure to enjoy your perusal of our history — HOLD! — Whether you accompany the word with a suitable gesticulation, we do not venture to guess. It is a question of your temperament, reader. — Whether you incline to the *choleric*, or the *melancholy* — the fire in the nerves easily kindled, or sluggish — *Allegro* or *Penseroso* — we cannot divine. But we hear your abrupt complaint, as distinct as though you stood at our shoulder. —

— Hold! Is this low business of the gossiping maid and her doltish swain to be no more than a repetition, in the *comic-pastoral* mode, of that same transaction, depicted in *Gothick* stile, in your chapter the fourth? And — your ire, reader, is increasing — And, you cry, is this narrative of yours to be endless scenes of *female inducement*, offered in the most indecent terms? Are we next to see Miss Arabella Farthingay attempt to procure the success of her literary endeavours, by *whoring*?

— Madam — Sir — Calm yourself — Resume your seat, we entreat you. — Read on, and when you reach the limit of the page, turn it over. — We confess, there is indeed a degree of kinship between this our present scene, and the earlier event, though we think it not so close. The one is perhaps a *country cousin* to the other. — We mean, that species of relations, whose names one knows — whose faces one might recollect, with a little effort — But as to what they are about — where they reside — the number and denomination of their children, Heaven help us! — Do not ask — they are only *country cousins*!

To the complaint of the repetition itself, we must give just acknowledgment; and we offer the following Apologia, which is in two parts. — First, we bid you remember the comedies of *Shakespear*; and in particular, those of witty Rosalind, and the affectionate disaffection 'twixt Beatrice and her Benedick; in each of which it pleases that incomparable author, to bring into his play, alongside the loves of the principal figures, as it were their *echo* or *shadow*, in the form of a subsidiary romance — Whose imperfections, and altered proportions, like a shilling engraving made after a priceless masterpiece, serve to emphasize the magnificence of the original. And in second place, we inform you, that we merely record the actual occurrences of our history; and so you must lay the blame for any deficiency in invention not at our door, but at the world's — For, as the preacher said, some thousands of years ago, there is nothing new under the sun; and we are inclined to think the events of the intervening centuries would not have changed his philosophy.

Look, now — Your expostulation, and our answer, have together caused us to miss several minutes of the conversation at the larder door.* It now appears the young lovers have settled their exchange to the satisfaction of both parties — Though, if we judge by outward looks, with much the lesser share of content, on the distaff side. — Ned Lumm sets to his task in all eagerness, heaving up the fraction of the old mill-stone — Whereas the fair maid seems all anxious impatience — From which observations, we must deduce, that whatever the future reward agreed between them, in the course of those minutes during which our attention was unfortunately diverted away, the lad has more pleasure in its anticipation than the lass. — As, indeed, is usually the case, when we compare the one obliged to pay a reward, with the one preparing to receive it.†

Inspired by the prospects newly arisen to his view, the vigorous swain fetches the larder door a great crack, splintering the tranquillity of the night like Jove's thunder-bolt. — At which there comes a feeble, trembling sort of shout — Who's there?

We pause our narrative a moment, for an *historical* illustration. —

When Buonaparte surveyed the disposition of the soldiers, as we suppose he must have, on the eve of the fateful battle at *Waterloo*, he will have said thus to himself — We translate from the French — Hum! Good! All is as I planned it! — Exactly as it was at *Austerlitz*, and *Jena*, and *Marengo*, and before each one of my series of triumphs — To-morrow, at my command, my dragoons will charge *there* — The foot will come up from the side, so — My cannons will strike *thus*, and *thus* — And *bof! hon hon hon!*‡ Victory must inevitably be mine! —

---

* We suspect there may be a lesson hereabouts, which we trust you will take to heart.

† Which might give us cause to doubt the popular adage, that *it is better to give than to receive.*

‡ These terms having no exact equivalent in English, we leave them untranslated.

For so it goes with STRATAGEMS, that the deadly error waiting to confound the plan, is necessarily invisible to its author. What the Emperor of France failed to see, on that last night of his liberty, we do not know. We merely observe, that the intention so clear to his thoughts — the plan of battle, on which he expended every labour of his formidable military intellect, for not only his own fate, but that of a continent, hung upon it — Must have been, in plain words, wrong. There lay before him, that night, some thing he overlooked — Some thing he could not, or would not, see — Blinded as he was, by the vision of a decisive triumph over the despised *Villainton* and his nation of shop-keepers.

All of which we mention, by way of excusing the fact, that the little female general of our present adventure has, in the conception of her own *Austerlitz*, entirely omitted to account for the existence of — Jem the stable-boy.

His voice it is, that now raises a tremulous *Who's there?* — The thunderous assault upon the innocent larder door, has disturbed his slumbers, where he lay in the loft above the stable.

— 'Tis the constable, says Ned, dropping the stone again.

In her extremity of confusion, Anny can only think to be rid of him, now his purpose is served. — For the way inside the house lies open! the door having received a wound which, like that fatal to Mercutio, is not so deep as a well, nor so wide as a church door, but is enough, and will serve.* — Go, Neddy! she says, intending a whisper, but in her agitation producing instead a breathless shriek.

— Anny? calls poor terrified Jem.

At this juncture, we must explain the second portion of the maid's STRATAGEM — Though we hesitate somewhat, out of respect for the lass — For, in truth, this second part evinces not much more genius than the *first*.

The door being broken, it had been her intention to leap within, and cry out, Oh! Help! Robbers! Present danger and destruction!

* *vide* the third Act of Romeo and Juliet.

&c., and so in all haste up-stairs, with every effort to rouse the supposed Mrs Peach — Thus once and for all to determine, whether the room under the roof be empty or no.

In the immediate crisis, produced by the unanticipated appearance of the stable-lad, her thoughts revert by a natural reflex into the course already prepared for them, as water will flow into a channel dug for the purpose.

— Help! cries she. — Robbery! Rescue! Help, Jem!

— Why then, says Ned, his terror of the constable receding — 'Tis only Jemmy Sixways, is it?

— Flee, Neddy, says Anny, attempting without the smallest success to propel him from the scene by the force of her arms.

— Nay, says Ned, for now the dread of arrest, transportation, hanging &c. is removed, his thoughts likewise return to the direction they have pursued, since he secured the maid's promise to — We cannot say precisely what was agreed — You it was, reader, who disturbed us at the critical moment.

— Nay, says he, It ain't robbery, for you said it weren't. Don't cry so.

— Be off, you great fool, Anny says, unable to disguise her disdain an instant longer. — If Jem sees what you did you'll be whipped.

— Jemmy Sixways won't tell tales of me, says Ned. — I'll crack his head clean open. The milksop.

— Then be whipped, for all I care, and hanged too, cries Anny, and she falls once again to shouting, Help, Murder, and the like.

— I'll have my promise, Ned says, and lays hands on the poor girl, causing her to shriek in good earnest. At which young Jem, who has descended from the stable-loft, and crept by unwilling and fearful steps in the direction of the disturbance, loses the little heart he has, for his imagination is a-whirl with visions of rape and murder — And he thinks it likely, that if Anny is to suffer the former, the latter doom must fall to his own part — Unless he set himself to escape it.

— I'll fetch the constable, he says, in no very loud voice, and turns on his heels, and flees into the road.

Up to the present moment, it will be agreed, that Anny's strata-gems have been attended with very little luck. But now Dame Fortuna proves her capricious nature, by arranging matters, so that there is an *hiatus* or lull in the girl's shrieking, at that very instant, which allows the word *constable* to come whispering through the ivy, and under the overhanging trees, and into the capacious ear of Ned Lumm — Where it alone, of all the words in the language, is able to make an impression sufficiently dread-ful, as can divert the owner of that ear from his efforts to secure the inducement previously offered — Whatever it may be.

He hesitates, suspended between love and fear, or, as the poets say, *burning* and *freezing*. — Anny seizes the moment, and pours into that interval all the vehemence of her passion, upbraiding him in the most determined language for his rude behaviour, and bemoaning the wicked folly that ever led her to seek help from his hands; and, in short, exhibiting so entire a change from her former complaisance, that her suitor is utterly dismayed, and his ardour quenched. — The fire subsides — The ice gains the upper hand. — Ned takes his leave, with many ungracious reflexions on the cursed nature of the female heart, which, being neither original, nor felicitous in their expression, nor of any philosophical merit, we shall not record.

Thus, and perhaps more by luck than any art of her own, Anny has atchieved every point of her great aim.

The house is indeed broken in, as though by robbery — And, no inconvenient witness being present, she may imagine she has just arrived at the scene.

It only now remains, to cry out in surprize — Rush in-doors — And up-stairs — Thinking only of the poor invalid above, at the mercy of who knows what criminal desperadoes — Mercy! Mrs Peach! Have they accosted you? — Is any injury done? — Fear not! it is only I, Anny, your faithful maid — Your husband, alas! is gone, but I will do every thing in my power —

How still is the house, and how dark!

And how full of whispers is the night!

And how Anny's heart is beating of a sudden, like the steam-engine in miniature, which last summer she saw exhibited at the Bridgwater fair! — When she opens her mouth to cry out — Why is it, that she seems to have no breath? — Almost as though a cold, ghostly hand were clasped at her throat!

— I shall go in on tip-toe first, she thinks, and light a candle.

There is not another light nor sound within. Once more Anny prepares herself to raise the alarm — Run to the stair — Mrs Peach! Mistress Eliza! —

And once more, she cannot.

There is a kind of nocturnal stillness, which *will not be broken*. It stares at you, reverent and awful as a stern face in an old portrait — Its eyes are on your back as well as your face — Its finger upon its lips. In its presence we feel, as we do in the silence of an empty church, that an invisible power slumbers, which we must not awaken, at any cost.

Anny creeps to the foot of the stair.

— There can't be any body in, she says to herself. — 'Tis quite impossible. — After all this *hallaballoo* — The smashing of the door — Not to stir one bit — However ill she may be — No — 'Tis impossible — Impossible —

Anny sets a foot on the stair.

— Quite impossible.

Another — And so by degrees, she ascends towards the forbidden door — While the Newcomen engine lodged in her bosom cranks, and clatters, and beats, as though set to drive twenty weaving frames.

She is expressly prohibited from knocking at the door.

On the very day she came into the service of Tho.s Peach, she was given this one solemn command, like Eve in the garden of Eden — Every thing you may do — Only the fruit of this one tree you may not eat — Mrs Peach's rest is ON NO ACCOUNT to be disturbed.

Whether our common ancestress experienced such torments of

indecision, before she succumbed to the serpent's blandishments, and plucked the fruit, as afflict our present heroine, we do not know. Milton, in the ninth book of his Paradise Lost, gives a very full account of the lady's doubtful hesitation and inward justification — But we are obliged to note, his poem is all *made up* — It is *invention*, every last word of it — Not in the least part to be relied upon, by the historian. Whatever the truth, certain it is that Anny delays long — Several times over, her little hand approaches the proscribed portal,* only to retreat again, without a touch.

— I shan't be found out, she says to herself, for there's no body within. — No one shall ever know I did it.

With such words she vies, in the phrase of Shakespear,

> to screw her courage to the sticking-post

until, at long last, and perhaps almost as much by accident as the exercise of valour, the knuckles tap on the wood.

How the tiny impression peals in her ears, like the kettle-drums of *Herr Handel!*

It is done —

The crime committed —

The great injunction breached — the apple is plucked, and eaten. But neither earth nor heavens cry out an echo of the blow.† All is silence and darkness still, save the beating *prestissimo* of Anny's heart, and the small radiance of her candle.

— Mrs Peach —

She whispers it aloud — Though it is barely above a breath, and would hardly have drawn the notice of the keenest ears in England through a closed door — so much the less, those of an invalid, supposedly not yet roused by the violent breaking of the house.

---

* That is, the bed-room door. — Our figures approach the obscure, in their sublimity. — It is in the nature of the enterprize, and cannot be helped.

† 'Earth felt the wound, &c.' — Milton.

Nevertheless, whisper she does, though she knows it be forbidden — Mrs Peach — It is I, the maid — May I be of assistance?

There is no answer — None at all.

Here Anny discovers, we are sorry to say, another flaw in her stratagem.

For when she applies her ear — and then, greatly emboldened, her eye — To the key-hole — She discovers — Nothing.

Nothing at all is revealed, by either means — Not a sound — Not a spark.

— It's just as I thought, she says to herself, in momentary triumph — There's no body there.

But in the very next instant, her supposed victory shews itself hollow — For, what has she learned, except what she KNEW ALREADY — which is, that she can produce no *positive* evidence of the actual existence of Mrs Eliza Peach?

All her night's work has come to this — That every thing beyond the forbidden door, remains no whit less mysterious, than it was in the morning.

It would be a different matter, thinks Anny, if I could *go within.*

The mere thought is sufficient to produce such a reflex of terror, as sends her rattling down the stair with her candle. For, her imagination having emptied the room of Mrs Eliza Peach, wife to her employer and lady invalid, there comes in her place, that thing of all things most sublime and terrible to the phantasy — a BLANK — An absence — The dark potency, from which all manner of fears are birthed, as children fear what may be found beneath the bed, when the lamp is extinguished.

Anny recalls, that in the night — at an hour not very unlike this present hour — She has heard her master, in the up-stairs room, behind the locked door — in conversation with — SOMETHING —

— Lord save us! she cries, and retreats from the stair.

In the course of which manoeuvre her eye happens to fall upon the nook behind the first four steps — An inconvenient and dusty angle of the house, where is stored —

Reader — Can you say, what object rests in that spot? We permit you a moment or two to search your recollection. It was mentioned in the course of our opening chapter, though *en passant* merely. We will not think the less of you, if the detail has slipped away from you. — Nay — Do not turn back the pages — We shall teaze you no further. It is — a CHEST —

We see, you remember it now — A *chest*, kept under lock and key by Mr Peach, to the frustration of the curious miss, who was heard in our first chapter to venture her belief, that some thing strange or dreadful must be sealed therein.

Having gained nothing at all by her chief stratagem, Anny on the instant conceives — a *second* plan.

This device, requires no besotted suitor — It may be put in train as soon as thought of — There is no body to interfere. — In short — It is utterly certain of success.

It is, that she will break the lock of the chest, and discover the contents.

What could be more natural, thinks she, than that some robbery be done in the house, now the door is broken? And who is there to do it, but *herself*? When her master returns, she will say, Oh, sir, look, the ruffians, they have struck the lock off that old chest of yours — The one you said was only full of old books. — I hope you have not lost any thing of great value!

Wise reader, we do not doubt that you have anticipated the difficulties attendant on this latter device, as you did in the case of the former. To name but the first — How is the lock to be struck off? It is no very grim an object, intended more to deter momentary curiosity than determined assault, but our Anny is no more than the greenest apprentice in the art of robbery — A bashful scholar, stammering out her *amo, amas* from the first page of her primer.

— I'll drop that stone on it, she says to herself.

The instrument, which in the enormous arms of Ned Lumm seemed but a feather, is to Anny a great anchor, or a cannon-ball, or — Enough of our metaphors — It is, in plain terms, a very great burden, which she carries in-doors with much discomfort, and not a few coarse terms.

And now, the dreadful silence of the house descends once more, and as it were murmurs in her ear — as though to say — Break me — And what will be roused? — So that for the second time, Anny is chaffed with indecision, and dare not do, what she cannot bear to leave undone. — Until, having several times set herself to lift the stone, only for her courage to fail, she raises it at last, and, while still possessed by doubtful terrors — Drops it by accident.

The clamour gives her a fright almost fatal. — Now — she thinks — Now the door will creak! — and Mrs Eliza Peach will come down in the dark — Pale as a spectre, clad in a night-dress — Pointing an accusing finger — WHO DARES DISTURB MY REST?

But the door above remains as fast as ever. — And, which is still more delightful to our trembling heroine, it appears the descent of the stone has once again proved a *fortunate fall* — For the brass lock is bent and cracked, and torn away a little from the chest! By swift experiment Anny discovers, that the point of the fire-iron will fit snugly into the crevice thus created. It is then a simple matter to apply force to one end of the iron — The shade of *Archimedes* rejoices, to see the principle of the *lever* applied with such perfect simplicity. —

Huzzah! — the lock is loose. —

Now nothing but fear and her own conscience stands between Anny and the opening of the chest. Or rather, nothing but fear — For as to the other matter, we are compelled to admit, it is a very feeble obstacle. Indeed, so great is the predominance of curiosity in the character of the maid, that even her dread at what she may be about to discover, detains her for only a moment. The deed, after all, is done — The crime committed — Ought I not, she reasons, now have my prize?

Recollect, reader, that when Anny made enquiry of Mr Peach concerning the mysterious chest, in our first chapter, she was told it only contained — More books. A reply, to which she gave not the least credit; for who would shut away a mere *book*, and that when the end-room is already furnished with thirty, or Heaven knows how many, of the mouldy old things, lined up in plain sight, and catching the dust?

Imagine, then, the surprize and dismay which pierce the unlucky girl to the heart, when she dares to raise the lid of the chest an inch — another inch — Wide enough to hold the candle to the aperture — She peers within, and sees — *Books!*

— Oh! she cries. — I am to be vexed in every thing!

There are some nine or twelve of the beastly volumes, great ugly wrinkled objects, big and black as bibles. There is a smell attached to them, which brings to Anny's mind a series of associations confused and unpleasant — chairs, beatings, parson's gowns — ink, and leather.

— Only more books! she says, and pouts. — Who'd rob a book?

Nevertheless, she examines her secret prize more closely. — There is a glimmer of light among the dull contents.

— Now, thinks Anny, *that* one, with the patterns stamped upon its covers — Perhaps it's done in gold, for it gleams in the candle. That might be precious metal, for I'm quite sure nothing else is.

She lays hands on the volume thus chased and tooled. It is a monstrous thing, for a book. — None of your neat trim quartos or octavos, but an huge clumsy antient beast — A fossil of bibliography, surviving from an age of giants.

The pattern, which has attracted Anny's covetous glance, is a five-pointed star in a circle, with many small symbols and hieroglyphs around the perimeter.

Beneath the covers, the paper is bent and a little stiff. The pages whisper and crackle as she turns them.

Here is the frontispiece — A writhing border of inky serpents and death's-head moths, enclosing a blind woman crowned by the moon, her bare feet resting upon open graves. —

Here are pages of writing, in black letters crammed and pointed like the stones of the church-yard — And here are pictures between them, in red ink as well as black. The pictures are no more decipherable than the letters, except where there are faces in them —

Horrible grinning faces —

Imps, and devils, with bat's ears, and tongues like fire —

Anny drops the book with a shriek, and takes up the candle, and runs to her own room behind the parlour. — Gets into bed — and pulls the covers over her head, swearing to God above that she will never in all her life commit robbery again — Promising, to go to church every Sunday, and mend her ways — And determined above all, to quit the house for ever, just as soon as the day comes.

In which uncomfortable state we must leave her. — We shall not moralise, upon the rewards of impertinent curiosity — Nor, for the present, make any remarks upon Mr Peach's tastes in bibliography — But must now briefly relate, what came of Jem's flight in search of the constable.

It being long after dark, and the merry folk of the village exhausted by drink and sport, the lad found it no easy matter to rouse them from their beds, though he stood by the well, and cried Help, Robbers Ho! with all the vigour he could muster — Which, alas, was little enough. But in time the village was awakened — And, as a great blaze grows from a meagre spark, the message brought by poor stammering Jem spread from house to house — Until all the people were wild with excitement, and formed what may be called the *mob*. — A body, which included none other than Ned Lumm, than whom no man was more eager to lay hold of torch and cudgel, and march in pursuit of the supposed house-breakers.

After much delay and argument, and a little disputation of the said cudgels, this army of justice set off along the road to Widdershins Bank, where they arrive not an hour after Anny's retreat to her bed, to her inexpressibly great relief. She runs out to meet them in the road — Embraces her father — her uncle — even Jem the stable-lad — Every body, it seems, excepting Ned Lumm, whose eye she avoids as rigorously, as he avoids hers. She is chaffed with questions, which she answers in no very clear terms.

115

— Oh — Robbers — A great gang of them — Three men, I'm sure — Three WILD men, they were — All black in the face — Swearing strange oaths. — They broke the house — They would have murdered me in my bed, I'm sure, but I ran away — The horrid ruffians! They might be any where —

Villains! cries the mob. — And up and down the road it goes, seeking its quarry, falling in ditches, setting hedges alight, &c., until for two miles around the country is a scene of utter confusion, echoing to *view halloo* and every other shout, while the torches are carried into barn and grove and field, so that the night is scattered over with spots of fire. — And into this scene of rustic *Pandemonium* rides Tho.s Peach — Who, for the many hours of his benighted journey, has been anticipating with heartfelt fervour the comfort and peace of home.

CHAPTER SEVEN

Permit us, reader, to express the hope, that you have never suffered the loathsome depredation of domestic *burglary*.

The crimes gathered under that name are to the peoples of this island, as an assault upon the household saints must be to the Spaniard, or, to the Frenchman, the despoliation of his cheese. — They strike to the heart of what we hold dearest — the sacred tranquillity, of our own parlour — That last refuge, where we may be sure of sitting at peace in our chair, and taking our tea, and suffering no disturbance!

The indignation of Mr Peach, at discovering the outrage committed upon his larder-door, may easily be imagined.

If, however — which God forbid! — you have indeed suffered the like misfortune, you may be tempted to reflect, that our hero has not so very much to complain of. For though he be ignorant of the circumstances, which by the irresistibly comprehensive power of our pen we have laid before you in our previous, and therefore cannot know, what you know, that the supposed robbery was in truth no more than a shadow or simulacrum of that despicable crime — Although, we say, he has only the testimony of his own eyes upon which to rely, and they assure him, that his door is broken in the night, and his house entered by violence — Nevertheless, it must be just as plain to him, as it is to you, that the offence of burglary here presents its mildest guise.

In short — Not a thing has been stolen.

Mr Peach counts his dining-forks, and his pewter, and his linens, and, with more attention, his papers and books. All are mustered as they were when he departed the house. The only mark of the invasion within-doors, is the cracking of the lock upon the chest, and the twisting and splitting of its frame by the application of the fire-iron. Yet within moments Mr Peach has set a candle by the stair, and examined the contents — those great withered remnants of leather and parchment — And discovered, that none is absent. Their antient repose has been barely disturbed. They have but shuffled around a little in their place of rest, and now they sleep again, in the dusky glimmer.

Ought Mr Peach not to think himself fortunate? — as far as any man may, who comes home to find his house robbed?

Has any such crime taken place at all, in strict philosophical consideration?

Since there is no theft, what inconvenience has he suffered, except the breaking of an old item of furniture, which lay out of notice behind the stair, and the partial destruction of a door at the side of the house? — a ledger of injuries, which requires no more reparation than a day or two of the carpenter's labour.

Tho.s Peach is, as we have already remarked, a man of some philosophy. — You, reader, may therefore imagine, that his natural indignation, upon discovering the crime, would be mitigated, when he sees no property is lost. You will guess his first thought is for his poor invalid wife, who must be presumed to have lain above-stairs, while the shocking intrusion took place below! — Alone, we know — Helpless and frightened, we must think. — Surely he will go up at once, to see she is unharmed, and comfort her with his return?

Mr Peach does no such thing.

Nor does he seem much relieved in his spirits, when he is finished inspecting his property.

He seats himself beside the candle, upon the stair. — And there he sits — With his head in his hands.

His eyes are open. He stares at shadows —

We cannot but think, that whatever obscurity he studies with such deep and silent attention, lies not *before* his eyes, but *behind* them. He has the look of one, sunk in gloomy reflexion — Meditating upon inward scenes, whose colouring is no less nocturnal than the darkness beyond the candle.

Should you think this behaviour surprizing — Perhaps, worse than surprizing — Reader, we shall only invite you to reserve your condemnation, for the present . The eccentricities of Mr Peach, are not without their causes. You will learn them in time, if you care to. – Though you may wish you had not —

Let us not strive to peer into obscurities, and decipher shadows — But attend to the progress of our narrative.

The essential point to be noted, is that Mr Peach remains much troubled by the assault upon his house.

When morning comes, he seeks the earliest opportunity to make enquiries — Which presents itself, in the person of Mrs Shin.

That lady is not ordinarily used to attend Mr Peach before noon, nor, indeed, for several hours thereafter. To-day, however, is no ordinary day. To-day the house at Widdershins Bank is the very centre of all the country thereabouts. — The *omphalos*, of that corner of Somerset-shire. All the world speaks of nothing else. Every thing and person connected to the house shares in the universal fame — With the greater share, according to the degree of connexion. Mrs Shin cannot wait until the evening. She would not have it said, that she is merely the cook, who tends to Mr Peach's table, and then goes home as soon as she may. No — she is the house-keeper — A person of significance. She must be present in person, to receive the house's new-found influence in its full glory, as the courtiers of the Sun King dared not remove themselves from his French majesty's palace at *Versailles*.

Mrs Shin is pleased to be able to satisfy every enquiry of Mr Peach's, for, she thanks God, there is not the least doubt, who the villains were. Authorities even higher than Mrs Shin are in agreement. The constables — Mrs Wainwright, the tavern-keeper's wife — Mr Shin himself — and no less a personage than Mrs Shin's neighbour, the widow Mrs Young, who by virtue of her great age, and the severe deafness which causes her to speak exclusively in *pronouncements*, because she cannot acknowledge any question, is accepted to be the final judge, on all questions of material fact.

All affirm, with one voice, that the perpetrators of the outrage at Widdershins Bank, are — The GYPSIES.

— The gypsies! cries Mr Peach, astonished.

— Curse their heathen thieving ways, says Mrs Shin.

— Is this information quite certain? says Mr Peach.

— It can hardly be doubted, says Mrs Shin. — It is all told to Samuel Sexton, for he's the constable, you know, with Toby Squire, and made proper, according to the law.

— Why then, these supposed gypsies have been apprehended in the night.

Mrs Shin bestows a look of pitying condescension on the master of the house. — Bless me, sir, no.

— Then who has made report of them to Mr Sexton?

— Why, little Anny, sir, and who else? For it was she by the house when they came, and frighted her half to death, all dressed in their rags and black in the face.

You, reader, smile at such rustic superstition. — Which we think makes it all the more remarkable, that Mr Peach does not, but appears to be very greatly impressed by this report, and says, he wishes to speak to Anny as soon as she arrives.

— You'll get no sense from that silly goose of a girl, begging your pardon, sir, and anyway, she swears she don't like the house, and won't return, and she goes crying up and down the village that the place is accursed.

We were so rash as to assert, that nothing had been lost in the supposed robbery. Your pardon, reader. — Every offence against the truth of history pains us. We ought to have said, that there is *one* article forever removed from the house at Widdershins Bank; that item being — Anny Pertwee, the maid.

You will recall, that near the close of our last, we left Anny with the covers pulled over her head, meditating on certain resolutions. Among them was the determination to *mend her ways*; which, being of all resolutions in this world the one most frequently made, and most swiftly and universally abandoned, we suspect it caused you to ignore the others, presuming them likewise to have been sworn in the heat of the moment, and forgotten on the tepid morrow. — We remind you, therefore, that the fair maid had also resolved, to quit the service of Mr Thomas Peach, at her earliest convenience.

In testament to her fortitude of spirit, we must record, that she has held fast to this inward promise. Anny has taken up her brush, and her cap, and all her little things, and quit the house.

Perhaps this augurs well, in the matter of her other resolution? —

— But is it quite certain, says Mr Peach, that Anny saw the men who broke my door, and that they were strangely dressed, and of a foreign appearance?

— If a body wished to be certain of a thing, says Mrs Shin, a body might go asking elsewhere, than such a pert giddy little piece as Anny. But however the dirty gypsies may look, they'll not be seen again, and I hope they haven't stole much that's dear to you, for sure as any thing you won't see it no more neither. Once they do their thieving they say certain of their heathen words, which make them small as your thumb, and they hide away among the nettles, and then on their way, and no Christian soul can say where.

— I shall be very much obliged to you, Mrs Shin, says Mr Peach, if you are able to learn any well-attested particulars of these supposed vagrants.

— I'm sure I don't know who supposes any thing, says Mrs Shin. — I hope I know better than to suppose, begging your pardon.

It is plain from Mrs Shin's manner, if not from her syntax, that she has taken some offence. Mr Peach makes some mollifying assurances, regarding his entire confidence in her opinion, but repeats nevertheless, that he will be grateful to hear any further report of the miscreants, particularly regarding their number, their manner of dress and speech — of what complexion they are — Whether they wear beards!

Mr Peach is so precise in his questions, that we cannot but wonder, whether he gives more credit to this nonsense of Mrs Shin and her gypsies, than it can possibly be worthy of receiving, from any man of sense.

For Tho.s Peach *is* a man of sense, is he not? — In the course of our six-chapter acquaintance, we have seen him behave with discrimination — With humanity. We have made you privy to his inward discourse, which we think was conducted entirely according to rational principles, and arranged in intelligible sequence.

We have seen him studying a book of sermons! —

Yet we ought not to forget, the reputation he has gained among his fellows of the Anti-Lapsarian Society — And, indeed, the decidedly eccentric character of that fraternity.

We must reserve judgment for the present. Within the course of two or three further chapters, we shall perhaps know more.

Meanwhile, let us exercise the less ambiguous faculty of *observation*, and watch our hero, as he goes about the day.

It is quite plain to see, that Mr Peach's troubles have not been lessened by his conversation with the house-keeper. He appears distracted, and anxious. He cannot settle himself to any single thing, but is perpetually rising from his chair — Glancing at the window, or going to stand in the door, whence he surveys the limits of the valley on either side.

When evening comes, he seems fearful of the shadows — Strains his hearing, as though to listen for whatever may be hidden among the murmurs of the wind — Starts at every sudden noise.

What alarm can he possibly have taken, from the house-keeper's ridiculous report? —

— My dear, says Mr Peach to his wife, when he is gone to bed, We shall have to remove ourselves from this house as soon as can be managed.

— Have we not just lately come here?

We have mentioned, that Mr Peach took up the tenancy of Widdershins Bank the Michaelmas before last, and has therefore lived in the house but a few months shy of two years. We must suppose, that by reason of her perpetual and unvarying confinement, Mrs Peach has no very good grasp of the passage of time.

— I had hoped to stay much longer. Perhaps for ever. But we shall find ourselves another retreat, if we must.

— You went to the landlord, I recall. Will he turn us out? I thought you were the gentleman's friend.

— No, my dear, no blame attaches to Mr Farthingay. I have spoken to him, though not without some adventures along the way, and we have secured a quarter's grace in the matter of the rent. — Here Mr Peach gives his wife the history of his visit to Grandison Hall, not forgetting the episode of the poetical Miss Farthingay, with which Mrs Peach is particularly delighted.

Reader — we see your doubtful look.

We suspect, you ask yourself — Was Mrs Peach then in the house, all along? — through all the noise and confusion of that sixth chapter of yours? — though the too-curious maid listened at the door, and spied at the key-hole, and detected — Not a thing?

Are Mr and Mrs Peach now in ordinary domestic conversation, as though there had been *no disturbance at all?*

Patience — good reader — patience. You will know every thing. — And sooner, perhaps, than you will wish, when the time comes.

For the present, let us merely note, that Mrs Peach neither remarks upon the nocturnal disturbance, nor complains of Mr Peach's absence, unexpectedly prolonged. Her talk is by every token quite as content and good-humoured, as we heard in our second chapter, before the door of the house, and the chest at the foot of the stair, were broken in pieces.

It is, in plain fact, much as though the lady has no suspicion of any such events at all! — And certain it is, that Mr Peach does not allude to them either.

The most he will say, is thus —

— I fear the house is not altogether safe.

— Alas! Are there beetles in the wood, and the roof is to come falling in about our heads? Or will the chimney not draw? What can it be, that you must have us removed at once?

— You are in a merry humour to-night.

— One of us ought to be. I feel you are low and solemn. I shall play the more cheerful part.

— Dearest Liza. You always know me best.

— And I always shall.

— Then I must endeavour, says Mr Peach, to shed my surly mood, for when you say such a thing, I think I care for nothing beyond this room, and have all I could ever wish for.

— Listen to us, like an old contented pair. I don't call you surly, Tom. Only a little glum to-day. But you may put your worry aside. Fetch the house-builders to mend the chimney and the rotten wood, and all will be well.

— Ah, my dear, the house is sound enough. I am fond of it, and shall be sorry to go. But though the roof and chimney are well enough, it will no longer serve us as a sanctuary. Do you recall the letter from Uncle Augustus?

— We were speaking of it just now, I think?

Mr Peach does not trouble to correct his wife's misapprehension. — If, he proceeds, my uncle has discovered our whereabouts, in this secluded place, despite all my efforts to avoid notice, then I can only think others may find us just as well.

— Poor Tom! You fear being plagued by visitors.

Mrs Peach remains merry — Mr Peach, quite otherwise.

— I fear, says he, the attention of those who don't wish me well.

— Are there such?

— Your father's people —

— Tom, my dear.

Whether this gentle ejaculation be emitted with a laugh, or a sigh — Amused, or weary, or unhappy — We cannot say. The lady's speech has a kind of faintness, or lightness. It wears not its passions on its surface — It has something of the delicacy of a veil. Her long illness, we suppose, has worn it down.

— I wish I could forget them, and not speak of it. I know it pains you. But their enmity will not be avoided merely by wishing.

— Are you still not reconciled with poor Papa?

— My dear, you must remember, your father is no more.

— I do remember. Poor Papa. But were you not reconciled before he died? I can't think he would keep angry so long. He knew I followed my heart when I chose you. You and he were always friends before. I remember how you would sit together at the back of the shop, and talk all the morning, and have his tea-drink of mint. I used to bring it in. I think it was one such day when I first set eyes on you.

Mr Peach is familiar with the circuitous courses described by his wife's conversation. In an ordinary night, he loves nothing better than to indulge the turns and windings of her talk, as one strolls with idle pleasure along the sinuous paths and secret arbours of a garden. On this occasion, however, he steps back into the straight road of his purpose. He is more than usually serious, we suspect. — Or it may be, that the subject of Mrs Peach's late father, is one he does not wish to linger on.

— However that may be, he says, I must look to the immediate future, and make our preparations.

— Well, Tom, says Mrs Peach, you know what must be done. I don't complain, so long as we go together.

— There is only one great obstacle, which is the want of money.

— Did you not say the rent is forgiven?

— That's no more than an expence spared, my dear. If we are to re-establish ourselves in some more distant spot, I must find positive means to obtain funds. There will be costs, and now the annuity is withheld, I see no present way to meet them.

— You might sell some of my things. I had some good cloaths of my mother's, when we were married. They are no use to me now, and might fetch a price, I'm sure.

— They were left behind in London.

— Were they? That was remiss of us.

— We removed in very great haste, my dear.

Mrs Peach seems to hesitate in her speech.

— I wonder now why that was, she says.

— There was some unpleasantness with your father. It is best forgotten.

— Poor Papa.

Mr Peach makes no reply.

— Tom?

— Yes, my dear?

— There you are. I thought you were gone.

— I am here.

— I feel I recall every thing. Yet when you say we hurried away from town, though I'm sure it was so, I can't remember it.

— It was at that time that you — Here Mr Peach's tongue halts, as though of its own accord, and he struggles with some inward emotion, as he seeks to compel it again. — It was then, he says, that you fell into your present condition.

— That is the explanation, I suppose.

Mr Peach is eager to return to his former topic. — Assuredly, he says, if I could find any thing to sell, it would be sold. But there is nothing —

— Nothing, he adds, after another moment's hesitation, To the purpose.

Mr Peach is not in the habit of telling falsehoods to his wife. Indeed, it is a thing he is scrupulous to avoid,* unless in respect of certain details, regarding the unfortunate demise of her late father — Which exception we may account for, in its proper place. Hence his addition of the cavilling words. — For he has thought of his books.

---

* A policy we cannot recommend, to those of our readers who chance to be husbands, nor indeed, *mutatis mutandis*, to wives. — We need not explain our reasons. You, married folk — you understand us perfectly.

We do not mean the twenty or thirty volumes, which he keeps in neat order in the end-room of the house. Were they bundled together, and offered as a single lot, they would fetch no great sum. There is nothing among them, to excite the avarice of the bibliomane.

But — those *other* objects — Those rare and curious tomes, collected in the chest beneath the stair — They have a certain value, to certain people. — To a very few people, a very great value.

— Yet, he says to himself, they are not suitable for my present need. If the danger be as immediate as I fear, I gain nothing from offering those volumes for sale. Such things are not to be hawked at any common market. I might have not much less labour attempting to dispose of them, than there was in acquiring them. — A matter of many months, perhaps, not a few weeks. — And I may have only days to spare.

— Besides — he thinks — *What if I must turn to them again?*

Gracious! — Is it the *gypsies* of Mrs Shin, which have infected our hero, with such a fever of dread?

And what can he have meant, by this last inward remark?

Mrs Peach seems not in the least perturbed by her husband's silence, which is the outward consequence of these reflexions. It is among the curious features of their nocturnal talk, that such *lacunae,* or intervals, are not infrequent, and cause no discomfort to either party, though they may be prolonged for several minutes at a time.

— You ought to find yourself a rich wife, she says.

Mr Peach sighs a little, and says, — You always advise it, and my answer is always the same.

— We are become a tiresome couple already. We shall repeat the same things for ever.

— I should not mind it.

— But this Miss Farthingay, says Mrs Peach, who is a poet. Is she the only surviving child?

— I believe she is.

— Then she is heir to that estate. Is she handsome?

— Tolerably handsome.

— Why, all you have to do is woo her. She won't refuse a man who commits her verses to heart on a single hearing. I'm sure a lady poet wants no other quality in an husband.

— Alas, my dear, the objections to your scheme are so numerous as to be insuperable. Firstly, it is too slow and doubtful a means of obtaining money, for there is all the wooing to be done before the marrying, and the banns to be published, to say nothing of the wedding itself; and only then may one begin to think of separating the wife from her riches, which may yet turn out an uncertain enterprize. Secondly, it is quite against my own inclinations. And, thirdly, which ought to be the first objection as well as the *final* one, I am not free. I'm married already, you see, and to the best and dearest of women.

— I feel I am not very much of a wife to you now, Tom.

— You are all the wife I shall ever desire, says Mr Peach, with the most heartfelt emphasis.

We here pass over certain further exchanges. The sentiments are pretty enough — But of no significance to our narrative, except to further illustrate what is already sufficiently plain, that Mr Peach and his wife are what is called an *happy couple*. — A condition of the most tremendous interest, to the large class of novel-readers; but to you, reader, whose judgment is raised in an higher sphere, a matter of no import whatsoever. Every person of literary discrimination knows, that there is nothing so insufferably tedious to read of, than the contentment of an *happy couple*.

— If you will not find another wife, says Mrs Peach, might you turn highwayman? It is the quicker way to get another's money.

— Very true. But I have not the temperament for it. An highwayman must have gallantry, and I'm only a dull bookish old man.

— You were gallant and bold enough, when you won me.

— If I was, it was only because the prize was so great. I should never rouse myself from dullness in pursuit of mere purses and pocket-watches. Besides, there is the same objection to this scheme, as to my turning lawyer, or doctor, or master-mariner, or any project of enrichment by means of a profession, which is, I have not time to master it. A novice highwayman fares no better than any other apprentice, I dare say.

— Then you won't marry money, and you won't earn it, and there's nothing to sell. I think you must beg for it.

— Perhaps, my dear.

— I have it! You shall approach your friends, the philanthropic gentlemen.

Mr Peach has thus far prolonged the conversation, more for the pleasure he finds in talking to his wife, than from any thought of profiting from her advice. We hasten to add, that he does not despise her intellectual accomplishments! — They could not be so happy, as this specimen of their chit-chat appears to shew, if he did. Mrs Peach's mother was a seamstress, and her father, though derived from a family of some standing in their native city of *Aleppo*, resided in London as a trader in antiquities, which is to say, a species of shop-keeper. She has had no particular education. — But she has a lively wit, and a good understanding. If Mr Peach does not expect wise counsel from her, it is not because he deems her incapable. — Rather he supposes, that being two years and more retired from the world, in her infirmity, she is no longer well enough versed in its ways, to advise how to navigate among them.

Yet, at this last suggestion of hers, he sits up a little straighter in the bed.

— Do you not, continues Mrs Peach, attend a society of such men?

— Indeed I do. I was there just lately. Mr Farthingay, the land-lord, is a member.

— Then the thing is settled. The gentlemen can't be philan-thropic, and refuse charity to one of their own number. You have only to go back to them with your begging-bowl, and refuse to leave before it's filled.

If he chose, Mr Peach might explain to his wife, that although the principles upon which the Anti-Lapsarian Society is founded be avowedly philanthropic, in that they tend to the betterment of mankind — if the tremendous project to restore our state of Original Perfection, may be comprehended by a phrase so common-place! — Nevertheless, the Society's business does not consist in building alms-houses, or hospitals for children or fallen women, nor in sending monies for the assistance of the displaced crofters of North Britain, nor for any of the destitute and starving who may be nearer at hand. He might also add, that to approach his brethren of the Society in the character of a mendicant, would be so utterly mortifying, that he would sooner adopt any of her former suggestions, whether threatening the public roads with a pair of pistols, or conjoining himself to some foolish widow.

He makes no such answer.

Her allusion to the brotherhood of the Anti-Lapsarians has reminded him, of one very significant circumstance attached to that fellowship, which is — That they have money.

We must pause our narrative for several moments, in order to explain a distinction, of some philosophical subtlety.

The difficulty, which Mr Peach has been revolving in his thoughts, and which has given rise to this curious nocturnal discussion with his wife, is not precisely as it might appear to the untutored eye. The question he poses himself is not, *How am I to obtain a moderate sum of money, in an immoderately brief span of time?* — For this question admits of no serious answer. The thing is *impossible.* — A conclusion you may confirm for yourself, by the simplest exercise of reason. Merely reflect, reader, that if it were *not* impossible — why, then — Every body would do it.

The true question — The essential difficulty — is of a more general nature. We might put it thus — *Where is money to be found?*

There is no scheme Mr Peach can conceive, by which he may *assure* himself of obtaining the sum he needs. He must instead be like the metal-diviner, who surveys the green expanse of a field, and feels by instinct the seams of gold secreted beneath.

He must find the place where money may lie hidden. — And then, he must go to the place — and, though there stands before him nothing but the plain ground, he must spread his hands across the earth, and await whatsoever his fingers may happen upon.

For money is a slippery thing. — It does not like to be confined by reason, law, and axiom. It is forever going off in an unexpected direction, or disappearing when looked for, or finding its way into elusive corners — Not unlike your cat. It will not stay where it is put — nor behave, according to your expectations, or your requirements — It will not come, when called. It is outside, when you think it within — Up-stairs, when you think it out of doors.

Above all, and most significant for Mr Peach's purposes, it has the habit of passing from place to place, or from hand to hand, by mysterious and unpredicted courses.

Hence it is, that all those numberless thousands, who convince themselves they have hit upon an infallible method to make themselves rich, atchieve only frustration and ruin. They have failed to understand the very distinction we here expound. If we may return to our simile — They approach money, as though it were a dog, to be taught, and trained, and made obedient, with the exercise of a little care and effort — and then, with no more than a whistle, and *Hey, Bounder! — come to heel —* presto! they imagine it sits at their feet, and follows wherever they go.

But money has, we insist, the *feline* nature. The only way, is to approach cautiously —

Affecting an incurious air —

With slow sidling steps — the gaze directed elsewhere — humming a tune, perhaps. —

Then, to sit as near as one may — and, *see whether it may come.*

Mr Peach has not, until prompted by Mrs Peach's remark, given any thought to the gentlemen of the Anti-Lapsarian Society, in his present predicament. Perhaps it is because they are several miles distant, in Bristol. — Perhaps, because they figure in his reflexions as acquaintances and friends, not as *rich men.* — Or it may

131

be a simple error of omission, to be accounted for by the general disturbance in his intellects, apparently produced by the fantastical gypsies of Mrs Shin. However it may be — he *is* now prompted — And in particular, he recollects certain parts of his conversation with Mr Selby White, as it was recorded in our third. — Above all, that gentleman's hints, concerning a quantity of *colonial silver*. —

He assures his wife her advice is invaluable. She is very pleased to hear it. — And so their talk continues, and becomes more pleasant to the parties themselves, though of no significance to our narrative, for which reason we shall take no further notice of it, and leave them to the enjoyments of an happy couple.

Once Mr Peach at last bids his wife good-night, and she falls silent — into that complete stillness, which so aroused, and equally frustrated, the imagination of fair Anny Pertwee — he does not, as is his usual custom, follow her at once to sleep. Though the hour is very late, he sits a while longer.

The room is perfectly dark and quiet. — No matter. Mr Peach is — thinking.

After several minutes, he rises, and goes to the stairs. Mrs Peach stirs not.

He lights a taper at the embers in the kitchen, and takes a candle to the end-room.* He sits himself at his homely *escrutoire*, and, though it be past the middle of the night, prepares pen and paper.

For some further minutes, he remains in an attitude of contemplation, the pen turning in his fingers — And then writes a direction to — Doctor Thorburn, of the Anti-Lapsarian Society, in Bristol!

Our curiosity is greatly roused. — We thought, Mr Peach hardly knew the American gentleman? Let us look over his shoulder, and read the lines he means to send.

---

* We wish we had a better name for it. — But to call it a *library*, or a *study*, would endow both room and house with an air of dignity, or grandeur, that must leave a misleading impression upon your imagination.

There are many, whose hearts are aflame with the same heavenly fire that burns in yours.

There are many, who also desire the change that you hope to see.

Though we must yet be secret — We are near — and we are prepared.

You are spoken of, as one who loves our cause.

Need I name it? It is —

L ____ Y

IF that word be sacred to you, as it is to us —

IF you would have it triumph in these lands, as it has in the glorious west —

THEN you will understand the import of these lines, and return your answer, as the paper instructs.

I do not salute you by name. We must tread carefully, but a little while longer. I give you those titles, which the honour of our cause bestows on all who love each other, as they love it. Not, sir — but —

BROTHER — and FRIEND.

To these extraordinary lines, Mr Peach adds the still more remarkable instruction, that any reply shall be directed to — JEREMIAH SIXWAYS — at Widdershins Bank, by C___ton B___, in Somerset-shire!

What can be the meaning of this? —

Hush! — do not look directly! — or you may *offend the cat.*

CHAPTER EIGHT

Mr Peach surveys his writing-desk on the following morning, and says to himself —

— I shall have to send to Bristol for a supply of paper.

Understand, reader. — We do not imply, that our hero has sat at the same chair, from the close of our previous chapter all through to the commencement of this. He has retired to sleep in the interval, though his rest cannot have been long, nor do we suppose it to have been very tranquil. It has fallen a good deal short of that easy and restorative repose, which is proverbially said to be the lot of the righteous man. Which is not to say, that his conscience must therefore be troubled. — We put no such faith in common proverbs, nor in any thing that is commonly said. It is with speech, as with many another commodity — That what you may meet any where, is of least worth, but that which is rare, is precious. Indeed, we suspect that *silence*, being the rarest of all, is — the *Sangreal*, or holy-grail, of the old romancers — the phoenix feather — The thing of incomparable price. For there is in all human creatures this incurable malady, that they must EVER BE TALKING. — And, *not to speak*, seems as deathly an embargo, as *not to breathe*. — Have you not observed, reader, how the world is plagued with our noise, like the perpetual buzzing of the bee-hive?

To our business. —

Neither the paltry refreshment of a few hours of sleep, nor the light of a new day, has eased Mr Peach's mind. He has passed much of the morning composing various further letters. — Plain and prosy, in comparison to the extraordinary document sent to the American Doctor — Yet in their own fashion, suggestive of the tumult in Mr Peach's brain. For he writes to enquire, whether any passage may swiftly be secured, to a remote harbour on the coast of *Cornwall* — to some part of *Ireland*, sufficiently distant from the principal cities of that island — or, to a deep recess in the wild *Norwegian* coast! — along with several other letters, pertaining to the business of removing his household.

Thus it is, that he is brought to the reflexion, with which we opened our chapter. — We have expended more ink than we might have, accounting for it. Do not be impatient, reader. The causes of things are profound — subtle —

We may as well offer a plain hint, that this matter of the supply of fresh paper, which Mr Peach has determined to request from Bristol, will prove more significant in our tale, than it here appears.

Never think, that we waste your time on trifles.

The practical difficulties of the morning, are not confined to the shortage of material for correspondence. Mr Peach is twice or thrice required to stand up from his desk, in order to attend to tedious domestic matters, such as the fetching of water, the emptying of the pot, &c. — All those duties, which until this morning fell to the lot of Anny Pertwee.

— It is a further point, he thinks, in favour of quitting the place as soon as I may. I shall find it very tiresome to occupy an house, where there is no house-maid. — And he goes to the door, and cries out, Jem! Jem! Where is the boy? — Reasoning, that though he has lost one servant, he need not be burdened by every toilsome necessity, when there yet remains another in his employ.

Jem is no where to be seen.

We have not hitherto had leisure to mark the character of the stable-lad. He is, in truth, all too easily disregarded. — He is not one of those, who leave a lasting impression on the eye, or the ear. To look at, he is a shy, rheumy, creeping boy, who hangs his head. To listen to, he is — Nothing at all, as often as not, for he steals away from company when he can, like a shadow banished by a cloud — And, when he cannot, and is called upon to speak, the halt in his tongue overcomes him. As Mrs Shin says, There's scarce a word to be had from his mouth, and those that are, you may be waiting till next Wednesday to have them. — By which the good-wife means, that because Jemmy Sixways says little, and that with a stammer, he is not worth hearing. — An opinion held universally — As all Mrs Shin's opinions must be, else she would discard them.

We, however, are no respecters of orthodoxy. — No more, we think, are you. We have watched the lad with some attention. We note how he sighs, when he is alone — How he will sometimes pass several silent minutes, in contemplation of a flower plucked from an hedgerow. — We have once or twice come across him scrambling among the branches, in search of the thrush's egg, or ascending the highest ridge of the country, and setting his gaze to the west, straining to discern the distant glitter of the sea. In short — we discern several marks of *sensibility* — That quality, which bestows so great a degree of interest upon sickly and retiring young ladies. Whether it can effect the same alchemy, upon a stammering country lad, with a dripping nose, we rather doubt. It must also be acknowledged, that those habits which shew to advantage in the simpering heroine of a romance, are not much prized in a domestic servant. — For, diverted as he is by the inward promptings of his soul, Jem is often liable to be absent when called for, as on the present occasion — Having abandoned his place in the stable or the cottage-garden, and wandered away, who knows where — to muse upon, who knows what.

It may be wondered, why the lad is not dismissed? — An enquiry, indeed, which Mrs Shin will often make of herself, aloud, within the hearing of Mr Peach.

That gentleman, however, is himself fond of walking about the country, as we may have remarked once or twice before now. He cannot find it in himself, to banish the boy from his position, for a fault Mr Peach must by nature look upon indulgently. — And besides — There are certain advantages, in a servant who is quiet, and too often absent — just as there are many objections to one always busy, and too often present — A comparison which has perpetually been before Mr Peach's eye, and indeed his ear, in the person of the garrulous and inquisitive Anny.

We have dwelt upon the dilatory habit of Jem the stable-boy, not only to provide you with a better understanding of his character, but also, because at this very moment in our narrative Mr Peach is reminded of the identical thing — And is struck by a curious notion, of how he may put the lad to use.

— I have observed, he says to Jem, when the boy is returned, That you are fond of walking about the country.

An harmless remark, you may think — But the soul of young Jem is, as we have said, a delicate thing. The blushing and stooping that follows, would honour the most prudish of virgins. — Jem feels himself reprimanded, and cannot manage any answer at all.

Mr Peach is undaunted. He knows well enough, that any interview with the boy will call for a great store of patience. — A quality he possesses above the common measure.

— I make no accusation, lad, says he. I should be an hypocrite if I did, for I love to go about in the open air myself. Nor do I reckon it an idle pursuit. It cultivates the habits of observation and attention. You, perhaps, may see, what others overlook; and those who speak least, see most.

By such expressions, Mr Peach hopes to ease the poor lad's halting tongue. Alas, Jem is so entirely unaccustomed to praise, that the good effects of a kindly manner, are *equalled* and *opposed* by the lad's surprize at such unfamiliar treatment, in accordance with Newton's famous principle. — And Mr Peach must proceed, as patiently as before.

— They say in the village, that you were the one to fetch the constables, when the house was robbed.

Jem is able to signal by a nod, that the report is correct.

— It was well done. I have you to thank, that little damage was done, and no harm came to Mrs Peach.

These further morsels of encouragement, and in particular the allusion to the lady, whose mysterious affliction must be of compelling interest to any feeling heart — are enough to soften Jem's terror, and enable him to stammer a few humble and grateful syllables.

— You never saw the thieves, I suppose?

Jem shakes his head.

— Nor heard them?

— Only — Jem begins.

— Did you hear any thing? I shall be curious to hear of it, if you did.

— Only the breaking of the door, sir.

— Ah.

— Like thunder. It woke me.

— I suppose you ran for the village, as soon as you were awake?

— Yes, sir.

— No doubt you were very frighted, to think house-breakers had come so near while you slept.

Jem rouses himself a little, at the suggestion of cowardice. — I shouldn't have ran, he says, except I heard Anny cry, Help, Murder, Save me, and the like. I feared she might come to harm.

— That was a noble thought. Then it appears you heard Anny's cries, as well as the crack of the door.

Jem fears he has been caught in a contradiction, and once more cannot speak.

— Never mind, boy. I think you did just what you ought to have done. I only wish to be sure, that you had no sign of the villains themselves, whether sight or sound.

Jem assures his master of it.

— I wonder, Jem, whether you have ever seen any body hereabouts, that you did not know, or thought strange? I know you are fond of walking in the woods and fields, and have a keen eye. Do you recall that you ever noticed one, or two, and asked yourself, Who might that fellow, or those fellows, be?

The boy is again quite confounded. His master's question is itself not so difficult of apprehension, nor of answer. — The confusion has another cause — Which is, that no body has ever once asked Jem what he does when he goes a-wandering, or what he thinks, or what he sees, or, indeed, has ever mentioned the circumstance, except to abuse him for it, and call him moony, or wool-gathering milksop, or breech-soaker, and pull his ears, and knock him in the dirt.

— You might have seen them only for an instant. Men strangely dressed, or with an outlandish air, stealing away from view as soon as noticed.

— The gypsies, sir?

— Would you know a gypsy, if you saw one?

The lad frowns, and plucks his lip, and concedes, that he might not. — Which Mr Peach thinks is to his credit. After some further gentle enquiry, Mr Peach is able to establish, that Jem has noticed no strangers, or foreigners, or persons otherwise out of the ordinary, on any occasion he can remember.

— But — the boy says, with a blush, and some other marks of sudden passion — But — sir — When I go walking, I shun the roads and the houses — I don't love company!

— Why, Jem — I don't blame you for it.

— Don't you, sir?

— Not at all. The beauties of nature appear to their best advantage, without the intrusions of mankind.

Jem appears greatly moved by this sentiment, trite though it be. — He clutches at his heart, and says — Oh — sir —

— I should like to make a request of you, Jem. I should like you to continue as you do now, that is, to wander in the country hereabouts, away from the roads and the common places. And I should like you to keep a careful watch, for any such man or men, as I have described. Any who appear to keep themselves from the general view — In the woods, perhaps, or other secret places. No ordinary eye would ever see them, but you, Jem, I think, do not look as others do.

— I?

— It is a matter of importance to me.

To be given a task, of *importance* — To be entrusted, with a gentleman's confidence! — For Jemmy Sixways, who, poor lad, has met only with varying proportions of indifference, disdain, and scorn, in his young life, these are revelations.

— Will you remember? says Mr Peach.

Jem's tongue cannot readily answer, but at last he swears — he will — he will.

— I am much obliged. And should you notice any such body, on no account are you to accost them, or follow them, but you must come straight and tell me.

— I will, sir — I won't —

— Then we are agreed. I shall depend on your vigilance. — Mr Peach is tempted to encourage the boy further, with sixpence — But remembers, that he must mind his pennies.

— You may depend, sir, cries Jem. — Only — only —

Mr Peach waits patiently, for the boy to unburden himself.

— Only, sometimes — When I go abroad, sir — I will watch, and be vigilant, yet sometimes — I don't know what I see —

— Why, Jem, what do you mean?

The boy's rising passion overcomes his halting tongue. — The sky, sir! he cries, throwing out his arms. — And the great world, all about!

Mr Peach regards him with surprize.

— Those are fine sights, to be sure, Jem. These hills afford many picturesque prospects. I have often stopped in my own walks, to enjoy their splendours.

Jem seems close to tears. — But have you not felt — Oh, sir! — I wish sometimes I weren't a man at all — But a bird of the air — A tree —

— A tree?

Jem bows his head, and can say no more. His cheek is crimson — His eye, wet.

Mr Peach studies the poor impassioned youth for several seconds, and then enquires, whether he knows his letters?

Jem nods.

— I'll give you a book, says Mr Peach.

— Sir?

— There is a book I should like you to read, from my own collection.

— I have my Bible, sir.

— I'm sure you do, lad. This is another book.

— I have the adventure of Christian too.

— There are books in the world, that are neither Bible nor Bunyan. This one is but lately written. It is called, The Sorrows of Werter.

Jem's further confusion is plain. He plucks at his smock, and looks at the earth, and says, I don't know that I ought.

— On the contrary, says Mr Peach, I am quite convinced you must. I shall give it to you to read, though not to keep. You must only promise to take great care of it, and return it unharmed, when it is finished.

In this eccentric manner is the interview with the stable-boy concluded. Jem is dispatched, with his volume of Goethe's romance, and his peculiar commission. — And, if it is the case, which we must now concede probable, that Mr Tho.s Peach of Widdershins Bank, though by every outward token a man of sense and reason, truly believes himself in danger from lurking *gypsies* — Then we very much doubt, whether young Jemmy Sixways will prove an hundred-eyed *Argos*, to keep immaculate watch over the house, and the pleasant country all around. — For the lad shews few marks of the martial spirit.

Reader — we hear your protest.

— What matter, you say, whether this whey-faced addle-brained puppy be suited to his task, or no? — when *there are no gypsies!* — The circumstances of the assault upon Mr Peach's house have been plainly reported in your sixth chapter, and it is perfectly evident, that prattling Anny tells her tales of swarthy burglars, for no purpose other than to disguise her own part in the business. All this nonsense of heathens and vagrants, is merely the superstition of swinish rustics. They might as well emulate their forefathers, and lay the blame upon witchcraft and devilry, and find some poor old woman to burn, or drown! — Good heavens — Is your Thomas Peach no wiser than these?

There is merit, we confess, in your complaint. We only remind you, that neither Jem nor Mr Peach knows one jot of the comical misadventures betwixt Anny and her Ned. We must allow them to proceed as they have agreed — The boy, sent out on his curious watch — The master, unable to rid himself of his mysterious fears. You must permit our narrative to proceed likewise. —

It is Mr Peach's usual custom, when conducting his correspondence, to await the arrival of Dick Wainwright the tavern-keeper's son, and give the lad any letters which are to be sent. On this day, he prefers not to wait, but rides to the inn himself, where, having entrusted various papers to the post-bag, he enquires generally, whether there be any further news of the miscreants supposed to have robbed his house.

The reception he meets, is not altogether as friendly as he expects. — An alteration for which, alas, we must blame the fair Anny Pertwee — Who has gone up and down the village, telling any that will hear — which is to say, every body — That Mr Peach is a man as ill-omened as his house — that there is something not natural in his domestic arrangements — that he is *not seen at church* — &c. Yet, though his reputation among his neighbours has gained a more sombre colouring, Mr Peach finds them willing enough to discuss the great events of the hour — That is, the plaguing of their homes and lands by a visitation of thieving strangers. Every tongue has its own tale, of the wicked devices of these gypsies. Not a soul doubts, but that the villains lurk near by. Goody Parson, the blacksmith's wife, has lost a silver spoon — Ben Boatman, the waggoner, a buckle — And each is as certain as the other, that their trinkets are stolen by the heathens, for every body knows, that gypsies prize silver above all other treasures, and use the metal to cast their fortunes and work their curses.

However, Mr Peach can find not a single soul, who will positively swear to have seen them, or who can say with certainty, where they hide. Ask where he may, he finds no confirmed evidence, that they exist at all. All is rumour, suggestion, and empty talk. — You may wonder, what else is to be expected, from the common-rooms of a village inn. We are inclined to share your opinion. — But Mr Peach departs at least somewhat satisfied, that if there have been malevolent travellers at his door, they are no longer any where in the immediate vicinity.

For two or three days, then, he has nothing to do, but wait. The letters are sent. They travel at the pace of the coach and the post-boy. Replies must be considered — composed — Sealed, and sent by the same methods. Until the uncertain hour of their return, Mr Peach cannot advance his enterprizes, of whatever sort they may be. He watches at his windows — Sets a table against the broken pantry-door, so that the house may not be entered by stealth in the night — Questions Jem each evening, whether the lad has observed any of those signs he was sent to watch for. — Though from the last exercise he gets no profit at all, for Jem is more distracted than ever he was, and his pale face more wan — His eye blank and dreamy — he sighs, more often than he speaks — Heaven help the boy!

We shall learn what ails him anon.

One evening, as the dusk creeps towards the western horizon, our hero sits in his chair, and expostulates with himself, thus. —

— Three days are now passed, and still I hear of not a single further circumstance to cause any alarm, whether by direct knowledge or indirect report.

— If those I fear have made an attempt on my house, only to find me absent, by a mere accident of fortune,* why have they not returned? — Is it not more plausible to think, that finding them-

---

* We might mention in passing, that Mr Peach has on several occasions remarked to himself, how *fortunate* he was to have been diverted from his home on the night of the supposed robbery, by his unexpected adventure in Bristol. Whether the encounter with Mr Farthingay's former ward proves to have been a lucky accident — Is a question we may perhaps reflect on, in future chapters.

selves sought for, they have fled the country?

— And yet —

It is a great weakness, in those of the *reflective* temperament, such as our Mr Peach, that they cannot persuade themselves of any thing, without bringing in the accursed *And yet!* — the counter-reason to all their reasons — The further question, which forbids them from ever settling upon a determined answer.

— And yet — thinks he — One or two men might easily conceal themselves from the general notice, for several days, among the woods hereabouts.

— But is it possible to imagine, that such visitors could pass entirely unobserved, in an English country parish, where every body knows one another's business, and nothing unexpected can occur, but the news of it spreads universally, with the invisible swiftness of an infection?

— Yet these may be no ordinary strangers — But adepts, in the arts of stealth and disguise.

Mysterious reflexions! — and, we dare say, not such as are usually to be found, in the mind of a British gentleman, as he sits in his parlour on a fine May evening.

Yet the scene we must now present, reader, is more curious still. We prepare the ground, to receive the rarer seed. — It is an element in our necromantic art.

Darkness covers the earth. — Or, those acres of it which concern us. Mr Peach remains in his chair, his thoughts turning one way — then, the other — From doubt to reassurance — From confidence, to uncertainty — The *perpetuum mobile* of the anxious mind — Until, by what paths we cannot say, or will not — He recalls a means, by which he may be resolved.

It is one of those summer nights, when the stillness of the air seems almost to oppress the hearing. So quiet is the house, that Mr Peach goes on tip-toe, as though fearing to disturb its rest. He steals thus to the foot of the stair, where he opens the cracked old chest.

He moves the topmost books aside.

Like the student of antiquities, who digs in the earth, Mr Peach seems to reach backwards through time itself, the deeper into his chest he goes. At the very bottom, where the candle-light hardly penetrates, the most antient of all the old volumes lies in a bed of shadow and dust. So decayed is it, that it might be the corpse of a book — No store of wisdom, preserved against time and ruin, but a thing forgotten and defunct — A grave-gift, dedicated to eternal silence, away from the world's light.

If there were once characters or figures stamped on its covers, they have long since worn away. The leather is blank and wrinkled with age — Its edges crumbling — Stained with spots of deeper black, as though touched in places by fire or corruption. An iron clasp bolts the volume shut. Sealing the clasp is a small lock. — This alone gives a little brightness to the dull dead thing, being a delicate brass object, and certainly belonging to the modern age — unlike the grim beast it serves to muzzle.

We shall suppose, it was put in place, by the volume's present owner. —

Mr Peach's eye falls only for a moment, upon that colossal relic — And hurries aside, as though something in the sight of it discountenances him.

He sets his hands instead upon its nearest neighbour, an huge handsome sturdy thing, evidently worn from age and long use, but so well-made, and well-preserved, that it looks fair to endure as long again. It is as broad as Mr Peach's two hands spread, and as long as his arm, and no less thick than the Bible, with commentaries. — The thing is, you may imagine, excessively heavy. Mr Peach groans to lift it. — But, lift it he does, and takes it to the end-room, where he sets it down, brushing away some accumulations of dust.

He lights another candle. One single taper cannot do, to peruse so wide a volume.

The binding is stamped with a series of Greek characters. Our knowledge of the tongue of Homer and Herodotus is a little scanty, but we declare with confidence nevertheless, that they spell no word in that language. They are — A Z P Ω H — that is, *Azroë*.

The pages within are very fine. — Perhaps the paper was polished before it was gathered and sewn, for it lies very smooth and close. There are several hundreds of sheets. — No wonder, that Mr Peach struggled to move the book!

He lifts it open.

We cannot say, he reads. It is true, that he turns several pages. — But no mortal creature could stop to scan the lines therein, without losing their reason, unless perhaps a reader that is mad to begin with. Look —

No — do not look, for your own wits' sake. — We shall describe the contents for you.

Every page that Mr Peach turns, presents the same appearance. Each one is printed from the upper margin to the bottom, and from the outer to the inner, with line upon unrelenting line of words — As though the volume were a miller's sack, into which language is poured like grains of flour. There is not a single pause to them to be seen, on any page. There is not so much as a stop or comma — No indentation, to give the eye respite — Neither paragraph nor period, that might order the teeming profusion of words. No letters *majuscule* — no decorative characters — Even the spaces between one word and the next are narrow. The mass of print confuses the eye. — Letter upon letter, and word after word, like the swarming creatures of an ant's nest. It is as though the compositor who set these pages, intended nothing more than to fill them with type — as though he resented the virgin paper, and wished to see it as near utterly blackened as his tools allowed.

Perhaps the *selection* of the words was entrusted to the same lunatic. It is quite certain, that no author guided him. The pages tell no history — record no thought — They do not even trouble to speak intelligibly for more than two or three words together. Every line presents no more than mere *vocabulary*. — Word upon word upon word, in entire disorder, without connexion, or sequence — without sense or grammar. — A *printed chaos*.

Here — Mr Peach pauses a moment, and runs his finger along some few lines. We shall transcribe them, as a specimen of this shapeless ocean of language. —

six leagues northwards shoe-laces according to your sister's opinion no crystalline translucence the cathedral at scodra no by water yes mulberry it is the reverse bound in stone three eighths is correct a sword certainly the blue but not the yellow pilgrimage turn aside he lies yesterday pig-bristles

— and in such stile, which is no stile at all, but the scattering of words like the droplets of mist at the base of a cataract, the volume proceeds, sheet after sheet, without interruption or remission, from its first page to its last.

Mr Peach closes the book again, and rests an hand upon the cover, in an attitude of doubtful contemplation.

— Well — he says to himself, at last — Most likely, nothing will come of it — But there's no harm in the attempt.

Thus resolved — he sits himself upright, and clears his throat — Hem —

He raps the cover three times with his knuckles, exactly as though knocking at a window, and pronounces the following, in a clear loud voice —

Azroë, Azroë, come to your door
Azroë, Azroë, answer me four

Is it a trick of our fancy? — or has the breathless stillness of the night, grown heavier — A stony silence, like that of the crypt?

Mr Peach now lays his palm upon the cover. He waits several moments, as though in anticipation, and then shrugs.

— I do not recall, he says to himself, that any reply was to be expected.

— Perhaps, he thinks, I ought to conduct a trial. — I might propose for my first question some simple matter, whose answer I know already.

— Or perhaps I ought to confess myself a credulous ass, and go quietly to bed.

A wise suggestion! but Mr Peach will not heed it. He sighs, and closes his eyes, and places both hands on the book, and recites —

Azroë, Azroë, never be done
Azroë, Azroë, hearken to one

He considers a moment, and then says, — In what place is the king's palace?

His eyes remain tight shut. He feels for the edge of the binding, and lifts it, and begins to turn through the pages.

— Now, he thinks, while the leaves whisper and curl under his blind manipulation, we shall see whether the word *Westminster* or *Whitehall* be printed any where in Monsieur Azroë's universal lexicon!

His hands cease their sightless journey through the book — Allowing it to fall open, upon a page, which yet he does not look at. He extends a single finger, and makes it wander over verso and recto, up and down and across, as thoughtless as a child scraping lines in sand.

— Although, he thinks, I suppose *Kew* would be as proper an answer.

He frowns — Indeed — he thinks — I ought to have positively declared, *which* king. Well — let us see —

He allows his hand to halt on the page, and opens his eyes.

At his finger's tip appear the words —

as you wish the ground marksmanship not yet

Mr Peach shakes his head.

— I am an ass, he thinks, to have expected any thing else. — Here is not even the name of a place. Monsieur Azroë may go back to his chest at once, and I to bed.

He is about to raise his finger from the page and close the book, when a further thought gives him pause.

— The very nearest words to my finger-tip, he thinks, are *the ground*. Is that not a fair answer to my question? However many kings there are in the world, all their palaces surely lie, upon *the ground*.

Mr Peach smiles at his own reasons. — This, he thinks, is why the world will never be done with the quackery of oracles and fortune-tellers. They may say whatever nonsense they please, and we fools will persuade ourselves of its wisdom.

— I might try the experiment again, he thinks, with a more careful choice of words. I am permitted four questions, after all.

A minute or two passes, while he considers it. The candle-flames rise quite straight. The very air seems hushed. —

Once more he closes his eyes, and lays his hands on the cover of the book.

Azroë, Azroë, never so true
Azroë, Azroë, hearken to two

Thinking of the loss of his female domestic, he says aloud — Who shall now sweep the floors of my house?

As his hands open the volume, and begin to pass among the pages, he thinks, There, Monsieur — An oracular question, for it looks to the unknown future — Yet a determinate one, for there are only two or three answers which may prove your worth. You may inform me, I shall perform the task myself — which I think most likely — Or that no one will — You shall not excuse your-self with Delphic ambiguities. Let us see how you fare, now. —

He selects a page — Drops his finger upon it, with a flourish — Opens his eyes.

The line above his finger reads

certainly nine year past my fellow servant infernal music no

Mr Peach frowns again, and looks more closely. The type is

small, and the blanks very narrow, as we have mentioned. — As best he can determine, his finger has stopped precisely between *my fellow servant* and *infernal music*.

— This is no answer, he says, aloud.

The book makes no protest. —

— *Infernal music*, Mr Peach says, does no house-work. A *servant* is an answer conformable to sense, but not *your fellow servant*. — You have no fellows, or not such, as may arrive at my house to sweep a floor. But if the plain word *servant* is meant, why has my hand not come to rest on that one word alone?

Mr Peach bends very close to the page. It seems to him that his finger indicates the two words equally, which lie adjacent — *servant infernal* —

He lifts his hand away.

— It is possible, he thinks, that my hand moved as I opened my eyes — That it lay only on *servant* before then.

— But what is it worth, to be told a servant shall sweep my floors? — Nor do I think it a good answer. For Anny will surely not return, and Mrs Shin would certainly not lower herself to the task, were I to ask her, which I shall not; nor would I engage Jem to it. I shall not bring in another servant, when I intend to quit the house as soon as I may. No — This is all mere nonsense.

Mr Peach rubs at his temples.

— And yet, he thinks, it is not so perfectly implausible an answer.

He closes the book again, and regards the characters stamped on its cover.

— I see, he says, you are a cunning imp, Monsieur, and will not have your authority put to the test like a school-boy.

The book neither acknowledges the compliment — Nor dismisses it. It is *only a book*. — Is it not?

— Either, says Mr Peach, I must come to my senses, and end this charade, and you must go back to your bed, and I up to mine — Or, I had better ask of you, the thing I truly desire to know.

The gentle flames quiver. No doubt some exhalation, emitted with the gentleman's words, has sent an invisible disturbance through the air about them.

He composes himself — Rests his hands on the book — And recites —

Azroë, Azroë, riddle-me-ree
Azroë, Azroë, hearken to three

And asks aloud — Am I at this present moment pursued by a stranger, or strangers, from a distant country?

The pages turn forward and back. Mr Peach waits much longer now, before daring to open his eyes. Here — he thinks — and then — No — and passes over two or three score leaves — Then returns again — His eyes tightly sealed all the while.

He wonders, whether he should close the book again, without looking.

At last he lets it lie open. The page is chosen — The finger scans, left and right — Comes to rest.

He takes particular care, to hold it very still.

He opens his eyes.

The finger-tip is poised, with the most exact precision, beneath a single word — *yes* —

Mr Peach rises abruptly. The candles dance in agitation.

He says to himself — It is the word most frequently appearing, in the whole book. See — there is scarce a line in which it is not found — It may be the merest chance, that my finger fell upon it. There are ten thousand places in this volume, where my hand might have come to rest, and received the same appearance of an answer, quite by accident.

Mr Peach now desires nothing so much, as to go straight up-stairs, and have some pleasant inconsequential intercourse with his wife, according to his usual custom, and then go to sleep.

But — he is permitted one further question.

We shall not attempt to describe his restless agonies of indecision. The outcome is, that he sits again — Spreads his palms over the book's cover — Closes his eyes — And, in a voice altogether less clear and careless than it was, pronounces his incantation and enquiry —

> *Azroë, Azroë, but a word more*
> *Azroë, Azroë, hearken to four*

— How may I escape those who pursue me?

The leaves murmur under his hand. It seems almost, that they laugh. — He turns them over near to the last page — Sends his finger to the extreme margin. With a sensation of dread, he opens his eyes.

His finger has fallen on the word, *no.*

He bends closer, to read the adjacent babble of print.

danuvius a beggar by no means unwelcome turnstile the buried wishbone

— By no means, he says, in a dreadful whisper. — I may escape, by no means.

A noise breaks the fearful silence of the house. — It is a small sudden clatter, like the nervous scratch of a mouse within the wainscot. It has sounded from the room up-stairs — whence no sound is ever heard.

Mr Peach leaps up from the chair — Throws the book closed — Hurries above.

At the door — at the very door, where Anny Pertwee so often contrived to listen, and never detected the slightest sound — He hears his wife's doubtful murmur — Tom? Tom?

He unlocks, and hastens within.

— Are you awake, my dear?

— Tom! there you are. For a moment I fancied —

There is no light at all. Mr Peach stands by the door. — He is perfectly accustomed, to speaking with his wife in the dark. But his habit is always, to take the candle to bed, and then to extinguish it, before he wakes her. In all the months she has been confined within this one room, he has never until now stood a few strides apart — and called to her, across a sightless abyss.

— What did you fancy, my love?

— The silliest thing. I felt, someone else had been here.

We cannot see Mr Peach's face, and therefore, we will not presume to say, what expression appears there. But we have the power, to lay as it were a finger on his heart. — It is constricted, and quickened — Seized by a sudden chill.

— It was you, Tom, that woke me, wasn't it?

— Yes — Liza — says Mr Peach — of course it was I.

— Where are you?

— Hush, my dear. Rest again. I have disturbed you unwontedly. It is not your hour.

— No — It is not.

— Rest, says he. — Be at peace. All is well.

With which comforting words, he steps away from the door, and into perfect invisibility. No more words are spoken — There is nothing to be seen, or to be heard. — We can narrate no more, with neither word nor deed to report, and shall therefore relieve you of all these obscurities, by quitting our chapter.

CHAPTER NINE

They begin to gather, and draw closer about us — Like flies of summer, each one in itself a thing minuscule and negligible, but when a multitude assembles, ah! — they darken the air, and trouble the ear. — We mean, those circumstances of our history, which hint at something *not rational* — not NATURAL —

We suspect you have already certain doubts, concerning Mrs Peach. — You are no ordinary reader.

Perhaps you feel — by mere tact — A sensation in your hands, as you turn the pages — Some presentiment, of what may lie ahead.

If you would part from us, while the way seems yet clear and straight ahead, and the weather untroubled — the hum of flies, no more than an inconvenience, dispersed to innocuous nothing by a wave of your arm — We shall think no worse of you. To-day, indeed, is as fine a day as may be imagined, in which to dawdle, and go no further on. The sun ascends towards a cloudless heaven, while soft breezes temper its heat, and all nature puts on her May finery. On such a day, any body might forget there ever were such mysterious fears — such obscure stumblings, in lightless rooms — such solemn charades of sortilege — as we met with, in our last. — Forget them, as we forget in an instant the turbulence of unhappy dreams, when our eyes open to the embrace of dawn.

The offending book — relic of unenlightened ages! — is put out of sight.

The house is filled with day-light. It presents the very picture of domestic peace and good order — Thanks to Mr Peach's own efforts. For, having determined that he must stay within-doors, in expectation of the replies to his written enquiries — and perhaps also for another reason, which we shall not mention, for in the spirit of this new morning we will not think of fantastical lurking foreigners haunting the woods — Remaining, we say, at home, he has set about the duties, formerly belonging to Anny Pertwee, with surprizing relish — Taking particular care, to sweep every room below-stairs, from corner to corner and back again — A labour he performs with the most determined satisfaction, as though to exemplify the old verse of Parson Herbert —

Who sweeps a room, as for Thy sake,
Makes that and th'action fine.

Mr Peach is resting from his toils, and contemplating the beauties of the after noon — his pleasant mood only a little clouded, by some impatient reflexions, on the idleness of Dick the innkeeper's boy — When he spies beyond the window, a person making their way down the valley-side opposite, in the extreme of haste. — Running — tripping — falling — up again — Coming pell-mell towards the house, as though pursued by the Furies.

It is young Jem Sixways. He runs in among the willows — Splashes through the stream, heedless of his shoes and stockings — Comes up to the road, and to the door, red in the face and dripping, and with scarce a breath left in his body. The ordinary reluctance of his mouth, to produce articulate speech, is thereby compounded. — Sir — he attempts to say — Sir — Alas, even that one syllable resists his efforts.

— Heavens, Jem! calm yourself.

Jem cannot — But points instead, along the road, with a force and emphasis of gesture, that would not shame the tragic stage.

Mr Peach's heart leaps in his chest, and then shrinks, touched by unseasonal cold. — He takes Jem by the shoulders. — Have you — he says — Jem, have you seen the men I told you to watch for?

Jem holds up a single digit. — One — he says, amid gasping breaths.

— One man only?

Jem answers with urgent nodding. — Poor lad — He may shake his brains loose from his skull, if he continues so!

— Only one, thinks Mr Peach. — I must not despair — I must rouse myself. — And he turns to go within, to fetch his fowling-piece and powder; but Jem seizes him by his sleeve and points again. — There! — he says — Him!

A single rider has come into view at the turn of the road.

The man is quite certainly no vagrant. He is neatly and fashionably dressed, and his horse is evidently a well-bred elegant animal. Nor does he shew the smallest sign, that he prefers to conceal himself from general notice. He rides quite comfortably in the road, under the plain light of the sun, like any gentleman going about his quotidian business. There is only one aspect of his appearance and bearing, which possibly corresponds to the description of those Jem was sent to look for. — And that is, that the man is a negro — And, unfortunately, the first person of his complexion, that silly Jemmy Sixways has ever set eyes on, in his life. — A novelty which, we fear, has confused itself, in the boy's imagination, with notions of gypsies, and foreigners, and every thing lying beyond the horizon of his knowledge.

The touch of winter recedes from Mr Peach's heart. He forgets fowling-piece and powder. — For the rider is no other than Caspar, attendant and amanuensis to Miss Arabella Farthingay.

— Go — says Mr Peach to Jem, rather more roughly than the lad might think he has deserved — Don't be a fool, but look to the gentleman's horse.

Jem has been sufficiently amazed, at the mere appearance of the unexpected traveller. We may imagine his astonishment, upon learning that this remarkable person is a visitor to the house! — he collects himself so far, as to obey the instruction, and take the animal's reins, as Caspar dismounts — but, we must confess, not much further.

— The stable-boy, says Caspar to Mr Peach, appears discomposed.

— He is afflicted with a stammer, says Mr Peach.

— I see, says Caspar. — I also surmise, that he has recently been immersed to the waist in unclean water.

— That is possible, Mr Peach concedes. — He is fond of nature.

The explanation suffices. — Caspar turns his attention from the stable behind him, to the house before. He offers a courteous and eloquent greeting, and explains, that he is sent on an embassy from Miss Farthingay.

— In the first place, he says, my lady offers her compliments to Mrs Peach, and hopes to hear good news of her health.

Mr Peach returns his thanks to Miss Farthingay for her kind enquiry, and, though he regrets he can report no improvement, invites Caspar to assure her, that Mrs Peach at least does no worse.

Caspar acknowledges the answer, with a dignified inclination of the head. — Permit me also, sir, he says, to present every condolence, on my own behalf. — His speech is as grave and magnificent as his posture. It produces an effect of tremendous solemnity, even in pronouncing so trite a sentiment.

— The situation of the house, he says, looking about, Is very remarkable, for its perfection of retirement.

— Indeed, says Mr Peach. — Mrs Peach's condition requires it. I trust you were not greatly inconvenienced, in finding your way here?

Caspar makes a broad smile, as though Mr Peach had just delivered an elegant witticism, of the sort that demands to be written down, for the amusement of posterity, by some attendant *Boswell.*

— Not in the least, he says. — I committed the roads to memory before I set out, though not, I regret to say, in the form of blank verse.

— I should hope not, Mr Peach says. — The distance from Grandison Hall to here would have resulted in a very considerable canto. Forgive me — You have had a long journey. Will you take some refreshment inside?

— You are hospitable, sir, says Caspar, with another bow. — I have come no more than three or four miles, from the inn beyond these hills, at the turnpike-road. Miss Farthingay has passed the last night there, awaiting Mr Farthingay's carriage from Bristol. Miss Farthingay observed that your house was near by, and engaged me to convey her best compliments, along with her gift. — At this word Caspar fetches from his bag a packet closed in paper and string, which from its form and dimensions Mr Peach guesses to consist of a single large book. — Miss Farthingay, Caspar continues, desires me to say, that she fears she was not gracious, on the occasion of your meeting some days past; and hopes you will accept this trifling token of her sincere regret, and her wish to make amends. — The man now holds the packet forth towards Mr Peach, with an elegant bend of the knee, and an accompanying inclination of the head, and, having adopted that posture, which might serve as an illustration, in a manual of the art of Deportment, remains quite motionless.

Mr Peach can hardly refuse. — Unless I take the gift from him, he thinks, this fellow might remain at my door in perpetuity, like a suppliant statue.

He accepts the present with a bow of his own. — You may assure Miss Farthingay, he says, that there is no need for amendment, since there has been no injury; nor do I recollect our previous encounter with any sentiments but the most serene satisfaction. My library is not as extensive as I could wish. Every addition is welcome. Miss Farthingay therefore gives much pleasure now, and gave no offence before. I must consider myself obliged, and not recompensed.

— I shall convey the sentiments, says Caspar, resuming his upright stance.

He studies the house with a slow considered look, as a connoisseur might examine the paintings at the Academy.

— Have you no dog, sir? he says.

— Sir, says Mr Peach, I have not.

— In a retired situation such as this, Caspar says, a dog would be a great comfort and convenience.

— Undoubtedly so, says Mr Peach. — But the indisposition of Mrs Peach is unfortunately such, as to forbid any domestic animal from the house.

Caspar discovers a pipe from somewhere about his person, and, though he has neither tobacco nor flame, puts it to his mouth, with the same contemplative air. He continues to examine the aspect and disposition of the cottage, as though it were his own dwelling.

— But, sir, he says, as though he disputed a problem of theology, Are you not then greatly troubled by the rats?

— We are not, says Mr Peach.

Caspar taps the pipe against his teeth.

— That, he says, is most curious.

Mr Peach is not accustomed to being addressed in this manner, by a servant. Nor, we think, is any gentleman. — However, unlike other gentlemen, our hero has grown somewhat out of the habit of being addressed at all, and has perhaps forgotten what is due to his station.

— Will not you take a dish of tea, he says, before returning to Miss Farthingay? I should not like to think you had journeyed several miles, only for the purpose of standing a few minutes at the door.

Caspar steps back. — I ought not to intrude in such an house, he says.

Mr Peach is surprized at this answer. — You need not fear any inconvenience to Mrs Peach, he says. — My wife is at rest above-stairs, and will not be troubled by any thing below. The remainder of the household is no more than myself and the stable-boy.* There would not be the least intrusion.

---

* A passing remark, of no great consequence, one might think. — We append this note, suspecting you would otherwise take no heed of it. Be so good as to remind yourself, reader, that Mr Peach here informs Caspar, of the persons of his household, that is, himself, Mrs Peach, and Jem, and *no other*. We may have cause to refer to the circumstance, in a future chapter.

Caspar glances towards the roof, and the covered windows that project above the eaves, with a curiously earnest look. — You are generous, sir, he says, but it is not my place.

— Well, I shall not press you. Return to Miss Farthingay, if you prefer, with no more than my expressions of sincerest regard and gratitude. Mr Farthingay intends to depart the country for some time, I understand?

— Mr Farthingay? Indeed, sir, no. The master is always either at Grandison Hall, or his house in town.*

— Did you not say that you and the lady await his carriage at the inn?

— Your pardon, sir. The carriage is indeed sent, but for Miss Farthingay's use only. She is to go to London, and I to accompany her.

— Then I wish her a good journey. I hope the occasion is a pleasant one.

Caspar places one hand at his back. — Miss Farthingay goes to London, he says, to be introduced among the family and society of her intended.

— Her intended!

Mr Peach receives this information, with a greater share of astonishment than might be expected. — It is hardly unheard of, that an handsome woman of marriageable age should find herself engaged. We suppose we must attribute his surprize to another cause — Though we shall not at present speculate, what it may be.

— I had not understood that Miss Farthingay had accepted a proposal, he says.

— The engagement is not yet announced. The alliance was suggested by Mrs Farthingay, during her last visit to Bath, as I

---

* Bristol. In the romances of Miss Edgeworth and Madame d'Arblay, we know, it is inconceivable to admit the existence of any *town*, except London. We need hardly remind you, that our narrative is of an altogether different nature.

understand. The gentleman is now to meet Miss Farthingay. I am told his family is of some distinction.

— Great Heavens! has the young lady herself no say in the matter?

Caspar draws the pipe from his mouth, and holds it up before his eyes for careful consideration, as though it were an object of rare interest.

— You will understand, sir, he says, that I must not speak of my lady's sentiments, except upon the matter which brings me to your house.

Mr Peach feels himself somewhat admonished. — Certainly — he says — Be so good as to convey my congratulations to Miss Farthingay, and my every wish for her future happiness.

— You may be sure of it, sir.

Yet Mr Peach cannot but reflect, as he sits that evening in his parlour, with the packet beside him, and a knife to loose the string, that he thought Miss Farthingay would have had more spirit, than to submit to an arrangement made so hastily, and in her absence, and perhaps without reference to her own sentiments! — His indignation is aroused, at the very thought of it. Indeed, he is rather more offended on the young lady's behalf, than might be strictly allowable, considering the slightness of their acquaintance.

— But is she really to be married to some witless peeling, scraped from the butt of the nobility? thinks he, as he cuts away the knot. — I ought to speak to Farthingay about it.

In this spirit of affectionate concern for Miss Farthingay's prospects, he unfolds the papers, between which he discovers a scattering of pressed and dried primroses, and inspects the book.

It is a fine heavy folio, comprised of several engravings of the principal towns, sights, and roads, of Somerset-shire. The title proclaims it *Gazetteer and Atlas* of the county. On a fly-leaf some lines are written, in an exact feminine hand: —

No more the trav'ller need rely
On versifying passer-by;

For every road is figured here —
The gift of one, whose wish sincere

Is that he ever find his way; —
Miss Arabella F _____ ay.

Our human sentiments, like sealing-wax, grow softer, and more impressionable, as they are heated. Having been already somewhat warmed, prior to reading these sentiments, Mr Peach finds them rather more affecting, than can be accounted for by their mere poetic merit; and he gathers up two or three of the yellow spring flowers, and incloses them between the leaves, at that place in the volume where he finds engraved a chart of the streams and roads, in the vicinity of St Dunstan's church, near Grandison Hall.

— An handsome gift! he thinks.

— Not much less handsome, than the *giver*. —

He brings the folio to the end-room, so it may become acquainted with its new fellows, in Mr Peach's library.*

Laying it upon his writing-table, he is, by inevitable operation of the law of *association of ideas*, reminded of the weightier and more forbidding volume, which occupied that same place the previous evening.

---

* Do not imagine, we speak figuratively. There is as evidently a society among books, as there is in a parliament of fowls, or a pack of hounds. Certain volumes do not love to be put too close to one another — Others, rejoice in propinquity. One may look well or ill, in the shadow of a particular neighbour. A slight modest book, must avoid overbearing company. — Poets must be kept well apart, or they will quarrel, as every body knows. These are matters of plain fact. — As axiomatic, to keepers of books, as the mysteries of shepherding are to any keeper of sheep.

The reminiscence is unwelcome. — He puts it off, with that small shake of the head, which we use to rid ourselves of an errant thought, as though such things were to be dislodged like insects. But, before it flies off — Mr Peach is struck by an interesting notion.

— Why — he thinks — Was not the question, which appeared to receive so positive an answer, whether I was *sought by strangers, from a distant land?* — And, lo! the very next day, I am visited at my own door, by an African. — Most likely he had his instruction the previous evening, for he said they passed the night at the inn. — So it happens, that old Azroë assures me I am sought by a man from a far-off country, perhaps at the very moment when Miss Farthingay has told Caspar he must find his way to this house!

Reader — We think you begin to apprehend, that Mr Tho.s Peach is not quite an ordinary man. — Or, perhaps, that his history is no record of every-day events — That the things he does, and will do — To say nothing of what he *has done* — a matter, we scarce dare hint at, and that only in the darkest terms —That these things, lie some distance out of the common road. — Perhaps, a very great distance.

Whether your apprehension be just, or no — We shall see.

Let us merely remark for now, that however singular our hero's character, he remains an human creature, subject to the fixed and universal laws of mankind. One particular such law, now shews its operation.

It is as true of Mr Peach, as of every man or woman who ever lived, or ever shall, that the fears which oppress him in the dark, are diminished by day-light. — That what we dread at midnight, we laugh at in the morning — So fickle and unfounded are our imaginings. You may try the experiment. — Betake yourself, along any unfamiliar path, at a nocturnal hour. Behold — every shadow terrifies you. Every half-glimpsed shape, appears to threaten. You start at every noise — You look over your shoulder with every step, and hurry along, and wish yourself home.

Now walk the same way, at noon-day. That grotesque silhouette, which you fancied a crouching beast, is but an old tree-stump. The impenetrable obscurities to your left and right, which your fearful imagination populated with bandits and monsters, shew themselves to be fields of harmless sheep. A twig snaps — An hare darts from the bush — Those sounds, which in darkness made you tremble, now pass without your notice.

Thus it is, that Mr Peach's mysterious fears, which for several days have preoccupied him, and kept him within-doors, and which induced him to the peculiar exercise of *bibliomancy* recorded in our last, begin to fade. The question he posed in the evening, and its answer, which by candle-light and silence together seemed such strong confirmation of his secret dread, now appear quite innocent. — Nay, foolish as well. — For — he reflects — one may put any construction one wishes, upon the pronouncements of a supposed *oracle*. — I have, he thinks, surrendered to a dread, conceived and nurtured no where but in my own mind. — And, after several further comfortable reflexions, in a similar vein, he decides he will resume his custom, of taking his evening walk amid the surrounding hills.

In which pleasant exercise we shall leave him, and close our chapter, as we determined to begin it, without admitting any further thoughts of lurking strangers, malevolent gypsies, or any ill dreams and terrors of the night. — For, at this season of the year, it will be some hours yet before darkness returns.

CHAPTER TEN

Like the rustic, who closes his eyes at sun-set, after his day of wholesome toil, and wakes again with the dawn, we omit the night altogether, by the simple method of opening our new chapter upon the following day.

We cannot promise an end to shadows and gloom. — We are no farmer, who has nothing to do with the hours of darkness, but sleep through them. But you shall find us this particular morning in a lighter mood, for we must now relate a somewhat motley adventure, which falls to the part of Jem the stable-boy, in the course of his wanderings.

Though Mr Peach's curious terror of hidden strangers is, as we reported in our last, partly diminished, it is not forgotten. Dismiss, if you please, the gossip of old Mrs Shin — Dismiss the ignorant rumouring of all the country folk — Agree, that all the business of the antient book is superstition and credulity, beneath the notice of a rational and scientific age — The fact yet remains, that Mr Peach's house was broken and entered, by *some body* — and remind yourself, that he knows not who.

So it is, that Jem is not yet relieved of his commission. Mr Peach reasons, there can be no harm in sending the boy abroad, to keep his eyes open, while he himself awaits the progress of his other endeavours — That is, the replies to his correspondence.

We have already expressed our doubt, whether the boy be suited to his task. We are sorry to report our suspicions justified. — We observe, indeed, that since his interview with Mr Peach, recorded in our eighth *supra*, Jem pursues his duties, with less vigour than ever before.

165

He comes down each morning from the stable-loft pale, and heavy-lidded — Blinking, as though he has barely slept. He is listless — feeble — Drained of all manly spirit. He droops, and sighs, and vanishes within the loft again, as often as he is able. — The cause of this alteration, we shall perhaps discover in its place. For the present, we may note that where he was once used to roam the woods and fields, musing on the glory of the created world, with all the eager passion of a young and feeling heart, he now leaves the stable with the greatest reluctance, and murmurs sad whispers, and walks slow, with his eye upon the ground. — When he walks at all — For, we are ashamed to say, that at the hour in which this interlude of ours begins, he is stretched out on the earth, under an hazel-tree — Fast asleep.

How long he has lain thus, while Mr Peach supposes him to be watching the country around, and *keeping his eyes open!* — we shall not positively declare. We would spare the lad some embarrassment, when we can. We are fond of him, we confess. — Besides, our necromantic sight comprehends some glimmers, of his future destiny — But, hush! we are forbidden to prophesy — lest we overreach the humble station of the *historian*, tethered to the diurnal earth, and rise, like Icarus, into regions from whence it is certain destruction to fall — or be cast down —

Let us say, Jem has slept sufficiently long, and deep, that a nearby disturbance brings him awake with a violent start.

Plucked without ceremony, from the mysteries of a passionate dream, he sits up in confusion, to find immediately before him the altogether less elevated prospect of a rough-looking fellow, who has approached him while he lay insensible. The stranger wears boots and a travelling-coat, each as much mud as leather or cloth. He looks down at Jem from under the brim of a wide hat, with no very friendly expression. So close he stands, it is quite possible that the shock which roused the poor surprized boy was administered directly, by one of the said boots.

— Were the enquiry not supererogatory, says this fellow, in accents whose melody of vowel and profusion of syllable instantly proclaim him a native of Wales, I would feel bound to demand of you, boy, what it is you do here, idling on uncultivated ground, and in that hour of the morning when Providence calls us all to the earning of our daily bread; but it is plain you do nothing at all, being asleep, which is, look you, a condition of being, and not of doing; and therefore the enquiry is supererogatory.

Jem is still in that new-woken state, where we barely know our left hand from our right. The Welshman's eloquent admonishment strikes his ears with no more meaning, than the singing of a bird. The stranger pauses only to allow himself a pious glance heavenwards, before continuing. —

— To close our ears to the summons of Providence is a grievous fault, and much to be regretted in one of tender years. I am recommending to you that you examine yourself inwardly, and with the greatest regard to instances and evidences of the sin of sloth, which is among the deadly, or mortal, sins; and proceed thereupon to the mending of your ways.

We think it doubtful, whether Jem has ever heard such a collection of words assembled in a single speech, in all his life. — The stupendous periods, in alliance with that natural state of bewilderment, proper to any body startled out of a deep slumber, render Jem incapable of any response, except blinking, and staring, and some inarticulate motions of the jaw.

The stranger opens his arms to the heavens, or rather, to the greenery of the hazel-tree, which stands more immediately above. — I trespass no farther, he says, upon the duties properly belonging to the spiritual doctor of this parish, whoever he may be. Though I do not know him, being myself a traveller in these parts of the country, I shall credit him a worthy shepherd, with good care of your soul. My purpose with you I shall confine within its necessary and secular limit, it being no more than to ask of you, to direct me to a certain house of this same parish, whose name is Widdershins Bank.

Jem's sluggish faculties are roused, at the pronouncement of so familiar a name — And yet still not sufficiently stimulated, that they are able to penetrate the thickets of language preceding those two concluding words, and arrive at a clear apprehension of the stranger's meaning.

The Welshman frowns. — By the disposition of your body, and other outward marks, I had taken you for a young sprout of my own species. But I recollect me that I found you unmoving in the earth, in a damp and shady nook, among the rootings of this tree, and I am wondering now if you are less a man than a mushroom. You lack the gift of spoken discourse, which the Universal Author by His grace has made the joy and boast of mankind alone, among all His creatures. Is your nature above the vegetable, boy? Have you within yourself the power to answer as I ask, and advise me the ways to that house of Widdershins Bank?

Jem has now collected himself so far as to perceive this much at least, that he is made sport of. — A sensation, alas! too familiar to the lad, who has been the butt of taunts and mocks, for as long as his memory knows. He will not have this traveller think him another lumpen dolt — a witless stock, like his brothers and sisters — like his old school-fellows — like every body he knows, saving perhaps his master Mr Peach — Not he, whose soul is full of mysterious urgings! He opens his mouth to tell the Welshman, that not only does he know the house, but every other yard of earth for many miles about, and that he could direct the man there as easy as snapping his fingers, were it not that they stood almost in sight of the place. — But of all this proud rejoinder, Jem produces no more than three words, before, to his grief and shame, the accursed catch on his tongue brings him short.

The Welshman pulls off his hat, and holds it to his breast, exposing some lengths of unclean hair.

— You suffer from the stammering! he cries.

Jem is about to acknowledge it, and proceed with his direction. — But no sooner have his lips parted, than the stranger raises an interrupting arm. — I shall not, he declares, require you to torment yourself with the efforts of speech. No — he says — for Jem has attempted to protest — No — It is a matter of only very small ingenuities, to devise another way of proceeding, that shall serve as profitably. We may have recourse to the indications of the head, look you, such as the nodding and the shaking, and also the indications of the arm, to signify the north, or the south, or the points between.

Jem answers, that no devices are necessary, except the ten words needed to explain that Widdershins Bank lies just below the very wood where they stand. — Or rather — he begins this answer — But the Welshman will have none of it, beyond the first syllable. — Spare yourself, lad, he cries — For Providence has so ordained our respective faculties and powers, that it is fitted for me to speak, and for you to listen. — Jem, though no theologian, doubts whether this be true, but the stranger will hear no argument, nor any thing, but the diapason of his own voice. Indeed, he seems highly pleased with the arrangement suggested — as who would not be pleased, to find that their own inclinations accord so well, with the dispositions of the Almighty? — Let us — he says, without waiting for any reply — Let us first establish, whether you know of the place I seek.

— Sir — says Jem — I live there.

— Hush, boy, says the Welshman, almost before the last stumbling syllable is out. — It cannot but be painful for you, to make trial of your tongue. You are to understand, I am not asking where it is that *you* live, no. Your home is a blessed spot, I trust, and health and fair fortune to all who dwell therein; but it is exclusively of Widdershins Bank I desire to know, and so I ask once more, whether that name and that house are familiar to you?

— Widdershins — he begins — with the intention of repeating, that it is the very place where he is in service. — But the Welshman is not to be diverted from his course.

— Precisely the name! I see you know the place, which was the first matter to be certain of; but, look you, it had been an easy thing to indicate so much by only a motion of the head, which was more comfortable and amenable to your own practices, while no less sufficient to mine.

169

— But — says Jem, who begins to find the stranger irksome —

The Welshman interrupts again, with a sweep of his arm. — Your hesitation is very pardonable, boy. I shall excuse you any further labour, in accounting for it. I am stranger to you, as to every man of this parish, or, let me say, every man but one, and even that one will not know me by the sight, when I stand at last at his door; for my claims upon his intimacies, and his upon mine, are not such as belong to the ordinary manners of acquaintance, but are founded on the great and mysterious workings of Providence.

Jem has made several attempts, in the course of this period, to bar the flooding tide of the Welshman's eloquence — the *Severn bore*, of his speech. — In vain. Such motions, once begun, are not to be reversed, by any means less potent than the operation of planets.

— I am indeed, the stranger continues, as though he had ascended the steps of an invisible pulpit, and had now the authority of divine service, to speak as long as he wishes, As the prophet of Israel said, a *stranger in a strange land*. Moreover, I confess I do not present in every point the manner and dress of a gentleman, nor do I ride in the public road, as the gentlemen do. To allay your doubts, I shall inform you, that my name is John Brown, and my history as honourable as any gentleman's; and for the reasons I am come from my own country in search of this house, they are not only unexceptionable, and honest, but indeed very natural reasons; and not only very natural, but I should say very necessary reasons.

Whereupon Mr Brown delivers himself of the whole history, which has led him to the spot, where poor young Jem sits before him, and 'cannot chuse but hear.'* Mindful of the progress of our narrative, we shall relay it in paraphrase, excising those elaborations of grammar, and those figures of rhetoric, for the copious use of which the natives of Wales are justly famed. He has been,

* Mr Coleridge's 'Antient Mariner.'

he says, in the service of His Majesty's navy, and fought many engagements in the lately concluded wars; returning from which, the frigate on which he served became separated from her fellows, by a violent storm, which blew twenty men overboard, and dismasted the ship, and drove it far into those southern latitudes, known to be frequented by *pirates*; a crew of whom, discovering the helpless vessel manned only by a remnant of exhausted and starving sailors, for the storm had also rotted their stores of salt-beef and biscuit, proceeded at once to board it, and in the merciless rapacity of plunder to slaughter every soul the tempest had spared; excepting only Mr Brown and one old shipmate, who by great good fortune were able to hide away in the jolly-boat, and row out of sight of the pirates after dark, when the scoundrels were rendered insensible by the quantities of rum consumed to celebrate the capture of their prize. For ten days and nights the jolly-boat floated alone upon the ocean. Mr Brown and his mate collected rain for their drink, and consumed the curious fish raw, having no means to make a fire; and, in consequence of this dangerous diet, the shipmate fell sick in his bowels, and died; only, with his final breath, urging Mr Brown, for the extremity of their circumstances had forged an unbreakable bond of friendship between them, that if he should chance to survive, and find his way back to good old Britain, he must not fail to seek out a bosom friend of his, residing at Widdershins Bank, in the parish of C___ton B___ in Somerset-shire; adding the assurance, that Mr Brown, if he should ever reach that place, would without fail be provided with whatever assistance he might need; for, said the dying man, this bosom friend owed him many and deep obligations, which could not fail to be repaid to anyone who requested them, in his name. By the grace of Heaven, Mr Brown continues, the little jolly-boat was rescued a few days after the poor man's demise; and so Mr Brown did indeed return alive to Britain, whereupon he was discharged from service, the peace of Versailles having been concluded, and so found himself, like many such unfortunates, in great want; whereupon he remembered the dying man's words, and determined to seek out this bosom friend, in Somerset-shire. But, naturally reticent of presenting an appearance so entirely unexpected, he had hoped to make some careful enquiries, as to what sort of man the bosom friend of his old shipmate might be, in order not to come altogether unprepared to the encounter; and this, Mr Brown explains, in conclusion, is the reason he does not advertise his arrival in the parish, but keeps himself apart from the taverns and the public roads.

Jem hears this great farrago of Welsh nonsense at first with impatience — then, with amazement — And at last, with some of the sympathy, natural to a feeling heart. — A tear starts in his eye, at the picture of the poor shipmate, dying a martyr to his bowels, upon the uncaring bosom of Neptune, with none to comfort him in his last affliction, but one single faithful friend!

— Now, boy, says Mr Brown, you know the length and breadth of the reasons, whereby I am come to this parish, God look kindly upon it; and so I have only to ask you once more, to shew into which way I shall direct my steps, that they may bring me to the house, where lives the bosom friend of my old shipmate.

Jem rises to his feet. — Sir — he says — 'Tis my own home —

— Odzounds! exclaims the Welshman, in a sudden passion of impatience — Have you yet chaff in your ears, or a brain of straw? I do not care to hear your stammering news of your dwelling-place. Your arm, boy, your arm! — Here Mr Brown lays hold of the limb in question, and shakes it, with some ferocity — Raise it — he says — Point it — And I shall be on my way.

At this rude treatment, a blush of shame and resentment rises to Jem's cheek. All sympathy is banished — He will attempt no more, to explain himself to the stranger. He suspects he will never be heard with patience. — An opinion, we are sorry to say, born of long and unhappy experience. By a surly motion of the hand, he indicates the valley below.

— A wonder! cries Mr Brown. — I see the fruits of my eloquence are not cast on utterly stony ground. Shall I make presumption that you are in your own person familiar with this place of Widdershins Bank?

Jem answers with an ungracious nod.

— Now look you, how well we proceed, says the Welshman, with great satisfaction. — Your limping tongue is no impediment at all. I shall catechize you further — *catechize*, boy, is to ask several questions — It is a word of the old churchmen. Are you sufficiently intimate with the house I seek, that you know some of those who inhabit it, by name and reputation, if no more?

Jem scowls — But nods again.

— That is very good, says Mr Brown. — Perhaps you have some measure of acquaintance with that very bosom friend of my old shipmate, who is the man I have come all this way to see? There is policy in the making of some enquiries concerning his character. You may indicate, boy, whether he be known to you as an upright and loyal man, who loves with equal obedience his masters spiritual and temporal, that is, his God, and his king. His name is — *Mr Jeremiah Sixways.*

Jem's amazement, at hearing his own name pronounced by the stranger, is not to be described.

Mr Brown examines him with renewed interest. — By several evident marks in your face, he says, I see the name is of some notoriety; I venture to say, of very great notoriety. Though whether for good or ill, must be established by further catechism.

Jem points to his own breast. — 'Tis I myself — he says.

— Great God! says Mr Brown, with swelling indignation. — Will you be yet incapable of opening your clumsy mouth, except to descant upon yourself, and your home, and I know not what else that belongs to you? I tell you, boy, it is of this Mr Sixways I wish to hear, not of such a clod of earth as you are.

— I'm him, says Jem, though every circumstance conspires against his speech. — I'm Jem Sixways — I live there — 'Tis I you seek!

Mr Brown frowns, and replaces his hat on his head, pulling the brim down low. He takes several steps back — Descending, perhaps, from the phantasmal pulpit, whence he has admonished and interrogated the poor stable-lad.

— The boy is a mere ass, he says. — I might have known as much.

We remark again, that insult and contempt have been the common currency of Jem's transactions with the world, his whole life long. He submits to Mr Brown's unkind judgment, with no more protest, than the stooping of his head.

— Or I dare say, the stranger continues, no less an ass than a knave. Is this your knavery, boy? — that you hear my tale, which ought to call forth your compassion, and are instead moved to impersonate the bosom friend of my old shipmate, by a boorish instinct of cunning? You have missed your mark, knave. — I am no such man, to be imposed upon, and cozened, and led by the nose, by so lean a scraping as you. I am a man of WALES — Do you understand me, boy? I am a WEST BRITON. I am not to be humbled, and deceived. Go — Get to your heels — For I am minded to give you such a thrashing, as will make you rue your impertinences. —

Jem needs no further inducements to take his leave — But flees straight home, without staying to hear any more of Mr Brown's threats, though they continue for some time at his back.

Mr Peach observes his progress, with great curiosity, and wonders what new alarm can have sent the boy lolloping down from the wood, like a great clumsy hare, a second time. — Jem hastens within-doors, gasping, and gesturing, in no very articulate manner. — But, once the breath is back in his body, he gives Mr Peach as full a relation of the encounter just described, as careful and patient questioning can elicit.

— You are certain, says Mr Peach, once the tale is told to its conclusion, That he gave his name as Brown?

— John Brown, sir. Most certain.

We observe in passing, that Jem's accurate recollection of this single point, is not altogether unremarkable. Re-peruse our account of the foregoing scene, and you will discover that the

Welshman announced his name but once. We think we would
have forgiven Jem, had he not been perfectly sure of it, amid the
torrents of language thundering about his ears.

There is more to this stooping country lad, than meets the eye. —

— And a Welshman?

— Yes, sir.

— How did you know him for a Welshman, Jem?

— He boasts of it. And I knew by his way of saying the words.
You know the way they says them, sir, all *hoop-me-dee* and
pilly-polly.

— I wonder, says Mr Peach, that a native of Wales should bear
so very *English* a name, as John Brown.

— 'Twas how he gave it, I swear.

— I don't doubt you. But I suspect the name to be an
imposture.

— A lie, sir?

— Indeed. An unknown fellow, lurking about in the wood,
away from the roads, and dressed in the roguish habit you describe,
may reasonably be suspected of some dishonesty. You are quite
sure he sought this house, and you yourself within it?

— He said it twenty time, Widdershins Bank this, and
Widdershins Bank that, but never would he hear me say I know
the house. He said Jemmy Sixways but once, but, sir, I think I
know my own name. Though I think there must be another Jem
Sixways besides me. I know I'm friend to no navy man. But he
would never hear me tell him so neither.

Mr Peach hems, and tuts, and paces back and forth across the
parlour. — I fear, my lad, he says, you have been spun a yarn, as
they say.

— All of it were lies?

— Tales of pirates and shipwreck are commonly found to be
so.

Jem stares very wide. — Sir — he says — Is this the villain you
set me to watch for? The same, who broke the house?

— I won't say as to that, says Mr Peach, and he looks out at the window, across the valley, where he sees no creature stirring but the daws and wood-doves. — But some species of villain, I believe he must be.

For Mr Peach can imagine only one explanation, that will account for the arrival of a stranger, with an assumed name and history, and a sneaking manner, who comes in search of Jem Sixways the stable-boy. — And that is, that the mysterious lines he sent to Doctor Thorburn, in Bristol, have been *intercepted.*

You will recall, reader, the very curious fact, that in the course of writing those lines, Mr Peach directed any reply to be sent to — Jeremiah Sixways, at Widdershins Bank, in Somerset-shire.

— Unless — he thinks — this supposed Brown, is himself the bearer of the reply, which I have for several days expected by letter instead.

— But if that is so — Why does he not come to the house?

— I am beset, he thinks, by puzzle and conundrum, on every side. — The sooner I am escaped from this place, and settled somewhere far beyond the reach of every body who seeks me, or asks after me, or remembers me — somewhere far from every vestige of my former existence! — the better it shall be.

The sun begins to dip westward.

No stranger comes to the door — Nor shews himself, any where within sight of the house.

Moreover — Another evening is almost come — And still, there is no sign of Dick the inn-keeper's son. — Confound him! — The boy has never been known for an idler — Nor has Mr Peach once incurred his resentment, by failing to reward him for his journey with an ha'penny, and a friendly word or two.

— I shall not sit another day waiting in my parlour, Mr Peach declares at last. — And with those words resolves, to ride to the tavern that very evening, where he hopes to discover something of the fate of his correspondence, and also to hear any rumours of the supposed Mr Brown, who has perhaps attracted some notice among the village society.

You also, reader, will be glad to pass some time beyond the

valley of Widdershins Bank. We have inclosed you within its confines, for some few chapters now, and we fear you have become as bewildered and doubtful as Mr Peach himself, concerning what may be passing in the world beyond.

Let us all go out together, and see what adventures we may meet. — We shall mark the occasion, by opening a new chapter.

CHAPTER ELEVEN

Eleven, the old counting-song informs us, is 'for the eleven that went to heaven.' — We fear our eleventh chapter sets a less *elevated* course. Had we suspected a touch of prudery in your constitution, reader, we should have advised you to avert your eyes. — Our next several pages, shall lead us into the realms of the profane.

Unholy anthems greet Mr Peach's ear, as he approaches the tavern. Every door and window is open, to let the sweet country air in, and the stench out, and by those apertures drunken songs ring across the village, as the pierced belfry emits the church-bell chimes. — Which of the two summons be more generally acknowledged, we should not like to guess, unless upon a Sunday.

Our hero makes his appearance in time to join the chorus of 'By the Back Stair' —

> With a *rum-bo-tum*
> My lady's b_m
> And fetch the sauce from the cellar, o!

— Mr Peach! is the universal cry. — Old Tom Peach! — His arrival is saluted with enthusiasm. — For though he is known to be a strange sober fellow, and, if the rumours be true, a scholar of mysterious arts, he has the one signal recommendation among the society of the country, that he is no canting Wesleyan, and has never been heard to trouble honest folk with talk of idleness, sottishness, hellfire, or the narrow way. Huzza's, are raised. — Pots, are also

178

raised — and sunken again — Pipes, offered. The chorus strikes up anew —

> With a *fee-fo-fum*
> Tom Peach's b_m
> And fetch the sauce from the cellar, o!

Libations must be made, in celebration of his coming, and each accompanied by further rounds, of the humorous song. Further offerings must then be proposed, and swallowed, to honour the king — The country — Confusion to their enemies — With a lusty 'Rule, Britannia!' given by all, not omitting Mr Peach. — These necessary ceremonies concluded, the musical entertainment resumes its witty character. 'Old Fishwife Fiddle' is given, and 'The Mouse in the Bush' — Each in due place, for their sequence is no less fixed and ordained, than the responses in the divine service.

The scene, in short, is such as haunts the night-mares of Methodists.

His duties to the company discharged, Mr Peach steers his course through the tumult of the public rooms, to where Mrs Wainwright the inn-keeper's wife keeps watch over her demesne, and, after paying his respects, observes, that he has not for these past several days received the usual visit of her boy Dick, bringing the post-bag.

— Mercy! cries the good woman — How is my child to ride his mule all as far as Widdershins Bank, when he's lying up-stairs with his poor head almost broke in three pieces, and like as not he mayn't ever rise from bed again?

Mr Peach express his surprize — his consternation — His sympathies, at the boy's unfortunate accident — And asks, how Dick came by such an injury?

— *You* may well ask, says Mrs Wainwright, with severity — You, Mr Peach — When it's on his way to your house that my poor Dick is set about, and pulled from the saddle, and thrown down so hard in the road it's God's mercy his head be not broken clean from his neck. You may fetch your own letters in future — Saving your pardon — I speak a little bold, I know, sir, but, a mother's grief! — Mrs Wainwright mops her nose, with her sleeve.

Mr Peach is very sorry he has been the cause of so tragic an accident, however unwittingly. He proffers his handkerchief.

— Mrs Wainwright accepts the token, and is somewhat mollified. — I told the boy, she says, be quick as ever you can, and keep your wits about you, for every body knows, the gypsies skulk about that cursed house — Your pardon — But I warned him so, that very morning, and look how my fears proved true — For all the good it did — A mother knows, sir! Oh! my poor Dick! &c.

Mr Peach has in an instant forgotten all the exclamations of a grieving parent — and all the noise of the room besides — The reek of tobacco, and spilt beer, and other effluvia — The whole rustic pandemonium.

— Madam — he says — Do you mean to say, the boy was assaulted in the road, near Widdershins Bank, by gypsies?

— Who else? — cried she — Who but the dirty rogues? Two or three of them, bold as you like, sir. They stop him in his way, and pull him down, and make away with the bag, and leave him there for dead. — My own son! What days we live in — God forgive us all —

Mr Peach's heart, which has for a day or two beaten quite contentedly in his breast, with its customary ease and warmth, feels again the chilling touch, and shrinks, as though seeking to hide itself deeper within its fortress of bone and flesh.

— I must speak to him, he says, interrupting Mrs Wainwright's lamentations — At once — If he cannot come down, be so good as to conduct me to his bed-side.

Mrs Wainwright receives this demand, as though Mr Peach had declared his wish to fetch her son a further clout on his skull. She exclaims in horror, and forbids it absolutely — Adding such exclamations, against the gentleman's unfeeling peremptory nature, that Mr Wainwright himself cannot but remark them, from another corner of the busy room, and is compelled to intervene. The inn-keeper guides his wife to a quiet place within, with apologies to Mr Peach. — Yet he insists equally firmly, though less furiously, that no interview with Dick is to be thought of. The boy lies near insensible — He thanks God, the danger is not so grave as Mistress Wainwright fears — Doctor Law himself has been so good as to examine the injury — But advises, that the boy must rest his cracked head for several days, without attempting speech, or motion. Nor has Mr Wainwright any more to tell, than what is generally known, which is, that Dick was on his way to Widdershins Bank with the letters and packets received from the Bristol mail, and was accosted, in his own account, by some vagrant ruffians, who knocked him from his mule, and made away with his bag; and all this at broad noon of the preceding day.

Mr Peach demands to know, where exactly the assault occurred — How close to his door — And, how many the assailants numbered, along with any other particulars the boy may have given. Mr Wainwright, who is a mournful sighing fellow, wishes he could oblige. — But cannot. — Dick made his own way home, with a bleeding head, and has said no more, than that he was struck down along the way to Widdershins Bank. How far along the way, no one knows — Perhaps not even the boy himself knows — For a blow to the head will often produce derangement of the memory. As for the perpetrators, Dick says only, that it was the *gypsies*, beyond which no further particulars are called for, since every body knows, those thieving villains have come to plague the parish. The constables are sent up and down the roads, with several other honest men besides, to beat the rogues from their hiding-places. — But — says Obadiah Wainwright, with a tremendous sigh — They will never be found — For the gypsies have feet like a crow's, and they climb up and sit in the tops of the trees, where no Christian can detect them. — I grieve, sir, he says, for the loss of your papers. — You are a great man for writing and reading, I know. A scholar — Here the inn-keeper favours Mr Peach with a somewhat suspicious look — Well — God keep the knaves from your house, sir.

Mr Peach cares not a jot for the loss of his papers. — A very remarkable circumstance! when we have informed you but a few pages since, that his chief purpose in riding to the inn, was to discover the fate of his expected correspondence. Yet he no longer thinks of it — Nor, we fear, of the dangerous state into which the unfortunate messenger-boy is fallen. This fresh news of *gypsies* has put every other thing out of his head. All his fears, are renewed. — All his mysterious doubts, muzzled near to silence by an handful of untroubled days, now come shrieking back.

— *They are here* — he thinks — They have come indeed — They have found me —

But, WHO? we hear you exclaim. — WHO, does this odd fellow fear, with so mortal a dread? — And — WHY?

Reader — your pardon — Every thing must be told, in its proper place. Be assured, we shall neither deceive you, nor disappoint you.

Besides — We cannot yet positively declare, that Mr Peach's terrors are any thing more, than the phantasies of a disordered imagination. — Remember, what the gentlemen of the Anti-Lapsarian Society say of him. Remember his books — his *wife* —

Furthermore — Observe now, how he occupies himself, for the concluding pages of this *profane* chapter.

Mr Peach hastens home, while the light yet lingers. Or rather, he urges the gelding to hasten, at a pace to which that animal can only be driven, by the most insistent and sustained persuasions. Mr Peach is well aware, how deeply the creature resents this treatment. — He risks feeling the expression of its resentment, at any moment — Yet continues to apply the said persuasions, with merciless rigour. Wherever the road is overhung by trees, or runs up beside a tangle of concealing shrubbery, he spurs the indignant beast to yet more strenuous efforts, and glances fearfully to his left and right — And behind — As though some strange-looking man might appear suddenly in his way — As though he rode across a lawless waste of bandits and savages, and not the good British lanes of Somerset-shire, on a fine May evening!

He comes to Widdershins Bank just as twilight gathers in the upper air. The shadows are already grown murky. — For, as the brightest fire consumes itself most rapidly, so the clear day darkens soonest.

The indignant gelding is stabled with perfunctory care. Jem comes tumbling down from the loft — Seemingly startled, from some private reverie — Unprepared, as is lately his habit, for the exercise of his duties. But in place of the justified admonishments, his tardiness deserves — or, indeed, even so little as a command, to look to the horse — He receives only one brief instruction, which is, that he must return immediately to the stable-loft, and *stay there until the morning!* — The which instruction Jem hastens to obey, since it accords exactly with his own wishes.

No more of him, for the present.

Mr Peach goes within-doors.

He lights no fire. — Not so much, as a single candle.

He brings his chair by the window, and sits himself there. — Watching the valley — and waiting — Pinching his lip — His brow troubled. — He waits thus, until the last of the day has fled the west, and the whole earth is blotted to inky nothing.

He rises. — Closes each shutter, feeling his way from one to the next, like a blind man in a stranger's rooms.

The broken door he cannot seal. It must be left as it is — Its crack, admitting the sounds of night — Restless airs —

He strikes his tinder at last, and lights a taper, and now conducts himself to — The old chest, beneath the stair.

He moves aside the topmost books, of incantation and astrology — Those whose pages struck inquisitive Anny with so dreadful a terror.

He reaches past the alchemical tomes — Past the compendia, of spells, and hiero-glyphs, and the names of invisible beings. — Past the deranged word-hoard of antient Azroë — Down, to the very bottom of the chest — Where lies the last withered and spotted monstrosity, closed with a small brass lock.

He lifts it up. Dust and decay spill from its covers, and stain his fingers dark.

Candle and book are brought to his desk. He sits there before them, a long while. — Meditating, we must think, upon some silent choice.

Consider what you do, Thomas Peach! Think well, upon what may come of it! — Upon *who*, may come!

The decision is made. — He puts his hands to his neck. A thin cord hangs there, hidden by collar or cravat. We had not noticed it before now. — He brings it over his head, and into his hand. Attached to the loop, is a delicate key. It is small and fine as the machinery of a pocket-watch — Fits without a sound, into the brass lock.

The mouldering book is unclasped. A strange odour rises from its parchment pages, when they greet the air again, after two years and more entombed. The smell is not earth and rot — but something more akin to smoke — Distant fire —

He dons a pair of black gloves. — Which would not be curious, except he is not going out-of-doors, and moreover, the gloves are thin and soft, like those more commonly found adorning a lady's hand.

Thus accoutred, he begins to turn the pages, one after the next. He seems to know what he seeks. His lips move a little, as he scans the wrinkled leaves — Though no sound escapes them.

What antient names he may mouth, as they pass under his veiled fingers — We do not ask. We do not now look over his shoulder. There are things, of which we chuse to remain ignorant.

He finds the desired page. His hands and lips come to rest. For several minutes, he studies the marks before his eyes. He prepares himself, perhaps — Or — *reminds himself.* —

Next, he fetches from a cabinet a bottle, and a square of black cloth, upon which are embroidered certain signs, of doubtful meaning. From the bottle he drinks, in the usual manner, though whatever the potation be, it leaves his lips stained an unwholesome blue. — The discolouration cannot possibly cause him any embarrassment, first, because there is no body present to witness it, and second, because it is in the next instant concealed, by Mr Peach placing the square of cloth over his head. — Indeed, the spectacle he presents, gloved and shrouded in this fashion, is so exceedingly ridiculous, as to forbid embarrassment altogether. — For no body could adopt this mode of dress, who gave any thought at all to his *appearance*.

But this is by the by.

The square of cloth is evidently of sufficient transparency, that Mr Peach is still able to read, for he bends above the book, and places a finger upon the chosen page, and begins to recite. —

Bego — bogo — imnaphi — bil —

We transcribe no further. We need not explain our reluctance — Our *refusal*. If you wish to learn the conjuration for yourself — which, in sober and solemn truth, we cannot advise — You must seek out the original.

Mr Peach intones the strange words, as loud as he dares. He stumbles over the syllables in several places, and his finger some-times slows, or halts. — As though there is labour in the read-ing — Or, as though his efforts meet with a certain resistance — Whether from within — from his own conscience — or, from the book itself! — we do not say.

His finger comes to the end of the page. His recitation is complete.

For some minutes, there is only silence, and stillness.

We hear no stroke of thunder. We see no spark of faery light. — No *djinni* has appeared in the end-room of the old cottage at Widdershins Bank, to say *Your wish is my command*, as we read in the Thousand and One Nights — Nor any other ghostly altera-tion is visible, in our scene.

Mr Peach removes the peculiar item of dress from his head, and wipes his lips clean, and replaces bottle and book. Within but a few moments, all is at it was before.

— As it was before! — we fancy we hear you exclaim, reader — Why do you trouble to inform me, that all is *as it was before*! As though I am to believe otherwise —! These are *not* the Thousand and One Nights — Nor is this antient Persia, nor any time or place of absurd superstition and grotesque mummery. This is our own enlightened nation of Britain, and within the memory of some yet living! — It cannot be possible, that any body should expect a palpable consequence to have derived from this absurd pantomime of your Mr Peach — Unless it were a child of eight years, and excit-able fancies, with their head full of Jack and his magical beans!

Reader — We beg you, be neither intemperate, nor hasty in your judgment. Remain patient — as we have urged you — And, observe.

Mr Peach takes up the candle, and peers one by one into every corner of the room, as though he expects to find, among the shadows —

We shall not guess, what Mr Peach expects to find.

He raises the light, and turns himself a full circle.

He calls out —

— Who has come?

The answer — if answer it be — We cannot think it is, and yet, the dreadful cry sounds out in the very next breath — is, a *scream* — of pain or terror — From above — Mrs Peach —

Mr Peach rushes to the stair — and up. — While he fumbles at the lock — See, how his hands shake, and the quivering light makes every shadow leap, as though the house were on a sudden filled with darting ghosts! — the scream sounds again — And Mrs Peach's voice comes crying after it, Thomas Peach! Thomas Peach! — Mrs Peach, we say, for no body else can be within, to emit the scream, or call the name, yet it is scarcely credible, that the voice we have heard only in frail whispers and murmurs, should now sound with such clarion strength. — Howling, as though for light and water, from the deepest cell of a dungeon — Thomas Peach!

— My dear — says he — Hush — I am here. — He has the door open, at last. He extinguishes the candle as he hurries in. — We think we have mentioned already, that Mrs Peach cannot *bear the light*. All within the room, is utter black. — Dearest Liza — he says, with two or three hesitant steps towards the bed — into the abyss of invisibility — How do you do? What has frighted you so? Your Tom is here.

— I have heard you — says the voice of Mrs Peach, clear, and determined, from the darkness.

It is so unlike her usual manner of speech, that although Mr Peach longs to rush to her, and give her comfort, his feet come to a stop. He cannot proceed so much as half a pace. Some iron horror has manacled his limbs.

— That is well — he says — I am close by, have no fear.

— You belong to me eternally, says Mrs Peach.

— I do, says Mr Peach, though with a trembling in his throat, hardly suited to so loving a sentiment — for Mrs Peach has intoned the words, not in the manner of one who plights her troth, but as though pronouncing some fatal sentence. — I am always yours, my dear, he says. — But what has woken you?

— I will help as you ask, says Mrs Peach.

Mr Peach's heart leaps and shakes, like a maddened bird, that will batter itself to death against the bars of its cage, rather than endure imprisonment.

— It is I who must help you, Liza, he says — And always shall.

Mrs Peach's voice pronounces three further words, each slow and full, as though they were the several strokes of an hammer on the bell.

— I shall come.

— My dear — says Mr Peach, with awful hesitation — You are here already. Something has woken you. — I think you are not quite yourself.

No answer comes now from the bed — from the black —

— Liza? says Mr Peach.

The shackles melt from his legs. Silence, perhaps, has dissolved them. He feels his way deeper into the room — Ducking his head, beneath the first of the oak beams — Liza?

— Tom? says Mrs Peach, in her habitual gentle murmur.

Mr Peach's sensation of relief, at the alteration in her tone, cannot easily be described.

— Yes, my dear, he says. He has reached the bed — puts his arm out, to steady himself against its familiar frame. — Are you calm now?

— Have I not been?

— You cried out. — I thought I heard you cry out.

— I have had a peculiar dream.

Mr Peach lays himself down. — Let us not talk of it.

— No — 'Tis already forgotten. Oh, Tom. I'm glad you are by. I shouldn't like to have waked alone.

Mr Peach answers with gentle words of his own. Forgive us, reader, that we do not record them. — Nor the remainder of their nocturnal conversation. It has no bearing on the progress of our narrative. — And, if the truth be told — We would linger not a sentence longer in the abyssal dark of this room, than our duty as historian requires — But hasten away from the foregoing scene — Thus —

CHAPTER TWELVE

Are you beside us still?

Do we declaim our tale to the empty air? — Like the lover, sighing her passion in the solitude of her closet — or the old desert fathers, in their rocky cells — Like the man engaged in private conversation, with his dog? —

No — There — We sense the touch of your hand, upon our page. We think we would know it among a thousand others! —

You have not yet given up Tho.s Peach, despite the evidence of our last chapter — Antient superstition, and unhallowed arts —

There are many who will smile at you, or sneer. Childish nonsense! — is the cry, of these superior persons. — Fit only for the nursery — for infants, or half-wits — For credulous savages, or mumbling Papists!

We shall not waste our breath, in disputing with our *superiors*. Though we may permit ourselves to mention, that we have sometimes noticed them, with our necromantic eye, as they go about their business. Look — Here is one, whose child is sick. Mark, how she puts several coins in the hand of that poor crippled beggar — The very same beggar, whom she passed without a look, day after day, when her darling boy was well. And *there*, is another — aboard ship, in rough weather — Hear, how he mutters his fervent pleas for the passing of the storm — Though on dry land he will assure you, with scientific complacency, that wind and waves are natural phaenomena, quite certainly not to be altered one whit by the hopes or prayers of man!

It is beyond doubt, that every person who ever lived, has at one time or another, in defiance of reason, judgment, and the plain evidence of their own senses, attempted to bargain with the universe, whether by appeals to the single deity, or propitiation of local spirits, or small acts of unthinking superstition. For what is human existence, but a perpetual stepping-on into uncertain futurity? — a succession of doubts, and fears, and hopes? We know not, what lies before us. — Yet we wish we did. And therefore we barter with time and circumstance — Rub the rabbit's-foot, and pin the horseshoe above the lintel — Light a candle to the saint, or leave a dish of milk at the step, for the pixies — Whisper our promises — *Only let me win her heart, and I shall be faithful for ever* — *My affairs must certainly prosper, for I have been sober and diligent* — &c. &c. — As though the great world should bend its ear to our little concerns — As though we, among all the countless millions who have lived, and live now, and are to come, were deserving of special care and favour. — As though we were more than a speck — a mote — A nothing, in the infinite chaos of existence.

But we must beg the pardon of those *superior* people, for daring a comparison between them, and the dust, which glitters an instant in the vision, and is then eternally lost. Forgive us, *mesdames* and *messieurs* — We have grown somewhat uncouth, in the many years' practice of our solitary trade, and forget the deference of falsehood, which is due to the great. We shall not speak of it again. —

Let us only express our satisfaction, that *you*, reader, continue in our company, and do not shun our narrative, though we fear it has turned *criminal*, under the Act of the 9th year of George II.*

---

* 9 Geo. II c. 5. — Popularly termed the 'Witchcraft Act.' We doubt whether the history of these islands affords many equal instances, of the genius of our legislators. In the enlightened year of 1735, it could no longer be admissible, to a wise and rational Parliament, that there should be a statute against the crimes of magic, and divination, and other forms of witchery; for every body now agreed, that there were no witches, and there was no magic. — And therefore it was instead made a crime, to *pretend* to do magic, and to be a witch! — A stroke of sublime invention — Worthy of deep study, by all who wish to understand the pre-eminent virtue of the mother of parliaments.

For Mr Peach has sought aid, or protection, or we know not what — from — Dare we say, whence it is sought? We know only, that he opened the book, which for two years had been kept under lock and key. —

But we shall think of the command given to Lot, before the destruction of Sodom, and 'look not behind.' Our narrative presses forward, and we must on with it.

We shall perhaps best interpret the events of our chapter preceding, according to the experimental method. — That is, by examining whether they produce any discernible consequence.

What will the morning bring?

The morning brings — further NEWS — and of the most tremendous import.

Mr Peach rises laggardly, and is only lately dressed, when word comes to Widdershins Bank, that — the *gypsy* has been found, and apprehended!

A farm-hand brings the tidings — A country simpleton, who wrings his hands in his smock, and has nothing more in his head, but that the wicked devilish thief is taken, and Mr Peach is to ride at once to the constable's house, to swear to his stolen property before the justice, so that there may be an hanging. The churl has fastened on this joyous prospect, as though it were the promise of a month of holidays. — An hangin', zurr! says he, stamping his feet in delight, and implores Mr Peach to hurry; for, in his imagination, if we may dignify his pinched and wooden faculties by that term, it only requires the gentleman's say-so, and neck shall be fitted to noose that very day.

Mr Peach hardly dares hope, that the aid he sought has arrived so soon. Yet if it should be, that the dreaded stranger is intercepted! — and in the very night, that a voice he fears to name spoke from the darkness, saying, *I will help you!* —

He enquires of the rustic messenger, what sort of appearance the imprisoned gypsy presents — whether notably strange, in complexion or dress. The simpleton has no answer. Mr Peach asks, what property it is, he must swear to. — For if his

191

long-expected correspondence is to be recovered, in the very same event, he will bless the day, no matter what power has encompassed it. The hind knows nothing of the goods, nor cares neither, but only repeats, that the gentleman is to hasten to the constable, and give his word to the squire, so the miscreant may swing.

From which we may infer, that the principles and proceedings of British justice, are not apprehended in all their majesty, by the common folk.

Mr Peach calls for Jem — Who has not yet arisen, and can only be summoned by several thundering blows struck against the stable — Demands the gelding be saddled — Leaves the stumbling blinking boy with the care of the house — And rides forthwith to the village.

The country people are in festival spirits, and aflame with the promise of the day. They cheer Mr Peach's arrival. — From the very tavern-door, where we saw him enter in our preceding, toasts are thrown out, as they were last night. We hope they are fresh in your remembrance, and need not be repeated — Mr Peach — King — country — confusion to the French — &c. Though the spring morning is yet young, several persons are already drunk. The rustic sports of *pitch-noggin* and *frog-in-your-breech*, are prosecuted with fervour, on every side. All is clamour and confusion. — We could wish for the brush of a *Breughel*, to portray it, but must pass on through the scene, until we arrive, with our hero, at the house of Samuel Sexton, appointed one of the constables of the parish.

Samuel is by trade a cooper, and by practice a maker of other wooden items. He keeps his barrels in an old poultry-barn behind the house, where, because it has but one narrow window, and a beam across the door, he has imprisoned the felon, until the arrival of Squire Furzedown the justice. Conscious of the momentous duty laid upon him, he has stood guard throughout the night, and kept the crowd from his door. Let them revel in the lanes, and be at their drunken pleasures. — Within the sphere of Samuel's authority, all shall be grave, and stern, and exact, as befits the solemnity of THE LAW.

Mrs Sexton has had the parlour dusted, and a bit of lace put over the chairs, and the children scrubbed or sent away, in preparation for the arrival of the dignitaries. Mr Peach is welcomed in — Pays his compliments — &c. — And asks of Samuel Sexton, the same questions he was so eager to have answered by the doltish clot, who came to his house; *viz.* what are the particulars of the prisoner, and what goods are recovered from the thief, that he is to swear to?

— Sir, answers the constable, that a villain is apprehended, and that some movables, belonging to honest folk, have been found about the person of the accused, I may say. — But, sir, any thing further, being in the nature of *evidence*, I may not bring it forth, except before his honour the justice.

— I suppose not, says Mr Peach, somewhat taken aback. — Though I don't ask that any thing be brought forth. I am only curious, whether this single person be confirmed a gypsy, for those antient travellers are not habitually of solitary habits; and I should also like to know, whether certain papers of mine are among the stolen materials. I have been very uneasy at the loss of them.

— Ah, sir, there you have hit on it. The very word. They are certainly *material* papers, for every thing, touching the nature of *evidence*, is greatly material, in questions of justice. And as to what is *confirmed*, or not confirmed, that, sir, must be for the law to decide, and determine, and so confirm. We must not anticipate, Mr Peach. We must only do as his honour directs, that it may be duly set down, and witnessed by authorities.

Mr Peach sees that this pillar of rectitude is immovable, and, having no other choice, resolves to wait.

Conversation turns to general matters, until Mr Peach, happening to glance at a window, notices a curious form of decoration behind the house. — In the muddy yard before the poultry-barn, within which the accused is held, a row of iron hoops is laid from one side to another, each overlapping its neighbour, as though to form the picture of a giant chain.

— My barrel-hoops, sir, says Samuel, observing Mr Peach's interest in the odd arrangement. — I thought it best to lay them all round the barn. It is well known, that gypsy enchantments cannot cross cold iron.

Mrs Sexton confirms this truth, with some encomia on her husband's wisdom.

— Then the person apprehended is acknowledged a gypsy? says Mr Peach, expecting, perhaps, that Mrs Sexton's tongue may be somewhat looser than her husband's, with regard to matters of evidence.

— Acknowledge! says Mrs Sexton, in a tone of contempt. — She don't acknowledge not a thing, the murky hussy.

Mr Sexton desires his wife's silence, and then explains, that the apprehended has not confessed to being a gypsy, nor to any thing else. — But, he says, it is certain the gypsies are lurking about the parish, and 'twas the gypsies that set about Dick Wainwright, as he says himself.

— The prisoner is a female? says Mr Peach, surprized.

— A filthy ragged young thing, says Mrs Sexton, and won't speak a Christian word to any one. I never saw such a face.

— You must not say so, says her husband. — You are not to speak any thing *prejudicial*, until the squire come.

— I don't care, says Mrs Sexton, I never saw the like, and I'll swear as much before any body.

— But, says Mr Peach, what is she taken for? Are we to suppose a young woman pulled the inn-keeper's boy from his saddle?

— Isn't that the very proof of her gypsy wickedness! cries Mrs Sexton. — Sure, she broke that poor child's head with the devil's help. But she'll not be doing any of her work here, for as well as the iron, she's sat in a barrel of water, and their curses don't cross water, unless it's salt, which you may be sure there's none of in that barrel.

Mr Peach rises. —

— Constable, he says, Am I to understand that your prisoner, a single female, has been shut up all the night, in standing water, in your poultry-barn?

— Only to her ankle.

— A young vagrant?

— Whether she belong to any parish, sir, is not yet certain, and, as a matter of *evidence*, must not yet be spoken of —

— Excuse me, good Mr Sexton, but I think you know your duty. You are not called upon to secure any person in so inhumane a manner, and particularly so, when she has confessed to no crime, and there can be no reasonable presumption of guilt.

The constable seems inclined to dispute the point; which shews very *lawyerly* in him, for, as you will know, reader, if you have ever been unlucky enough to come before the law, there is no truth so utterly plain and incontrovertible, that the gentlemen of that profession will not subject it to argument, when the mood is upon them. His deliberations are, however, forestalled by his wife, who exclaims, She don't confess, only because she won't say a thing, not even to give her own name when asked, which the law says she must, and I hope the squire'll hang her just for that. Only asking for ink and paper! — Such a face!

The constable again suspects that his wife's conversation is encroaching upon matters *evidential*, and desires, not very politely, that she hold her tongue.

A brief altercation follows, between husband and wife. — It is identical to numberless other altercations, which occur daily between husbands and wives, in every place where the dread institution of matrimony is established; and being therefore of no possible interest, we omit it.

Mr Peach halts its progress, by demanding to know whether it is indeed the case, that the prisoner requested the use of ink and paper? — which Mrs Sexton confirms, perhaps out of spite for her husband, who repeats his insistence that she must not speak of such things, and goes so far as to guarantee she shall not, by banishing her from the room, under threat of a cudgelling.

Alas for him, the insurrection against his authority is not thereby quelled, but begins instead to stir in another quarter. Mr Peach has now heard more than enough to suspect, that some ridiculous error has been perpetrated by this rustic officer, and he will not stand by, while a poor young woman is treated in the fashion described, no matter how low her estate, nor what offence she be guilty of; the less so, if she is at the very least of such a condition in life, as to be familiar with the use of ink and paper, and indeed to feel the want of those items above every other, in such an extremity! — In truth, we think Mr Peach has become not a little curious to see this supposed gypsy for himself.

He insists on being escorted to the poultry-barn. — The constable is reluctant in the extreme, but can hardly have recourse to that same decisive argument, against a gentleman, which he employed with success against his wife, *viz.* the threat of his cudgel. Mr Peach lets slip a number of hints, that the treatment of the prisoner may not accord with those antient rights, established in the Great Charter of King John — adding, that one might be disposed to suggest as much in the presence of Squire Furzedown. — And so Mr Sexton consents to accompany the gentleman to the domestic gaol.

That edifice is some five yards across, and three deep — A low, dirty, cold hovel. A sufficiently miserable situation! — yet Mr Peach observes with horror, when the door is thrown open, that the prisoner has been further tormented, by being fastened to a chair, sat within the circumference of an half-made barrel, which is filled to a depth of two foot with water.

But this is not the extremity of his surprize. — For, when the poor creature raises her head, to see who has opened the door, Mr Peach is beyond measure astonished to discover, none other than the same young woman, whom he encountered, in similarly inhumane confinement, in the house of Mr Davis, in Bristol!

At her former appearance in our narrative, we fancy she presented the very image of horror. We saw her then, set about with the most barbarous trappings, fit for a depraved lunatic, and yet beneath them, she bore the dress and general appearance of a young lady of good education. — A contrast, or *juxtaposition*, by which the scene was made more fearful and grotesque.

We need no *Gothick* stile to paint this her new portrait. Here is only an extreme of degradation. — We require the pencil of an *Hogarth*, not a *Fuseli*. Her cloaths are filthy and torn — her features wild — her limbs scratched and muddied — her hair like a bramble-bush. The imagination of that incomparable British satirist, never conjured a figure brought so low. You have seen his engravings of the drunken bawds of *Gin-lane* — And thought them the very bottom, of all depictions of miserable disgusting humanity. But the present creature is sunk still lower. She seems barely above the animal. — She sits with her feet drawn up under her, like a slovenly child, though we can hardly complain of her deportment, when any other posture would require that she immerse herself to the shins in cold water, for the seat of the chair is but a few inches clear above the surface.

Mr Peach turns on the constable.

— Is this Christian? he says, with unfeigned indignation. — Is this British justice? I am ashamed to witness it. You shall unbind her immediately, and bring her in-doors to be warmed and dried, and she must be provided with some decent cloaths before the squire is to see her.

— 'Tis no common prisoner, protests Samuel. — She might lay a curse on my house, or change into a frog, and escape.

— In the first place, I must say, that your superstitious fears ought to disqualify you from the office you hold, for the agent of justice is to be guided by reason and law, and not his grandmothers' tales. And in the second place, I assure you that this poor child is no gypsy, for she is known to me personally.

— Is that so? cries Samuel.

— I hope you have not so entirely forgotten what becomes a constable, as to contradict the word of a gentleman? — Mr Peach offers this rebuke with no affectation of dignity, but rather in a mild tone, and perhaps thereby affects Samuel more deeply. — As the pained reproof of a gentle master, touches the errant pupil with a more sincere shame, than the thundering of the school-room tyrant.

The constable begs the gentleman's pardon — You ought only to have said so before, sir.

— So I would have, had I been allowed sight of this unhappy wretch. I could hardly know her, before I saw her. Release her immediately, or I shall do so myself. I will answer for it, that she gives no trouble.

Mr Peach's confidence, which is, we confess, largely assumed, falters a little at this last declaration. — For he cannot forget the howling fury which possessed the young person, towards the conclusion of their previous interview. He meets her eye, with what he hopes is a significant look, as though to say, *Behave yourself, and we shall both be the better for it.*

To his very great surprise, the miserable confined creature returns a distinct nod of her head.

At Mr Peach's demand, Samuel loosens the fetters of hemp, which have fastened her to the chair, though he performs this humane deed with no very good grace, and adds several mutters of *Now mind yourself, hussy*, and *Remember where you are*, and the like. He stands over her, and wags a finger, saying, — It's your own fault you gave no answers, or you'd have escaped this treatment, you know.

— Constable, says Mr Peach, I must tell you that this young person suffers from a deformity of the mouth, which renders her unable to speak, except with the greatest difficulty. No doubt it was for that reason she made the painful effort to request paper and ink; and if you had provided them, as would have been merely reasonable, and no hardship to you, she would doubtless have written the answer to any thing you put to her, and thereby much trouble would have been avoided, which must instead be laid to your account. However, all this must be explained in the presence of his honour, and I shall say no more about it *now*. — With this severe hint, he demands again that the prisoner be removed in-doors, and suitably cloathed.

All this while she watches, with a fixed look — Fearless and unwavering.

— I have seen an hawk stare so, Mr Peach thinks.

The besmirched and ragged creature is now led to the house, where she is treated in accordance with Mr Peach's instructions — To the great disgust of Mrs Sexton.

Our hero now has some minutes, in which to consider, *what he is doing*, and *what he shall do next*.

He has acted to free the poor young woman, almost upon impulse. — An instinct of charity, we should like to think; for what person, possessed of that noblest of virtues, upon seeing a fellow-creature reduced to such a state, would not wish to raise them out of it? — But when we examine Mr Peach's heart and mind, we must acknowledge, that his intervention on the prisoner's behalf has been equally prompted, by an instinct of *surprize* — That suspension of reason and deliberation, which so often occurs, in the presence of an event utterly unexpected. Mr Peach, as we have remarked before, is not blessed with rapidity of the faculties — That quality, which is often called *brilliance*, for it shines on a sudden, and throws off sparks. He is — permit us to pursue our metaphor — He is no gem-stone, that catches the light, and reflects it in an hundred new colours, in every direction — But rather a *shingle*, smooth, dark, and obdurate —

We think we must abandon our analogy, as being overly poetical.

Let us merely say, that only now, while he and Samuel Sexton await the squire, in somewhat formal silence, is Mr Peach able to reflect on the extraordinary happenstance, that the person apprehended for the theft of his papers should be that very same unfortunate, whom he presumed shut up in an asylum several days past; and only now does he consider, what he shall say before the justice.

We shall not describe the outcome of his reflexions. — It will become evident, in our next pages.

A commotion in the road signals the arrival of Squire Furzedown. He comes in his carriage, and is attended, beyond his usual equipage, by the curate from a village near his own estates, who will serve as clerk. The squire is a lean phlegmatic man of sixty, more respected than loved. He is known to be punctilious and somewhat cold, though fair, and temperate, and an upholder of those *antient liberties*, which are enjoyed by all Britons, high and low, and make them the most fortunate nation upon earth, in their own estimations. He accepts tea — Enquires after the health of Mrs Peach — Commends the constable in general terms for his diligence — Says what he ought, and no more than what he ought, which is, we think, no insignificant accomplishment, in a justice.

We pass over these scenes of polite sociability, and advance to the commencement of proceedings. Squire Furzedown orders a seat to be prepared for the curate, and invites Mrs Sexton, her older children, and the domestics, to withdraw, and so assumes his station.

Now, at last, the worthy constable is invited to submit his precious *evidence*. — Which, in summary, is: that about ten o'clock of the night previous, a dirty vagrant woman was apprehended in the parish roads, and found to have about her person a packet, known to have been violently robbed from the inn-keeper's boy not two days past; that the woman will give no account of herself, nor any explanation of how she came by the goods, nor say any thing at all, but persists in an obdurate silence; that it is widely known, that the country is presently troubled by gypsies, who are suspected of various offences; that the prisoner, being of the meanest appearance, and refusing to answer to lawful authority, is likely one of the troublesome thieving heathens; but, however that may be, she is certainly caught in possession of stolen property, and must answer to justice. — In the course of this account the goods are produced. Mr Peach, who listens with attention, is delighted to see that the object in question is a substantial parcel, directed to him, which must certainly represent that quantity of blank paper he had requested from Bristol.* He is a little disappointed, that there are no other papers. There is no sign of any letter, such as might inclose a reply from Doctor Thorburn, or an answer to his other enquiries. Nevertheless, when invited to swear to the goods, he does so, to the satisfaction of the constable, who had begun to fear, that the gentleman intended to *obstruct the course of justice.*

— That is very good, says the squire. — And is it also sworn, that the property was found upon the prisoner's person?

— It is, your honour, says Samuel.

— I must understand, then, that you apprehended her yourself, Mr Sexton?

Samuel lifts himself several times upon his toes, as though straining to leave the earth, in the buoyancy of his pride, like an hot-air balloon — Indeed, your honour, he says. — I have gone searching about the parish for these vile gypsies, as is my duty, and I found the prisoner sleeping under Farmer Shepherd's barn, and took her up with my own hands.

The squire nods, and waits several moments, so that Mr Sexton's commendable vigilance may be memorialised by the clerk.

The accused is now required to be brought in.

The dirt is not altogether washed from her face and arms, and with the Gordian puzzle of her hair, there is nothing to be done. But she is dried, and presented in plain decent cloaths — belonging, we suspect, to one of the daughters of the house — And makes a tolerable appearance. She bears herself with a certain modest and humble carriage, quite astonishing to the eye of Mr Peach, who has only beheld her in the most loathsome confinement. In her every motion there is a delicacy quite correct. — Were it not for her wild and haggard person, we might almost think it charming.

— Well, now, young woman, says the justice, with a severity more paternal than judicial, for he is not an hard-hearted man,

* *vide* p. 134.

You are accused of the theft of a gentleman's property, which is a very serious crime, and I am the person appointed to decide your innocence or guilt, and pronounce the sentence of the law upon you; do you understand?

She stands as before, and makes no answer, by word nor gesture.

Hem — says the squire — looking over his nose — You must answer me, you know, when I put a question to you, for if you do not, it is in my power to have you committed to the gaol, for the offence of *contempt of court*.

Mr Peach stands — Sir, he says, I believe I may be able to assist —

The squire interrupts. — Mr Peach, says he, I do not find it recorded, that you are appointed counsel to the prisoner, and therefore she must do without your assistance. — Young lady — the squire turns again to the accused, and assumes a more encouraging aspect — Do not be afraid — You must first tell me only your name, and where you live; after that we shall proceed to the charge, and you may speak whatever you have to say in your defence.

Mr Peach says — May I humbly request to address the bench, your honour, upon a matter directly concerned with the furtherance of this proceeding?

— The gentleman declares as how he knows the hussy, saving your honour, says Samuel.

— That is so, says Mr Peach, and I am obliged also to inform your honour, that the poor young creature suffers a deformation of the organs of speech, from which she is barely able to pronounce a word, without dreadful effort and pain. Her name is Clarissa Riddle, belonging to the parish of St Dunstan in this county. And I may invite your honour to bring this action to a swift and easy end, for Miss Riddle is in my own employ, as house-maid. I confess I am surprized to discover her in such a state and place, and shall have her answer for it, to my own satisfaction; but there can be no question that any theft has been committed, for I sent Miss Riddle to collect that packet on my behalf; and I therefore withdraw any action, by which she may be answerable to the law for my property.

The squire pushes his fingers together at the tips, and says, with no very friendly look towards the constable, Then on what cause have I been called away from my breakfast-table?

The constable's complexion is turning gouty. He sees his prey slipping from his grasp, by some lawyerly subtlety or trick, which he cannot quite penetrate, and resents the more on that account.

Mr Peach takes advantage of poor Mr Sexton's bafflement, to continue his address to the squire. — Your honour, neither myself nor the worthy constable knew that the person apprehended last night was Miss Riddle, until this last hour. I do not doubt that the whole business may be blamed upon Miss Riddle's unfortunate defect of speech. It is regrettable that her request for ink and paper was not honoured. To speak even so many words must have cost her great pain, yet she might have been spared the further trials of imprisonment, had she been permitted to write her explanation. But it shall be for you, sir, to consider, whether Mr Sexton has done his duty.

Samuel has by the end of this speech atchieved a sun-set colour. His worst suspicions are confirmed — He sees, that not only will Mr Peach rob him of his prisoner, but will contrive to blame the constable himself for it — Nay, your honour, he cries, All that may be as it is, but there's Dick Wainwright the inn-keeper's boy who swears he was set upon by gypsies, and they stole that very packet from him.

— Swears, does he? says the squire, his frown gathering. — I look to every corner of this room, Mr Sexton, and I see no Master Richard Wainwright, to swear to any matter under the sun. Or shall I understand that you mean to present the affidavit of this Dick Wainwright?

— Why, he's laid up at home, and half-killed, because of the attack on him.

— Excuse me, your honour, interjects Mr Peach, whose calm demeanour forms a striking contrast with the excitable Samuel, and one which must surely be to his advantage, in the eyes of justice. — I believe it was said, that the supposed robbery was committed on the inn-keeper's boy about noon, two days past?

— Supposed, is it? cries the constable, in a passion — And do you *suppose*, the boy's head is not broken near in three pieces?

— I cannot speak to that, says Mr Peach, for I have no knowledge of the events, but what comes by *hearsay*. — He accompanies this last word, with a significant glance towards Squire Furzedown. — However, he continues, I may declare with certainty that this young person cannot have had any part in any such accident, however it may be supposed to have occurred, for she passed all that day at my own house, in the ordinary performance of her domestic duties. I may also add, that if Master Richard Wainwright will swear he was set upon by the gypsies, there can be no case for this young person to answer. She is quite evidently *not a gypsy*.

Hardly the oration, of a *Demosthenes*, or a *Cicero*! yet it is more than sufficient to confound Samuel Sexton, who can find no reply at all. — The delay is fatal to his cause. — Squire Furzedown has heard enough. He is not a man, to prolong his business without reason. He prefers the law swift, sharp, and decisive, as the executioner's axe — An instrument he would have wielded with great satisfaction, we think, had he lived in a former age.

The proceedings are concluded, with little further ceremony, and all the parties depart the home of the downcast constable. — The squire, by his carriage — Mr Peach, on his gelding — And Miss Riddle, as we must now call her, on the same animal, mounted before him.

She has returned the borrowed cloaths, in accordance with the peremptory and insulting demand of Mrs Sexton, who is still more displeased with the outcome of the morning than her husband, having taken the most violent dislike to the filthy gypsy trollop, as she will call the former prisoner; who is therefore clad once more in her smeared and tattered dress, which corresponds rather better with the rest of her outward shew, though the picture be no very elegant one.

Mr Peach has invited her to share the saddle, partly from pity of her impoverished appearance, and also, because she has no shoes, nor even stockings — But chiefly, because he is somewhat fearful of the attentions of the mob.

The people of the village have gathered outside Samuel Sexton's house, anticipating the execution of justice. They have huzza'd the departure of the squire — Taking it for a sign, that all the formal business is finished. — They are much less pleased, at the appearance of the prisoner, astride Mr Peach's gelding. — There are hesitant cheers — Perhaps, this is a procession to the place of judgment? The more worldly among them know, that this is how matters are conducted at the famous gibbet of *Tyburn*, in London, where the gallant highwaymen go laughing to their deaths, throwing gold coins to the crowd.

When it appears, that no such performance is likely, but that Mr Peach is simply riding home, and taking the ill-looking slovenly witch with him — the cheers turn to cries of disappointment — And then, to fury. Stones are raised — Cudgels are fetched — And Mr Peach's doubts, seem likely to be well founded.

But a mob, though a fearful thing, when raised, and impossible of controul, is sluggish. Like a great boulder atop a precipice, it cannot be stopped when once in motion, and will pursue its path, crushing any thing interposed; but to set it on its way, requires the application of much sustained effort.* The assembled rustics are not capable of it. Before they can gather their strength, in the spirit of a just vengeance — Mr Peach has set his heels to the gelding — The gelding, though filled with bitter resentment, finds it useless to protest — And he, and the animal, and the former prisoner, are free of the village.

---

* A truth but lately demonstrated, in these our latter days, by the infamous Lord *Gordon*. Should you be reluctant to look for proof of our axiom, in the history of so vile a character, you may find several nobler examples, in Gibbon's Decline and Fall of Rome.

So concludes Mr Peach's transaction, with the majesty of JUSTICE. — An authority, to which we fear he has paid less reverence, than it must demand.

We cannot be altogether certain, whether his behaviour in our eleventh chapter contravenes that statute of 9 Geo. II, to which we alluded some pages earlier. But, alas, our best efforts cannot absolve him of his offences, in this our twelfth. — For, reader, it will not have escaped your notice, that his testimony before Squire Furzedown, though motivated by the most humane and generous impulse, has several times strayed beyond the bounds of perfect truth.

In plain words, we suspect our hero to have perjured himself.

It is not the historian's task, to *condemn* — Nor even, if we consider it rightly, to *judge*. Our first purpose must always be, to know the actions of men, and enquire, as best we can, after their profound and secret causes, and illuminate their consequences. — In accordance with which solemn principles, we shall at present remark no further upon Mr Peach's surprizing behaviour, but proceed with our narrative; which we propose to do, in a new chapter.

CHAPTER THIRTEEN

Our scene now changes to the open road.

The fields are empty, every man having laid down his hoe, or tethered his ox, or put aside his pot, to attend the anticipated hanging. The fowls and the smaller beasts rejoice, at the unprotected seed. — We suppose they do — Our business is not with them.

We present instead the picture of the solitary horse, now progressing at a sullen walk, and meditating its revenges — And the pair of riders — All making their way, towards the steep-sided valley of Widdershins Bank. At a suitable distance from the village, Mr Peach draws up the gelding, which comes readily to its stop, and dismounts.

— Madam, he says, I trust you know the manage of an horse. I think we will each be more comfortable, if we do not share the saddle. I shall walk ahead.

The young woman says not a word, but dismounts also, and gestures to him, to resume his place.

— You need not fear to speak in my presence. You will remember our former encounter, as I do, though remembrance must shy away from circumstances so unpleasant. I know you well capable of language, and I have seen the deformity of your mouth. If you are shy of it, I may avert my eyes, for your convenience. — With a somewhat ceremonial air, Mr Peach turns on his heels, and directs his look towards a fine old elm that overlooks the road.

Were he not certain otherwise, he might think the wretched dirty figure behind him had been magicked away, and an elegant young lady of good breeding had dropped from the heavens in her place; for the voice that addresses his back is sweet and finely-tuned.

— I am sensible of your kindness, sir, and still more conscious of the gratitude I owe you, for your actions before the justice. You have taken pains for my sake, which I, who am a stranger to you, have no right to claim. Heaven shall bless you for it. I however must trouble you no further.

— As to that, says Mr Peach, to the outward eye addressing himself to the lower branches of the elm-tree, I hope the bond of simple humanity is sufficient to cancel any obligation you may feel, for I think any person not utterly wanting in sympathy for his fellow-creatures would have wished to relieve a friendless young woman from such treatment.

— That you think so, sir, is further credit to the goodness of your heart. But I fear you have pursued your generosity to an excess, on my behalf, and overstepped the mark of virtue. On that account, if no other, I am obliged to be no further encumbrance to you. I would not willingly be the occasion of behaviour a gentleman of honour must have cause to regret.

Mr Peach begins to wonder whether he has been mistaken, in supposing this to be the same person, formerly encountered in the house of Mr Davis. — For her every sentence seems to breathe modest virtue and gentle accomplishment.

— I am not certain of your meaning, madam, he says, to the elm-tree. — I assure you, nothing of what has passed threatens to trouble my conscience.

— Sir, though I hesitate to recall the event to your hearing, I fear that in the exercise of your humanity you have been led to bring false witness. I cannot be so ungrateful as to hold the accusation against you; but your own recollection must recoil from it.

— Madam, says Mr Peach, the text of the commandment, forbids us to bear false witness *against our neighbour*; and though I confess I was somewhat free with the truth before the squire just now, I bore no witness *against* any body, nor spoke to any malicious purpose whatsoever. My intention was merely to relieve you from an oppression, which I do not think you deserve, and an accusation, which I believe to have been unjust.

— I must not pass judgment, sir, nor express any sentiment other than perfect gratitude. Nevertheless, you were put upon oath, and swore to a falsehood.

— Rest assured, madam, that I have done worse, and in a better cause. May I remark that I find this method of conversation somewhat ridiculous? Will you permit me to face you? You cannot think I will object to the sight of your deformity, when you take my character to be as *black* as you paint it.

There comes no immediate answer. Mr Peach continues — To be frank, madam, I wish very much to speak with you, on some matters which have engaged my curiosity. If we are to continue in conversation, we shall both surely prefer a more comfortable arrangement.

— Very well, says she, after a brief interval, and so Mr Peach turns again, almost expecting to see a different creature altogether. — And finds the ragged filthy beggarly creature before his eye, as before.

— If, sir —

She neither bows nor averts her head — and Mr Peach is again presented, with that grotesque vision, which struck him with so profound an horror, in the attic-room of Mr Davis's house in Bristol. It is amazement enough, that such a voice, and such sentiments, should proceed from such a person. But that they should be emitted from such an orifice! — like a granite sea-cave, all *black*! — Yet Mr Peach has prepared himself for the sight, and makes no involuntary start of disgust. Indeed, it is as well he has already armed his fortitude, for the young woman's next words threaten to undo it again. —

— If, sir, she says, you mean that you wish now to receive those favours, which I formerly promised, in return for securing my liberty, you need not resort to gentlemanly circumlocutions.

Mr Peach requires several moments, before he is able to reply.

— The construction you put upon my words and actions astonishes me, madam. I did not intend to allude to a suggestion, which would dishonour me still more in the acceptance, than it lowers you in the offer. The extremity of your circumstances on that occasion may excuse it; but I must ask that you never refer to it again, nor think to use such language, which is a far worse stain on your tongue, than your unfortunate accident of the flesh.

The young person appears not in the least abashed at his reproof. — And why should she be? thinks Mr Peach — For though her every word speaks of grace and delicacy of temperament, I know it is all sham. The evidence of my own eyes shews a most abandoned and desperate creature, nor can I forget how she once howled, and cursed, and threatened, like a very devil.

— Sir, says she, you need require no such undertaking of me; for though I am grateful to you, and shall for ever be sensible of my obligation, we are strangers to one another, and must now go our separate ways.

Mr Peach's sentiments soften at once — or rather — His *curiosity* reasserts itself, with the keenest pang — Or perhaps both sensations arise together.

— And where do you propose to go? I know a little of your history, madam. You have no home. That you escaped the asylum, I rejoice with you, for it is perfectly evident that your wits are sound; but I cannot help but remark, that you have cast your lot upon the unsheltered roads, which is a cruel and comfortless state, and most of all for a solitary female. You have not even shoes to your feet. At the very least, you must consent to accompany me homewards, where you shall rest in warmth and tolerable comfort, until you have some better prospect.

The young woman is silent a while. Her face betrays no expression at all, that Mr Peach can interpret. He thinks again — as he thought before, in the house at Bristol — that there is a darkness in it — An *inward* darkness, as though the hideous stain in her mouth, were the visible sign of some imperceptible blackening in her mind.

— I shall ride home with you, she says, if you will consent to answer one question. I hope you will answer honestly, though I shall not make you *swear* to it.

Mr Peach is surprized, at the boldness of the jest — Or would be surprized, if he had expected her to continue in humble and deferential discourse — But he feels, he knows not what to expect of her. — This creature is, he thinks, a perfect *cameleon*.

He promises to abide by her condition.

— My question, she says, is, How you named me Clarissa Riddle, before the justice?

— Is it not your right name?

— It is; but how you know it, I cannot guess. We have no acquaintance; yet you say you know my history, and my name, and have told a plain lie on my behalf, and now you offer to shelter me in your own house. I must ask what unknown connexion there is between us, that accounts for this behaviour to a wretched friendless creature — indeed, one as wretched as any that walks the earth!

— Why, says Mr Peach, if that is all you require from me, we shall be on our way in an instant. There is no mystery to it. I have heard a little of your upbringing, from Mr Farthingay; and from that I was able to guess your baptismal name.* Your sirname you revealed yourself, in the course of our former interview.† There it is, in ten words.

Miss Riddle, as we must now call her, makes no move towards the saddle, but says, Are you a friend of that Mr Farthingay?

— Madam — I understand your doubts. Have no fear. — The gentleman is no more than an acquaintance. Permit me to add, that the little knowledge I have of your education in his house, inclines me to think you have some cause to resent it. I assure you, neither he nor any person else need know what has become of you, if that is your wish. My wife and I exist in a state of tranquil retirement. Mrs Peach is confined to her bed, by the extreme frailty of her health, and therefore we have no society, but exist in

---

* That is, Clarissa, after the heroine of Richardson, in imitation of whom Mr Farthingay intended the bastard infant to be educated.
† p. 71.

an happy seclusion, which I think will be no more displeasing to you than it is to myself. Besides, our bargain is struck. I have answered your question, and therefore you must ride.

His assurances are evidently sufficient. With some further expressions of gratitude, eminently polite and correct, Miss Riddle ascends again to the saddle, while Mr Peach goes afoot before her, and leads the gelding on, at a slow walk. — A pace which, in the animal's estimation, is perfectly sufficient, to convey any body any where. — And, in justice to its natural wisdom, we must confess, that its opinion is borne out by the event, for Mr Peach and Miss Riddle proceed on to his house, quite comfortably, if not so quickly as they might have — And without further incident.

Jem! — Jemmy! — Up, lad! Hasten to your duties, for the master returns, with an unexpected visitor! —

Jem is no where to be seen.

The stable, in truth, presents no very neat appearance. — Nor the house. — Nor, the visitor.

It is to the credit of Mr Peach's humanity, that he applies himself exclusively to the remedy of the latter. — There is water, though he must draw it himself, and lay the fire to warm it — There are the other necessities of bathing. — The greatest difficulty lies in the matter of clean cloaths. After a period of reflexion, Mr Peach decides this want is best supplied by recourse to the property of the stable-boy, which, though meagre, includes a pair of stockings, and a shirt, such as our country people wear. He will not deny, that he thereby commits a theft. — Though he thinks Jem bears a portion of the blame for the loss of his chattels, by his not being present to defend them, when he ought to have been.

The transformation effected in the outward form of Miss Riddle, is such, as the old alchemists might have dreamed of.

We will not go so far as to say, that the base metal is transmuted into *gold*. — But only, that the young woman emerges from the crucible of her inundation and refinement, a creature entirely unrecognizable as she who entered it. Gone is the raggle-taggle gypsy girl. — In her place, a plain neat person, washed clean, and made to seem younger than her seventeen years by the ill-fitting boyish garb. If the vengeful mob were to come from the village, and beat down Mr Peach's door — his other door, we should say, for one is already beaten down — We think she could stand before them in broad day-light, and not a soul would know her, or think to lay a finger on her, but take her for some poor aukward country child, in the employ of the mysterious Mr Peach — Provided that she never opened her mouth.

— Sir — says she — Your kindness quite overdoes me. Is your wife not to be consulted? I ought to have paid respect before now to the lady of the house. — I have not heard her voice.

— Mrs Peach's infirmity, says Mr Peach, is such that she rests all through the day, and must never be disturbed, except by myself, at any hour whatsoever.

Miss Riddle casts a glance at the ceiling. — Is she in the house at present? I had thought she must be away.

— She is always in the house.

— In the room above?

— Yes. You will oblige me, Miss Riddle, if you will not continue the subject.

Miss Riddle frowns a little, as though in uncertain contemplation, but makes a gracious apology.

— Let us talk instead of your own history, says our hero, offering a simple dish of tea, which he has prepared while the young lady was occupied with her rustic toilette. — I wish very much to learn what became of you after our previous meeting, if you will forgive the allusion to circumstances so eminently distressing. I must also say, that I am eager to know how you came to be in possession of the packet of papers, intended for me. I assure you I harbour no resentment. If you will do me the favour of an explanation merely, I shall be quite satisfied.

— Sir, says Miss Riddle, that you have interested yourself in the trials of a friendless wretch, is proof of an uncommon kindness, which demands every expression of gratitude and obligation that lies within my power; and that you have so far pursued that kindness, as to rescue me from degradation and unjust punishment, and now to provide me with those comforts I have so long been denied, renders the obligation so great, that I could not hope to cancel it, were I the wealthiest duchess in the land. Yet, sir, believe me when I tell you, that I am a cursed unhappy creature, and my history is nothing but misery and despair. For your own sake, do not involve yourself in it any further, than you already have! — Though you are a gentleman, I see your means are modest; and your wife is grievously ill. Attend to her, and concern yourself no more, with one who can bring you only misfortune, when she wishes you nothing but its opposite!

Says Mr Peach to himself — I can well believe this woman was educated in daily intercourse with the epistles of *Clarissa.*

He answers aloud — We may dismiss your objections in a moment, if that is the sum of them. I am so well acquainted with misfortune, that I count myself something of a connoisseur, and shall be well pleased to discover any new varieties of it, which you may bring to my attention. Mrs Peach will not mind my absence from her bed-side. Her infirmity is such, that she passes all but a few hours nearly insensible. — There are in this world happy and prosperous people, who shun intercourse with the unfortunate and destitute, for fear of contagion, I suppose; but my wife and I are not of their number. I assure you, child, whatever your curse may be, I do not fear it in the least.

Miss Riddle looks long at him, and says, That is not the answer I expected.

Mr Peach lays his hands on his knees, and leans forward in the chair, and says, Miss Riddle, I think you have not often been dealt with fairly.

A lengthy silence ensues.

Our books of conversation inform us, that such *lacunae* are of all things to be feared, and shunned. True sociability, they say, consists in the ceaseless exchange of speech; and his company is most prized, who can be relied upon to maintain a ceaseless flow of sallies, and *bons mots*, and opinions on every subject under the sun, provided only that all of them are things no other person is known to have said before; as though the single purpose of human language was to *make noise* — Thus protecting us from silence, within which state terrors must surely lurk. If it is so, then we shall presume Mr Peach and Miss Riddle to be equally at ease, in the presence of that abyssal dread — For neither the one nor the other shews any sign of discomfort.

But, at last — prompted by, we know not what — Miss Riddle consents to give her tale.

We might record it in her own words, for she is not prolix — But some parts of it, are not of the greatest importance to our narrative, and so we shall deliver the significant matter in paraphrase. — She was, she says, conducted from the house of Mr Davis, in Bristol, to the asylum wherein she was for ever to be confined, some few miles beyond the city, on the day after her strange interview with Mr Peach. Her captors spared her the odious garment, in which they had previously restrained her. This circumstance she credits to the good advice of the gentleman, for, by adopting a submissive and complaisant manner, in accordance with his suggestion, she made the men ashamed of their barbaric treatment, so that they not only omitted to replace the strait-waistcoat, but by degrees relaxed all the severity of their supervision; until, soothed and dulled by the motion of the carriage, and by the effects of a pot drained at the ale-house in the course of their journey, they fell into a stupor. Miss Riddle was then able to loosen the rope, with which her ankles had been fastened, and, divesting herself of her shoes, leap from the carriage, while it was yet in motion. — A desperate endeavour! and yet, she says, no injury that might have befallen her in the attempt, presented a worse prospect, than the dreadful sentence awaiting her had she not essayed it. The postillion raised the alarm at once; but the difficulty of stopping the horses, and rousing the drunken attendants, sufficiently delayed any pursuit, that she was able to atchieve the shelter of a copse beside the road, before the chase was effectively begun. Unencumbered by shoes, and shedding every other inconvenient article of dress, she fled into the wood. The disadvantages of her age and sex were more than outweighed, by the ease of her passage among the bushes, and the desperation which drove her. She escaped her pursuers, passed the night concealed in an hedge, and from then on committed herself to the fortunes of the road; a dangerous prospect for a solitary female, and yet, she says, so exquisite was the joy of liberty, after a life of domestic imprisonment, that she looked on the hardships of vagrancy and indigence as mere trifles, and never for a moment thought to complain of her fate.

Having no knowledge of the country, she sought only to avoid the busy haunts of men. She knew that Grandison Hall lay to the south and east of Bristol, and so was resolved to go northwards and westwards, as best she could judge by the rising and setting of the sun. — Mr Peach does not tell her, that such a course would infallibly have led her to the inhospitable mountains of Wales; nor that her navigation has been so far in error, as to have led her *south* of the city, and indeed to a parcel of land, which, though several miles disjunct, nevertheless forms a part of Mr Farthingay's own estate! — He has no wish to alarm the young woman, with whom, in truth, he feels a mysterious and inarticulate sympathy. — Indeed, as she tells her story, recounting such extraordinary events with unaffected simplicity, and no little ease and grace of expression, he begins to form an idea — Which we shall not at present describe, since the conception will shew itself by its own plain light, in our next chapter.

The conclusion of the tale is, that Miss Riddle came by accident into this country, and would have wandered out of it again, had it not been for the events, which led to Mr Peach's packet being discovered in her possession, and her confinement under suspicion of violent robbery.

In the morning of the previous day, she says, she came across a boy lying injured in the road, having apparently taken a fall from his mount.* She endeavoured to assist him, but found him wounded in the head, and delirious, so that he mistook her efforts, and raved at her, and she was forced to leave him.

— This circumstance, thinks Mr Peach, may well account for the story, that young Dick believes himself to have been set about by gypsies; for, in the delirium caused by a violent blow to the brain, it is eminently likely that the sudden appearance of a wild and dirty-looking vagrant woman might have induced such a phantasy.

She says, that at that time she took particular note of a bag, lying beside him in the road; for she looked within it herself, in case it might contain any thing she could use, to bind the wound at his temples; but it was only full of letters and papers.

— Letters? repeats Mr Peach, leaning forward with interest. — You are certain there were letters, as well as the large packet?

Miss Riddle casts down her eyes, and seems somewhat uneasy. — Perhaps, she says — I think there were — I could not swear to it.

— Then you did not take note of the direction of any letter, among those in the boy's bag?

— Sir, I opened the bag in haste, and closed it as quickly, when I saw it contained nothing for my purpose. You will understand that I did not stop to read the papers over.

— Yet this packet of mine was upon your person, when you were apprehended by the constable. — Mr Peach indicates with a gesture the parcel in question. It sits half-opened upon the table, for he has already taken the trouble to assure himself of its contents, which are, as he presumed, the quantity of plain blank paper that he requested from Bristol.

---

* This unfortunate, reader, we shall suppose to be that Dick Wainwright, the inn-keeper's boy, who was to have delivered to Mr Peach's house the reply of Doctor Thorburn, along with the quantity of blank paper. — We hope you will forgive us these parenthetical glosses, upon the body of our narrative. It is not that we doubt your attentiveness, nor your powers of apprehension. — But we ourselves are conscious of the murky intricacies of our tale, and our instinct is always, to shed whatever light we can.

Miss Riddle clasps her hands in her lap.

— My state was desperate, she says.

— My dear child, I am neither accuser nor judge.

— I had been in the bare roads for days. You cannot conceive the hunger — the exhaustion —

— The sufferings you have endured within my sight would excuse far worse acts, than the theft of a quantity of paper.

— I cannot deny the theft. I hope I shall be credited with equal sincerity, when I say I am truly glad to see your property restored. You of all men I would not wish to offend. It was a moment of weakness — Feminine weakness, sir. I shall always be ashamed —

— Miss Riddle, says Mr Peach, you need not use such language. No harm is done. Indeed, your account of these events has greatly eased my mind, for reasons you cannot know. My only present concern is to learn the fate of certain letters, which I believe to have been in young Dick's bag, along with this packet.

Miss Riddle raises her head, so that when she answers, Mr Peach is struck once more by the ghastly vision of her mouth. — I cannot say what other papers might have been within, or what became of them. I suppose they must be lost.

Mr Peach expresses his disappointment, with no more than a mild sigh, and several taps of his fingers, upon the arm of the chair.

— I would not have you think me a common thief, says Miss Riddle, with animation. — I regret the action. My nature is not yet wholly evil. — I am convinced of it. Do not condemn me — I implore you!

Mr Peach ceases his tapping. — My dear Miss Riddle — I am no more your confessor, than your judge. Be easy — Drink some tea. You have not touched the cup.

Miss Riddle breathes deeply, and seems to draw herself inward, like the *sensitive-plant*, which by mysterious vegetable sympathy curls away from the touch. — Thank you, sir, she says, in a low voice, and takes up the drink — though without raising it to her lips.

218

Thinks Mr Peach — I might have saved myself the trouble of preparing it. The silly girl has not so much as tasted a drop.

There passes another of those intervals of mutual silence, upon which we have already remarked.

— Well — says Mr Peach — I am glad to see you calm again. I hope you will rest here to-night? You must be greatly fatigued by your trials, and the ill-use you have endured. We shall consider your future prospects in the morning, when you will perhaps consent to hear a proposal of mine on that subject.

Miss Riddle puts down her cup, and rises. Mr Peach will not sit, while a lady stands — He will honour her upbringing and gentle manner of speech, despite her barbarous appearance — He rises also.

Miss Riddle falls to her knees. — Mr Peach, quite astonished, does not.

— Sir, says she, throwing out her arms, I am entirely at your mercy. If you are the one fate has chosen, to lift my curse — as I must believe you are — You may direct me, as you wish.

— Great heavens, child! Come up to your feet again at once.

— If you command it, says she, and stands, but holds her head low.

— What is the explanation for this absurd behaviour? All I have done, is press a dish of tea upon you, which you have not taken, and offered a brief respite from the perils of vagrancy, which is no more than any person would, in common humanity. Whence comes this talk of fate, and curses? I must forbid it — Nor will I receive prostrations, like an antient potentate. Come — No more of it.

Miss Riddle glances again towards the ceiling, and then to Mr Peach himself, with a curious look. We might almost call it sly — Suggestive, of some cunning and secret thought.

— Sir — says she — Is this not the magician's house, of which I have heard so much?

— The magician's house! cries Mr Peach, in the last degree of amazement.

— I cannot think it mere accident, Miss Riddle continues, that we are met a second time, in such circumstances, and that you have brought me under your roof.

— What else but mere accident? — when I thought you far away, and committed to an asylum — if I gave any thought to your fate at all? — when I knew no better, who was shut up in Samuel Sexton's poultry-barn, than you could have guessed who would enter it this morning? You are under some extraordinary misapprehension, madam. I pray you, dismiss it immediately. A magician! — I am quite astonished. You are a person of education. — This is some phrenzy, brought on by your ill-treatment.

— I beg your pardon, says Miss Riddle — Pray, do not be angry.

Mr Peach continues to mutter his surprize and indignation — A magician's house! — And shakes his head, and murmurs *Hem!*, and *Nonsense!* — Perhaps it is the repeated shaking of the head, that causes a thought to ascend, like a single perfect bubble, into the surface region of his brain. We are certain, there is a more intimate connexion between *mental* events, and *bodily* motions, than is generally acknowledged, by the doctors and philosophers. — But we shall return to the subject, on another occasion. — For this new thought of Mr Peach's is a very significant one, and we must allow him to express it, without delay.

— Did you say just now, that you have *heard much* of your absurd notion, of a magician's house?

— Did I, sir?

— I think you did. — Am I to understand, such an house is common rumour about the country?

— I wonder you do not know as much yourself. I have heard it spoken of every where. An houseless wanderer hears much talk, not intended for her ears. The magician's house is the universal gossip.

Mr Peach's indignation is forgotten. A new light, is dawning in his understanding. — The sensation is much as the Methodists describe it, we suppose, though the illumination be of a different nature.

— Miss Riddle, he says, forgive me, if I spoke intemperately, in my surprize. I should be greatly obliged to learn what the country people say about this supposed house.

— Then I hope you will equally forgive me, for answering freely, sir. They say only that there is a man, who lives alone, and keeps above-stairs a wife, whom no one ever sees, and below-stairs his books of magic. I dared think I might have come to such an house, sir. Indeed, I may say — I dared hope. —

Mr Peach is not at all inclined to be offended, at this very free treatment of his domestic affairs. He is now all contentment. — He admits, his may be the intended house, but advises Miss Riddle, quite good-humouredly, of what she must already know, that country gossip is compounded of ignorance, superstition, and malice. — Adding, that the same good folk who swear him a Somerset *John Dee*,* will declare *her* a gypsy, with equal certainty, and just as good authority. Once more he advises her, to put the nonsense from her head, and so dismisses her to her rest, which he invites her to take, in the room formerly set aside for the use of Anny Pertwee. — That fair maid being now in the fore-front of his thoughts, as you shall shortly hear.

The day turns mild and sweet. Mr Peach moves his chair by the open door, where he sits himself with a cup of wine, and Cowper's Task, to enjoy the warm air of the declining after-noon.

How shall we account for this sudden access of leisurely ease and contentment, after so many days of curious hesitations, and mysterious fears?

Why — it is the simplest thing in the world.

Mr Peach has reasoned thus: —

If it is rumoured about the parish, that there are books of magic in his house, then some body must have instigated the rumour; and who is better suited to play that part, both by their own nature, and by the advantage of their former situation, than garrulous Anny Pertwee, his quondam house-maid?

---

* The famous astrologer and cunning man, of Elizabeth's reign.

And what has put the idea of magic books in her head, if not *her own discovery* of the contents of his old chest, at the foot of the stair?

From which it follows, that Anny may be presumed to have made such a discovery. — And therefore, that the robbery perpetrated upon Mr Peach's house, was not the work of any strangers, of foreign appearance and manner, supposed by the rustics to be gypsies, but was done by — Anny Pertwee herself.

Mr Peach revolves these interesting conclusions in his thoughts, while alternately musing upon the homely verses of Cowper, and so passes some pleasant hours, interrupted only by the return of the errant Jem. The lad's cloaths are smeared with the embrace of earth, and his face sallow with weeping. He presents so unfortunate a picture, that Mr Peach cannot bear to give him the reprimand his truancy deserves. — Why — he says — Jem — Whatever is the matter? In reply to which tears burst forth from the boy's eyes — Oh — Sir, he says, clutching his breast — I have gone to lay down at the spring — For there is within me a veiled thought — A twilight, sir! of the mind! — And, delivered of this perfectly obscure explanation, he sighs piteously, and rushes to the stable-loft.

— I see, thinks Mr Peach, that I shall have to take away his *Goethe*. —

Yet our hero has no disposition to be stern, in his new-found holiday mood. He remembers his own youth — And is indulgent. — Perhaps, he says to himself, I may turn the lad's brain-sickness to advantage. I might promise him *a yellow waistcoat* at Christmas-time, if he can shew himself diligent until then.*

---

* There are fashions in *literature*, as well as in *dress* and *coiffure*, and they rage with no less fury, nor expire less suddenly. In the last decade but one of the century preceding, the Sorrows of Werter were borne to the very height of popularity, all over Europe, and every poetical young man from *Kopenhaven* to *Rome* longed to wear the yellow waistcoat and blue tail-coat of their idol, and to blow out their brains. — Which fashion, if it had continued long, would infallibly have been of great detriment to the literary atchievements of our own century, though it might have increased the wealth of *tailors*. But the fire which burns hottest, is soonest exhausted, and now no body remembers Werter and

Somewhat before her usual hour, Mrs Shin arrives, with a leg of mutton and several turnips — Or what not — It may be a pig's cheeks and bread — We cannot be always attending to such things — Let us merely record, that she arrives. She has heard the news from the village, which accounts for her unusual haste. — For if, as every body now knows, Mr Peach has been bewitched by a gypsy trollop, who has unfortunately escaped hanging, but must now certainly be burnt at the stake instead — Then she, that is Mrs Shin, ought to be first to confirm it. She has brought with her the Pilgrim's Progress. — She cannot read it, but knows, it is an holy book. The family Bible would have suited better to ward off gypsy magic, but is, alas, too weighty to be tucked about her person. She has also a butter-knife, in lieu of a mirror, which would have been inconvenient also. — The knife is lately polished, and thus sufficiently *reflective* to return any spells, in the direction whence they come. Further, she has tied several red ribbons in her bonnet, to signify the blood of the Saviour. Thus girt about with the armour of righteousness, she enters the house — And finds there, only Mr Peach, no more bewitched than herself.

There is no heathenish black gypsy harridan to be seen — But only a surly ill-looking girl in borrowed cloaths. Well — says Mrs Shin — And where have you come from, young baggage? — For you're no daughter of any family hereabouts. — You must excuse her, says Mr Peach — She has a deformity of the mouth, and prefers not to speak! — Mrs Shin has never heard the like. Her suspicions are renewed. When Mr Peach comes in to speak with her, in the kitchen, she dares an allusion, though in the most general terms, to the events of the morning — Remarking, as though it were a matter of indifference to her, that there are some in the village, who will murmur of a gentleman riding away from the constable's house, with the gypsy thief upon his own horse — though she for her own part knows better, she thanks God, than

---

his sorrows. — Hence our *foot-note*. — You understand, reader, we ornament our pages thus, for your sake, not our own.

to talk so, of a gentleman's doings — Yet where the nasty trollop has hid herself, she cannot but wonder — She hopes she will never find herself under the same roof as such a thing! Amen, says Mr Peach, and bids Mrs Shin be easy, for, as she can see herself, there is no gypsy in the house. — To which very reasonable remark he adds, some moderately severe strictures, upon the idleness and folly of village gossip. Mrs Shin is abashed, and has no answer.

— On the matter of the gypsies, Mrs Shin, adds Mr Peach, I should like to ask your advice.

Mrs Shin is mollified, by this mark of her employer's good sense.

— It is only Anny Pertwee who has seen the rascals, as I understand?

Mrs Shin is a little reluctant to agree as much, and relates several other well-attested instances of the villains' wickedness. — But, on further examination, must confess that none of them are supported by ocular evidence.

— I wonder, says Mr Peach, how Anny knew them for gypsies.

— Bless me, sir, did I not tell you already, that she saw them in the house? And heard them whispering in their heathenish tongue, Lord save us. Saying how they'd break your old chest and steal what they should find, then be away before any body might catch 'em.

— Does Anny say so?

— Aye, sir, she told it all to the constables. And Samuel Sexton told it all to Mr Shin, so I've heard every word if it, as true as what have you.

— She heard them speaking in a strange language?

— Aye, sir.

— Saying, that they meant to rob the chest?

— Aye.

— That is curious, that Anny heard them confess their plot, in a foreign tongue.

— Lord, sir, says Mrs Shin, in great pity at Mr Peach's ignorance — Every body knows the gypsies don't use the proper words of the Bible.

Mr Peach nods humbly, and thanks Mrs Shin, and compliments

her upon her knowledge of these matters, and others.

And now Mr Peach's contentment is complete, and he looks back upon his restless worries, and strange terrors, as one dismisses the phantom torments of a dream. All that seemed certain, is now shewn to be baseless. Every morsel of news, or rumour, or suspicion, which formerly appeared to add its substance to the strong edifice of proof, now dissolves to flimsy shadow.

In short — *There are no gypsies* — No lurking rogues, of foreign appearance, who might have been taken for such. The dread, which has haunted him, is banished!

He considers each piece of evidence in turn. —

The first, and original, suggestion, that Mr Peach's house was found and set upon by mysterious strangers, was the testimony of Anny herself, on the night of the robbery. That testimony is now found to be mere absurdity. The events of that night admit of another explanation, more conformable to all the evidence. — It was Anny herself, that broke the lock upon the chest. — Anny herself, that disturbed the books within. — None but Anny Pertwee, who now spreads the word up and down the parish, that Thomas Peach keeps wicked books below the stair.

The next supposed confirmation, of the presence of some malign foreigner, was provided by the bookish imp *Azroë* — If we suppose such a creature to exist, and to be gifted with oracular power. Mr Peach is inclined to smile at himself, for having ever imagined such things. Why, even if his fingers were guided, as they traversed the pages of close-printed nonsense, by any thing more than mere chance — blind whim — The answers might still as easily be applied to the subsequent visit of Caspar — For the courteous negro might well be supposed *a stranger from a distant land, seeking Mr Peach's house*, whom Mr Peach could escape *by no means*.

The last piece of evidence, that gave credence to Mr Peach's fears, was found in the tale of Dick the inn-keeper's boy, supposed to have been assaulted by gypsies in the roads near by. A report, which struck Mr Peach with dreadful horror! — and yet how swiftly has he learned, that it too is perfectly unfounded! — For he has now heard the story of young Dick's misadventure, from an immediate witness.

Mr Peach goes to bed that night, in entire satisfaction. He is much pleased at the curious accident, by which he is reacquainted with Miss Riddle. Indeed, he is now determined to pursue the acquaintance, in a manner which you shall learn of, in our next.

Thus, in the most remarkable circumstances, is a connexion resumed, which both Mr Peach and yourself, good reader, must have thought impossible of renewal.

If you are wise, reader, you will reserve your judgment, as to whether the accident be fortunate or unfortunate — or whether it be accident *at all* — Until you are better acquainted with the young person.

You are at a certain disadvantage — In that you receive from our pages a more vivid impression of her *language*, which we are able to report exactly and fully, than of her *person*, which may only be presented by description, at one remove from the flesh — And thus you hear her speak fair, while avoiding sight of her hideous mouth.

Let us see what Miss Riddle is about.

— Why — you exclaim — Surely the young woman is asleep! Mr Peach has betaken himself to bed — Passed some time, in pleasant conversation with Mrs Peach, and bid her rest again. — It is the dead of night. — Think of the trials Miss Riddle has endured, this day. — You cannot mean to intrude this questionable narrative of yours, into the bed-room of a sleeping girl!

But, reader, Miss Riddle is *not* asleep. Look —

There is no light, but what enters the windows from the moon-lit clouds above — But see — A shadowed figure, seated in the parlour. — It is she. She *listens* —

Or so we suppose —

Reader, we have here to make an important confession.

We must freely acknowledge, that we cannot always declare

with certainty, what Miss Riddle does.

We may observe her. — We shall watch, and carefully — Our powers are such, that no scene or act of these events can be hidden from us, if we chuse to attend to them. She cannot lift a finger — Nay, cannot take a breath — But we will see it, and report it, if we wish.

But as to those *inward springs* of action — Her feelings, and her contemplations — They remain DARK —

The other personages of our narrative, are open books before us. We have shewn you their thoughts — Turned them inside-out, like the lecturers in anatomy — For, unlike your ordinary writer of histories, who must deduce the secrets of temperament, and character, and private impulse, from the outward evidence of word and deed, we in the trade of *necromantic history** may peer into the chambers of the soul, and the caverns of the brain, and give a voice to unspoken thoughts, or inarticulate sensations. You have witnessed us at our work — Transcribing the contemplations of our hero — but also, taking soundings of shallower vessels, such as fair Anny, and goodwife Shin. Yet, in the case of Miss Riddle — A blindness descends.

We fear, there may be an explanation. — Do not hurry to learn it!

For now, let us watch her, as close as we may. We may perhaps make some inferences, as to what she is about. —

Thus, we have deduced that she *listens*, because she sits very still, but quite awake, and with every sign of alertness and attention. However, her listening is not like the eaves-dropping of the fair Anny. There is no anxious turning of the ear this way and that — No straining towards the foot of the stair — No effort, to make out what is spoken in the room above — Nor any guilty dread of discovery.

---

* An arcane profession, conducted beneath a veil! — We cannot with any certainty number our brothers and sisters in the art, still less name them. There is ONE, incomparably great! beside whom we know ourselves to be a mere fumbling apprentice. But their true name — where they are to be found — even, whether they be man or woman — We shall never learn.

From all of which we shall infer, that Miss Riddle's only purpose is to await the conclusion of Mr Peach's gentle discourse with his wife, and to satisfy herself, that they are both asleep.

Our inference is just — For, see now — When every hint of a noise from above is silenced, and utter stillness possesses the house — Only then, does the shadow rise from the chair — And begins to move about.

She is dressed as she was, in the rude cloaths belonging to Jem. Her stockinged feet are noiseless as a cat's. She goes first to the kitchen. No embers remain. — She could not light a candle, but she goes well enough without. Some cloaths of Mrs Shin's hang by the grate. She takes one, and ties its corners, to make a sack — Then tip-toes through the parlour, and into the small room at the end of the house, which serves Mr Peach for a rustic study.

There is the table, which Mr Peach has pressed into service as his *escrutoire*. Here are his pens, and blotting-paper, and ink-stand. Miss Riddle explores them with her fingers, as we fancy a blind man might. Here, too, is that substantial parcel of blank sheets, of whose misadventures we have heard much.

This packet she takes — and — Puts into her sack —

Is the paper to be robbed from Mr Peach, a second time?

We cannot but think, that Miss Riddle means to *steal away* — and steal Mr Peach's goods into the bargain.

A poor return! to make herself guilty of that very same crime, in excusing her from which Mr Peach willingly perjured himself!

The moralists will shake their white heads — And compose an epigram.

Is the character of Miss Riddle then settled? Is the girl as Mr Farthingay pronounced her? — as she feared to pronounce herself — Irredeemably WICKED?

Your suspicions are not groundless, reader, and your indignation on Mr Peach's behalf does you credit. — But, let us be patient, and watch a while longer.

The silent questing hands have left the table, and now busy themselves among the gentleman's books. She picks them out from the case, one by one.

It cannot be, that she means to occupy herself in reading! — The light is very faint. — And besides, she does not open the covers, but only lifts each book in turn, in her arms, as though *weighing* them.* One after another she lifts them, up and down, and then replaces them. — Until, after having investigated the entirety of Mr Peach's modest library, she returns to the *largest* and *weightiest* single volume — Which happens to be, that very *Gazetteer and Atlas* of the county of Somersetshire, printed in handsome folio, which was recently presented to him, by the hand of Caspar, as a gift from Miss Arabella Farthingay.

Miss Riddle puts the book into her sack, alongside the parcel of papers.

Horresco referens! —

She appears satisfied — And leaves the room, with the purloined items slung at her back. And, behold — She directs her course now, towards the door!

Alas, there appears no possibility of doubt. She will quietly leave the house — Pausing, perhaps, to add her own filthy ragged garments to the bundle — Which will be the only objects therein, properly reckoned her own. All else, not excepting the very cloaths on her back — mere *robbery*.

She halts again to listen, at the bottom of the stair. — We suppose she must confirm that Mr and Mrs Peach are fast asleep, before risking the opening of the door, which will necessarily occasion some noise.

Her foot meets an obstacle.

We need not tell you what it is. — You are now well acquainted with that chest, in which Mr Peach keeps his rare and antient

---

* An ingenious method of exercising literary judgment, and not without advantages; yet we cannot altogether recommend it.

volumes of arcane superstition. — A container, you will also recall, which is no longer closed by any lock.

What female heart doth gold despise?

exclaims Gray, in his funerary ode; and,

What cat's averse to fish?

— an exquisite pair of examples, of *questions that supply their own answer.* — For our present purpose, we may add a third, though with less poetry. — *What burglar can overlook an unlocked chest?*

Miss Riddle sits to inspect this new discovery.

The lid is lifted. — All is shadow here, but her fingers discover, what her eyes cannot — the heavy tomes within. She lifts one in her hand — Weighs it — Then, impelled by what motive we cannot say, carries it back to the end-room, and stands by the mismatched windows, where such radiance as the night affords enters the house.

At this very instant — strange chance! — the clouds are blown from the face of the moon, and its reflected light pours over the occult pages —

She turns them over. —

Not for her, the horror of Anny Pertwee, in the same circumstances! Miss Clarissa Riddle reads on, unmoved. — Or, scans the pages — We cannot think she *reads*, the black-letter, and the fusty Latin — to say nothing of the other languages, which we must not name. Yet she studies them with attention — Returns it to the chest, and brings another volume out to the moonlight —

Are her base instincts sufficiently refined, that she knows these books to be more precious than the rest?

Dreadful thought! — that a girl of seventeen, should have acquired such expertise in the art of thieving!

Of all Mr Peach's worldly goods, the sum of which, we are not ashamed to admit, is modest enough, he would least willingly be parted from this dozen or so of curious old tomes. Is this how his generous behaviour to Miss Riddle is to be repaid? — by the expropriation of his dearest possessions?

But — What is this? —

The presumed burglar has finished with her lengthy study of the books. One by one, she removes them from the seat by the window — Not to her sack — But, replaces them in the chest. And in the very order, in which she extracted them! so that if any body happened to look in upon them, it might appear they had not been disturbed at all.

And, now! —

She unties the simple sack — takes out the *Atlas* — And returns it also, to the very place on the table, whence it was just now removed.

The sack itself is next unfolded, and becomes once more a plain square of cloth. She hangs it by the grate, in the kitchen. — All this she does, as quiet as the rest.

She *undoes* her actions, as stealthily as they were *done*. No body observes her — None but we — And of us, she cannot be conscious. We are but shadows of futurity — Bodiless as thought —

Every article, which it appears she intended to steal, is replaced. And now she returns to the narrow bed, in the room behind the parlour, formerly occupied by Anny Pertwee. — Where she lays herself down — And is still.

What has occasioned her change of heart?

Has her heart indeed changed? — We cannot be sure of it. We know as little of what passes therein, as we did before.

Has she even an heart *at all*? — In the place where we observe such an organ, in the other persons of our narrative, we find an obscurity. A veil shrouds it — A fog of night.

Any thing might be concealed within — or — NOTHING.

We suspend our tale accordingly, and conclude the chapter.

CHAPTER FOURTEEN

The restoration of Mr Peach's ease and contentment has many advantages, not the least of which is, that he no longer feels compelled to quit the house at Widdershins Bank.

To be spared all the trouble and expence of a removal, is certainly a very great blessing. There is, however, one difficulty, which arises as a consequence. — Our sublunary existence being so ordained, that we may never experience the full cup of pleasure, unmixed with a single drop of pain — Else this *earth* of ours would be an *heaven* — Which, it is plainly not — Despite the efforts of the Anti-Lapsarian Society.

The difficulty is, that Mr Peach now feels the want of an house-maid.

He has pondered this domestic puzzle through the night, in his habitual fashion — That is to say, slowly, and with philosophic care. His conclusion is, that the answer presents itself under his very roof, in the person of — Miss Clarissa Riddle.

Thus it is, that, in the morning, he stands before that curious young person, in his parlour, and addresses her in the following terms.

— I invite you, madam, to consider your prospects in the world. It is evident you possess many advantages of education and accomplishment, and have been raised in the expectation of no mean station in life. But it must be just as evident that such expectations are at present exceedingly remote. As you approach your years of vigour, there lies before you no immediate course, but the privations of a vagrant existence. If we look further ahead, I fear we shall discover equally little prospect of that life of decent and sufficient comfort, which is the very least your upbringing and your natural parts have intended you for. I hope I shall be excused for saying, that your unfortunate disfigurement has rendered you unsuited to ordinary society; still less to that state which it is decreed a woman must occupy, if she is to be afforded a secure place in the world. You will say, in answer, that you do not regret it. You have expressed a desire for mere liberty of person, above all other things. Yet, Miss Riddle, you cannot be ignorant of the dangers which inevitably await you, should you cast yourself once more into the embrace of desperate unhoused beggary. The freedom you prize is precious to you, because it is new. It will not always be so. When its lustre fades, what will be left to you, but daily misery, and the perpetual terror of something worse? Neither nature nor your education has fitted you for the open fields, still less for the poor-house. In mere justice to yourself, you ought to seek a way of life which permits you some enjoyment of the pleasures of health and youth. Reflect on it, and you will see that a specious liberty of your person, without the least security from want, or any protection against the first villain who inclines to offend it, is no liberty at all.

Mr Peach clears his throat — And wipes his brow.

He continues — It happens, that while you are, I hope I have persuaded you, in want of some secure means of living, I am myself in need of a female domestic. Do not, I pray, be offended! — I cannot pretend that your education has fitted you for a position in service. It shall be for you alone to consider what you see here about you — An house of peaceful seclusion, untroubled by wider society; no wealth, pomposity, or ambition of grandeur; a place where your unfortunate circumstances will attract neither curiosity nor derision. You are not used to menial tasks. Whether they are a worse oppression than sleeping under hedges, and fearing the vigilance of constables, and the rudeness of every passer-by, and the violence of lawless rogues, I do not presume to decide. — You have the liberty of your own opinion;

and as to the liberty of your person, Miss Riddle, there lies the door, and beyond it the road, and nothing shall prevent you from passing through the one, and making your way along the other. The earth is all before you, where to chuse your way.* You will be neither indentured nor confined. You would have only a room, and cloaths, and wages, all honestly earned, and safe for so long as you desire to enjoy them. Say nothing at once — Mr Peach interjects in haste, for now Miss Riddle rises from her chair — Consider every thing, that I have said, at your leisure. You shall stay, I hope, another day. You need not give your answer before the evening — or to-morrow —

But Miss Riddle is not offended. On the contrary — Though she has got up from the chair, to interrupt Mr Peach's lengthy oration, her answer is only — to accept the proposal, at once! without the least hesitation — And with every mark of sincere gratitude.

This person, is to be our hero's new house-maid! — You marvel at his recklessness, reader. — We know you have your reasons, to doubt Miss Riddle's character. We might protest, that Mr Peach is ignorant of those events you have witnessed below-stairs in the night — But you will say, and with some justice — That he has heard her described as a lunatic — a criminal — a devil, in human form; that he has witnessed her, in a state of intemperate rage; that he has heard coarse and filthy language, from her disfigured mouth — Indeed, that he knows enough of the circumstances of her young life, to deduce, that she is unlikely to exhibit those virtues of humble uncomplaining dutifulness and deference, which are usually reckoned the first requirements in a servant.

We suppose these objections must have occurred to him, during his philosophic deliberations. And yet, his decision was made — And is now enacted.

The wisdom, or otherwise, of this choice, we shall observe in what follows.

* In the transports of his rhetoric, Mr Peach alludes to the exquisite conclusion of the Paradise Lost.

For now, all is honest satisfaction on his part, and modest complaisance on hers. The wages are suggested, and accepted at once, with becoming appreciation. Mr Peach regrets he cannot do more, his means being at present much straitened. Miss Riddle says —

A moment, if you please.

Miss Riddle, we have called her hitherto, for we thought it right to adopt a polite form of address, while we remained uncertain of her station. Though we knew her vagrant, we remembered nevertheless, that she had been raised in a gentleman's house, and in some form as his own child. But now! — it would be ridiculous, to belabour a *maid*, with this title, on every page of ours. — We do not mean to insult the profession — Nor to suggest, that a girl who accepts a *wage*, thereby gives up her *dignity*. We only wish to avoid a ridiculous sentence — Such as, *Miss Riddle sweeps out the fire-place* — *Miss Riddle washes the window* — We would no more be caught with such stuff at the tip of our pen, than we would write, *Old George Hanover signs the bills of state* — *Billy Pitt addresses the Commons* — or the like. Since the young woman is to become a more familiar presence in our pages, we shall henceforth refer to her, in more familiar manner. Her baptismal name, is, as you know, Clarissa, but, as she says to Mr Peach —

— I was always called Clary.

— That will do very well, says he. — And we agree with him.

Where were we? — On the matter of the wages, Clary is so modest as to declare, they will do very well, and indeed she would accept less, if to do so would aid Mr Peach in the management of his expenditure; for, she says, she has no desire for trinkets and baubles, and is content with an humble sustenance.

Such sentiments, in the mouth of one whom we know to have countenanced the most shameless robbery! — Is this not gross hypocrisy, stained as black as the organ from which it proceeds?

Nonetheless, we are compelled to observe, that Clary now makes every effort to impress upon Mr Peach her gratitude for his offer, and her determination that he shall not regret it. She sets to her duties willingly — Without sly looks, or idleness. — Remember, that we may watch her, though Mr Peach's attention is elsewhere engaged. We see her as she goes about the house — And do not, through all the morning, detect the smallest sign, that she resents her position, or will take advantage of her employer's generosity — Or, that she plans any further *theft*.

Clary hesitates to speak to Jem, or before him, and it is left to Mr Peach, to explain the cause of her reticence. So far from conceiving any distaste for the maid, or for her affliction, the lad is entranced. He has been used to the teazing and chaffing of Anny Pertwee, who would mock his stammer, and make him her sport, and not trouble to conceal her opinion, that he was a poor stick of a boy, and barely worth her notice. Clary's silence is most welcome to him. — Better — it is *romantic* — In Jem's poor passionate heart, the deformity which afflicts her appears a mark, like that of Cain — The sign of a fate, which sets her apart from common humanity — Lifts her, into a mysterious realm of noble and inexpressible tragedy — &c. &c. — You know your Werter — Or, if not, you have certainly read your Childe Harold, or your poems of Landon — You may supply the rest.

It must also be acknowledged, that the person of Clary makes no little impression, upon the baser parts of the constitution of Jemmy Sixways.* She is not pretty, in the common estimation, as Anny is; but, he is a fellow of sixteen — She is young, and female, and in health and vigour — It is enough — More than enough.

The addition to Mr Peach's household is resented only, by Mrs Shin. She has taken an instant and immovable dislike to the young visitor, in the previous evening, as you have read in our previous. When she now learns, that the ugly thing is to take up a position at Widdershins Bank! she is thoroughly out of humour, and takes no pains to conceal it. She was wont to sit in the kitchen with

---

* As, indeed, we think the person of Charlotte made a great impression on the vulgar sensations of Werter; although, amid his paeans upon the purity and nobility of her soul, he unfortunately omits to mention it.

Anny, who, though a giddy foolish girl, was not deficient in the art Mrs Shin prizes above all others, *viz.* conversation upon matters of popular interest. What can be the use of a maid, *who will not talk at all*? — Nay, will not even open her mouth to eat, while Mrs Shin is in the kitchen?

— You'll not do for this house, baggage, says she, bending over the creature's ear. — And I'll be sure to tell the gentleman. Don't think he don't care for my opinion neither, for he do, you'll see. You may be on your way home, wherever you make it, sooner than the cock crows.

But though Mr Peach listens patiently to Mrs Shin's complaint, he says only, Well, well, we shall see what we think to-morrow — And sends her home to Mr Shin, with no very clear indication, that he has afforded her opinion the deference it demands.

— Perhaps, says she to herself, the master still suffers a touch of the gypsy spell? — Finding comfort in this explanation, she proceeds on her way, better satisfied — And so makes her exit from our pages.

Bid her ample back farewell, reader — You shall not see it, nor any other aspect of goodwife Shin, ever again.

— Might I offer a suggestion? says Clary, towards the end of this first day of her honest employment.

— Certainly, says Mr Peach.

— You alluded to some difficulties in your present circumstances. I wonder whether it would be convenient, to dispense with the services of the woman who provides your table.

— Mrs Shin?

— Yes, sir. I can manage the kitchen as well, or better, if I may say so, and I would consider it a part of my duties, and expect no further emoluments.

— I could not consider such an arrangement. The position you have consented to requires enough of your labours. I should be a tyrant, to impose any further.

— It cannot be an imposition, when I make the suggestion myself.

Mr Peach does not deny it; but observes, that the requirement to go to town on market-day, and otherwise to supply the necessaries of the table, would surely be unpleasant to her, for she could not discharge it without intercourse of speech, thereby exposing her deformity to vulgar fascination and disgust; and he adds besides, that he would in any event be unwilling to dismiss Mrs Shin, for the wages she receives from him form no great portion of his own expences, but, he believes, make up no small part of her pleasures. The value to *her* being proportionately greater than the inconvenience to *him*, he believes he ought not to deprive her of it.

— You must be a philosopher, sir, to weigh your deeds so exactly. Or a man of religion, to place another's needs higher than your own.

— Do we not all weigh our actions? Or how else do we act at all? As for the virtue of selflessness, I do not think I may claim any extraordinary share of it; nor, if I could, would that proclaim me a good Christian, for pagans and heathens no doubt care as much, and as little, for their neighbours, as church-going folk.

— Then, sir, says Clary, you do not confine your philosophy to the teachings of the church?

— Let us not discuss it, says Mr Peach. — I am already too much sensible, that you are employed beneath your accomplishments. If we are to dispute theology, I should be still more embarrassed to see you with broom and pan.

Nevertheless, Mr Peach is delighted with his philosophical maid. That she goes about her work readily, would give him satisfaction enough. That she is rational, fair of speech, and acquainted with the forms of conversation, elevates her almost to the Platonic *eidos*, or *Idea*, of the domestic servant. — He desires her to name any particular request she may have, which would make her situation more convenient or comfortable.

Somewhat to his surprize, she answers without hesitation. — She wishes, she says, for a supply of — ink and paper.

Mr Peach is happy to comply. — So it is arranged — And for the present, we need say no more about Mr Peach's household oeconomy.

How curious, that the reappearance of Clarissa Riddle, should have at one stroke resolved so many of the fears and troubles by which Mr Peach has been beset!

And how remarkable, that this perfectly unexpected and fortunate accident, should have followed immediately upon Mr Peach's invocation of *supernatural* aid! — You will have noticed, reader, that the morning of Mr Peach's visit to the constable, came on the heels of that night, in which he unlocked the last and eldest of his secret volumes. —

Let us not think, that his every wish is granted — That every cloud, is banished from the horizon of his prospects — That his tale is come to a resolution, like the end of the comedy, when every confusion is explained, and every hindrance overcome, and there is nothing for the hero to do, but marry the heroine — A final deed, which, according to the comic authors, forbids all future disquiet, and represents the sum and terminus of joy and good fortune — As all the audience must agree, since they sit beside their spouses.

You will recall, reader, the very first scene of our narrative. — How long ago it seems!

You have not forgotten, the unkind behaviour of Mr Peach's uncle Augustus. — Nor, alas, has Mr Peach. He would forget it, if he could afford to, with as much relish, as can possibly be attached to so *negative* an act, as forgetting. — But he cannot. He must still find some means, whereby he may compensate for the loss of the annuity, settled upon him in his late father's will.

In plain terms — He has not resolved his want of money.

We read in our seventh chapter of certain epistolary schemes, effected with the intention of supplying that want. The exact nature of those schemes, we confess, we have not enquired into. — Our narrative was overtaken, by all this business of the chimerical GYPSIES, or mysterious foreigners unknown — And consequently

239

plunged into a murky fog, of sortilege, and Welshmen, and antient ritual. — Heavens! — it will be a relief, to return our attention to so prosaic an obstacle, as the want of an hundred pounds *per annum*!

In this matter, unfortunately, the reappearance of Clary, which has otherwise proved so lucky a chance — if chance it be — Is, of no use. For we remember, that the above-mentioned schemes, were to be conducted by letters; and Clary has testified, that any letters directed to Widdershins Bank, which may have been in the bag of Dick Wainwright, are — lost. We must therefore think Mr Peach's projects frustrated, and his hopes dashed.

But we shall not throw a pall over our scene, by dwelling on those few clouds, that obscure a prospect otherwise bright with summer cheer. The close of day finds all the house of Widdershins Bank at peace. — Clary, in the little room next the larder, which she may now call her own. — Jem, awake with a candle in the stable-loft, reading over and again the passionate effusions of love-struck Werter. — Mr Peach a-bed — and Mrs Peach quite herself again — Which, as she answers, when he observes as much, is scarce a surprize. — How should I be other than myself, Tom? she says, teazing. —

Mr Peach does not answer. — He has no wish to allude to that night, when she cried out from the room above, in tones of horror, and spoke strange promises, in an unfamiliar voice. — And, on this fine May evening — no more do we.

CHAPTER FIFTEEN

We told you, did we not, that you had heard the last of Mrs Shin? — We ought to have said, The last of her, considered *in propria persona*. She will be alluded to on occasion, in future pages. But she will not appear *herself* — because — She is drowned.

Mr Peach receives the tragic news, two days after the events of our last. Mrs Shin was making her way homeward, and in the twilight must have lost her footing, beside the pond, and unfortunately fallen in; whereupon her skirts became heavy, and entangled in the marshy herbage, and pulled her down in the water — Never to rise.

It is rumoured, perhaps with rather less of Christian charity than the occasion demands, that she may have been drunk. She had been at the tavern — But what of that? She was always at the tavern, and for two score years passed nevertheless the pond at the bottom of the old lane, without falling in.

Poor Mrs Shin!

— Sir — says Clary to Mr Peach — she is looking still more ridiculous this morning, for she has put her borrowed cloaths out to dry, they having been wetted in some accident of the previous day, and has requested the use of a tattered smock of Jem's, which hangs on her more like a sack than a garment — Sir, says she, will you consider again the suggestion I put to you yesterday, and allow me to take on the duties of house-keeping?

Mr Peach looks her up and down, and says — Clary, we must provide you with some suitable dress.

— That will be an expence to you, at a time when every unexpected outlay must be unwelcome. But reflect, sir, how much may be saved, if you are not required to pay for the services of a cook. It will be no hardship to me to assume the duties, which are, after all, not very burdensome.

An unheard-of thing! that a servant should plead for an increase in her work — without any mention, of an addition to her wages!

Mr Peach is a little surprized, that Clary should offer herself in Mrs Shin's place, so soon after the poor woman's untimely end. A decent interval, he thinks, might have been appropriate. — And yet — an house-keeper he must have; and he cannot dispute the oeconomy of Clary's proposal.

He agrees, therefore, with the proviso, that three days in each fortnight, he will betake himself to the tavern, or elsewhere, so that she is not required to labour every waking hour.

— I prefer to be occupied, she says — And I am never tired.

Mr Peach cannot deny it. The house is neat, and clean, and every thing is in good order, yet at the end of the day Clary shews no marks of fatigue.

— And how do you proceed with your literary labours, Clary?

— Sir?

— You have the paper and ink you requested, I think?

— Oh! well enough, sir. Indeed, I wonder whether you might spare a little more of each?

Mr Peach considers whether to jest, that she, like the god-mother for whom she is named,* must be *always writing*. — But reflects, that any allusion to her upbringing at Grandison Hall, and in particular to the eccentric system of education imposed upon her, by Mr Farthingay, is likely to be unpleasant, and therefore cannot be amusing.

— I have no objection, says he.

— You are very good, says she.

---

* That is, Richardson's Miss Clarissa Harlowe.

Mr Peach's private opinion, is that *he* ought rather to be grateful to *her*; for her stile of speech, and the ease and breadth of her discourse, bespeak a young person who could scarcely be expected to content herself with so humble an occupation, as she has willingly assumed; yet he cannot find a single complaint to make of her. — What is more, the experiment agreed upon, whereby she assumes the duties formerly undertaken by the unfortunate Mrs Shin, proves an entire success. Mr Peach will not allow that she should go to the market, or to Mr Butcher the dairy-farmer, or to Mrs Milken, who bakes the bread — firstly, because he fears her appearance abroad must excite attention and ridicule, and second, because she will not open her mouth, before any but him and Jem — Which must infallibly produce great difficulties, in the execution of such quotidian tasks as purchasing cabbages and eggs. He therefore attends to such transactions himself, to the amusement of his neighbours. — But all the occupations of the kitchen itself, are managed by Clary, and with the most satisfactory results.

Why should we dwell on the particulars of these menial arrangements? — which are not generally thought to rank among those events, worthy the notice of history? — Reader — It is to explain the cause, whereby Mr Peach is now often to be found travelling the parish roads, following the sad demise of Mrs Shin. — An alteration in his habits, which may be significant, in relation to the next occurrence we must relate.

Behold another fine morning, in the month of May. — Our history has not yet advanced beyond that sweet season, though the parched airs of June draw near. Mr Peach has gone out, to procure his daily bread; finding, in common with all his fellow-mortals, that it is better to beg that necessity from the baker, than from the Almighty, despite the instruction recorded as gospel, in the sixth chapter of St Matthew. He is returning by his now accustomed route, when he comes upon a stranger, who stands in the shade of a spreading beech, leaning upon the trunk, and smoking a pipe.

Mr Peach anticipates no more from the accident, than a mutual exchange of *Good-days*, and a touch of the hat; and is therefore much surprized, to be accosted by name.

— By tarnation! cries the stranger, in accents which proclaim him beyond doubt a native of Wales, before the last consonant has escaped his lips. — By Washington! Do these old fraternal eyes deceive me, or is it not Mr Thomas Peach, of Widdershins Bank? I think my sight is not yet so weakened, by the glare that reflects from the mighty expanse of *Lake Ontario*, as to be mistaken.

The man wears a travelling-coat, not of the cleanest, and his boots exhibit a similar degree of intimacy with the dust of the roads. In contrast with these rough and well-worn articles of dress, he sports a peruke, of a stile in fashion some fifteen or twenty years before the time of our story, such as you may see in several portraits from the brush of *Gainsborough*; and, atop the peruke, a three-cornered hat, pinned with a rosette in the colours of red, blue, and white; which same tricolor is displayed also by his cravat. The buttons of his breeches are newly polished, and likewise his brass spectacles — though these last items attract Mr Peach's attention, less from their brightness and neatness, than because of the very curious fact, that they contain no glass, but are merely a pair of circular window-frames, through which the stranger observes him.

Mr Peach draws up the gelding. — You have the advantage of me, sir, he says.

— That I do, friend, that I do, as surely as old Washington had the advantage, when he crossed the Delaware! My name, sir – brother — is George Jefferson, and I would count it a mighty friendliness, if you would stop a moment, and consent to share this pipe with me. The tobacco is the finest Virginia has to offer. I think I can smell that county's forests, and plains, and mountains, and desarts, with every puff! There is not a finer odour in all the olfactory kingdom, by tarnation!

We have remarked more than once, that Mr Peach's wits are not rapid. They are comprehensive — But, according to the pattern often found in nature,* what they gain in *expansiveness*, they lose in *agility*. Thus, although he is immediately suspicious of Mr Jefferson, he cannot at once determine the precise direction, where his suspicions tend. — I must continue the conversation, he thinks, in some neutral and diffident fashion, until I better understand its import.

— I shall be very glad to, Mr Jefferson, he says, dismounting. — For it seems we are acquainted; though I fear I cannot recall the occasion of our previous meeting. I beg your pardon for the lapse.

— An egregious supererogation! cries the Welshman, with a flourish of his pipe. — Not the least apology is to be thought of, for, indeed, there is no lapse that has occurred. I have not had the brotherly honour of your society before now. Your name, however, is known to me. — The man offers the pipe, as though to share it were the most natural thing in the world. Mr Peach, having accepted the offer *in verbo*, feels bound to do likewise *in re*, and takes it from him. The stranger adopts a more intimate tone. — Let it be spoken only between true friends and brothers such as ourselves, says he — I confess I had hoped to meet you. — His voice descends as near to murmur as it is capable of, taking into account the splendour of elocution so naturally abundant among the natives of Wales. — For, he continues, with a significant look, I have heard, that Thomas Peach, of the parish of C___ton, is — a TRUE FRIEND OF LIBERTY.

Mr Peach draws on the pipe. — His wits have lumbered to their feet, and begun to exercise themselves a little; making so much progress, as to recollect Jem's story of the mysterious Welshman, lurking about his house.

— Now, thinks he, during the interval afforded by his emitting a puff of smoke, and observing how it dissipates into the invisible air — Now, this fellow has some purpose with me, which I cannot guess at. The politic course, is therefore to humour him, in the hopes that he may be encouraged to expose himself.

* The *elephant*, and the *walrus*, &c.

— Liberty, he says aloud, is no doubt among the highest blessings of civilization, and a condition greatly preferable to its opposite.

Mr Jefferson squints through his empty spectacles, and then winks, and waggles his bewigged head.

— Now, sir — says he — Sir — brother — Circumspection is much to be advised, by Washington, and lauded also; but we shall not have reason to call upon it here, between true friends, such as we are. — He taps the rosette in his hat, and winks again, most expressively. — I speak of — His voice becomes a thunderous whisper, if such a thing may be imagined* — the TRUE LIBERTY.

— The false one, says Mr Peach, returning the pipe, Is indeed a lamentable thing.

— Why, cries Mr Jefferson, there you have it! You strike, sir — brother — in the very exact heart of my meaning. I could not myself have expressed it so well, in an hundred days, or the time it would take a man to ride from the fort at *Ticonderoga*, to *York-town*. The false liberty! — well said, by the tea of Boston harbour, well said indeed. There is in very truth such an untrue thing, Mr friend Peach, a vile false thing, and it goeth about the world like the sun. But there are those — The man looks about, and then indicates himself and Mr Peach, with a gesture of the pipe, though he could hardly refer to any body else, the road being otherwise quite deserted — There are those, among the many ways of this beleaguered world, who maintain the distinction, between the false and the true. The true liberty, brother! — I imbibed my love of it, with every drop of the waters of the *Susquehannah*, whose sweet streams nourished the blessed days of my earliest life.

---

* Betake yourself sufficiently far west of the Severn — And enter into conversation upon one of those subjects, which inspires the people of that country with the utmost earnestness — such as, the heroism of Glendower, or the superior merit of the antient Welsh poetry, or the wholesomeness and manly vigour of the sheep-farmer's existence — And you shall soon be afforded an example, of the effect we mean to describe.

— I take it you are an American, sir?

— By Washington! by Franklin! I have that incomparable honour, and I make no mightier boast. — He offers an enthusiastic hand, which Mr Peach accepts. — George Jefferson, sir friend, of the county of Pennsylvania. — Ask not which parish of the county — The name would be unknown to you, I am so bold as to venture, for it is a part of the territory, but lately acquired by treaty from the tribe of the *Ham-pea-bannocks*.

— It is curious, says Mr Peach, with a friendly air, That the manner of speech of that county, appears very similar in my ears to the distinctive accents of Wales.

— Do you think so? cries Mr Jefferson, somewhat too hastily. — The circumstance is easily accounted for. — Nothing could be more natural! — Let me give you to understand the nature of my birth and upbringing — sir — brother — The very truth of it is, that the mother in whose womb I grew, was a squaw of that same *Ham-pea-bannock* tribe. — But being afterwards promised by the great chieftain of those people, to another man, she left my father and myself, though I was then a mere infant. It is entirely customary among the tribes of the Americas. — You may easily read of a thousand such incidents, in several of the most verifiable accounts of the travellers. — And so, being separated from the maternal breast, I was raised by a serving-woman of my father's house. She nurtured me like a second mother. She was a woman of *Dolgellau* — Her accents, the purest strain of the antient Welsh, as uncorrupted as the mountain streams. — Here Mr Jefferson's eyes begin to water, and take on a dreamy cast. He dabs his cheeks with his sleeve. — Why, he continues, and so it is, and not in the least way surprizing, that I grew up speaking with a touch of the same music upon my tongue. But do not doubt, my friend — I am an American, and as great a lover of the LIBERTY as any who praise the name of Washington, by tarnation!

— I am glad to hear it, says Mr Peach. — But I must ask, whether you have any particular business with me? I cannot think it likely, that you have traversed the waters of the Pacific, only in hopes of this chance encounter.

— The Pacific, says Mr Jefferson, is indeed very wide. But I would be content to sail all the oceans of the world, when there awaits me in my final haven a FRIEND of TRUE LIBERTY. Indeed, brother friend, the grand purpose, for which I abandoned my ancestral home of Pennsylvania, and bade farewell, perhaps for ever, to the *Ham-pea-bannocks* and their fields of buffaloes, is no less than to seek out one of the very greatest of our number! — to whom I bring a message of such importance, that it must be spoken in his ear alone.

— Indeed! says Mr Peach. — And who is this man, for whose sake you have come so far?

— Need I speak his name aloud, good friend? I am advised, on the informations of many of those, who hold the liberty the dearest, that he is an intimate and confidant of yours. — Seek out our true brother Thomas Peach, of Widdershins Bank, in Somersetshire! they told me — Make your introductions to that liberty-loving man, and from him you shall learn, where you may find — JEREMIAH SIXWAYS.

Mr Peach affects tremendous astonishment. — Mr Jefferson — he says — I am surprized at you. That name — spoken in the public road! —

He is gratified to discover, that Mr Jefferson snaps up this bait as eagerly, as any trout snaps at the hooked fly. The supposed American is profuse in apology — winks, and waggles, and nods, with the utmost enthusiasm — And, to save us the trouble of recording further pages of his nonsense, we may only say that Mr Peach gives him to understand, that he is indeed an intimate of the said Mr Sixways — Persuades him of the need for the utmost discretion — But hints, that he may be able to arrange an interview between Mr Jefferson, and the gentleman he seeks — Though the meeting must be prepared with all possible secrecy, and will necessarily require some time to encompass. In short, Mr Peach has at last understood, what the Welshman wants, and therefore dangles before him the prospect of obtaining it, while postponing the hour of satisfaction. — Like any coquette — Though, in truth, we need not leap to the abuse of the fairer sex, in search of our simile; for to promise, and withhold — to offer, but delay — is the wise stratagem, of all who find themselves with the power to provide a thing, that another desires, and will pay for. Do not dismiss it as coquetry — For is this not the whole art of *commerce*? — which is universally held, to be a necessary and noble pursuit, and productive of the wealth of nations, and the contentment of mankind.

We digress. — We have been too much in the company of this Mr Jefferson, and fear we have caught a touch of his dilatory distemper.

Let us dismiss him, then, without further ceremony. He leaves Mr Peach with the information, that he may be sought again at the inn, where he has taken lodging. Mr Peach promises for his part that Mr Jefferson will shortly hear from him, to his advantage.

It is not the first lie Mr Peach has spoken in the course of our pages. — Nor will it be the last.

Does he fear no judgment for his sins? —

He does NOT. — Before our final chapter is ended, you shall understand why.

But to our present narrative. — Behold him now, walking in the road. He leads the doleful gelding by the reins, as though the beast were lame, and incapable of bearing him. The picture thus presented, is not a little comical. — Our hero, in his black breeches and coat, stepping slowly, a mild frown upon his brow — The animal plodding behind, as disconsolate as ever, though relieved of the weight of its rider. But Mr Peach cares not, how ridiculous he appears. — He is — thinking.

There is a kinship, between the motion of ambulation, and the motion of *thought*.

Attempt the experiment yourself. — Conjure before your imagination, a problem of mathematics — or of ethics — or any quandary or dilemma you chuse — And then, set yourself at the pace of a run. We will stake our head, you cannot solve it, while you jog on. Every thing is hurry and bustle. Time becomes importunate — Distraction crowds upon you. — Now, try the same challenge, atop an horse — Or in your cabriolet. — Perhaps in this case, we do not wager our very head; but we are confident nevertheless — You will be uneasy. The problem will rattle away from you. The rapidity and discomfort of your motion will interpose itself, between your brain, and the puzzle it pursues. It is like attempting to think with the *tooth-ache*.

But now, put on your boots, and open the door, and *walk*. — Do you not feel at once, how the easy constant pace of your feet, encourages the steady advance of your thought?

If you do not — We are heartily sorry for you.

Mr Peach, we say again, chuses to walk, because he is required to think.

— This fellow, says he to himself — This Mr Jefferson — is plainly no more an American, than I am a Dutchman. And because he gives a false account of himself, I must presume every other thing he says dishonest.

— And so, like the ingenious old Frenchman *Descartes*, I must endeavour to determine what remains certain, when all is to be doubted.

Mr Peach walks on a quarter-mile, pondering as he goes. — Until he reaches the conclusion, that there are three points he can assert with confidence, concerning the supposed George Jefferson; which are, first, that he is a Welshman; second, that he is a liar; and in the third place, that he wishes to gain admittance to Jeremiah Sixways, at Widdershins Bank.

We suppose, reader, you have not forgotten, the curious interlude recorded in our tenth chapter. Mr Peach assuredly has not. — He thinks of the Welshman, whom young Jem reported meeting in the woods, and whose stories of storms and pirates appeared quite fanciful; who likewise had come to the country, in search of — Jeremiah Sixways.

Mr Peach's conclusion is as secure, as that famous *cogito, ergo sum* of the old French philosopher. — Beyond doubt, he says to himself, these two rogues are one and the same man — And this Jefferson, *alias* Brown, is watching my house, and skulking after poor Jemmy, for some secret purpose.

Jem Sixways! — an obscure and harmless youth, of no possible concern to any body outside the meagre society of his family, and his employer, and two or three old play-fellows. — In truth, of little enough interest even to those few. What mystery is there about the sighing stuttering lad, that can have attracted the attention of this Welshman?

There is only one answer conceivable. Mr Peach arrives at it, within fifteen or twenty paces. — We do not doubt you have reached it yourself — Provided you have got up from your seat, and *walked* a turn or two about your room, or garden, or whatever pleasant retreat you have selected, to indulge the pleasures of our history.

It is — That the peculiar letter, which Mr Peach sent to Doctor Thorburn, has, as he feared, been — INTERCEPTED.

You will recall, that in the said letter, the Doctor was invited to direct any reply, to — Jeremiah Sixways, of Widdershins Bank, in Somerset-shire.

Perhaps you have also not forgotten, that the lines, written by Mr Peach, as though from the hand of Jer. Sixways, had something of a *democratic* hue. — Expressive of an enthusiasm for certain *liberties*, in excess of the sacred and sufficient freedoms, which are the pride of every Briton.

It is not at all inconceivable, that some features of Mr Jefferson's manner and discourse, might have taken their cue, from those expressions. —

Mr Peach remembers also the hints of his friend Mr Selby White, to the effect that the Doctor had aroused the suspicions of the ministry.

— Doctor Thorburn's correspondence, thinks Mr Peach, is *watched*. — The letters he receives are read by other eyes, before they reach his.

— The lines I sent him were reported — And now some sneaking rascal is sent, to discover the conspiracy, of which the Doctor is suspected. —

— In conclusion. — This pretended Mr Jefferson is no more than — a government SPY.

Here Mr Peach stops walking, and takes several breaths, to compose himself.

The gelding stops also — And rejoices.

— A spy! exclaims Mr Peach, aloud. — Am I to be beset, by such a low wheedling snivelling wretch, as a spy!

He thinks — I must find some means to be rid of the rogue.

Mr Peach! — Have a care, what you wish for! — Consider, how your former wishes have been satisfied — Or, *by whom* —

Yet we do not condemn his sentiments. What gentleman of liberal spirit — in this land, where the rights of a gentleman are sacrosanct — can tolerate the thought, that he is spied upon?

Or, what lady?

Mr Peach resumes his homeward journey.

By the time he attains the verdant slopes of Widdershins Bank, he has come to some further conclusions, of a more practical character. It is evident, that any project he may now intend, whether in pursuit of money, or to what purpose soever, cannot be conducted by letters. His correspondence is not safe. It is certainly observed, and followed — perhaps opened, and copied —

Intolerable oppression!

This first conclusion, leads to another, significant to the future course of our tale.

Mr Peach determines that, being unable to apply to the Doctor in writing, he must instead attend him in person. That is to say — he will shortly make another journey, to Bristol.

Thus resolved, he continues along the road, to his house.

Jem! — Jemmy!

The stable-boy is absent once again.

— Clary?

A perfect stillness envelops the house. Neither lad nor maid comes to his call — Nor is any where, to be seen.

Mr Peach stables the gelding himself, with several murmured expressions of his displeasure. He goes within-doors. — All is silent. Clary has VANISHED.

Mr Peach frowns. — Do you likewise, reader?

To explain this state of affairs, we must now relate an event, which occurred within the house, while Mr Peach was abroad, and the eye of our narrative directed elsewhere. — The which occurrence shall take its place, at the head of a new chapter.

CHAPTER SIXTEEN

Reverse thy course, bright cart of *Phoebus*, by several degrees of inclination, towards thy Orient home! — Thus —

It is done. — Our narrative returns to those hours of the morning, while Mr Peach is yet abroad.

No sooner has his horse trudged from view, than Jem retires to his loft, and, with trembling hand, and palpitating heart, and who knows what motions of his other parts, sinks into enraptured study of his Werter. In which reverie he remains, heedless of the passing day, until roused, after an unknown interval, by the noise of an approaching rider.

— The master is returned! thinks he, and hurries down, fearful of rebuke. — How cruel! he thinks, is the world, that the exercise of the body, which is the lot of every dumb animal, is deemed fit for praise, while the motions of the *soul* are called idleness, though they touch the highest faculty implanted in man!

Young Jem's meditations have turned somewhat lofty, as you see.

But the rider is not Mr Peach. — A visitor is a rare sight, in this unfrequented valley, and a returning visitor rarer yet. Jem is thus doubly amazed, to see the same handsomely dressed negro, whose previous appearance in the road, in our ninth chapter, caused him to run pell-mell to Mr Peach, with a report of the dreaded mysterious stranger.

Caspar dismounts, and hands Jem the reins, with a polite request that he be announced to the master of the house.

Though amazed, Jem is not on this occasion abashed. He has of late been less inclined, to cower and stutter in the presence of his fellow-man. — For, he thinks, are not all human creatures *equal*, in the sight of God, and of Nature? — and is not a *feeling heart* a worthier accomplishment, than any title of wealth or station? — &c. — So he answers with a bold upright bearing, and a steady tongue.

— The master's out to market.

Caspar looks to Jem — To the house — To Jem again.

Having assured himself that no further information is forthcoming, he places his arm behind his back, and enquires, whether Mr Peach is expected at home this after-noon?

— He may be — says Jem — Or — He may not — The future is veiled from our mortal eyes!

Caspar stands quite unmoving, while he considers this remarkable reply, for several seconds.

— That is so, boy, he says. — But it is generally found, that he who goes to market, shall very likely return therefrom; and in that expectation, I require you to convey to Mr Thomas Peach the message, that Miss Arabella Farthingay presents her compliments, and to Mrs Peach as well, and desires the pleasure of calling on them in the after-noon.

— Alas! cries Jem — The mistress can receive no callers. — The lad accompanies this exclamation with a sigh, and an heavenward look, each equally tragical, and lets the reins of Caspar's mount fall from his hands, as he clasps them to his breast.

Caspar is unable to maintain the dignity of his deportment. He lays his head to the side, and frowns.

— Are you quite well, boy? he says.

Now — This brief exchange has taken place, as you will have understood, by the side of the road, where stands the stable. Clary is within the house, a little way off. — She has paused in her work, upon hearing the indistinct noise of conversation, and so proceeds to the door, and opens it, to see for herself who it is that has stopped to talk with Jem.

Caspar hears the door open, and looks again towards the house. —

In the ordinary way of our narrative, we should not linger over such petty actions. — Else how would our tale advance at all? But, consider — The present moment is far from insignificant — Very far.

Be pleased to remember, that Miss Clarissa Riddle was raised, and for seventeen years lived exclusively, in the household of Mr Farthingay. — That household, where Caspar is in service.

She knows him *at once* — In the first glance.

But *he* —

We cannot suppose he does *not* know her. A person familiar from all the years, since he came into Mr Farthingay's employ! — Yet consider, how utterly changed she appears. Instead of the elegant figure of a wealthy gentleman's ward, she is presented in the meanest and most common guise — Clad in a plain linen smock, with all her hair undressed, and her legs bare, for the day is warm. — Consider also, that she stands inside the door, shadowed from the bright day without; and, that Caspar knows Miss Clarissa Riddle to have been sent from Grandison Hall, to be shut up in an asylum.

Remember one thing further. — A trivial matter, we thought it at the time, though we took pains to mark it, in the course of our ninth chapter.* — It is, that Caspar has already been apprized by Mr Peach of the persons of his household, that is, himself, his wife, and Jem — and *no one else*.

Reflect on all this, and you may imagine, that Caspar observes the shadowed form — at once familiar and strange — loosely garbed in white, and standing for a silent moment at the door, before retreating from view — And is not certain what he has seen. He thinks he saw Clarissa Riddle — Yet it cannot have been her. Perhaps it was some form of her — Some wordless image — Altered — Impossible —

* *vide* p. 159.

Perhaps, a ghostly simulacrum. — Her *spirit* —

All this, in no more than a moment of mutual regard — For no sooner has Clary seen who is come, than she withdraws from Caspar's view.

The vision is gone. — That gentleman takes up the harness of his horse, and rides away again without further ceremony, pausing only to repeat his message, and to cast a single uncertain backward glance, towards the door of the house — Which stands open and empty, like the frame of a picture, inclosing no canvas.

A little while after, Clary comes out to Jem, to ask what was the visitor's business.

This event fills the lad's poor feeling heart with such an excess of painful delight, and exquisite misery, that he can scarce look her in the face, nor answer three words together. She bestows on him certain encouragements — a soft look — A gentle hand upon his cheek. — We shall not trouble to record them all, except to say they seem to be offered with as much contentment on her part, as they are received with ecstasy upon his. — And so in due course he explains the errand, which brought Caspar to the house.

— Miss Arabella Farthingay intends to come here, this very after-noon?

Jem repeats the message — Is surprized, that Clary appears familiar with the lady's name — But discovers no more, firstly, because his wits are quite unsettled, by the encouragements we have just now alluded to, and secondly, because Clary goes straight within again, and closes the door. Jem is left gazing after her, with as great an excess of mysterious emotion, as Caspar experienced in the same act, some little time ago. — Though the nature of the emotion is certainly quite different.

The lad returns to his book, and finds a page, which he has marked for his especial attention, by turning down the corner of the leaf. He has read these words so many times over, that each of them is indelibly graved in his spirit. — It is that page, in which Werter first sets eyes on the fair Lotte, and receives in his heart the wound, that is to destroy him!

Jem fancies he feels the arrow, in his own breast. —

He murmurs the words — Ten times over — Sighs — Tears cloud his vision. He can endure it no more. — Descends from the loft, and goes to the window of the house — Peers in —

Clary is no where to be seen.

The cause of her behaviour, though mysterious to poor Jem, must be quite plain to you, reader. Miss Arabella Farthingay is expected at the house, within a few hours. — The daughter of that same family, from which Clary escaped. — We need say no more.

— Ah! cries the stable-lad — Are you an angel, who has fled this earth? — And, having delivered himself of this tragical apostrophe, he bursts a-weeping, and runs off to the woods, to lay himself down by the spring, and muse upon the torments of existence.

Thus it is, that Mr Peach comes home, from his curious encounter with Mr George Jefferson, to an empty house. — Emptied of all, we should say, but Mrs Peach. His wife is present still, as she is always present. — Her *presence* such, as can barely be distinguished from *absence*.

But we must not make light of the subject. The mystery of Mrs Peach's infirmity nears its solution — Perhaps, within this very chapter. We shall learn then, whether it be a matter for jesting or no. —

Mr Peach is still alone in his house — alone, but for Mrs Peach — When Miss Arabella Farthingay arrives, in the company of her perpetual attendant.

Mr Peach has of course had no word of their coming, nor made any preparations. He is not, indeed, inclined to company, having been for some hours entirely preoccupied by the unexplained absence of his domestics. Nevertheless, he is sincerely pleased at their arrival.

— My dear Miss Farthingay — he cries, going out to the road — This is a pleasure as delightful as unexpected. — I must apologize for the rustic reception. Allow me to take the horses. My stable-boy has vanished unaccountably — But we shall manage quite well without — Welcome, Miss Farthingay, to Widdershins Bank!

Though dressed for travelling, the lady nevertheless appears more magnificent, than he has heretofore seen her. Her hair is piled high, and arranged with care — Her dress new, and *a la mode*. — Jewels dangle at her ears — Of magnificent purity, though not of ostentatious size.

— The pleasure is entirely mine, Mr Peach, says she. — But were you not expecting us? I sent Caspar this morning with the message. He spoke to your boy, I think.

Caspar remains astride his horse, behind the lady. He holds himself quite still, and fixes a respectful gaze, upon nothing at all.

— No matter, says Mr Peach, no matter at all. You are just as welcome unannounced as announced. — I must only beg your pardon for the entire want of preparations. But you see, my house is no place of ceremony — Nothing need interfere with the sincere pleasure your visit brings. — Please — Come within. — Mr Peach offers his hand, to help the lady from the saddle.

— There has been a misunderstanding, I fear, says she, with a look towards Caspar, which he appears studious not to acknowledge. She accepts the hand, and descends. — I shall accept your invitation notwithstanding. I have been most particularly eager to see you again, Mr Peach.

The gentleman is flattered by the sentiment. — With further polite apologies and reciprocations, his hospitality is accepted, and Miss Farthingay and Caspar come to the house.

It is only now that Mr Peach reflects, how fortuitous is Clary's absence. He could not possibly have brought Miss Farthingay and the maid under one roof — Miss Farthingay, who might once have known her almost as a sister!

The lady pauses at the threshold.

— I trust, she says, that Mrs Peach will not be at all inconvenienced, by unexpected company?

— Not in the least, says Mr Peach, and explains that his wife must remain above-stairs, perfectly undisturbed, but that whatever passes below will be no intrusion on her rest.

Mr Peach knows by experience, that the general run of persons, on hearing this information, will look aside, and murmur the usual hurried condolences; for there is something in the condition of sickness, which produces in the healthy an effect of embarrassment, as though to speak of it were ill-omened. — He is therefore a little surprized at Miss Farthingay. She answers him with a clear countenance. — A look almost penetrating, as though she hears more meaning in Mr Peach's words, than he intended.

— Mrs Peach remains the same as ever?

— She does, says Mr Peach.

— There is no decline, God forbid, yet no remission, nor improvement?

— Just as you say, Miss Farthingay. — I do not complain of it.

Miss Farthingay's steady gaze continues to suggest a significance he cannot grasp. — It must be a very great grief to you, she says. — But there is comfort, I must think, in constancy. The evil we are familiar with is less to be dreaded, than unknown dangers.

Miss Farthingay's sentiments are unexceptionable, and yet Mr Peach feels some aukwardness, and manages no more eloquent a reply, than to murmur his appreciation for her kindness, in general terms, and to ask whether she will enter the parlour, and accept a dish of tea.

— Will you permit one further question, concerning your wife? says she. — We have dispensed with ceremony, have we not? — I hope I may be forgiven.

Mr Peach assures her, she may speak quite freely.

— I only wonder, she says, whether Mrs Peach's baptismal name is Eliza?

Mr Peach cannot hide his surprize. — Why — he says — Yes — It is — But I cannot imagine — Forgive me, madam —

Miss Farthingay lays an hand on his arm, and steps in the house. — Good Mr Peach, she says, I shall trouble you no more with questions on a subject which can only give you pain. I wished only to satisfy myself concerning a very curious coincidence, which I have learned of during my sojourn in town. You know, sir, I am afflicted with the habit of speaking more freely than I ought. I shall at least promise to inflict no more verses upon you. — Let us enjoy tea, and talk of inconsequential things. I have been in London, and am therefore the very index of every thing worth knowing. I have at my fingers' ends all the talk of the town.

— Heavens — Miss Farthingay — I had quite forgot the occasion of your journey.* — Mr Peach conducts her into the parlour with a bow, and, looking to her hand, observes the ring upon her fourth finger. — I hope, he says, I may wish you joy?

— You may indeed, she says.

— Madam, I do so, and every good wish besides.

— I must accustom myself to *madam* now, I suppose. It has such an ugly sound. It makes me think of old age, and hypocrisy.

— You are equally remote from the one, says Mr Peach, as the other.

Miss Farthingay sighs, and seats herself, while Caspar, having surveyed the parlour, as though searching it for some concealed presence, places himself at a respectful distance beside the chair. — How gallant you are, Mr Peach, she says.

— I intended no gallantry. Each half of the compliment is plain common-sense. Your frankness you confess yourself; and as for old age, if you are within sight of it, then what hope is there for me?

— You are not so very old, says the lady, except in spirit. The soul and flesh age very differently, I believe.

Mr Peach does not agree. — Like any person who has passed thirty, he knows, that youth is another country, though they who dwell there never know it. But he keeps his opinion to himself, for he sees now that Miss Farthingay's temper is not cheerful, and he has no wish to try her.

---

* Be pleased to recall, reader, the previous visit of the man-servant Caspar, recorded in our ninth, during which that gentleman mentioned, that Miss Farthingay went to London, to be introduced among the family of her intended husband.

— For my part, she says, I cannot tell whether I must be married because I am no longer young, or whether I feel old, because I must be married.

Mr Peach cannot but remark, that the lady is very far from being in that state of giddy excitement and delightful anticipation, which is commonly supposed to be the lot of a young female, who has secured for herself the much-desired prospect of legal enslavement to an husband for the term of her natural life. With an air carefully polite, he observes, that he is pleased to hear her visit to town has met with an happy outcome.

— But, sir — If you are to *madam* me, Mr Peach, then I shall *sir* you — Do you not know, that London is the very *omphalos* of all gay society and fruitful endeavour? It was inevitable that my journey should end in profit. — Do you know the town, sir?

— I spent many of my younger years there. Mrs Peach and I had our household in London, before her illness compelled our retirement.

— I beg your pardon, Mr Peach. I must maintain my resolution, to speak of other things. — And so, while Mr Peach is occupied in preparing the dish of tea — a task which, his domestics being absent, he must necessarily perform himself — they carry on their conversation upon general subjects, while Caspar maintains a perfect, though watchful, silence.

In the ordinary course of things, such talk holds little relish for Mr Peach. He tolerates it to-day, since it is certainly preferable to the former subject of conversation, in which Miss Farthingay shewed such an interest, that is, the malady of Mrs Peach; and also because the lady herself appears unwilling to allude to that recent event, which one supposes ought to be close to her heart, *viz.* her own engagement. Nevertheless, he cannot altogether conceal his indifference to the news of the town; for, after several minutes of such talk, Miss Farthingay observes —

— It is pleasant to discuss these things with a person who has no opinion.

Mr Peach acknowledges the sally.

— You think I teaze you. I do not, I assure you. In London, the fever of party burns so hot, that every body must be either passionately in favour of a thing, or violently opposed to it, according to whether it be claimed by the ministers or the opposition. Nothing is allowed to lie beyond the two camps. The painters and poets and musicians are all owned by one faction or the other. Science and philosophy are either for Pitt or for Fox. I witnessed a dispute at a milliner's, over whether a certain hat was sufficiently patriotic. Each person holds to their opinion with the utmost ferocity. It is a wonder they do not all kill each other in duels. Whereas you, Mr Peach, are equally phlegmatic upon every subject. It is a great relief to me, although I fear it must be tedious to you, to speak of things which do not touch the heart.

— Permit me to say, Miss Farthingay, that no conversation with you can possibly be tedious.

— My permission is granted. — You may bestow your compliments in future, without hesitation. If I am to be *madam*, and *lady*, I must grow suitably vain and proud.

— May I speak as freely, on another subject?

— I would never have it otherwise.

— I fear it pertains to matters of the heart. You will not be pleased to hear it.

— Perhaps not. — But I shall bear it. I must, in justice, must I not? — for you have patiently submitted to all my talk on subjects which have been of no interest to either of us.

— Then, madam, with your pardon, I must ask, whether your own inclinations are not to be consulted in the matter of your marriage? I cannot help but observe, that you appear to accept the alliance as a thing to be tolerated, and endured, and as though it had been decreed by a power beyond your controul. Are not your prospects of happiness worthy of consideration?

— Happiness! exclaims Miss Farthingay, as though the word were a bitter jest.

— Do you care so little for it? Many reckon it a prize worth the pursuit.

— I think not many of those *many* are women, Mr Peach.

Mr Peach opens his mouth to answer — And closes it again.

— If the world were ordered to my inclination, continues Miss Farthingay, I might go on as I am, and be quite content. But the world does not permit me to be three-and-twenty for the rest of my days. I must be married, whether I will or no; and because my father is wealthy, but without influence, I must be attached to a man with influence and too little wealth, for the world also decrees that the purpose of a wife is to supply a deficiency in a man's affairs.

— I think, says Mr Peach, these are not the sentiments you will put into the mouth of your Clorinda.

— A woman may write in verse, Mr Peach, but she must live in prose.

Mr Peach is on the point of replying, that a woman has surely an equal title to happiness, as a man — or, that there are such things as *prose romances* — or some such gentle contradiction — But he feels once more, that the answer will not look well in him, and is silent.

— Do not look so solemn, I pray, Miss Farthingay says, with some effort at her usual vivacity of temper. — I am really quite content. Mr Stocks will do as well for an husband as any. He is tolerably good-natured, and possesses the very great recommendation, that his chief concern in life is to acquire favour and position, which occupy his thoughts so exclusively that I hope he will not be much concerned with his wife.

Mr Peach sits very straight. — The happy man, whom you have done the great honour of accepting, is a Mr Stocks?

— Indeed. — I guess by your look that the name is familiar.

Miss Farthingay's own gaze is suddenly attentive. Mr Peach turns aside, in some confusion. — Perhaps — he says — I thought for a moment — But I am doubtless mistaken. Though who does not know the name of Sir Nigylle Stocks? He is a great man in the ministry. — His renown has perhaps caused my mistake.

— If so, says Miss Farthingay, your mistake has brought you

nearer the truth than you suspect. I am to be a relative of Sir Nigylle. My intended is Mr Stokesay Stocks, a younger cousin to the peer, or a cousin in the second degree, or perhaps it is the third. Mama is always reminding me of it, and I continue to forget. You are surprized, Mr Peach.

— I? — No — Excuse me, madam. I congratulate you, on so distinguished a match.

— Mama is indeed in transports. She was introduced to Mr Stocks's family, in Bath, at the public ball, on her last visit there. An invitation to London was secured. I need not tire you with the particulars of the arrangement. These things are always done after the pattern, are they not? The alliance was proposed, and deemed advisable. I have been courted with enthusiasm. I was presented to the family in London. Chiefly, to Sir Nigylle. — It is a connexion of which they are jealously proud, and, indeed, on which they pin all Mr Stokesay Stocks's hopes of preferment. We dined at Stokesay House, in the grandest stile.

Mr Peach's confusion has redoubled. A strange pallor has come over his countenance.

Miss Farthingay observes him carefully — As though conscious there is something in her words, which affects him deeply.

— I know, Mr Peach, she says, that you derive no entertainment from the tattle of the town. But I think I must nevertheless tell you a story I heard, at Stokesay House. I may even say, it would be very remiss of me, were I not to repeat it to you.

— How so, madam? says Mr Peach.

— Caspar — says Miss Farthingay — Would you to look to the horses, and wait there, until I come?

The attendant bows without a word, and quits the room, and the house. Miss Farthingay waits until he is gone. — Mr Peach sits, as though turned to stone.

What can this behaviour mean?

Let us listen to Miss Farthingay. — For by the look in her eye — serious, and penetrating — We guess, that *she* knows the significance, of the story she has to tell. — The story, she will permit no one to hear, but Mr Peach himself — Not even her discreet and devoted Caspar.

— Among the company at Stokesay House, she says, I was introduced to the Lady Sophonisba Stocks. Mr Peach — It was from her, I had the tale. It is a very unhappy one. I confess I was much affected in hearing it.

Mr Peach makes no reply.

Miss Farthingay speaks very gently. — You might prefer not to hear so sad an history, enduring as you do the daily grief of your wife's illness. — Understand me, sir. You need only forbid me speak, and I shall honour your wish, for ever.

Mr Peach looks up. He meets the lady's eye in silence — Passes several moments, in reflexions equally wordless.

At last he speaks. — Miss Farthingay, I now see that the whole purpose of your visit to-day was to relate this story. I do not believe you would have formed that purpose, without the careful exercise of your judgment. Your judgment I have learned to respect; and therefore I am content to listen.

— Have you? I cannot imagine what my judgment has done, to earn your admiration. I myself find it a very unruly faculty. I hope with all my heart it has not disgraced itself, in the present instance. To lose your respect, Mr Peach, or, God forfend it, your acquaintance entirely, would be a great sorrow to me. Yet if we are to continue acquainted, as is my earnest wish, I cannot see any other course, except to repeat to you what I heard from the Lady Sophonisba.

Mr Peach again bids her proceed.

Miss Farthingay puts aside the dish of tea.

— Lady Sophonisba's husband, says she, is the nephew of Sir Nigylle, and a very rich man. You know how such people talk — The boasting, and grasping, and flaunting of any name, that reflects any glory onto themselves. Or perhaps you do not know it, Mr Peach, in which event I congratulate you, for I find it barely supportable. — The lady mentioned in passing that her own uncle is one Augustus Peach, who has been of signal service to the ministry. I could not help remarking the curious fact, that her maiden name was Peach. I told her I had but lately made the acquaintance of a gentleman of the same name, a Mr Thomas Peach of Somerset-shire. Lady Sophonisba was much amused at the coincidence, and said, it was her own brother's name. —

Here Miss Farthingay pauses a moment, to observe Mr Peach. He remains still — pale, but silent — And so, she continues.

— I agreed it was a very quaint thing, that there should be two men, with the same name, each connected after a fashion to this gathering at Stokesay House. Lady Sophonisba became serious, and said she ought not to smile at it, for her brother's history was very tragical.

Miss Farthingay pauses again, and then says — I hope I may take your silence, Mr Peach, as permission to continue.

Mr Peach nods.

— The lady's brother, says Miss Farthingay — This other Mr Thomas Peach — was, as I understood it, a man of scholarly habits. The family had intended him for the church. By the uncle's influence a good living had been procured for him, with every prospect of future preferment; awaiting only the death of the incumbent, which was soon expected. But when the time came for him to take his orders, and succeed to the position, he refused both it and them. His choice instead was to continue in the pursuit of certain obscure studies. Lady Sophonisba spoke of them in contemptuous terms. She called them fusty, and heretical, and the like. The best I could deduce from her remarks, was that he had devoted himself to antiquities, and the antient beliefs of remote peoples. — Subjects which must excite the soul of a poet, in proportion as they disgust the society of a Stokesay House. For my own part, I thought it very noble of this Mr Thomas Peach — this *other* Mr Thomas Peach — to have willingly surrendered a life of ease, and secure advancement, from the mere thirst of knowledge. — But forgive me — I ought to give the tale without commentary. I only thought it proper to mention that I did not share the opinion of Lady Sophonisba.

Miss Farthingay continues. — This other Mr Peach, her brother, retired into a modest obscurity, and for several years occupied himself exclusively in his studies. As a natural consequence of his pursuits, he became acquainted with many scholars and antiquarians of the city. Collectors of rare books, and merchants from distant harbours — Those who have copied the hiero-glyphs, and deciphered tongues as old as mankind. — There was among them a certain Turk, a Levantine, a trader in antiquities of the East. The lady Sophonisba never spoke his name. Her brother, she said, became an intimate of this gentleman, and his family. The Turk had settled in London, and married a dress-maker of the town, with whom he had a daughter, who was now of age, and used to help in the business. — Mr Peach — Shall I continue?

Mr Peach nods once more, though his heart is ice. —

— An attachment quickly grew up, between the Turk's daughter, and this other Mr Thomas Peach, as passionate on one side as the other. But the happiness of the pair was not shared by the father. He, alas, had promised his child to another, by an arrangement of many years' standing, contracted when the poor girl was barely lettered. She was to be wed to the son of a family of wealth and influence, in her father's native city; a family of such great influence that he could not, or would not, countenance any objection to their wishes, though she begged him to revoke the arrangement, and leave her free to follow her heart. But he would not be moved. — So the daughter, unable to win her father's favour, resolved to go without it, and eloped from his house, to marry Mr Peach — that other Mr Peach.

— Their union, proceeds Miss Farthingay, must have been a very happy one, if I am to judge by the expressions of the Lady Sophonisba. She did not appear to me the sort of woman given to romantic sentiments, yet she said she never knew so well-matched a pair as her brother and his Turkish wife. The young bride's name, she happened to mention, was Eliza. —

Miss Farthingay occupies herself for some moments with taking a drink of tea.

She speaks very gently.

— I say, it *was* Eliza. — I do not say, it *is*.

— I understand you, Miss Farthingay, says Mr Peach, in a very low voice. — You may continue your tale.

— Dear Mr Peach. — I only repeat what I heard, though I know all too well that such terrible events ought not to be reduced to conjecture and hearsay. — It is supposed that the implacable resentment of her father broke the poor girl's heart. Month after month of her marriage passed, and still he refused to forgive her. He would not readmit her to the family. He persisted in the cruel accusation that she had shamed him by her elopement, and was never more to be called his daughter. I do not wonder that the weight of such tyrannical displeasure became insupportable. I grieve to say, that after two years of his oppression, she could endure it no longer, but — Forgive me, Mr Peach, I beg you, for the dreadful recitation — She took her own life.

Miss Farthingay's voice, which nature made bright and vivacious, has fallen to a bare murmur.

Mr Peach presses his fingertips together, and closes his eyes, like one who seeks to forestall the flow of tears.

— If that had been all the tragedy of the tale, Miss Farthingay continues, it would have been quite enough for me. I am not one of those who takes their morbid pleasure in hearing of others' misery. It is otherwise, I fear, with Lady Sophonisba Stocks. She was unaccountably eager to give all the remainder. — How the father was found hung by his neck in his own house, but a fortnight after his unhappy daughter met the same end. It is natural to think he had been overcome by remorse, though there were some who hinted, that another hand had been at work. The family to whom his daughter had been promised, in his native city, were mortally offended. It was said they had made an open declaration, that only death could absolve the dishonour done to their name. Lady Sophonisba had heard of emissaries sent, from their city, to be the instruments of an unspeakable private revenge. — But all this must be supposition and phantasy. The only part of her conclusion, which I found worthy of interest, was that her brother vanished from London, immediately after the death of his cruel father-in-law. Indeed, Lady Sophonisba would have it that he vanished not only from the town, but every other place as well. She swore her brother had hidden himself to such good effect that not a single person knew where he had gone. His own family — She herself — could not so much as say whether he was alive or dead. — To which, Mr Peach, I would have answered, had I thought it right to answer at all, that a man bearing the burden of such a loss, could not be censured for desiring to escape all human society. I myself should never wish to intrude upon the private grief of one who had suffered so. Understand me, dear sir. — Whatever consolation he sought, I would judge him perfectly entitled to seek — Whatever respite it brought him, I would wish upon him an hundred-fold. In particular — I would, with all my heart — With *all my heart*, Mr Peach — I would bid him embrace the consolations of *imagination* —

Mr Peach cannot sit. — Impelled by inward emotion, he rises to his feet. Miss Farthingay rises also, but continues to speak, with the most fervent emphasis. —

— I am a poet. — And what is poetry, but the effort to rouse the noblest of our human affections, in the service of the shadows of phantasy, which only live and love, in the mind of she who writes, and they who read? If this man, whom fate and human malice had robbed of so dear a spouse, were to alleviate the torment of his loss, by *imagining his wife yet lived* —

— Miss Farthingay — begins Mr Peach — though his voice cracks. —

— My dear sir — My dear friend, I hope I may call you. — I shall say no more. I have dared very greatly in saying even thus much. We need never allude to it again. — But you must allow me to assure you, that if it is ever mentioned, among the family to whom I am soon to be united, that my father has a tenant, who happens to bear the same name as the Lady Sophonisba's brother, I will smile, as they will, at the curious event, and maintain, what you and I each know, that there is not the least connexion between that unfortunate brother, and Mr Thomas Peach, of Widdershins Bank. —

Mr Peach takes three rapid steps across the parlour — Seizes Miss Farthingay's hand, with rising emotion — And, having performed that gesture upon mere impulse, has no idea at all, of what he shall do next. — So stands, with his head hanging low, and the lady's bejewelled hand clasped between his two plain ones, until she softly withdraws it.

— Thank you, Mr Peach, for hearing me with patience. I think we must now depart, with even less ceremony than attended our arrival. — Not a word, if you please. When next I have the pleasure of your company, I expect to be a married lady, and we shall each have to conduct ourselves accordingly — Formal and perfectly polite. Let us prepare for it by saying no more, on *this* occasion. Good-day to you, sir. — And my best compliments to Mrs Peach also. If I may perhaps not hope to hear she is *recovered*, I rejoice to know, that she will *do no worse*. — There is no need to attend at the door. I am quite content to remove myself. — Caspar! —

With which words Miss Arabella Farthingay makes her exit, and goes out into the warm after-noon, to where her attendant waits in the road, holding the horses; and so the two of them ride away, leaving Mr Peach alone once more, in the empty house.

CHAPTER SEVENTEEN

Mr Peach has not got up from his chair, when Jem returns. — Nor yet, when Clary slips within, by the broken door at the side, though the shadows grow long, and the rooks begin to seek their roosts.

All that while he has sat, with his outward look fixed upon the ash of the untended fire. There is no mystery in the cold cinders, to have occupied him so long. The true objects of his contemplation are all *within* — In the secret expanses of his remembrance. He takes his soundings in

the dark backward and abysm of time.*

— I must beg your pardon for my absence, says Clary, standing at the door. — I shall return the day's wages.

Mr Peach looks up.

— Clary, he says, as though only then reminded, that there exists such a person in the world.

— Yes, sir. — Are you unwell? I could warm a little wine with some honey.

— You were forewarned, I suppose, of the visit of Miss Farthingay?

Clary plucks at her smock.

— I could not have Bella see me. I knew not what else to do but take myself away.

---

* Shakespear's Tempest.

— It was wisely done, says Mr Peach, though his tone is gloomy. — You may keep your wages.

— Is Bella to visit often?

Mr Peach's spirits are heavy, and he has no relish for conversation. — I think, he says, Miss Farthingay will take great pains never to come under this roof again. I should like to spend the remainder of the evening in solitude. You may keep to your room. I will take no supper to-day.

Clary bobs her head, but, instead of withdrawing, stands a moment longer at the door.

— I fear the visit was not an happy one, she says.

The tide of Mr Peach's emotions will be contained no longer. It reaches the height — Trickles over — Then all at once, pours forth like a cataract.

— Be thankful — says he, in a trembling voice — That, when the ghosts of *your* past miseries approach, you have only to walk out the door, to escape them. — Be grateful, Clary! that you have torn away every tie, which might have bound you to the misfortunes of your former days. Be grateful that you are young — That the shadows behind you are a child's troubles, of such brief duration, that they never grew substantial, nor have attached themselves unbreakably at your heels, like chains of iron! Flee them whenever you may. — I shall never chide you for it. Nay, I shall bid you run the faster. For when we cannot escape what lies behind — It becomes a living darkness at our back, and haunts without mercy — without respite —

— Sir — Clary says, with an equal access of passion — I could flee ten times an hundred miles from Grandison Hall, and never be rid of its horrors. I have left no shadows behind — I cannot leave them — I carry them within myself. My shadow is myself — And will be, wherever I go — Unless *you*, sir — Unless you banish its haunting, and save me!

To this Mr Peach has no reply. — Which we do not think very surprizing.

— Leave me, he says, at last. — I must be alone.

273

Clary retires without another word, to the small room behind the parlour.

Mr Peach is left to his gloomy meditations, until the day draws to its close, and he retires also, to —

Reader —

Shall we say, that Mr Peach remains in solitude, when he goes at last to his bed?

Or — shall we *not*?

Of one thing you must be certain. You have heard the report of it yourself, in our last. You may enquire where ever else you please, and will, we assure you, hear in every place the same truth repeated.

It is confirmed, beyond doubt, that the wife of Mr Thomas Peach, scholar and antiquarian, formerly of London — that same Mr Thomas Peach, who is nephew to Augustus Peach, and brother to Sophonisba — who married Eliza, daughter to a merchant of Aleppo; — That, we say, the wife of Mr Thomas Peach, is DEAD. — Discovered hung by the neck, in their own house, some two years past. — Presumed dead by her own hand, from the grief inflicted by a parent's unkindness. — Presumed so, since no one can say otherwise —

No one, save Mr Thomas Peach himself —

Whatever the cause — The effect remains the same — Mrs Eliza Peach, is *no more*.

Yet you have heard her speak! —

Recall, that we advised you, near the outset of our narrative, not to be too hasty with your conclusions, concerning our hero's marital state. —

We can no longer equivocate. We must reveal the truth at last. — And yet, how can we confess in plain language, a thing, which is almost beyond the sense of words?

We shall describe to you, the exact manner of Mr Peach's conversations, with his wife. —

Each night, he ascends the stair. — Locks the door at his back, for such frail intimacies brook no disturbance from the every-day world — Lights no candle, for the same reason. Finding his way by touch, and by habit, he extracts five items, from a box, kept in the old oak wardrobe.

The items are, a tooth; a lock of black hair; a ring, set with a single stone of modest size; a pin; and a small shallow bowl.

He kneels by the bed. — There is a table adjacent, marked all over, like the walls and beams of the room, with many lines of writing, in white chalk. Here he places ring, hair, and tooth. He commences murmuring certain words. — They are the same words, written again and again, on every surface facing the bed. Do not ask what they are. — We know, for we cannot help but hear them, as we overwatch the scene, night after night, but we wish we could forget them, and no inducement, no threats, nor tortures, can ever bring us to repeat them! — As Mr Peach whispers the terrible phrase, he pricks his thumb with the pin, and lets a drop of his blood fall in the bowl.

And, then —

Then Mrs Peach comes.

She does not come, in the flesh.

The mortal substance of Mrs Eliza Peach is beyond recall, except for that tooth, and the lock of black hair. Mrs Peach is — DEAD — and laid in the unceremonious ground.

Nevertheless, it is she who comes. It is she who speaks. — She, to whom Mr Peach replies.

Our eye may be baffled by the perpetual shadow of the room, but our ear cannot be deceived. We know the very tenor of Mrs Peach's voice. — Easy and soft, as befits a sound produced by no mortal instrument.

They converse again this night, as every night. It is the chit-chat of any fond familiar couple. If we suspected you doubted us, we would set down every word of it, and, like certain gentlemen at the bar, wear down your doubts with the mere dullness of our recitation, until they were all exhausted. But you must not disbelieve us. If you do — close the book at once. Proceed not a page further. — For, if you imagine we have deceived you — if you recollect those previous chapters, in which we have recorded some of the talk between Mr Peach and his wife, and think, it was all merely our invention — Why, then you may as well doubt every word we tell you.

Perhaps there never was such a person as Tho.s Peach, nor such a county as Somerset-shire — perhaps there never was a year seventeen hundred and eighty-five — Perhaps we ourselves do not exist — AND NOR DO YOU.

The plain truth is, that Mr Peach *speaks with his dead wife.*

— You are low again to-day, Tom.

— Am I, my dear?

— You may hide it from yourself, but not from me. Had you not troubles about the house, and money? I believe you told me of it just now.

— You are quite right.

— So I thought. I am always right. Like the Pope, in Rome.

Though Mr Peach is not much in the mood for levity, he smiles a little, and is silently thankful for Mrs Peach's merry disposition.

— The Pope would not agree with you on certain points of doctrine, I venture. But if you were to dispute with him, I would certainly take your party.

— I hope you would. A poor sort of husband, not to support his own wife, against the Pope!

— Very true.

— You may count on me always to take your part also. What is it that weighs upon you so to-day? Tell me, and I shall dismiss it for you. Are we still to be cast out of the house? I shall refuse to be moved.

— I am taking what measures I can to prevent it. Another journey to Bristol will be necessary. But I wasn't thinking of it to-day. If I am heavy, I fear there is another reason.

— Another! what further troubles have you run into?

— No difficulties, Liza, I promise you. Only I had this afternoon a visitor come from London. It could not but remind me of the life we had there.

— Then what has made you sad? I'm sure I remember every day of it, and can think of not one morsel to regret. Our little house, in D____-road, by the Salutation and Cat! — were we not each quite happy there?

— We were, every moment. But to remember past happiness, is also to be reminded that it *is* past. — Mr Peach sighs.

— I don't find it so.

— I am glad to hear it.

— I have only to think of those days, and I feel their delight at my fingers' ends. Oh, Tom, only remember those times when I and you —

Reader, we shall not continue to set down what we hear. It is enough to know, that we hear it. — As we have heard the like, across the course of some hundreds of other nights, in the low room above-stairs. — The *nocturnal conversation*, between Tho.s Peach, Esq., and his late beloved.

The above fragments of their talk are, nevertheless, worthy of your consideration. Set aside your wonder, that Mrs Peach speaks *at all*, and reflect upon what you have just heard her say. — Recollect, indeed, that it is not the first time she has been heard to express such joyful sentiments, while thinking of her married life.

— Very pretty — you mutter to yourself, perhaps — Very pretty indeed — But I can discover no special significance, in such common-place language!

Reader — Ask yourself thus. —

Are these the sentiments, of one so oppressed by grief and shame, that they drove her to *self-slaughter*?

Is this Mrs Peach, who remembers so fondly the years of her marriage, and declares them to have been uniformly happy — this Mrs Peach, whose temper is playful and teasing — Is this the same woman, who, according to popular opinion, put a noose to her own neck, rather than endure the misery of a father's unyielding resentment?

Or — Is there *another* explanation, for her tragic demise?

We bid you attend closely. — We approach the heart, of several mysteries.

What if Eliza Peach did *not* take her own life?

What if her life was taken *from* her — By other hands — Secret, and invisible, and merciless?

What if those to whom she had been promised — that family of influence and renown, in her father's city of Aleppo — Could not, or would not, forget the stain upon their honour, made by her defiance? — Could not, or would not, permit the blot to endure — But must wash it away, in the BLOOD of the offending party?

What if that family engaged the services of — that fabled brotherhood of assassins — the *hashishin*?

The *hashishin*! — Syllables shrouded in terror, and whispered with dread!

None who enters that secret guild, is ever seen again. No tale escapes from among them, to give the historian any hint where they may be found, or who commands them, or what antient charters they follow.

To the ears of the world, they are no more than a rumour — a fire-side tale, to frighten children with — Nay, a mere phantasy — an invention, no more to be found in nature, than the cave of *Aladdin*, or the ship of *Sinbad* — Every where dismissed as an old and superstitious fable — Were it not for the signature, left by their hand — written in characters of *blood*. — Evidence as incontrovertible, as death itself.

Perhaps there was heard a murmur of dark silk over moonlit stone — Perhaps, the perfumed smoke wavered, as though a body had passed by, disturbing for a moment the desart air. — No trace else — But, lo! the cloaked fist reaches out, from its place of perfect concealment — immaculate in speed and silence, like the forked viper — and — STRIKES! — And melts away, as swiftly as it came — Leaving only whisper, and rumour, and dread — And, on the marble floor, the victim. — The blood emptied from his heart, or the breath choked from her mouth!

The one singled out by the *hashishin*, is as certainly doomed, as though he hung by an hair above the fathomless abyss. From the hour the bargain is struck, and the price paid — no matter where in the world he may fly — he walks as it were within his own coffin. It matters not, how high the walls he hides beneath. It profits him not, to set a guard at every door and window. He may offer his soul to God, or to the Devil, with anguished prayers, if only the one power or the other will save him from his fate. — Neither avails him. For he may be said to have heard the words, which poor mad Cowper* heard uttered by a divine voice, in his torments of delirium — *Actum est de te, periisti* — WITH YOU IT IS DECIDED: YOU SHALL PERISH.

We are not privy to every detail of the hideous transaction. Our historian eye is tethered, to the circuits transcribed by the life of Mr Tho.s Peach, in *space*, as well as in *time*. We cannot peer among the streets and houses of Aleppo. For all we know, you are better acquainted with them than we. — That fabled Levant, where great cities grew, and arts and commerce flourished, when the inhabitants of these rude islands were yet sunk in barbarism, and worshipped stumps and stones!

We know only so much — That a bargain *was* struck. The price was paid, to the deadly brotherhood. — Their emissaries were dispatched, to London, where Mr and Mrs Peach had established themselves, in modest means, though rich in the bliss of love.

Barely twenty months had they, to enjoy the happiness of well-matched souls, before the relentless hatred of their invisible enemy found them out — and struck. —

The verdict publicly recorded, was death by suicide. You have heard Miss Farthingay's report of the common opinion. — Mrs Peach had been disavowed by her family. The grief of it must have been insupportable, and led her to such distraction of mind, that she hanged herself.

Mr Peach, though in the extremest agony of loss, knew otherwise.

* The amiable poet, author of 'The Task,' &c.

Not a single circumstance, pointed to the horrid truth of *murder*. Yet he knew nevertheless. — He knew his wife's cheerful and contented disposition. He knew her heart, better than any other, and was certain, that it nourished no poisoned seed, which might have grown into so mortal a violence of despair.

In the midnight of his soul, he looked about him — And saw only *one* hand at work, in the execution of the foul deed — *One* person, who in their fixed and unrelenting hatred might have compassed the death of Mrs Peach — their own child! — *One* man, on whom he determined to exact the awful justice, the law would not provide!

Merely a few days after the death of the daughter, the father too was discovered hanged. — As you have heard.

This second tragedy also, was declared a suicide.

Reader — We shall say no more about it. The dreadful act, to which Mr Peach may have been driven, in his misery and grief, is not our present subject. We make no accusation. — We judge not — nor do we excuse. — Nor speculate, concerning the nature of the deed — by what powers it may have been aided, and encompassed. —

But you may now guess — if you chuse to — Why it was, that Mr Thomas Peach left London in haste, and in secret, and retired to a place so humble and secluded, as Widdershins Bank.

What is more to our purpose, you may perhaps now understand, why he was much affected by that part of his uncle's letter, which mentioned that he was enquired after, by associates of his quondam father-in-law. — And why a British country gentleman, of modest rank, and no particular renown, lives in terror of *strangers*, of *mysterious or foreign appearance*!

Meanwhile — we are very glad to see, that you have not quit our pages in disgust, because we have introduced among our *dramatis personae*, a dead woman.

Experience teaches us this incontrovertible truth of human nature, that we may accustom ourselves to any thing, if sufficiently exposed to it. Indeed, now the first transports of incredulity are past, perhaps your curiosity begins to awaken. It is, after all, a remarkable occurrence. — At this very instant, you, good reader, hold in your hands, in the form of our book, a *proof* — That in the frame of our natures there is an immortal soul, which expires not with the flesh. — An article of *faith*, for very many — of *belief*, for a much smaller number — but of *knowledge*, for *none*! save Thomas Peach himself — Until now.

We should not be surprized to discover, that certain questions begin to occur to you. —

Perhaps some of them shall be answered, before the end of our last chapter.

But for the present, we shall leave Mr Peach to his rest, or to whatever fraction of rest is allowed him, among his unwished-for remembrances of sorrows and sins gone by.

For us, too, it will be at best a brief respite. — For the tragic events we have at last exposed, will no more lie quietly in the past, than poor Eliza Peach in her unconsecrated plot of earth. Their consequences persist — Their reach is long — And the visitation feared by Mr Peach is, alas, much closer to hand than he dreams. — As he and you shall discover together, from a most unexpected source, in our next chapter.

CHAPTER EIGHTEEN

On, then, with our narrative! — Once more we spin the planetary orb beneath us, bringing the island of Britain out of shadow, and into the light of the vernal sun. It is morning, up and down our fair kingdom. — Nor any corner of it fairer, on this particular day, than our little nook of Somerset-shire, for the fields and wooded banks are in their finest spring dress, under a Venetian sky.

Into this picture we must now introduce an entirely new personage, and one who has no small part to play, in the crisis that follows.

A *new* personage, we say, though you have heard his name, once or twice. But now he is to appear in his own person, flesh and blood. — His blood, indeed, is of particular prominence, for it will be heated beyond its usual condition, in the course of our scene. — Leeches would have been called for, in those days, to draw off the excess.

To our purpose —

The morning, we have already mentioned, is very fine. It is that rare weather, in these vaporous and cloud-kissed isles of ours, which positively demands that a gentleman of leisure, however idle, must take his exercise. And lo! here is an excellent specimen of a leisured gentleman, riding into the secluded valley of Widdershins Bank.

We know his type at a glance — By the costly elegance of his dress, and the size and splendour, of the animal betwixt his legs — By the careless curls upon his bare head, and the fresh, well-fed complexion, belonging to those who feel no want, nor ever will. — And, most of all, by a certain upright ease in his carriage, as though his mortal substance is infused by the very quintessence of *superiority*. It holds him high, and makes him overlook every neighbouring object; for, according to the laws of nature, when one thing is superior, every thing beside it must necessarily be *inferior*. — We see the instinctive apprehension of this simple law, written in the face of our rider, and emitted in every direction from his person, like the magnetic fluid in the aether.

He rides without haste. If we were called upon to judge, we would guess the preponderance of idleness in nature to be above the median, even among the general class of gentlemen of leisure. His figure, we admit to be well-formed, strong, manly, and youthful. But it is evident from these mere few moments of observation, that the exercise he is presently taking, falls very much more to his horse's part than his own. He goes at the exact pace, indicating one who has *nothing to do*. Were it slower, we should suspect some reluctance — a pensive tardiness — A mind preyed on, by unwelcome thoughts of what awaits at the terminus of the ride. Were it more rapid — Well — we need not enumerate all the purposes, served by the varying degrees of haste. No — our rider is, with the most exquisite precision of science, poised so exactly between hurry and delay, that there can be not the slightest suggestion of either. — Do you not hear, that the very intervals of the horse's shoes upon the earth spell out a message, in the language of motion? which says, *I ride thus, because I wish to, but I might as well be doing any thing else — or nothing — 'Tis all one to me, whether I stop or go on — I don't care — Heigh ho!*

The languid pace, concerning which we have been so particular, brings our rider over the rise in the road, and down to the verdant bottom of the valley, where the elder-trees flourish their adornment of white lace.

Now, it so happens, that Clary has gone out to cut some switches of willow, from the coppice beside the stream; and, while our rider is yet some little distance from the house, she steps onto the road before him, with a bundle of sticks in her arms. For her greater convenience in traversing the damp ground, she has divested herself of her stockings, and is clad only in a shirt of Jem's, belted by a length of horse-leather.

We have described the effect produced by these humble farmer's weeds, upon the person of Clarissa Riddle, as highly ridiculous. — But we must acknowledge, that on a late spring day, amid the wholesome Arcadian delights of this modest landskip — the winding track, and the low neat house in the middle distance, and the pleasantly disposed masses of the trees, together not unworthy of the brush of a *Ruysdael* — The appearance she makes, with her legs as bare as her head, and a loose white smock girdled at the waist, has a certain sylvan charm. — She might, at a distance, do for one of the pretty shepherdesses, that disport themselves among the canvasses of *Poussin*. By a trick of the light, and the day's air, the simplicity of her dress shews not so much risible, as — *classical*.

— Upon my word! says the gentleman of leisure, and halts his passage, in order to cast several lengthy glances of appreciation at the vision before him.

Against our every expectation, Clary lowers her head, and makes a kind of curtsey, and stands aside to let the gentleman pass, with a murmur of — Good after-noon, my lord.

The leisurely rider continues his examination. He is in no hurry to ride on —Nor, indeed, to do any thing, as we have explained already. At this very instant, he can think of no occupation more interesting, than looking at the bare legs of a young country woman. — Therefore — look at them, he shall.

The gentleman's behaviour does not surprize us. It is quite otherwise, with Clary. — We have not heretofore noticed in her character many indications, of a modest and deferential temper. Yet here she stands, in the grasses and weeds beside the road, to all appearances waiting for the gentleman to ride past; and her head is bowed low, as though she dared not give offence, by presuming to look upon his magnificence. — Although it may be, that she adopts this posture, in order to conceal her *mouth* from the rider's gaze.

The gentleman's inspection proceeds.

The maid continues to wait. —

It is quite unexpected. This humble patience — Where has it sprung from? We would not be much more greatly astonished, were she to pull a penny-whistle from her pocket, and play a jig.

We have also observed, that Clary is reluctant in the extreme, to speak in the presence of strangers. An hesitation quite forgivable, considering the effect produced by the sight of her organs of speech, upon those not forewarned of her disfigurement. Yet, behold! not only does she submit, without complaint, to the gentleman's unhurried investigation — But, after an interval, addresses him, though with her head still low, and somewhat averted.

— If it please you, my lord, she says, I must take these switches to the house.

— That house there?

— My master's house, my lord.

— Your master's, hey? What's your name, girl?

— Clarissa, sir. — She curtseys once more, as far as her inelegant dress allows.

Has she gone down to the coppice of osiers, and been stolen away by the fairies, and *replaced*, by this meek and blushing changeling? —

We assure you, reader, she has not.

Our rider, you may well imagine, shares none of our surprise. He thinks it the most natural thing in the world, that the country hinds should bow to him, and speak low, and call him lord. Indeed, he particularly expects this behaviour, from the *female* hinds; among certain other expectations, which we shall not at present specify.

— A pretty name, says he.

— My lord, says she.

— A pretty name, for a pretty thing. Do you see this guinea? — He plucks a coin from a purse, and turns it in the sun.

— Oh, sir, says Clary, in tones of awe-struck wonder, and turning up her face, I never saw so shining a coin.

There can be no further doubt. — Either Miss Clarissa Riddle has struck her head on a tree, and lost her wits by the blow; or — She acts a part.

Have we not once before had cause to call her a *perfect camel-eon?* — We think, the latter explanation is much the likelier.

Perhaps we ought not to wonder at it. For, when we consider the matter, is not the whole engine of society — the machinery, which links the greater parts to the least — the design, which determines how each element must move, within the orbit of the next — To speak without metaphor — is not our whole *system* of pre-eminence, and rank, and deference, and obedience, sustained entirely by the acting of parts? The great man must play the great man, or his lustre tarnishes, and he falls from greatness. The servant must bob and look down, or she loses her place. The tradesman must flatter those whose custom he solicits, and bully those whose services he requires, or he shall get no where with either. — It is no very original observation, we acknowledge, but, as with many a common-place, it has turned somewhat worn and stale, only because it remains serviceable.

But we must resume our narrative. — For, in raising her head to eye the guinea, and praise its golden gleam, like some rustic goggling at the tawdry gilt of a strolling player, Clary has allowed the gentleman a glimpse of her face.

— By Jove! says he — You are bruised about the lips!

— Oh, no, says she, hanging her head again, It's only my birth-mark, which I had since I was born.

— Let me see, Clarissa.

— 'Tis fearful ugly, my lord.

You must imagine, reader, the beauty of the day, and of the scene. All the warm gold of a summer sun floods into the pleasant valley bottom. Even the white dust of the road, appears to shine. Amid this glory of nature, the stain upon Clary's face shews with far less of horror, than we have seen in it heretofore.

You may also consider, that the gentleman's interest in Clary's person perhaps tends less towards her mouth, than her *inferior* parts.

For one reason or another — He appears not much discomposed by the view of her face. Indeed, he is disposed to be gallant, and descend to a compliment.

— I say it is not. You are altogether a pretty thing. You should like a coin like this, I think, Clarissa.

— I wouldn't dare like it.

— You might very well dare like it, and you might dare use it, too, and buy a pretty dress, don't you know. Does your master treat you badly, that you have nothing to wear?

— Lord, no, sir, he's a good master.

— I hope he does not beat you about the cheeks, and fetch you that bruise.

— Lord, no, she says, and hangs her head down once more, as though in shame. — 'Tis only my old mark.

A *cameleon* indeed! — Had we never seen her before this moment, we would swear, she was nothing but a plain doltish Jill, with no more wits than her milking-pail.

The gentleman does not require her to raise her head again. If others chuse to address him, in a servile attitude, he will not object. — Moreover, there is a certain pleasing charm, in the disposition of her neck and shoulders, and the fall of the maid's unbound hair. — It draws the eye, *downwards*.

The gentleman fancies he might like just such a maid, about his own house.

— You might have this guinea, he says. — He tosses it in the air, idly, and catches it again, just as idly.

We here anticipate a protest. — It may be objected, that the latter act, that is, the catching of the coin, cannot but be *idle*, because it requires no *effort* — the labour being all performed, by that force of attraction, which compels all raised objects to return earthwards. — And therefore, that our application of the adverb is a redundancy. Nevertheless, we maintain that there is something essentially *lazy*, in the mere manner of the gentleman's holding out his hand, to receive the falling coin. — It is as though he knows, by right, that the grand universal force, whose mysteries have been penetrated by the genius of *Newton*, will do by him as it ought, and return his money to its proper place.

— I don't dream of such things, my lord.

— Don't you? Perhaps you might.

— Please you, sir, I'm to take these switches to the house.

— You shall tell me its name first. I might chuse to ride this way again.

— The house's name, my lord? This is called Widdershins Bank.

— Upon my word!

The gentleman looks about, with a satisfied air. — It appears, that Clary has named the very place he proposed to himself as the object of his journey — Insofar as his ride may be said to have had any thing so *definite*, as a purpose.

— Might I take in the switches, sir?

— I think your pretty arms were made to hold something better, Clarissa. But you may walk, and I shall ride behind you. I wish to look at your master's house.

Such may indeed be his desire, but we think it equally possible, that he wishes to keep other objects in view, by directing Clary to walk on her way in front. Be that as it may — The short distance is traversed without further incident, and our gentleman of leisure comes up alongside Mr Peach's dwelling, which he surveys with an inexpressive look. His countenance, we may add, is not naturally expressive. It has the dullness of contentment — Like a love poem, addressed to a three-years' spouse.

— Here is where you ply your broom, Clarissa, and wash the pots?

— I oughtn't speak so long with a fine lord in the road, before the house. — Clary pronounces this becoming sentiment with a sort of simper.

Reader — If you are in some difficulty, imagining the Miss Clarissa Riddle, with whom you are already acquainted, in the character of a *simperer* — Believe us, when we repeat, we should not have credited it ourselves, were we not witnessing it with our own necromantic gaze.

— You know you need not fear any impropriety. A fine gentleman always acts with honour. You may speak with me, or do any thing, girl, and it will all be quite honourable, don't you know.

— I must go in, says Clary again.

— Must you? — I shall give you leave, if you must. But tell me first, should you like to be maid in a great house, where every thing is fine, instead of this draughty old relic?

— I don't know, my lord.

— Think upon it, while you sweep. You might be like — what d'ye call her — in the nurse's tale. D__n me, I forget her name — The poor humble baggage that sweeps the floors, and is made a princess, with fine cloaths and pretty shoes.

— Like Pamela, my lord?*

— Silly piece. 'Tis some French name, or Italian — 'Tis not the name of some village drab.

Mr Peach now emerges, having heard from within the unexpected noise of conversation in the road. At his appearance, Clary beats a swift and demure retreat, towards the broken larder door. We would be curious to observe her, for the next several minutes — if only to assure ourselves, that she resumes the character, in which we have formerly known her — or, *one* of those characters — But our story requires us to attend to the gentlemen.

Mr Peach greets the visitor with due courtesy.

— I suppose you are the tenant here? says the latter. — I did not expect to find a gentleman.

---

* Clary's allusion to the heroine of Richardson, is hardly consistent with the character of the sheep-witted rustic, which she appears to have adopted, during these last several pages. Yet there is no danger of arousing the gentleman's suspicion. — For he seems perfectly ignorant of that famous tale, of *Virtue Rewarded*. We would guess, his library is not extensive.

Mr Peach conceals his surprize at this somewhat less than courteous observation — And merely agrees, that the house is his.

— This is Widdershins Bank, they say?

Mr Peach will not contradict them.

The visitor turns himself as far to one side as he may, without any suggestion of discomfort, and then to the other; and having thus completed his survey of the surroundings, says, — The land is poor. But, you know, it might be inclosed, and cultivated, and then be of some use. I have seen mutton and wool in these parts.

— May I enquire, sir, whether you have any business, that brings you to my door?

— Oh! business! none in the world! Only passing, you know, and looking, and happened to fall in with that girl of yours. Curate, I suppose?

— No, sir, she is the house-maid.

Mr Peach's answer is accompanied with not the smallest alteration in his habitual sober and somewhat melancholy air; so that the visitor is for several moments at a loss to know, whether it constitutes a jest; it being impossible to construe the words otherwise, according to reason and grammar — And yet he detects no index of a sporting sally, such as a smile, or a wink, or a slap of the sides, or a good hearty *Ha-ha!* — These being the currency of wit and jolly persiflage, among his fellow bucks and rake-hells. The interval of some seconds, to which we have alluded, proves insufficient to resolve the puzzle; and so our gentleman, who is not in the habit of applying an excess of mental effort, where it is unwarranted, gives it up.

— But, yourself, sir, he says. — I think you are the curate? Your dress, sir. I'm the devil of a fellow for noticing things. Man of the cloth, hey? Your humble dwelling honours it, sir. — Honours the vocation. I hate to see these puffed-up parsons. Buckles, and equipages! — Not Biblical.

— There are carriages mentioned in the Old Testament, I believe, says Mr Peach, though not, to my recollection, in the

New. As to buckles, I think it is said of the Baptist, that he professed himself unfit to latch the shoes of the Saviour. But I cannot speak with authority on the scriptures, for I am not the curate.

— No, indeed? — The gentleman appears not the least out of countenance, to discover that his powers of *noticing* have misled him. — Whom do I have the honour?

Mr Peach finds himself disinclined to shew this visitor the courtesy, which that gentleman appears to consider unnecessary on his own part. He makes the very slightest of bows, and turns on his heel without ceremony, saying only, My name, sir, is Thomas Peach, and I have business to attend to within-doors, and so wish you good-day.

— No! exclaims the visitor. — Thomas Peach! the very name!

Mr Peach halts again.

Whether it is the gentleman's sudden outburst of animation, that holds him back. — Or whether, it is an *instinct of danger* — a romantic notion! yet not, we think, altogether without foundation in nature — We cannot say — And no more can he.

— *Peach*, d'ye say? — and *Thomas*, before it?

— Has the name some meaning to you, sir?

— Why, it's the very devil of an amusing thing, and just happened this morning! I passed a brace of blackguards at a gate. Murky-looking scoundrels — And, what d'ye think they say to me? *Thomas Peach* — *Thomas Peach!* Nor in the king's English neither, they spoke like foreign fellows, I knew it by their moustaches. It sounded just like *doormouse, fish*, ha! ha! ha! Thought they were mad beggars, ha! Doormouse! Fish! Be off with you, rascals, I says, I've no mouse nor fish nor beef nor bread, nor any thing for such as you. I was of a mind to give them a fine whipping. But, you know, they bow, and pull their moustaches, and have on with their *Thomas Peach* — *Where lives Thomas Peach?* — *We seek Thomas Peach* —

The gentleman continues his anecdote, with which he is evidently delighted. Mr Peach does not hear him.

We need not tell you why. —

His vision swims, and grows dark. — He has the distinct phantasy, that his feet have sunk some inches in the earth, and the cold ground opens below him, preparing to receive the rest.

— And, by thunder, the gentleman continues, to conclude his comical tale — Very same day — Along the road — Stop to pass the while with a pretty maid — Turn over the next card, and here you are! Thomas Peach himself! Or — shall I say — Doormouse, Fish, ha, ha! Nothing has ever been so amusing. Acquaintances of yours, the moustachio'd rogues, I suppose? But no, sir, I only jest, ha!

Mr Peach has so far collected himself, as to be able to enquire when the interesting encounter occurred, and how far off?

The leisurely gentleman is vague. — He is not much concerned with either time, or distance, having so great a store of the former, that he is easily able to expend it in overcoming any hindrance, presented by the latter. The best Mr Peach is able to ascertain, is that the men were met several hours past, and some miles distant.

He thinks — They may be nearby, *now*.

— It will be *to-night*, he thinks. — Or, *to-day*. — Only pray, that they wait until the hours of darkness!

— Ha — says the gentleman, infinitely contented — Well, sir — Mr Thomas Peach — I am delighted to know you, sir — To see Mr Doormouse Fish, going on *two* legs! ha, ha, ha! Excellent! going, upon two legs! For the mouse goes on four, and the other on none at all — D__n me, it's as good as the old riddle of the sphinx!* And besides, your girl is a charming piece. — Though, you ought to cloathe her better, you know. For if she goes about with her naked legs, it may fall to some other fellow to — cover her — ha! ha! Upon my word, this is the wittiest day. I am Stokesay Stocks, sir, and honoured — honoured. We shall know each other

---

* A *classical* jest, which like this our fine gentleman's *modern* one, turns upon numbers of legs. — But you know your Sophocles, reader. We need not tell you, that the author of that old riddle, did not end well. Whether our new jester be similarly fated — We shall see.

better. You may remember my name. — In short time I expect to be master at Grandison Hall, and this land belongs to that estate, you know. We shall improve it — Cultivate it. What d'ye say, sir — Shall we turn the higher fields over to *doormice* — and make below a pool for *fish*? — Ha!

The gentleman, who thus reveals himself to be the intended husband of Miss Arabella Farthingay, and whose day's ride, we may infer, has been intended as a leisurely survey of those estates, which are in time to become his inheritance, continues a little further in this humorous vein, and then, takes his leave, and departs, immensely satisfied with his adventure.

You may well imagine, that the sentiments of Tho.s Peach, are of a very different water.

The day, so long dreaded — the day, of NEMESIS — Beyond question, it has come at last.

The emissaries of his vengeful enemies are close by his very door.

— Yet, thinks he — I am greatly fortunate, that I have by mere accident been granted some warning — Some foresight, of their approach. My beloved Eliza had no such fortune —

And yet, what hope has he? What avails it, that he knows the men are near? — perhaps, observing him, from the shadows of the woods above, at this very instant! —

The *hashishin* are merciless — Relentless — Unfailing —

Is this to be the END, of Thomas Peach?

He might be wise, to embrace a philosophical resignation — Faced with a sentence so certain, and so near. But he is *not* resigned. No — Not while he yet lives — Not while there is any prospect of life, however dark and remote. He has perhaps some few hours, to save himself. — The advantage may count for nothing, but he must try it. He must devise some *plan*. —

Alas! have we not already remarked, that Mr Peach is not blessed with rapidity of wits? Give him but his leisure, and he will unlock any conundrum — resolve any block. — Yet when each passing second beats in his ear, like the funereal drum-beat, which calls the condemned man to the gallows, his contemplations flounder, and his thoughts go racing about the caverns of his brain in frantic disorder, as rats scamper this way and that, in the belly of a burning ship. He racks his brains. — His brains rack him in return — Each tormenting the other, and as fruitlessly. — He imagines the silken cord at his neck — or perhaps it will be four inches of steel, cold as ice. — My Eliza! he cries, in despair — Soon I shall join you!

— Yet — he thinks — what if I *shall not?* —

The prospect that he might lose his beloved a second time, drives him to a phrenzy. He must find a means of escape. — He must *live.* —

There is no *Newton*, who will calculate the laws that govern the motions of the mind. We have each within us a Chaos, like that which went before creation, impenetrable to order and light. — From somewhere within that abysm, impelled by some force no art of ours can name — an IDEA arises.

There is, Mr Peach sees, one unexpected conjunction of circumstances — one stroke of wayward fortune — which he may turn to his advantage. — One single possibility, of saving himself from the assassins, *for ever.* —

He regards his idea, for a fraction of an instant, with confusion — with awe — with desperate gratitude — And then, embraces it.

There is not time to ask himself, whether it is a *wise* idea. You, reader, may have your reservations, once you have seen it put into effect. But Mr Peach can neither hesitate nor scruple.

He stands for several seconds quite still, with his eyes shut fast.

He is contemplating each precise thing, that must now be performed.

He thinks — I must first send a letter to the inn, with all possible haste.

— Jem must leave the house, he thinks. — I shall send him to his family, for a day.

— And Clary too — She must be commanded to go, and not return before noon to-morrow.

— But Clary has no other place to go.

— Yet leave she must. She has been used to spending the night abroad. — It is only one night.

— And Jem may take the letter to the inn, with a packet of my cloaths, before he goes home. He must hurry — I shall tell him to run every step. There is not a moment to be lost.

Mr Peach goes to the door, to call for Jem, and instruct him to carry the letter, with all possible haste — And then remembers, that he has not yet written it.

He admonishes himself. — Be calm, Thomas — For any misstep now will be your *last*.

We must now attend, with great care, to our hero's every motion. —

He fetches his riding-coat, and his hat, and a pair of his own black breeches. These articles he assembles in a small pile, to make a package, which he ties up in cloth and string. He then seats himself at his *escrutoire*, and, after another pause, to settle both hand and heart, takes up pen and paper, and writes a few rapid lines.

We shall peer over his shoulder, while the ink dries, and read the sheet ourselves. —

> *Brother Jefferson,*
> *In haste and confidence I send you this instruction, and the packet accompanying, by the hand of one who knows not the contents.*
> *Do not entrust him with any reply, but on receipt come* at once *to my house, at Widdershins Bank. Our mutual friend J____ S_____ desires to meet you here, in perfect secrecy.*
> *He instructs, that you must be disguised, and appear as though you yourself were T___ P___, the occupant of the house. You will find in the packet every thing requisite. Be sure to dress yourself before you leave, remembering in particular the hat. Avoid all notice. If you are challenged, say only that you are T___ P___, and on your way home.*
> *Our friend J_____ S_____ is most particular in these*

*commands. Follow them in every point. Fail in any part, and
he may not attend.*

*The house will be empty. Do not announce yourself, but
enter directly, by the door under the hill, at the right side,
which is broken in. Take the seat in the parlour, by the fire. A
bottle and a glass will be left for you. Our brother S____ will
arrive, as soon as he is able. He must evade observation, and
may be very late. You are to* remain in the chair *until he
comes.*

Your watchword will be — I am T___ P___ —

Maintain the disguise, and you may be certain of his trust.

*I write in urgency, and say no more, except to greet you in
the name of the TRUE L_____Y, and bid you hasten to
comply with the instructions of*

Your friend in brotherhood

T____ P_____

Mr Peach reads over the lines but once. They will have to
suffice. — He has no time for second thoughts.

He calls Jem out from the stable, and gives the lad his instructions, with the most particular emphasis. Every thing now hangs
upon the boy. — Jem must run to the inn, with the letter, and the
packet of Mr Peach's cloaths, and deliver them into the hands of
a Mr George Jefferson, and no other. — And then, he is to go
directly home, to his family, at their farm under Rowberrow Hill,
and not return to Widdershins Bank before noon of the next day.

The passionate urgency, with which this command is delivered,
makes a deep impression on Jem's susceptible heart. Though the
boy is not much pleased to be sent away from the house, and still
less, at the prospect of a reunion with his relations, his reluctance
is quite overcome by Mr Peach's manner. Indeed, no persuasion
could be more effective, upon a person of Jem's temperament,
than to tell him, that he holds his master's fate in his hands! —
And so the lad departs at a jog, perfectly convinced of the mysterious solemnity of his errand, and determined to play his part.

— Now for the maid, thinks Mr Peach.

He finds her at work by the washing-tub below the house.

— Put those by, Clary, and attend to me.

Clary rises to her feet. — If, sir, she begins, that gentleman has complained to you of my behaviour, permit me to observe —

She says no more. — She has seen the wild look in Mr Peach's eye.

— You must dress yourself in proper cloaths at once. — I am sorry to say I require you to leave the house, for one night only. I regret there is not time to make arrangements for your lodging elsewhere. You may go wherever you please — So long as it is some miles distant from here, and you do not return until mid-day to-morrow. But you must go at once. — I am not at liberty to explain my reasons.

Clary studies Mr Peach, with that expression of hers, whose meaning we shall never properly describe — For we do not know it ourselves. It is at once frank, and secret — Penetrating, and mysterious — and we know not what besides.

— You require the house to yourself, for the hours of darkness, she says.

— It will be but a single night, and need never be repeated.

— May I then dare to hope, sir, that you have considered my pleas, and intend to grant it?

— I do not understand you.

— I must guess that you intend to make use of the night, in the exercise of those arts of yours, which may save me from the cursed fate I endure.

— You are quite mistaken, says Mr Peach.

— If you say so, sir, I shall not contradict you.

Mr Peach cannot lose time in further efforts, to convince his maid that he is not a magician. — I cannot stay, he says, to hear your absurd suppositions. You must dress yourself instantly, and be away.

— Sir, says she, I have no cloaths to dress in.

Mr Peach had forgotten it. — Take what you wish, of Jem's, or of mine. It will be a warm night. A coat of my own ought to suffice.

— Thank you, says she. — I wonder, sir, since you have been so generous as to suggest it, whether I might request the use of two or three other items? I shall be very content to pass a night in a manner convenient to me, if you will consent to spare them.

With Jem, thinks Mr Peach, I have only to give the order, and it is done. With this eccentric house-maid, every command must be negotiated, like a treaty between warring nations. — Name them, he says, but be quick about it. I have not time to be bartering with you.

— Then in the first place, I wonder whether I might be permitted the use of the horse?

— You are perpetually a surprize to me, Clary. Where do you intend to remove yourself, that you require the horse to reach it?

— Sir — You have said, that you are not to liberty to explain your reasons. Allow me the same privilege, if you will. I shall be quite content to account for my intentions, when you are ready to do the same.

We say again — Clary does not, and surely never will, comport herself as a servant should!

If you are shocked at her boldness, in delivering so pert an answer to her master — a master, to whom she owes so much! — Consider — whether this frank and spirited freedom of language, be not preferable, to a fawning servility, or grudging obedience, which conceals under the mask of compliance, a rebellious and contradictory temper. Your own Sally or Joan may bring you your chocolate, with a bob and a curtsey, and an humble *if you please*. — Do you therefore dream, that there is in her heart the same respectful obedience, which the outward shew exhibits? Of course, you do not. — You know she sneers on her way out of the room, and goes down-stairs, and gossips on your failings with the valet and the scullery-girl. We would an hundred times rather have a Clary in our house, than any such smirking hypocrite. — One *like* Clary, we should say. — The true Clarissa Riddle herself, we would not have within ten leagues of our person, not if she brought with her the fabled riches of *El Dorado*. Heaven forfend! —

— Very well — says Mr Peach — Take the gelding, if it will hasten your departure.

— You are very kind, sir. Might I beg the indulgence of two further requests? I should be particularly grateful for the use of a quantity of the powder from your fowling-piece. It will put my mind at ease, if I am to spend a night again under the open sky. I might also consult that fine new Atlas, which you keep in your study, to acquaint myself with the roads.

Mr Peach cannot help asking what use the powder will be, in her defence, when she has not asked for the fowling-piece itself?

— If we were each to explain ourselves fully, sir, much time would be lost, and I think you are in haste.

For reasons which hardly need mentioning, Mr Peach is not minded to dispute with her, nor even correct her insolence. — There may be occasion to question this creature to-morrow, he thinks — If I live to see the dawn — For now, I must have her gone! — He unlocks the casket, and fetches a pouch of gun-powder, while Clary goes to the end-room, and begins turning over the leaves of the Gazetteer and Atlas, with her left fingers.*

Handing her the pouch, Mr Peach observes that she has opened the book to a page, portraying a map of that part of the county between Bath and Frome, where Grandison Hall is found.

— I had not thought you would turn to those places, he says.

— I could not help but look. See, there is the market town, and there St Dunstan's church, and the bridge beside. They are all laid out below, in miniature, as though I were an eagle. — I know every turning of that road, so. There is the house itself. But all these other pages are only lines and spots of ink to my eyes. Where is this valley, where we stand?

— Let me shew you, Clary. — Mr Peach turns some leaves, and

---

* We are not certain whether we have yet recorded the fact, that Miss Riddle favours the *sinister* hand. — Let it be noted.

points out the depiction of Widdershins Bank, and its neighbouring country.

Clary is strangely enchanted by the volume. She asks Mr Peach to demonstrate, with his finger, upon the paper, how the land lies between his house, and her former home of Grandison Hall; and she watches with great attention as he traces out the several roads.

— You need not fear straying near your former home, Mr Peach says. — It is several miles off, as you see. To-night you need only ride an hour from here, and then conceal yourself wherever you chuse, until the height of day to-morrow.

— I shall go exactly where I intend, now that I have seen this book. — She closes the volume. — Behold, she says — I shut the pages, and am no more the eagle, but have fallen to earth. — You are good, sir, to accommodate me. I know you are impatient. — I will be on my way.

Mr Peach stops her, moved by a strange impulse of the heart.

— One word more, Clary, he says.

— Sir?

— If any accident befall me to-night — You will know, if it does — Keep the horse, with my blessing. It shall be yours, wherever you go after.

Clary studies him again, with her fathomless look.

— Do you fear, sir, a fatal catastrophe?

— No, says he — I should not have spoken so. I am distracted. — All will be well. Be on your way now.

She addresses him with the utmost earnestness. She seems for a moment the image of those prophetic spirits, which the hero of the Odyssey summons from the land of the dead, in the eleventh book of that antient poem. — Believe me, she says — You need not fear death. Only dread a *worse* fate. — Let not my curse fall upon you as well, sir. — Have a care what you do to-night!

For a moment she seems to struggle, with an inward emotion. — But, before Mr Peach can answer, she turns her back — Is gone from the house, without a backward glance — And rides away.

CHAPTER NINETEEN

Now it remains only for Mr Peach, to make his very last preparations.

He seals the door, with key, bar, and bolt. He replaces his books in the case, and all his papers in the drawers, and makes every thing neat and proper in the parlour. Though the evening is yet warm, he lights the fire, and piles the hearth with wood, so it may burn several hours. He puts a taper to a new candle, and sets it on the mantel.

When all else is ready, he fetches a bottle of Rhenish wine, and a glass, and leaves them by the fire-side chair.

The little stage thus set, Mr Peach has no more to do, but await the entrances of the actors.

The sun is not yet down. — In these last days of May, it is reluctant to leave the upper air, and lingers over the hills to the west, as though to admire the gold it has painted them.

A scene of perfect tranquillity — The image, of an *English* Eden — And yet, what horrors of darkness it presages —

Though, we say, the dark is not yet come, Mr Peach ascends the stair — Unlocks the room above, where we have never seen him enter before night.

He steps as quiet as he may. He does not fetch the tooth, or the lock of hair, ring, pin, or bowl. He is not here, to pull aside the veil, between the quick and the dead. —

He only goes to his bed, without undressing. — There he lies — and waits.

The summer night falls, soft and slow.

Reader — We might, if we chose, conduct your steps outside, into that sublime quiet.

The moon is new, and dull. Those same clouds, which tempered the day's heat, now occlude the stars. All the world is become a variety of grey, like the tabby-cat. Substance and shadow are intermingled — so 'each seem'd either.'* — In the woods, limb and bough and leaf appear no more determinate, than the whispering vacancies between. The roads meet the air above, like the sea beneath a fog — no horizon, but a blur.

We might shew you, if we wished, the solitary rider — pressing his mount, from the inn, towards the valley of Widdershins Bank. He has received the letter brought by Jem the stable-boy, and hastens to his appointed meeting — All ignorant, of what awaits! —

We might also point out, those lighter, fleeting shadows — Look — There — You saw them but for a moment — The shape of an arm — The step of a foot, on the dewy grass — Were there not *two*? — though moving so swift and secret, that they scarce seemed bodies at all, but might almost have been exhalations of the darkness —

Approaching the house —

But we do not shew you these — Or the rest.

Understand us, reader. —

The slaughter of Agamemnon, by his vengeful wife, and her ambitious paramour —

The despair, in which Oedipus, king of Thebes, plucks out his own eyes —

The murder of gentle Duncan, at the hand of his host —

Are these catastrophes not each more dreadful, because those three masters of the tragic art — mighty Aeschylus, and wise Sophocles, and *Shakespear*, to whom we attach no single epithet, because, like the world itself, every quality that there is, dwells in

* We allude to the incomparable depiction of Death the king of terrors, in the second book of the Paradise Lost.

him — More dreadful, we say, because the authors have left each of them, *unseen*?

Our imagination is led, towards the crisis — The moment of horror — Like the calf, to the place of sacrifice. We watch the inexorable approach of disaster. — We *feel* it. — And yet — we are not permitted, to *see* it. The deed itself, is withheld from display.

At the very centre of the orbit of tragedy — The dark star of fate — we witness — NOTHING —

No view of the act — No spectacle, of blood and cruelty. — We come to the terminus of our descent, and discover only — emptiness — Look down, and see that there is no road beneath our feet — We stand above a fathomless void — Suspended without support —

Mr Peach lies in his bed, perfectly still.

He hears a man enter the house, by the side, where the door is broken. — A man, who cannot know, that he has perhaps but a few more minutes to live.

The house, as we have said before, is strongly built, and keeps its secrets. Mr Peach perhaps fancies he catches the clink of bottle against glass — But he cannot be sure.

The twilight makes its peaceful surrender to utter dark.

All seems still —

In such an hush, every sudden noise is magnified. Mr Peach has fallen in a trance, between sleep and waking — When he hears, quite sudden, the pushing back of a chair —

The visitor below has heard, that *some other enters the house* —

He calls out the watchword, quite distinctly —

— *I am Thomas Peach!*

CHAPTER TWENTY

And then —
   SILENCE.

CHAPTER TWENTY-ONE

The play is done.

Fire and candle yet burn. — Bottle and glass stand by the chair, as they did — Though not in their state of original perfection; for a finger's depth of Mr Peach's Rhenish now sits in the glass, while the bottle is half-emptied. — A Dutch painter of two hundred years ago, might have made play with these objects, we think, in this dusky light.

There is a man in the chair, dressed in the breeches and riding-coat, of Tho.s Peach.

Our old master averts his eyes with a shudder. — Here is no subject for his canvas! He is a painter of the *stilleven* — the still life, or, as the French say, *nature morte*. He shrinks from the view, of DEATH ITSELF — The terrible fixity of the human frame, emptied of its animating spirit — made a mere *object* —

Those gloomy daubers, who loved to decorate their canvases with the *memento mori*, in order to remind their patrons, of the transience of human fortunes — a moral enjoyed with particular complacency, by those whom the said fortunes have made wealthy — Those flattering artists, we say, were used to present their silent sermon, in the form of a death's head, or skull. — An acceptable element, in a decorous composition; for the bare bone of our mortal body, is a sight we tolerate with equanimity. — It appeals to our intellect, and not our instinct. It is as it were a *sign* — an idea, and not the thing itself. But, the *dead flesh*! — the corpse, preserving in every outward detail the figure of man, or woman, or — Heaven forfend! — child — Yet in its simulacrum of life seeming to mock, the very thing it appears to shew — This is a sight from which we recoil. We cannot bear it — Here — My dear surgeon — and you, the undertaker — here is your payment — Only rid us of *the body*, by your mercy, in all haste!

We shall not attempt to depict the man in the chair.

Ought we even call him a man?

Until this past hour or two, he deserved the name. We do not yet know, what other title properly belonged to him — what name baptismal — For we set no store by his *suet-pudding* of John Brown, and George Jefferson, and what have you. Yet he was a man, under every disguise and lie.

Now even that designation is effaced.

We do not enquire too deeply, into the nature of the operation, by which he is un-christened. Let us only remark, that we see no blood, nor any sign of violence.

The *hashishin* have done their work, we suppose, with a silken cord. Perhaps they are sworn to leave no trace. —

But of them we shall say no more. They have passed through our pages, like the vision of an opiate dream — And are gone — Vanished, as though they never were.

Where, then, is Mr Peach?

Why — he is behind the house; and has set a lantern hanging from a branch, by whose light he is — Digging a grave.

Our narrative, we confess, has taken a *Gothick* turn. —

Do not think, reader, that we intend to linger over the horrid scenery of these nocturnal *tableaux*. — The chair, with its ghastly occupant — The man, toiling at his morbid task, watched by the bat and the screech-owl.* We shall not labour to supply you, with

---

* A judicious acquaintance of ours happens to be by, while we write, and observes, that the bat, being blind, cannot be said to *watch*. We commend the exactness of their judgment — But, unfortunately, are made of stubborn metal. We are one of those, who, when advised upon any course of action, will resist it, merely because of the advice. Thus our bat remains witness to the scene. — Content yourself, madam — Or, if you cannot — *Write your own book.*

those sensations of delicious horror, which are meat and drink to a certain class of readers. Look more closely at Mr Peach. — Do you not see, that there is very little of the *romantic*, in the occupation of grave-digging? Ask any fellow who has turned the earth, and they will confirm it. — It is toilsome, unforgiving work, and no more thrilling a spectacle, than the operas of the Frenchman *Lully*, which, indeed, require as great a length of time to atchieve their purpose, and are similarly well-suited, for laying a man to rest.

We shall resume our narrative, therefore, at the moment when Mr Peach's digging is interrupted.

The cause, which prompts him to lift the spade to his shoulder, and recover his breath, is the intrusion of a noise as perfectly unwelcome, as it is unexpected — The sound of a rider in the road.

We do not know the exact hour of the night. — Though, beyond doubt, it is that period of deep darkness, when no body ought to be abroad. In London, perhaps, or another substantial metropolis, we would not raise a brow, at the passing of the watchman, or a thief or two, or some miserable drab of the streets. We need hardly say — This is not London.

Mr Peach extinguishes the lantern.

Reflect for but a moment, on his present occupation, and the condition of his parlour, and you will understand, that he has no wish to attract the attention of any passer-by.

The horse continues to approach. Its gait is slow, and even. — It comes beside the house — where — It stops.

We have not, thus far in our chapter, attempted to describe the state of mind of Mr Tho.s Peach, at this interesting moment in his history. We are somewhat reluctant — For, we confess, it does not look well in a man, who has recently contrived the murder of a fellow-creature, and is at present digging for that same unfortunate his final resting-place, secret, unmarked, and unhallowed — It does not, we say, look well in him, that he is near giddy with pleasure, and humming as he digs. If such be the case — we do not positively say, it *is* the case — though put us to the question, and we will not deny it — If so, let us at least allow him this much in way of mitigation, that he has within these past few hours escaped, what had appeared to be certain death. In such a circumstance, might not the animal spirits rise, by mere reflex, from being sunk under the weight of mortal danger, to an uncommon height?

We think, they might.

Be that as it may — Mr Peach is now plucked down from his elevation, by this wholly unanticipated crisis.

— Confound it — thinks he — Have I crossed over the rapids of a deep and mighty river, and come safely to the far bank, only to be tripped by accident into some humble muddy ditch, and drowned there instead?

It is among the curiosities of Tho.s Peach, that he grows somewhat extravagant in metaphor, when called upon to apostrophize his fate, in inward discourse. — An habit none would guess, who observed only the moderate and rational outward demeanour, which he presents to the world. But, *still waters run deep.* —

We have run into an hydrological confusion — And must extract ourselves, by proceeding in plain words. —

Mr Peach is dismayed, at the extraordinarily unlucky chance, which seems to have brought a traveller to his house, at this hour, of all hours. He tightens his hold on the spade, and conceals himself among the shadows at the side of the house, where the foliage overhangs thickly.

The horse is being led to his very stable. The traveller has said no word — Nor carries any light.

Now, our first thought may be, that any body, who goes about the country at such an hour, and in such a fashion, and who approaches a man's house, giving no notice of their arrival, and disdaining the benefit of a lantern, must certainly have no good intentions. It would be quite natural to think, that Mr Peach makes this very inference, and will prepare himself accordingly, perhaps by raising the head of the spade, *en garde* —

However — Mr Peach has no common mind.

— This person, he thinks, approaches my house without light; but I do not perceive them to stumble, or hesitate; therefore it is likely, they are familiar with the place.

— And besides, I thought I knew the gait of the horse.

A few more moments confirm his guess — Revealing, that the figure who approaches the broken door, under the half-occluded starlight, is none other than the maid Clary! — though he does not know her in the very first instant, because her outward appearance has again undergone a surprizing alteration.

Briefly — the young woman is quite naked.

Mr Peach is sufficiently astonished — how many times, have we recorded our hero's *astonishment*, at the behaviour of Miss Clarissa Riddle! — That for several further moments, he is uncertain how to proceed; during which interval Clary enters the house, by the broken door at the side.

The spell is broken. — Mr Peach is immediately mindful of what she will discover within, and goes to the door, where he calls out: —

— My explicit instruction was that you should not return before noon the next day.

There is a sound from within, expressive of surprize, and then Clary is heard to answer.

— I remember it, sir, but I met with a series of accidents, which compelled me to return home unexpectedly.

— That is very unfortunate, says Mr Peach. — I must ask that you quit the house again, at once, as we agreed.

— There is a dead man in the parlour, wearing your cloaths.

— We shall not discuss it.

Mr Peach hears some movement within, and Clary's voice comes again.

— His face, says she, is not familiar to me. Though his features are distorted by his last agonies.

— I insist, says Mr Peach, with some vehemence, That you come away at once.

Several light footsteps bring Clary to the cracked door.

— Heavens! exclaims Mr Peach — Are you not yet dressed?

— Forgive me, sir, she says, quite without embarrassment at the condition in which she presents herself. — The accident I alluded to rendered my cloaths very dirty and smokey. I thought to wash them at once.

— Be so good as to spare your explanations until you are able to make a decent appearance.

— Your command was to come out of the house immediately.

— I will not have you indulge Jesuitical sophistries at my expence, Clary.

— Sir, I wish only to oblige. I shall go back in if you desire it. But is this sight not pleasant to you?

— I cannot be gratified by the charms of your person, when I am disgusted at the abandon with which they are displayed. Go and dress yourself.

— Well, I shall, though I am surprized to hear these virtuous exhortations, when there is a man murdered within.

Mr Peach cannot withhold his protest. — It was not I who killed him!

— Was it not? says Clary. — Then we ought both to go in-doors. The criminal may yet be abroad. Or shall we go together, to the justice's house?

— Do you dare to mock me, child?

— No, sir!

Mr Peach feels his ire rising. It is a sensation, as unwelcome to him as it is unfamiliar. — You have no right, he says, to presume to know what has been done here, or on what cause, or to speak a single word about it.

— You mistake me, again, says she. We fancy, we hear the note of gathering passion in her voice also. — I do not mock, or judge. But let it be so — I shall be silent — You know, sir, I am used to the *muzzle*.

— Must you only refrain from talking of things not your concern, because you are commanded to? Is there no drop of natural discretion — Of decency — Of any thing, in your nature, to make you hesitate of your own accord? But why do I even ask the question, when you stand thus before me, utterly without shame?

So far from being abashed at the rebuke, Clary holds her head straighter, and spreads her arms. A wild spirit has entered her — A spirit of midnight, and deeds that hide from the sun.

— What do you see, she cries, that I should be ashamed of? And do not protest to me, that you are a *married man.*

— Abandoned wretch!

— Yes! — Abandoned! — Beyond hope of redemption! And will you now curse me, and cast me out as well? — You, who swore a false oath before my face, and conjure with the dead, and now have done — *This?* — Clary gestures into the house behind her, with a furious sweep of her arm. — Do *you*, she cries, put on the mask of virtue, and shun the vile Miss Riddle? Then I will not stop to fetch the cloaths you lent me — No — I quit the house as I am, and go naked into the night, for the world is all hypocrisy and deceit, and I will have no more to do with any corner of it.

— Great Heaven! exclaims Mr Peach. — I don't mean to put you out of doors. — Is it so much to ask, that you dress yourself, and conduct yourself with a minimum of consideration? What ill fate rules us to-night, that has brought you back to the house, and in this spirit, when I only wished to be left to my dreadful business alone!

Clary becomes calmer. Perhaps it is the grief in Mr Peach's cry, that tempers her rage. — As though for the first time sensible of her appearance, she folds her arms before her.

— Sir, she says, with some hesitation — Do you not know?

Mr Peach turns away in despair. — I do not understand your meaning, child.

— You ask, what evil power directs us. — But I think you know it, as I do.

Mr Peach sighs. — This language, again, Clary?

311

— I think you may not exclaim against your ill fate in one breath, and deny it in the next.

— May a man not imprecate his misfortune, when he is unlucky, without then declaring he is in service to the Devil?

— Do you call it misfortune, sir? There is a man murdered in your house. Is that *unlucky*? Are the trials I have suffered, and the miseries of my nature, to be dismissed as *ill luck*? There is a power, that compels you and I into its course. — Can you not feel it? If· we do not confess it between us — Are we not doomed to perish, each, alone?

A glimmer of noctural radiance falls about them. Beyond it, the earth is all dark. Perhaps the profound night calls to some answering abyss, *within* our hero — as, in the sublime language of the psalm, *deep calls to deep*. For something speaks out of him — Thoughts, which have always shunned the ordinary intercourse of the day.

— Miss Riddle, says he — You have, it is true, been very unfortunate in your life. I too have met with suffering and misery — But with this difference, that being twice your years, I have known them twice as long, and become perfectly acquainted with their real natures. They are not to be blamed on powers beyond this world. It is no malign demon that makes us suffer, nor the influence of opposed planets, but the ordinary vagaries of chance, and the inexhaustible ill-will of our fellow men. Your case is an evident example. — I have heard the history of your birth, and the misbegotten project of your god-father. Allow it but a moment's thought, and you will admit that all the extremities you have been put to, flow in rational though unhappy succession from their causes. The natural freedom and impatience of your temper, chafing over the years against a controul so all-encompassing and artificial, led you to your absolute rebellion. Why need you presume a diabolical agency? — Your character, Miss Riddle, on the one hand, and on the other, the eccentric determination of Mr Farthingay, have been like two volatile materials; and the system of education devised for you was the crucible in which they were thrown together; and the result was a violent reaction. — A result inevitable, and quite natural. No hand but nature's produced the eruptions, which have caused you so much distress, and propelled you to vagrancy, and the misadventures of the friendless roads. The same is true of the events of *to-night*. — I do not deny that murder has been done. I did not do it; but reason and justice compel me to admit that I encompassed the poor wretch's death, as surely as if I had strangled him myself. Yet no evil power guided my hand. — No devil prompted me. This dreadful act is merely the last desperate consequence of the same misfortunes, which have pursued me two year and more, and whose beginnings are no more obscure than the origins of your own. I know what I have done. I shall bear it in my conscience, beside the memory of another such crime. Whatever guilt lies in my deeds, I do not seek to avoid it; and to whatever punishment may follow, I will cheerfully submit. But of one thing I am certain, Clary. — There are no invisible powers that contend for my soul. Neither bliss nor hell-fire awaits me, at the discretion of an eternal judge. The heavens are empty! — If there was once an Author and Mover of this world, He has seen our microscopes, and steam-engines, and encyclopaedias, and found, that we have no more need of Him. You and I must each face our trials, without crying that we are given to the Devil, and doomed to *spiritual* death. I do not think myself wicked and lost, because I have to-night brought about the death of a lying rogue, in order to save myself. No more are you an accursed creature, because you have been angry and unhappy. For the sake of whatever light there is to be found in this cruel existence, let us be decent, and quiet, and comfortable, and let us not torment ourselves with talk of *evil powers*, but live as best we can, without fearing the shadow we cast behind!

Several silent moments follow, in the wake of this remarkable oration. —

Sir — says Clary — be so good as to follow me to my room.

Mr Peach sighs again. — I see, he says, I have wasted my breath.

— You misunderstand me, she says. — Look — I will go first, and dress. Only come after in a few moments. I will shew you your error. — You may see, with your own eyes.

— There is work to attend to. The hours of darkness are not long in this season. I must be finished before the night.

Clary's voice now comes from within. — You need only come for a little time, sir. But ten words. — I will help you afterwards. The corpse will be more easily managed by four arms than two. Please, enter, sir. I am cloathed, and have lit the candle.

Mr Peach stands by the broken door. He is possessed by another thought, of a *nocturnal* cast. — This strange wild girl, he says to himself, whom I so blithely brought into my house, I do not understand at all. She might do any thing, as Mr Farthingay feared. She may be quite mad. For all I know, she will brain me with the candle-stick.

She calls again. — Come, and see for yourself the cause of what you are pleased to call my *deformity*.

Mr Peach hesitates a moment longer. —

The wise anglers tell us, that for each several species of the denizens of stream and pond, there is a particular lure which must be offered. You shall tie your bait in one fashion, to tempt the spotted trout from her nook; in another, to bring up the dace; while the lurking chub will ignore each of these, until you flick the water with your third knot, shaped to catch her greedy eye.

The bait, which is irresistible to Tho.s Peach,* is SECRET KNOWLEDGE.

Had he lived in antient times, we fancy he would have donned the druid's robe — Or held his office in a dusty temple of *Egypt*, murmuring incantations to deities with the heads of cats and birds.

Clary promises him the solution, to a mystery. He has stood unmoved before her nakedness. — But *this* — he cannot resist.

In the little room behind the parlour there is only the bed, and a plain night-table, where she has set the candle. Her few possessions lie alongside. When Anny Pertwee was the tenant, there was a

---

* We have with some difficulty restrained ourselves from renaming him Mr Thomas *Perch*, for the temporary purpose of our metaphor. — The gravity of the situation, we think, forbids it.

hand-mirror in a wooden stand, and a comb, and a brush, and a dish for unguents, and two or three other trinkets, and a New Testament with the Psalms. Little enough — but a scene of Sybarite excess, compared to the Spartan austerity now displayed. The only objects to be seen, are those Clary has had from Mr Peach, *viz.* the items she formerly requested; several sheets of paper, and a pot of ink.

This latter container, she takes up in her left hand.

— Look, sir, she says — and —

DRINKS it.

She swallows. — A fresh black stain shines on her lip! She picks up a leaf of paper, to wipe her mouth.

— Tell me, sir, she says, Is this the *natural* and *rational* consequence of my temperament, and my upbringing? —

Now she tears a strip from the paper.

Mr Peach is a man with an instinctive love, for the materials of reading and writing. The careless treatment of a book causes him inward pain. — Wilful damage to paper, likewise, though in a lesser degree. — He starts forward at the tearing of the leaf, saying, — Clary —

She puts the scrap to her mouth, and — EATS it.

Mr Peach is left agape.

— This, says Clary, is how I live. Now tell me again, that I am merely an *unfortunate* woman.

She pulls off another strip from the paper, and takes it hungrily from her own fingers, and tears it with her teeth, and swallows it down.

— For a year past I have tasted no food nor drink but this, nor had any other appetite. Nothing sustains me except ink and paper. I was bred from my birth, sir, to live after the pattern of a book. — And now — I do.

Mr Peach's sensations are not to be described.

— No one else in the world has witnessed my shame, she says. You are the first to know it. Will you continue to deny, that my fate no longer runs in the course of nature? Will you insist that I am not accursed?

— This cannot be, says Mr Peach.

— Yet, it is. Ask yourself — have you ever seen bread or water touch my lips? Have you once known me to take even the smallest morsel of ordinary refreshment? You have not. I ask you for little wages. What should a creature such as I want with money? Recall the only request I made of you, sir. I wanted only, what I must die if deprived of — paper and ink!

Amid his stupefaction, Mr Peach cannot help a trivial thought. — I did find it curious, he reflects, that when she asked for ink and paper, she never requested *a pen.*

Clary observes her master speechless, and continues. — Had you not been so generous as to provide me with what I asked, I fear I would have committed depredations upon your library. I have stolen books — letters — Pulled the bills from walls, and the banns from church porches. Other vagrants beg for scraps, or rob the barns for their sustenance. I only scoured the land for printed paper. The village churches have given me their charity, without knowing it. Hymn-books and Bibles — Without these I would have famished, and died in the roads, like the robin in winter. There was a day I thought I would expire indeed. I had wandered far from villages and churches — All around were only the hovels of unlettered hinds. — I came to a cross-roads, in my last extremity, and did not know which way I should turn, and thought to lie down there and breathe my last. By a miracle — an *infernal* miracle, for the power that wrought my fate, and holds me to it, is surely evil — I caught the scent of paper. I dug in the very earth where I had laid my head — and found several sheets of manuscript concealed there — As if the very ground had been taught to breed the unnatural crop —

Cries Mr Peach — You disinterred my uncle's letter!

Clary returns his look with equal amazement. — Am I to understand, sir, that *you* buried those papers there?

Mr Peach cannot confess it aloud. — But the truth of it is written quite plainly in his face.*

---

* You have perhaps forgotten the incident, reader. We recorded it as long ago, as our third chapter. — *vide* p. 36.

— You cannot continue to deny me, says Clary. — Your fate is bound to mine. You have saved me not only from torture, and from imprisonment, but from death itself. You alone of all men have seen me, and not shunned me in horror. Do not persist in refusing, what your soul must know to be the truth!

Mr Peach is for a moment seriously alarmed, at the threat of a passionate embrace; for the young creature's feelings are running hot as the Bath waters, and her behaviour might in an instant take a melodramatic turn. — It is danger enough, to compel him to recollect himself, and reassert his reason.

— I think, says he, you must confide in me fully, and explain the whole history of this strange affliction. We might sit in comfort by the fire. — There is a flagon of wine already open.

— Sir, says she, there is a corpse by the fire, and besides, I cannot drink such thin bright stuff.

— No, says Mr Peach — He is sensible of his lingering confusion — Of course —

— If I may suggest it, says she, we might carry the body out to its grave, and then you may rest from the exertion, and listen to my tale.

— Do you not shrink from the prospect of such horrid work?

— I? I am a thing set apart from nature, by some horrid decree, which has left upon me the mark of darkness. The maidenly delicacy to which I was bred has long since abandoned me. I have no more fear of the dead, than *you*. — Clary accompanies these last words, with a momentary glance towards the ceiling. —

Mr Peach is possessed with the most urgent wish, *not* to know her meaning. — Well, then, he says, let us remove the body.

The fire now burns red and dim. The effects of its livid radiance, and pronounced shadows, upon a face bearing the characteristic signs of death by *asphyxiation*, may be imagined — Or, if you prefer, may not be — We shall think no worse of you, if you prefer not to linger over so ghastly a spectacle.

Mr Peach shudders, to see what he has wrought.

Clary appears quite unmoved. — We must first divest him of

those articles of clothing properly yours, she says. — We might also keep the boots.

— Heavens, Clary! let us not pick over the wretched man's effects, like human jackals!

— Might I at least be permitted the papers he has at his breast? I need not explain my purpose.

— I see no papers.

— They are concealed beneath his shirt. Perhaps he has a wallet there. — I can smell them, as an animal scents its food.

Receiving no reply, Clary turns to Mr Peach, and sees that he stares at her, with an expression compounded of incredulity and revulsion.

— I am a beast, sir, she says, with perfect simplicity, as another young person of her sex might say, *I am betrothed*, or *I am fond of dancing*. — I am become a b__h in Satan's kennel.

Mr Peach shakes his head, to dismiss these syllables from his ears, before they proceed any further along those intricate tunnels, and make a lasting impression in the plastic substance of his brain. — Let us see, he says.

Clary proves to be correct. There is a wallet hanging from the dead man's neck, hidden beneath his shirt. She opens it hungrily, and discovers leaves of writing within.

— I must look over them first, says Mr Peach, before you — Before —

He cannot say it.

There are two sheets. The larger is a commission, sealed by a great office of the state. It names the bearer as one Jenkyn Scrimgeour; declares him to be engaged on the king's business; and requires that he be provided with every assistance, by all lesser authorities of the kingdom.

The remaining paper is a private missive. Mr Peach unfolds it, and reads —

Scrimgeour —
I have seen your last report. I shall give these matters my
personal attention. You are to expend every effort to discover

the principal figures in this nest of traitors. I wish to have their names, and the places at which they habitually meet. Present yourself as a party interested in their purpose, and gain admittance to their confidence. Do not yet attempt to interfere with their scheme. They must be persuaded of your trustworthiness.

I shall be particularly eager to learn of this Jer. Sixways, and any of his intimates.

Your stay in Somerset will be extended. The inclosed funds are adequate to your immediate requirements.

Do not approach Doctor T____n himself. I have word that he knows himself watched.

My name must never be mentioned, nor the interest of the ministry suspected.

You shall be rewarded commensurate with the information you acquire.

No signature is appended. The only subscriptions are, a date, within the past week, and an address, indicating the office of the Home Secretary, in London.

Mr Peach studies the lines with care, while Clary disposes of the sealed commission, by the grotesque method already demonstrated. He wishes to fix in his mind the inferences he must derive from it, *viz.*: that the supposed Mr Jefferson was really a Mr Scrimgeour, and a spy in the pay of government; that he had interested himself in Doctor Thorburn, among others, at the ministry's behest; that by the authority of his commission he had intercepted Mr Peach's letter, and so become convinced of the existence of a cabal of *democrats*, with Jeremiah Sixways at its head. Once he is satisfied that no other construction can be put upon what he has read, he gives the paper to Clary.

We shall not narrate the particulars of Mr Jenkyn Scrimgeour's jouney to his grave. It is a scene lacking any shred of that dignity, which we human creatures feel by awful instinct ought to attend the mortal remains of the departed. There are accidents — Obstructions — Limbs, tumbling at inconvenient angles — The head knocking against the wainscot. Gasps of exertion — Sweat — Muttered oaths — And, the *door*! the broken door! It is a passage not at all convenient, for admitting a large and lifeless object. The contortions required — The lifting, and levering, and tipping — No — Indeed, we shall not describe any of it. We avert our gaze — and count to several hundred. — And resume our tale, with Mr Tho.s Peach and Miss Clarissa Riddle seated again, in the parlour.

The candle burns on. The fire, however, is extinguished — For both parties, as a consequence of those efforts we have forborne to observe, are excessively warm.

Mr Peach is not a man of appetites. Nevertheless, he swallows a glass of Rhenish in a single draught — Closes his eyes, and exhales — And pours another.

Now, he says — Let us hear how you arrived at the strange condition, in which you find yourself. But, I beg you, confine yourself exclusively to the facts of your story. We shall have no more talk of diabolic influence, or any thing else not witnessed with your own eyes and ears.

— And if the facts admit of no natural explanation, are we not to admit an influence beyond nature? Your wife —

Mr Peach raises a school-masterly hand. — Perhaps, Clary, perhaps, he says. He is too much exhausted, to become angry. — But, he says, we may as well *begin* with the mere facts, and of your own case, if you please, not mine. — I understand that you were not born as you are now. When Mr Farthingay spoke to me, immediately before the occasion of our first interview, he alluded to a change in your behaviour, within the past year.

— I doubt his language was so delicate.

— Well, but let us have your own words, not his.

— Sir, she says, all my life I was taught to imitate another's voice, and denied words of my own. You are the first who has ever wished to hear them.

Mr Peach is curiously touched by this declaration. — And bids her continue.

— I hardly know how to tell my own story, she says. — I look within myself, and see only pages — Endless pages, of another woman's words. — Speaking of herself, not of me. No — they are not a woman's words at all, but a man's, speaking in a woman's voice. I wonder, where am *I*, amid all this writing?

— My dear child, says Mr Peach. — You need only describe to me a chain of events. Tell me how you ceased to nourish yourself as people do, and began your new practice instead.

— Very well. — The alteration began in the winter before last, at the time of my sixteenth birth-day, which falls, I may tell you, on New Year's Day. Some months before then, I had begun to notice, that the life I led was no state of perfection, as for the whole of my conscious existence I had been taught to believe, but a tormenting imposition, compounded of hypocrisy, falsehood, and tyranny. The virtues I had been taught to imitate I saw practised by no one around me. The sentiments and actions I was instructed to adopt, I discovered to be absolutely unsuited to my own situation, while those I was encouraged to condemn, took hold of my innermost thoughts, and would not be dislodged. I had been taught to meditate upon each word I read. But the consequence of my habit of reflexion, was that I came gradually to know that the Clarissa Harlowe, every letter of whose pen I had revered as gospel, was an *invention*. — That the virtuous spirit expressed in those pages I studied every day of my life, was not her own, but a form of words, written down by a man, whose name was Samuel Richardson, and who had but recently lived in London, and made his living by his impostures. — That the machinations of Mr Lovelace, and the fiery resentment of Miss Howe, and the cruelties of Mr James Harlowe, were all likewise produced from the pen of the same Richardson. It is difficult to express the significance of this revelation —

— And, Clary, says Mr Peach, interrupting in a mild tone, That is the very reason why I encourage you to limit yourself to the plain facts of your history, as far as you may.

— I understand you, sir, and will endeavour to. — Then I shall only say that the day came — not at once, in a Damascene revelation; but slowly, as my wits grew to maturity — When I saw that my own existence was little more than — Sir — Excuse my hesitation — I can find no better language, than to say I thought *myself a book* — An invention, made only of others' words — As though it was not my unknown parents who had made me, but a pen, continually writing. I knew there was another life. — I saw it around me — The servants, labouring, and gossiping, and busy with petty things — Bella, who was never forced to undergo what I endured. My god-mother and god-father, full of vanity and folly — Even, sir! the animals — the dogs and horses — Even the trees and clouds I spied from the window, while I sat with the hated *book* open upon the table before me. — All these things belonged to a world not made of letters — Not ordered by Mr Richardson's story, of the depredations of vice, and the feeble resistance of unbending virtue. Myself, sir — I knew I was flesh and blood, but the flesh had no connexion with any thing I had been taught to be. Miss Harlowe seemed to *have no body*, whereas I — When I felt my corporeal being, I thought only of Mr Lovelace.* I dreamed of his hands, tearing the pages — Of his voice, coming from my mouth —

— Clary —

— Excuse me, sir. — She draws in a long breath, and resumes. — My condition, she says, became insupportable to me. I grew defiant. I refused to be educated, as I had been. I questioned the authority I had been taught to revere, and, in questioning, overthrew it. I determined to escape, and so found myself physically confined. My window was barred. The doors were locked around me at night. A servant was set to attend me at all times. All the behaviour, which I had been taught was necessary, because it was right, was now forced on me, by means of threats and punishments, which grew more severe the longer I refused to comply. I had been the favoured

---

* The seducer and rake, who is the villain of Richardson's Clarissa.

child, and the object of universal love and affection in the house; I became within a few weeks of my seventeenth birth-day no better than an indentured slave. I could not be compelled to exhibit a virtue I no longer acknowledged. I would not pretend to be a thing I knew I was *not*. — And so my god-father's plan, which I had followed since infancy, as docile as any dumb creature, was wholly destroyed. In the face of my refusal to be Miss Harlowe, he could do nothing; and without that purpose, I had no reason to exist at all, in his eyes. All efforts to return me to my former obedience were given up. I was shut in like a Bedlamite, and left to the resentful and brutish care of the household servants. You may imagine, sir, that I saw no better prospect, than to end my own existence. I wanted the courage to destroy myself by swift and violent means. So, I refused food. — I shall not disgust you, by reciting every detail of my struggle with this resolution. My determination proved stronger than my hunger. — Stronger, even, than the instinct for self-preservation, which nature has implanted in all living things. I became weak, and faint, and only roused myself when my captors came to force food upon me, at which times I would fight with extraordinary strength — My struggles animated by hatred for my condition, and my history, and for the world. That was the last and most efficacious lesson I derived from that paper paragon, Miss Clarissa Harlowe. — If she could determine to *die*, of her just resentment, then so could I!

— Poor creature, murmurs Mr Peach. — We think, he is not referring to Miss Harlowe.

— But you wish me to tell only the events which actually occurred. I shall now have great difficulty in doing so. Whether the visions which came to my phantasy, at the extreme limit of existence, are the stuff of history, I cannot determine. Nor, I may say, can you. — In my extremity of deprivation I fell at last into the insensibility I had sought. But it was not extinction. — The outward senses were closed, but I knew another state of being. — I recall it quite vividly. I felt myself no longer a corporeal creature at all. I seemed to be in truth, what I had discovered myself to be in figure — a being composed of mere *words*. It is no analogy, sir — No metaphor — It is the most exact truth of what I remember. All around was blackness. There was no form or dimension in myself, or the place I was. There was only — Forgive me; there is an horror in the recollection I cannot adequately express! — I felt I was thin and empty as air, and all that kept me from utter nothingness, was the shape of characters — Letters, sir — Words. I knew, that if the hand that wrote my being were to lift the pen — Or the voice that spoke me, paused for breath — I would disappear — I would die, and be nothing. It seemed to me I existed in this state for a time not measured in ordinary duration. It might have been for ever that I floated upon the margin of existence. But I became aware of a change. — Or, the truth of my new condition revealed itself, slowly. I felt — No — I *knew* — that there was an *author* —

Clary falls silent. The flame of the candle, which has trembled at her breath, making the shadows flicker, becomes straight and calm again.

— The author you allude to, says Mr Peach, is not Mr Richardson, I think.

The remark is perhaps intended to be gently humorous. If so — It misses its mark.

— There is not one person in the world I wish well, says Clary, except you, sir, and so I may say with perfect truth, that I hope you remain always as ignorant of what I underwent, as you now shew yourself to be.

Mr Peach feels himself rebuked.

Clary continues — It is a profound horror — profound beyond description — To feel another presence, within oneself. To know that I only continued my existence, at the whim of this other. — To feel myself *the work of his hand* — My every thought and act and motion no more than as he writes it. If this remains only a jest to you, count yourself blessed.

— I had not meant to make light of your sufferings. Perhaps we may proceed with the account of how you woke from your visions.

— My recollection is somewhat imperfect. I was very weak, I know. I had been at the border between living and dying. I believe it is not impossible that I crossed it —

Mr Peach raises his hand again.

Well — says Clary — If you will hear nothing but plain facts, then there is no more to say but I awoke, and discovered I had no appetite except that I have now; and it has been so from that day to this.

— But how did you make the discovery? There must have been an instinctive reluctance, to perform an act at which your former nature would have revolted.

— On the contrary, I recall no hesitation. I woke from my dreams. I was alone. There was a Bible by the bed. It had long been the belief of the servants that I was possessed by unholy spirits —

Mr Peach recalls, that Mr Farthingay had expressed that very opinion.

— And, while I lay confined, they would sometimes read the gospel to me, in hopes of exorcizing the evil within. I found the book there. I suppose I was hungry — I remember no hesitation in pulling out some pages, and feeding on them. They were in the Book of Isaiah, I believe.

— Were you not surprised at your own actions?

Clary pauses in thought before answering. — I think I was not. It seems to me now that I have always been as I am, though I know the truth is otherwise. Meat and water look strange to me. When I was changed — In that vision, while I lay insensible — I was changed *entirely*. *He* owns me, to the bottom of my soul. —

— You refer to the supposed author, whose presence you imagined, in your delirium?

— You may speak of it as though it were merely the phrenzy of an illness. But you cannot deny the change that was wrought. You have now seen the evidence — The consequence —

By the law of the association of ideas, which causes us to recollect a certain thought, when the circumstances obtaining at its first occurrence happen to be repeated, Mr Peach involuntarily remembers his first view of Clary.* He is reminded of his initial thought, that she was not an human creature at all, but a species of ghastly mannequin.

— No, he says, I cannot deny it.

— Then, says she — Since a change is wrought — and it is evident that I am made unnatural — Are you not also compelled to ask — *Who has wrought it?*

Mr Peach finds he cannot answer.

— Just as I know, you are compelled to ask — By what power is my wife brought back to me? Sir — Do not raise your hand to silence me now. I do not ask you to confide in me. I have exposed my secret to you — But you may keep your own. I only require you to confess, that you have suspected — that you *know*, and must acknowledge — a power and a presence, not of this earth.

Mr Peach would give all the little he has, to deny it — To suppress his confession, deep within the silent recess of his most inward soul. Yet —

He nods his head. A small gesture — but the meaning is plain.

To his great surprize, Clary reaches across the space between the chairs, and lays an hand on his.

— Then we both know, that we are not alone in the world.

— I am very tired, he says. — It cannot be long until dawn.

Clary rises.

— I must wash the cloaths, she says. — They are dirtied all over, with soot and smoke. I shall be quiet as I can.

— Do you never rest?

— Rarely, sir, since the time I have spoken of. If I were to sleep — I fear what visions might return.

---

* The particular circumstances repeated, being: the darkness surrounding; the single candle-light; the small inclosed room, and Clary seated near its centre; together with the pervasive air of sinister dread, on this occasion abetted by the recent act of murder.

— Many of us fear 'what dreams may come,' but none can voluntarily forgo sleep, no matter how we long to.

— None but I, she says.

Mr Peach wishes he could refute her. — But he cannot. He has observed her tireless vigour himself.

— Good-night, sir. I am grateful to you for hearing my history with patience. It is quite natural that you are reluctant to acknowledge its meaning. — But consider this. — You yourself tell me, that God has washed His hands of the earth. Do you not then think it the more likely, that His antagonist should rise again, to claim the abandoned field?

The conversation is concluded, and our chapter with it.

We shall put down our pen, for it is very late with us also. But though we write no more to-night — We shall not yet attempt to sleep —

CHAPTER TWENTY-TWO

The world, says Sophocles, is all mystery, yet there exists nothing more mysterious than man.

A sentiment we judge no less certain, in Somerset-shire, in the year 1785, than it was in Athens, some two thousand years before, when the tragedian penned his Oedipus. We have presented twenty-one chapters'-worth of Tho.s Peach, Esq., in the course of which you have observed in him many marks of humanity and good sense. Perhaps, from time to time, you have found him a little contrary in his opinions, though mildly expressed — Perhaps, a little more hasty to speak his mind, than the most punctilious civility can approve. Certainly, we admit some eccentric colouring to his habits and interests. — But it is an age of discovery, and curiosity, and enthusiasm, and invention! — Eccentricity is almost become the prerogative, of the English gentleman. Mr Humphrey Davy concocts chemical vapours, and inhales them himself, to try their effects. Mr William Herschel sits every night at his telescope, until Uranus wanders at last into his enraptured view. Mr Beckford commands the building of a vast folly on his estate at Fonthill, making brick and stone answer to his opiate visions. — And Mr Thomas Peach, a sober country gentleman of modest means and quiet pursuits, is — a MURDERER.

The playwrights and romancers will have it, that persons of this class are villains head to toe. They scowl, and leer, and stroke their moustaches, and strike wicked poses. — Scheming, and snapping their fingers in the face of conscience, and caring for nothing, but their greedy and depraved desires.

Ask yourself, reader — for you are now equipped to judge — Whether Tho.s Peach be such a man?

You must agree, he is not. — In which case, there is some error in the system of human understanding, on which our popular literature is founded; for a MURDERER Mr Peach most certainly is.

My learned friends — Gentlemen of the bar — You object, that though Mr Peach may have in some wise *encompassed* the death of Mr Jenkyn Scrimgeour, by means of the ingenious device, where he introduced that man into his parlour in his own place, to receive the dread sentence of the *hashishin* — He nevertheless in no wise performed the fatal act, *himself* — And must therefore be acquitted, of the crime of murder.

We will not hear your arguments. We know you, sirs. — We understand, that for a sufficient fee, you will be pleased to maintain, that Mr Peach was not in the house at the time of the murder — That he was aboard a lugger, off the Exmoor coast — That he is, in fact, the crown prince of Roumania — Or any other *fol-de-rol* you think may befuddle the jury. But our accusation, does not allude to the death of the Welsh spy. — We mean the *other* mortal crime, which we fear we must lay at Mr Peach's door.

Did you mark his confession, reader, amid the surprizes of our preceding? —

You did.

And have you also deduced, what Mr Peach did not make explicit, in conversation with Clary; that is, the particular deed of slaughter, committed some two years past, which he acknowledges his own? — The identity, of the *victim?* —

You do not wish to speak of it? — Very well.

Let us on with our narrative.

We do not know that we ought to say, a cloud is lifted from Mr Peach. The desperate stratagem, conceived in hurry in our eighteenth chapter, and executed among the three words of our twentieth, has succeeded, and triumphantly. The assassins, sent from distant shores, have returned, believing their commission complete. — The sword, suspended above his head by a mere hair, is harmlessly sheathed. — Or rather, has dropped upon another. Under other circumstances, we would count this a perfect transformation in his fortunes — Every trace of the threatened storm passed, and nothing but clear skies, to the horizon.

But we cannot forget certain other things. — For example — that, in the very same night of Mr Peach's escape from the mortal sentence pronounced upon him, he discovered himself to be sharing his house with —

With — What? —

A cursed creature? — A woman, possessed by unholy agency? —

Mr Peach ponders this very question, the next day, but comes no nearer an answer, than you have.

Perhaps he is fortunate, that there is a further problem before him, whose solution is a matter of urgency. We have for the past several chapters again lost sight of his *mundane* difficulties, distracted as we have been by things *supernatural* — or, if we may mint a fresh coin in the currency of this our English tongue, things *infra-natural* — For we are inclined to agree with Clary, that the obscurities of our narrative derive rather from the darkness of the abyss, than 'excessive bright.'* Nevertheless, it is the nature of every-day troubles, that they will not be gainsaid, nor long ignored, no matter what tragedies of grandeur and pathos occur alongside. — King Oedipus himself no doubt had to eat, and mend his shoes. — And Thomas Peach, you will recall, must find the means to pay his rent.

His domestic oeconomy is, to be sure, altered to his advantage, by the curious fact, that his new house-maid requires no food, and supplies the place of the late unfortunate Mrs Shin, without also receiving that worthy's wages. But the diminishment of expenditure counts for little, when the income is — nil.

Therefore Mr Peach's thoughts turn once more, to his former project, involving his correspondence with Doctor Thorburn, in Bristol.

---

* Milton. — We think this is not the first time we have alluded to the line. Its originality, and its splendour, must excuse the recourse.

Our first view of this project, in our seventh chapter, was attended with uncertainty. We guess, reader, that in those distant pages, you would not have countenanced the notion, of our Mr Peach engaging himself in a fraudulent scheme. — Alas! you can have no such scruples, now you have arrived in the noxious swamps of our twenty-second. A man capable of extinguishing the life of his fellow-mortals, will surely not hesitate to extract some pounds from their purses, by dishonest means! — Let us be candid, then. Mr Peach has taken the American doctor, for what is called his *mark*, in the parlance of the swaggering cullies. His initial efforts have been obstructed, as you will have deduced for yourself, by the unexpected interventions of the deceased Mr Jenkyn Scrimgeour, who has intercepted letters to and from Doctor Thorburn, on behalf of His Majesty's ministers of state.

— Well, then — says Mr Peach to himself — It is as I suspected. I cannot pursue my plan by means of correspondence, and must now approach the Doctor, in person.

— Besides — he adds, considering it further — There may be some advantage, in discovering Mr Scrimgeour's activities, and the interest of the ministry. The information will no doubt be useful to Doctor Thorburn; and he who brings it, may thereby appear in the light of a trusted friend.

Oh! the subtle machinations, of this mild and sober-seeming Mr Peach! — The *Machiavel*, of the Mendip Hills!

We shake our head at it. — And refer once more, to the antient opinion of Sophocles, with which our chapter began.

It is agreed that Clary shall accompany Mr Peach on the journey to Bristol. He can hardly leave her within-doors, with Mrs Peach. — Nor, upon reflexion, is Mr Peach inclined to tempt her appetites with the freedom of his library. Besides, he wishes to procure for her some more suitable cloaths, which he may do while he is in town. The impropriety of travelling in the company of a single female servant, will be lessened, by the extreme reserve with which she necessarily conducts herself in public. — She herself is quite amenable to the journey, despite her distaste for society. Perhaps the promise of two or three new dresses is irresistible, to her female heart. — Though we do not think it the likeliest explanation.

Jem is informed of the plan, upon his return.* He is delighted at the news that Mr Peach will be some days absent — then, utterly dashed! to hear that Clary goes with their master. With a piteous cry of — What a theatre of misery is this life! — he retires to the stable-loft; and the sounds of sighing, and groaning, and weeping, are emitted therefrom, in inarticulate stanzas, for some time following.

— The poor lad is enamoured of you, I fear, says Mr Peach to Clary.

— Permit me, sir, to go and offer him some consolation, while you make your preparations for departure.

Mr Peach is surprized. — Do you return his affections? he says.

— His affections! No! — Clary laughs.

We have mentioned before, have we not? the unpleasant effect produced, when that mouth is opened in a laugh.

— What should I care for the affections of a silly boy? The consolations I refer to are much more to my taste, and I think also to his.

Reader — What do you say? —

You would have us omit this portion of our narrative also? —

It is our wish to oblige you in every thing, when we may. We concede, that neither this conversation, nor the events subsequently occurring in the stable-loft, of which the said dialogue is the *efficient* or *motive* cause, are strictly necessary to our tale.

We shall defer to your request, and interrupt our course. —

But — look! — How delicate a construction, is the machinery of this narrative of ours! How carefully contrived, its parts! — and how exquisitely fitted! — And now you ask us, to place a

---

* You will recall, that his instructions were to absent himself from the house until the after-noon of the following day, once he had delivered the fatal invitation to Mr Jefferson, *alias* Scrimgeour, *alias* Brown, at the inn.

finger upon the nodding ratchet — To hold back for a moment, the stepwise march of the wheel. We suppose, you have your reasons. — Whether they savour somewhat of *prudery*, we shall not at present consider. — We have accepted them, and with good grace, we dare add. But now, the subtle balance of our artefact is upset. Its organization is disturbed —

The regular motion, which carries us on, is thrown out. The cogs scrape and strain — The springs are checked to bursting — LO! —

All flies into confusion! —

And, we are whirled away, from our present scene —

Hurled into the giddy air — tumbling head under heel —

What is this? — Mr Peach, and Clary, and the house at Widdershins Bank, are suddenly no where to be seen! Unknown faces pass below us — And strange fields — Whose they be, and where, we know not — We are sick, with sudden motion — 'Chaos is come again' —

Now — we descend — our headlong course slows — And the eye of our narrative alights once more on the earth — several miles, from where we were — And fixes on —

A scene, of hideous RUIN!

Mercy — Reader, what have you done?

Before us lies the disfigured remnant of a fine country house. The glass of its many windows is all burst out, and the leads melted into sad contortions. Its masonry is blackened — in one corner, entirely fallen away, as though the house had collapsed like an ill-baked pudding. What was once the roof, shield against the elements, is now a torn lattice of charred twigs, no more proof against wind and rain than an umbrella fashioned from a net.

Some few persons stand about, wringing their hands, or gawking. — The hand-wringers have the look of domestics, and we may take them to be the lesser folk of the house, who now have nothing to do but stand in stupefaction. The gawkers may perhaps be curious people of the neighbouring country — Drawn to the place in the night, by the great fury of the conflagration, which made an hellish glow behind their shutters, and spread abroad its unceasing roar of destruction, and covered their dwellings with a blanket of foul smoke, and a sprinkling of ashes.

In short — This is some rich man's seat, which has in the past night suffered the fate of Gomorrah — The dreadful depredation, of FIRE.

The surroundings buildings — stable, and barns, and the like — appear untouched, by which we deduce, that the inferno took hold within the house, and was contained, before its fury spread. But, having only one building on which to sate its hunger, it has feasted in full. The quondam palace of splendour is utterly ravaged. —

Even in its ruin, there is somewhat about it not wholly unfamiliar — Do you not think so too? The proportions, of the facade — The line of the roof —

Perhaps, your unfortunate interruption to the workings of our tale, has not thrown us *entirely* off course?

Observe — Also — Some of the bystanders — There are two or three among them, who seem to smile behind their hands, and are heard to mutter, that *pride goeth before a fall* — That those who will insist on interfering with things ordained by God, may hardly complain, to find their presumption noticed, and punished.

Bless us! — This charred heap, is surely all that now remains, of *Grandison Hall*!

We think we should hardly have known it, so thoroughly has the heat worked its terrible alchemy. And yet — there, is the modest flight of steps, which Mr Peach ascended, to make his entrance into Mr Farthingay's house — There, the lintel under which he passed. The stone of both has resisted the fire, though the doors between are bent and bowed, like the iron of London Bridge in the song.

And hence the grim satisfaction, which, to the dishonour of human nature, we mark in the faces of some few of the onlookers. You recall, do you not, reader, that Mr Farthingay incurred the resentment of his neighbours, by daring to re-christen the house, when he took possession of it? Some have not forgotten the slight. — Nay, have nurtured it, as quarrelsome neighbours will; and now their looks bespeak a flint-hearted complacency, that Providence has vindicated their grudge, and blotted the presumptuous name of Grandison Hall from the surface of Somerset-shire.

Are there such men? — and such women?

That there are, we know, as well as you — And for the same reason — Because such low-spirited cavilling knaves are also *our* neighbours — And yours, as well.

We dare to hope, they would not have allowed themselves the spiteful luxury of their satisfaction, had the tragic events of the night extended so far, as to encompass the loss of human life. But, by good fortune, the house was for the most part vacated. Mr and Mrs Farthingay have repaired two days since to their town house, in Bristol, in order to oversee some preparations for the engagement of their daughter. The young lady accompanied her parents. — The chief persons of the household being thus removed, it follows that a good many of lesser standing went with them; and the remaining servants were all quartered outside the house, or in such peripheral rooms, that they were able to escape before the blaze could reach them. A count has been taken, and no body is missing. — Tears of relief are shed. — The only victims are reckoned to be some unfortunate spaniels, who were so indulged by Mrs Farthingay, that they were permitted to sleep in her bed, even in her absence, and so were shut within her chamber; thus receiving as reward for their favoured position, a fiery martyrdom.

But we must exert ourselves, to bring our narrative away from this scene, and restore it to its proper course.

While we make the necessary efforts — You may linger some moments, and gather from the general hubbub what further particulars you may, concerning these events. The knowledge may prove useful — For we have an inkling, that we have not been deposited before the ruin of Grandison Hall, altogether by accident. Our tale is governed by a mysterious coherence. We do not ourselves fully understand the nature of this unifying power — We shrink, from enquiring further — These are the deep secrets of *necromantic history*, forever veiled from the eyes of the profane. Nevertheless — Some purpose may be served, by this unexpected diversion of ours.

Glean what you may, then, before we depart. Pass by the gawking vultures, for the present. — Listen instead to the servants.

Many are still overcome, with horror and distress, and do little more, than weep in one another's clutches, and wail the loss of wigs and petticoats. Some speak of the dreadful suddenness and ferocity of the fire. Two or three agree, that they were roused from sleep by a thunderous report, like the discharge of — a pistol, says one — a musket, says another — A third swears, it was loud as a bombardment of cannons. And the sulfurous reek of smoke! — like hell-fire itself, says this same third witness. — Perhaps we shall be suspicious of her testimony, for we think her as ignorant of the precise odour of the infernal flames, as she is of the noise of a cannonade. All, however, are united in the opinion, that *they are not to blame*. — Mingle a little longer, and you shall hear the same story repeated. Every body was asleep — No one knocked over a lantern, or left a careless flame untended. The fire began in the upper portion of the house. The stair and the bed-rooms were all a-blaze, before any body knew a thing. — Thank Heaven, the master and mistress were not at home, nor the young mistress neither! — Her proud negro — We don't much care to praise the good Lord, that *he* was absent — Let him shift for himself, as he do well enough at any road, nor do I mind who hears me say so. — He's gone with Miss Arabella to town — he goes with her all over — Aye — There's one, who won't rejoice to see young mistress wed! — Hum — Only madam's poor dogs are all burned up alive — I would have braved the flame to rescue them, but my ankles are all swollen with a dropsy — It was all we had to do to save ourselves! — so sudden it came on. Surely there's no explaining it — A blast of lightning, maybe, for I think I did hear a mighty report. — Or — *the Devil himself* — Madam will often be a-going to Bath, you know, and there it is all balls, and dancing. — I heard a preacher say that all who dissipate at Bath, are d____d, and will burn in the eternal fire — Mercy! — Joan Catchpole swears she saw a fiend running about the house, sooty black and shrieking — Depend upon it, master and mistress are punished by Heaven — Or the young mistress — for going her ways with *him* — Black as pitch! — Yet it's very hard that my own poor things are all burnt up, for the great folks' sins —

CHAPTER TWENTY-THREE

THUS! —

All is righted once more! — And our tale resumes its proper progress.

We cannot begin again, exactly in that place where we were halted. Some damage has unavoidably occurred, to the *continuity* of our narrative. An interval has passed, of uncertain length. — No matter. We are satisfied, that nothing significant has been done, or said, in that period. The bulk of it, we assume to have been taken up by the tedious occupations of travel, and the yet more dull business of making arrangements for lodging, and provision, in the place of arrival; affairs, which the ingenuity of *Smollett* may persuade you, are capable of furnishing an endless series of accidents amusing, pathetic, and grotesque,* but which your own experience will assure you, are nothing of the sort. Whatever character the journey may have borne, the plain result of it is, that Mr Tho.s Peach is again at BRISTOL.

We shall spare you any further evocation of the town. We have exercised our pen to that end, in a former chapter. Our words

---

* Such as are found in that author's Expedition of Humphry Clinker, wherein we learn, that a man may not so much arrive at a country inn, without chancing upon his niece's lover disguised as a strolling player, or his own long-lost bastard child, or an eccentric Scotchman with a fund of entertaining conversation, or what have you else. — Proof, we think, of the extremities to which a purveyor of narratives must resort, when he is obliged to *invent* all his matter, and has not the *necromantic historian's* recourse to mere TRUTH.

there, may do as well *here*. — We hope they were sufficiently well chosen, to serve more than once.

The lodgings Mr Peach has secured lie a mile or two outside the city, in a somewhat neglected village inn. To speak frankly, it is an house unknown to the fashionable world, being neither convenient nor commodious, and, indeed, barely suited to a gentleman, no matter how reduced his circumstances. Mr Peach's reasons for accommodating himself thus are twofold. — The first and chief consideration, is that the two rooms are to be had very cheaply. The second, which may indeed be accounted the cause of the first, is that to which we have just now alluded, *viz.* the obscurity of the situation. For Mr Peach is joined on his travels, by a single female attendant, which is a circumstance liable to attract some notice. Moreover, the eccentricities of Miss Clarissa Riddle's manner and appearance, cannot be entirely concealed from public knowledge. — And so he chuses to endure the curiosity of ten or twenty, in a village, rather than exposing himself to the gossip of hundreds, in the metropolis.

His first business must be, to procure for Clary some articles of clothing, that will allow her to appear in the streets without exciting the amusement of the polite, and the ridicule of the vulgar. To this end he has visited the dress-makers of the lower town, employing every artifice of diplomacy, until he finds one who will extend him the privilege of a gentleman. — That is, to have the goods he desires on credit.

It is a curious fact, that only those possessed of sufficient wealth, should be able to have the things they can easily afford, without paying for them. — An arrangement which appears to defy natural justice — Though it be sanctioned by Holy Writ, which declares, that *whosoever hath, to him shall be given, and he shall have more abundance.** But this is by the by. — Let us do Mr Peach the justice of recording, that at this hour of our narrative, he is not one of those who *hath* — Has, indeed, barely any thing,

* Matt. ch.13 v.12.

at all, discounting his books — And is only able to procure credit, because he presents the appearance of a gentleman, and, which is the more effective cause, by a free and frequent use of the name of Mr Davis, of the Anti-Lapsarian Society. — A man of known worth, and hence a talisman to the shop-keepers.

But we had not meant to dwell on these negotiations. We must hasten on — We are precluded, alas, from a full description of the articles obtained. — Let us merely say, that Clary is now accoutred in a stile, suitable to a young woman of modest decency, with the exception only, that there is a *veil* of plain lace attached to her bonnet. The addition of this piece to the ensemble defies the canons of fashion, for nothing else in her dress suggests a purpose either funereal, or bridal. It must inevitably prompt some whispers — But Mr Peach will endure them, for the sake of hiding Clary's ink-blackened lips from the general view.

We have twenty chapters and more behind us! — yet only now do we see Miss Riddle, presented to her advantage.

She will never be what is called an *handsome woman.* — Her figure, nevertheless, must be admitted excellent. — And her bearing — There is little in it, of that feminine grace, which the world demands. But, study it with more attention. — Cast not your look over her, as though you survey the couples at a ball, to see which makes the prettiest impression. Employ rather the vision of the painter, who sees within the outward form, the shapes of the soul. — And now confess, that Clary compels the searching gaze to linger. We might say, that though she is not *beautiful*, she touches the *sublime*. Not the less so, because she is veiled — It gives her image something of the air of those Egyptian heads, in the British Museum. You have admired them, reader — Their imperious stillness — Forbidding serenity —

Or — should we only say, that proper dress shews well on her, and that she is as pleasant to look at, as every healthy and well-bred person of seventeen years?

You may decide, reader, which account better suits your imagination. — We shall be content with your choice.

So to our narrative —

We return to Mr Peach, as he and Clary ascend the thorough-fares of the city, making their way through the various crowd, towards those elegant squares and avenues lately raised on the higher ground. Mr Peach seeks the house of Doctor Thorburn, where he hopes to procure an invitation. Clary is in search of — We know not what — Her desires remain obscure to us.

We toy with the thought of expatiating upon the veil she wears. It has the makings of a fine simile. — But we have spoken already, of the secrecy of Miss Riddle, and ought not to indulge ourselves in repetition; particularly at present, when our proper narrative is but lately resumed, after an unexpected diversion. On, then. —

Mr Peach nods to a few, with whom he is distantly familiar — Wishes still fewer, a good-day — And proceeds, ignored by and ignoring most — When a cry comes across the crowd —

— By Jove! Is that a fish, walking in the street? Or is it a door-mouse? Ha, ha!

Mr Peach casts around for some means of instant escape. — There is none.

— Come, my dear — says the voice of Mr Stokesay Stocks — Mr Peach now sees that gentleman's hat, and the golden curls of his head beneath it, over the common throng, and approaching. He cannot yet discern the companion, whom Mr Stocks addresses in such intimate terms. Mr Stocks has not lowered his voice. — Why should he? — If his words are not meant for all the world, it is all the world's business to shut its ears — Not his, to alter his tone. — Come — cries he — here's a fellow you must meet. Hi, sir! Good-day. — Upon my soul, is that your maid?

The crowds part before him, allowing Mr Peach to see, that the companion on Mr Stocks's arm is his intended bride, Miss Arabella Farthingay.

— My dear — says Mr Stocks — What would you think, if I told you this gentleman is — Mr Doormouse Fish? Ha, ha, ha!

Miss Farthingay does not say what she would think, though we deduce from her look, that she would be — indeed, she *is* — less amused, than her companion. The natural vivacity, which marked her previous appearances in our narrative, is absent from her demeanour. She is pale, and downcast, and acknowledges Mr Peach in a low voice.

— Good-day to you, Mr Peach.

Mr Stocks is amazed, to find them already acquainted — And not a little disappointed also, at a circumstance which threatens to diminish the humour of his anecdote. But he is one of those who never suffers disappointment long. — Happy man! The useful resilience of his temper encourages him to indulge his joke in full, whatever the risk that it may fail at the last. Some minutes thus pass, while he gives Miss Farthingay the whole comedy of the two foreign rascals in the road, and their misapprehension of Mr Peach's name, &c. — Meanwhile, Mr Peach is beset by several anxieties, which tumble one upon the other, each clamouring for his attention, in the persistent and distracting manner of small children, or dogs of any size. A most unpleasant sensation, for a man of a methodical cast of mind! — At one sleeve tugs the thought, that Miss Farthingay must not expose him, as the brother of that Sophonisba, and the nephew of that Augustus, connected to Mr Stocks's family in London. — In his confusion he cannot recall why — It is to do with the history of poor Eliza. — He is prevented from giving it proper consideration, by the urgent plucking of his other sleeve — we speak in metaphor — If the mind may be said to have an *eye*, why may it not also have an *elbow*? and so, if you please, we shall say, that his *mind's elbow* is tugged at — By the urgent necessity, of interposing himself between Miss Farthingay and Clary! — For, if the young lady were to recognize in the figure of Mr Peach's servant, the very girl, who was raised in her own father's household — Why, then —

Mr Peach cannot at the spur of the moment imagine the precise consequence. It is hard, to think in haste. — Doubly hard, with an harried and distracted mind. — Trebly hard, we might say, when decorum requires, that the body in which the thinking brain is housed, occupy itself with appearing to attend to Mr Stocks's

anecdote. Mr Peach can endure no more — He turns aside from
Mr Stocks for a moment, glancing behind, to ensure that Clary's
head is veiled, and averted. —

And so discovers, that Clary is *not there* — Not behind, nor
beside, nor any where in view at all — But has fled the scene.

Mr Stocks has not quite brought his joke to its climax, when he
observes that Mr Peach no longer attends.

— Well! says he, good-humouredly — I see, my dear, you
already know the gentleman is Thomas Peach — not Doormouse
Fish at all — But, sir, have you mislaid your companion? I thought
you were walking with a lady.

— Indeed, Mr Peach? says Miss Farthingay. — Is Mrs Peach
then sufficiently recovered, that she takes her exercise in the town?
I am very pleased to hear it.

— By Jove! says Mr Stocks — Then the gentleman is a married
man, and you are also acquainted with Mrs Peach — Mrs
Fish — ha!

— No — Madam — says Mr Peach — Mrs Peach is still
confined, alas. — That was my maid —

— A-ha! cries Mr Stocks, in even higher good-humour, for it
seems to him this encounter is as full of surprizing coincidence,
and unexpected discoveries, as the last Act of a play — I met the
very girl, ha'nt I? But where has she got to? I should like to give
her a shilling, in honour of — Here Mr Stocks looks about
himself, pausing a moment. — He is uncertain of the precise
occasion, to be honoured. — This lucky chance! he says. — What
was the little creature's name? — 'Twas C— something —

— Charlotte, says Mr Peach, hastily, for he would not encourage Miss Farthingay's thoughts to turn to her father's quondam
ward. — She has gone ahead — I required some things of her.

— You've dressed her in good cloaths, I see, says Mr Stocks. —
Was that not my very last advice to you? It was, you know, my
dear — When this gentleman and I parted — I said the very
thing — Come to town, I said, and get some things for your girl —
And, by thunder, here you are! Ha, ha. Nothing could be so

remarkable. And a friend of my dear Arabella, to cap it all! Is it not just like a play? Don't you think so, my dear?

— It is a little like, says Miss Farthingay.

— Ha! says Mr Stocks, striking his cane upon the ground, in the excitement of inspiration — And, like a play, it ends in — A wedding!

Mr Peach bows, and offers the couple his congratulations.

— My dear Arabella, says Mr Stocks, has done me the honour — The very greatest honour. — He smiles on her. In his look there is infinite satisfaction and happiness, not in the least diminished, by the entire want of any reciprocal marks of delight in hers.

Mr Peach repeats the felicitations.

— Why — says Mr Stocks, once more giving the unoffending street a blow with the heel of his cane — And you shall come to the wedding! Shan't he, Bella, dear? And Mrs Peach also.

— Your presences would make the joyful day more happy still, says Miss Farthingay, with the same pale look, as though to give life to that paradox of prince Hamlet's wicked uncle, *dirge in marriage.**

— D'ye know — You shall not be the only *Peaches* there. We shall have a *dish of peaches*, at our wedding, ha, ha, ha! — Do you recall those people of my cousin Sir Nigylle? They are Peaches too, 'pon my word. Sir — I must explain it — it is the most amusing thing in the world. My relation in London is Sir Nigylle Stocks, and, you know, there is some cousin of his — or a niece — or it may be by marriage — But no matter — The great jest of it is, that their name is also Peach! What do you think, Bella? shall we call them, the *town Peach*, and the *country Peach*? We must do something, or we shan't know who we speak of. By Jove! — it is exactly like the play. I'm sure I saw it once, where two fellows had the same name, and all the comedy that followed. Excellent — excellent!

* 'With mirth in funeral, and with dirge in marriage.'

— The invitation, says Mr Peach, bowing once more, Is very gracious. Though I fear the indisposition of Mrs Peach requires so much of my duty, that I cannot often expend the remainder in happier engagements. Has the joyful day been named, and the place?

— We have postponed all thoughts of it, says Miss Farthingay, out of respect for the late dreadful accident.

— An accident? cries Mr Peach. — Forgive me — Is all well?

— Terrible — says Mr Stocks, shaking his head, and repeats — Terrible — Though there appears no more shadow in his countenance, than there was sun-shine in his intended's, when she spoke of her *joyful day*.

— You have not heard, then, that Grandison Hall is destroyed by fire.

Mr Peach is all astonishment and horror. — My dear Miss Farthingay, he says, offering his hand, by an instinct of sympathy.

— But two nights ago, says she.

— I dread to ask, says Mr Peach — Your parents? —

— Thank Heaven, they were not at home.

— Dreadful, says Mr Stocks.

— None were lost, says Miss Farthingay. — But, nevertheless — So much is ruined. My library —

— I am unspeakably grieved for you, says Mr Peach.

— Terrible, says Mr Stocks, like the chorus in a Greek play, which stands as it were in the margin of the stage, and makes its comment, while the principal actors proceed with the drama. — A great tragedy.

— In the circumstances, says Miss Farthingay, our nuptials are not to be thought of.

— Naturally so, says Mr Peach. — Mr and Mrs Farthingay must be greatly distressed. I should ask you to express to them my sincere sympathies, and regards. I am at their service, and yours, in any thing.

— You are very kind, says Miss Farthingay.

— You know, sir, says Mr Stocks, you might do it yourself, come to that. There's to be a dinner to-night. Shall Mr Peach not join us, Bella? And Mrs Peach also? It shall be at Mr Farthingay's house, in ____-Square. It is to celebrate the engagement. There are several odd old fellows invited. — Shall we not include Mr Peach? We shall have capital amusement. — Mr Stocks here takes the hand of his intended from Mr Peach, and pats it, with a comfortable smile, as though to share with her the thought, that the violent destruction of her father's estate is but a trifle, next to the anticipated pleasures of Bristol society.

Mr Peach expresses himself obliged — But thinks he must decline to present himself to Mr and Mrs Farthingay, at such a time. Mr Stocks will not hear of it — And so the exchange continues, with neither side likely to gain the advantage, until Miss Farthingay intervenes.

— Sir, she says, Mama and Papa have decided that the occasion ought to proceed, because the buffet is already engaged, and the wine paid for. You need not fear they are disinclined to society. I shall not speak for my own part, except to say that whatever pleasure I may have in the assembly would only be increased if you were present.

— Why, Bella, cries Mr Stocks — You don't need a library, when you talk so much like a book yourself! Is she not a fine talker, Mr Peach? She was used to write verses. Were you not, dear? — Had you not once a little book of poems? You may smile, sir, but it's quite true, I assure you. Ask her father — He will tell you the same.

Mr Peach has not thought of a smile, since the inception of the encounter.

— Heigh-ho! well, you must please yourself, continues Mr Stocks. He is all indulgent cheer. He would have all the world please themselves — Just as he does. — But, he says, we shall expect you — I shall tell old Farthingay — And Bella will have you there, won't you, dear? I see you are old friends already. We shall all be better acquainted — &c. — Mr Stocks's further

346

remarks are of no consequence, and we shall remove ourselves from his company, a little before our hero is able to do likewise.

As for Clary — she is utterly vanished from the scene. Mr Peach looks among the nearby streets, but neither sees her, nor hears any murmured reports, of a veiled woman hurrying one way or another.

— Well, he thinks, she's a strange creature, and must go her own way. — And with this tolerant opinion, he proceeds to the house of Doctor Thorburn, meditating no further on his maid and her mysteries, but bending all his thoughts to his chief purpose.

His efforts are in vain. — The Doctor is not at home.

It is generally understood to-day, and was still more universally acknowledged, in the year of which we write, that to arrive at a gentleman's door, and be informed, that he is *not at home*, may have several meanings, among them some quite contradictory. It may mean, that the gentleman is — Not at home. But it may equally well mean that he *is* at home — That is, the very inverse of the apparent sense of the words — And that he merely wishes to be considered absent, should any body come visiting. Between these extremes lie other gradations of meaning — As, for example, that he *may* be found to be at home, if the valet or footman, who speaks the words, were to receive some form of persuasion — Or that he *is* at home to one visitor, but *not* to another — Or, that he is presently engaged with his mistress — Or is still drunk. The breadth of possibility, comprehended by those three syllables, is remarkable — Equalled only, among formulae as brief, by those three other oft-spoken words, *I love thee*, which are also found to signify any thing, between their plain meaning, and its exact opposite.

Mr Peach desires to know, when he may hope to call on Doctor Thorburn? — Oh — I don't know — To-morrow, or another day — The fellow evidently thinks it no concern of his. Had Mr Peach arrived in a barouche, or even a chair, the case might have been otherwise. Or, were he to resort to that method of persuasion, alluded to just now, he should perhaps have hopes of a definite answer. But he does not. — We shall candidly admit, he *cannot*. — His straits are such, that even those small considerations, which permit the man of moderate means to ease his path through the world, are not to be dispensed with, unless quite necessary.

Mr Peach says, he will return in the evening, and in meantime hopes that Doctor Thorburn may be advised of his presence in town, on a matter of very particular interest to the Doctor.

The fellow is bored — But rouses himself sufficiently, to advise Mr Peach, not to return in the evening, because the Doctor is engaged. He requests Mr Peach's card. — Mr Peach has no card — A confession, which propels the fellow's brow into a motion, expressive of the most profound pity and contempt.

By this time a small gathering of onlookers has assembled in the street, to amuse themselves with the scene. Mr Peach, as we have often remarked, is neither vain, nor proud. But he is by natural temper averse to being made the object of public interest, whether its tenor be scornful, or admiring, or of whatever quality at all. He tips his hat, and moves on — And walks all the way back to his lodging beyond the town, without a stop.

We have already noticed the interesting correspondence, or sympathy, between those two most elementary pleasures of human existence, *walking* and *thinking*.

Had Mr Peach mounted in a carriage, upon being turned away from Doctor Thorburn's house — Had he been jolted and buffeted by the cobbles on his way to the inn, and then taken his ill-humoured disappointment into the parlour, and thrown himself in a chair, and called for mutton and brandy — In such circumstances, we have no doubt, that the failure of his enterprize would have festered in him. He would have brooded on the injury, like the cat that licks her wound — His temper worsening by the hour — Until his whole project would have appeared in ruins before him, hopeless of rescue, and his future course nothing but a desart of lifeless despair. But, being compelled to walk a mile and more, and, in the course of that mile, exchanging the stench and tumult of the town, for the sweet summer fields — His mind runs free of the rebuff. It will not stay confined within the circuit of disappointment — But wanders, at large. — He meditates upon the unfortunate choice made by Miss Farthingay — and on the dreadful accident suffered by her parents — And so his brain goes along with his legs, until, without any particular effort of reason, he recalls Mr Stocks's remark, that the evening's entertainment at Mr Farthingay's town-house, is to be attended by *several odd old fellows*, and guesses, that this may very well be an allusion to the members of the Anti-Lapsarian Society — Mr Farthingay's dearest and most distinguished Bristol friends being his colleagues in that philanthropic assembly; and he then recalls the insolent butler's information, that Doctor Thorburn is engaged this evening; and so at last arrives at the thought, that — The Doctor is very likely one of those, invited to the house of Mr Farthingay!

Mr Peach had not intended to take up the invitation, so freely offered by Mr Stocks. Despite the gentle entreaty of Miss Farthingay, he has been unable to persuade himself, that he may properly appear at a gathering, where he had not been expected. Nor, we must add, has the prospect of celebrating the engagement between the happy pair afforded him much pleasure.

However, now that it admits the possibility of approaching Doctor Thorburn, the forthcoming dinner appears in a very different light.

In short — By the time he has entered the village, where his lodging lies, he has determined to wait upon Mr and Mrs Farthingay, at their house in town, that same evening.

He communicates the intention to Clary, who is likewise returned to the inn, having fled the sight of Miss Farthingay, and walked all the way to the inn, alone, and in new shoes. — From which adventure she has suffered no worse indignities, than the rude laughter of a few boys, and some pinching and bruising at her heel.

— Was that gentleman who accosted you Bella's intended husband? she asks.

— I fear so, says Mr Peach.

— I thought she had too much spirit to accept a booby and a coxcomb.

— Your acquaintance with the lady extends much beyond mine. Yet I think I would have come to the same conclusion, had I spoken with her but once.

— Is the man also so heartless, that he forbids her to wear her mourning?

Mr Peach regards her curiously. — Why, Clary — Did you expect to see Miss Farthingay in mourning?

Clary appears hesitant for a moment, and then replies, I heard, sir, that her father's house was lately destroyed in a sudden explosion.

— And from where did you hear this news?

— From the common rumour. Is it not true?

— It is true indeed, alas, though I myself only heard it from the mouth of Miss Farthingay, just now.

— Poor girl. Though she had not much cause to love her parents, the shock of such a loss must be keenly felt.

— I am glad to inform you that rumour has so far misled you, Clary. Mr and Mrs Farthingay are quite unhurt. By good fortune they are at their house in Bristol, and so escaped the fire.

Clary's black mouth opens in surprize, and her eyes seem to flash with some inward and noctilucent lightning — The picture for a moment as horrific a sight, as human features may be thought capable of producing. Mr Peach cannot escape the sudden impression, that if the book of Genesis speak true, and human-kind be fashioned in the likeness of God, then here before him is the very image of the vengeful deity, who consumed whole cities in fire, and drowned the world.

— Excuse me, sir, says she, and turns aside. — I had thought, from noticing Bella's unhappy look, that some such tragedy — Clary's speech has become halting. — But, she says, the Farthingays are still — Are alive? Is it certain?

— I think I should not have been invited to dine with them otherwise.

— They have had a fortunate escape, she says.

350

— I fear you are disappointed to hear they have not perished.

Clary is silent, and will not meet Mr Peach's eye.

— It is a cruel and unhappy thought, he says, to wish the death of another.

— So says the man, who confessed himself a murderer.

Mr Peach is taken aback by the sting of her rebuke — Well — says he — Let us not contend for dishonour, but agree to rejoice in the escape of Mr and Mrs Farthingay, if only for their child's sake. You do not wish *her* ill, I hope?

The storm passes from Clary's look. — Mr Peach is greatly relieved. — What this creature may be capable of, he thinks, I do not wish to know.

— Bella, she says, was often good to me, when the gulf between us allowed it. Will she really be married to that fool?

— It is the wish of her parents, he says, and will be a very advantageous match.

— He spoke to me in the road at home. He would have sat and begged like a dog, for a look at my a__e.

Mr Peach indicates, by means of a pained expression, that he prefers not to discuss the matter further.

— Might you not have wooed Miss Bella yourself, sir? She has wit and discernment, and will be very rich.

— I shall lose my breath, I suppose, if I condemn your impertinence. You know I am married already.

— Are you, sir?

Clary's look is piercing. — She knows, thinks Mr Peach — She has known, since she first set foot in my house. There is some kinship between her unnatural existence and my Eliza's — She has my secret, by instinct.

Says she — I observe your devotion to your wife, and admire you for it. But I fear it will be your downfall.

Mr Peach feels his indignation rising. — I have forbid you to speak of this, he says, but I see there is no restraint that can curb your black mouth. — If I cannot *demand* that you do not speak of my wife, may I *request* it?

— I mean no insult, nor contempt. You are very good, sir — Your heart is good. But I know — You hold a door open between yourself and Mrs Peach. So long as you do so, there are others, that will make use of the passage. You cannot do it at all, without their knowledge — their assistance —

Mr Peach is seized by a very great desire, to hear no more — To be elsewhere. Even the dinner in honour of Miss Farthingay's ill-chosen engagement, may be preferable to the conversation of his cursed inhuman maid! —

We shall allow him to try the experiment. —

Once again, therefore, we propel our narrative forward, across an interval of no interest to us — And return our hero to town, as the evening begins to cool — Revealing him, at the house of Mr and Mrs Farthingay.

No expence was to have been stinted, to honour the announcement of their daughter's union, to a young shoot of one of the first families in the land. — A somewhat obscure shoot — shaded, as it were, by the more prominent growth, that luxuriates elsewhere in the arbour — But, nevertheless — The mere name of *Stocks*, has a kind of prominence in the chronicle of the kingdom — Is printed in BOLD, in the largest type, where no eye can fail to remark it — Is listed, indeed, near the top-mast of the page — we confound our metaphors in our enthusiasm — Listed, we say, not many lines beneath the greatest name of all, that royal GEORGE, to whom the addition of a sirname, would be unpardonable superfluity. Sir Nigylle Stocks is said to command such influence, that nothing is done in the whole island of Britain, without his knowledge. — Nothing of importance, that is to say — Nothing worthy the chronicler's note. Though young Stokesay Stocks is at present several spheres removed from that celestial orbit, in which his great relative moves, dispensing the fortunes of those beneath — Nevertheless, Mr Farthingay *has hopes* — Mrs Farthingay counts them nearer to *certainties* — That the day will come, when a post among the burgeoning ministry of placemen shall be opened for his advancement, and he may paint a coronet on the door of his carriage, and their child will be LADY STOCKS.

A prospect so momentous, requires the most lavish, though elegant, celebrations. The house has for several days been given over in turn to the carpenters, and the painters, and the lace-makers, and the purveyors of sweet blooms, and the pastry-cooks, and the best musicians of the town. All was in readiness — Or, almost all — the remainder, carefully hidden from the vigilant eye of Mrs Farthingay — when news of the conflagration came to Bristol. — Mrs Farthingay was staggered, and took to her bed — Mr Farthingay, to his pipe and bottle. — The engagement must certainly be postponed. The carpenters have been called back, to take away the charming platform, done in the stile of a Grecian temple, with strict adherence to the second* of the orders of architecture, on which the blessed couple were to be revealed, while sugar-puff and lilac petals rained down on them from the belly of a plaster swan, and oboes and viols played a serenade. The swags of muslin have been folded away, though kept, for another occasion. The players of oboe and viol are advised, that they will not be required.

But the ice, and the syllabubs, and the pastry crowns — All the splendid victuals — These things, being transitory, cannot be sent whence they came, or put aside for a month. — And the wine! — It will keep, if it must; but why must it?

Mr Farthingay thinks there is no oeconomy in ordering the wine to the cellar, when the viands and sweets must be consumed. — Mrs Farthingay remains in her bed.

The celebration is ordered to proceed, though in more solemn mood. The engagement will not be announced. — It shall instead, be *murmured*. Every body will be informed, certainly, but by discreet degrees. Congratulations may be presented to the young people — In sober fashion. Mrs Farthingay will recover her spirits, in order to receive the compliments of her acquaintance, upon securing so excellent a match for her daughter. — But all shall be

---

* The Ionic.

done, without pageantry — As it were, in the *minor* key — The occasion is to be a *sarabande*, in place of a bright joyous *gavotte*.

Mr Peach arrives to find the assembly in curious equipoise, between gaiety and solemnity. In this aspect, it corresponds well with the handsome young couple, whose union it heralds. — For, as he found them in the street, he observes them again, in the parental home — He, brim-ful of social cheer — She, with a certain heaviness of spirit.

Mr Peach's own sentiments, we are pleased to say, tend more to joy than sorrow. — First, because he is most warmly welcomed by Mr Farthingay, though he had not been expected before that very after-noon; and then, because he is informed, that Doctor Thorburn is to be among the company, beside several other companions of the Anti-Lapsarian fraternity.

The welcome news he has, from Mr Farthingay himself.

— In our hour of trial — declares that gentleman, embracing Mr Peach repeatedly — When we are sorely tested — What a comfort is found, in the society of our *friends*. — Mr Farthingay, in pronouncing this last word, clasps Mr Peach by the shoulders, and shakes him, with all the fervour of elevated emotion.

Mr Peach, when his jaw has ceased a-rattling, expresses his sense of Mr Farthingay's loss.

Mr Farthingay leans close. — Quite *blown up*! he says. — I shall have to rebuild, from the very ground. The years — The expence!

Mr Peach is sympathetic.

— The Almighty has decreed, Mr Peach, that all my projects shall come to nothing. For what sin of mine, I know not — But beyond doubt, I am singled out for wrath. I am the most unfortunate of men.

Mr Peach is not willing to assume the role of Eliphaz the Temanite, and advise Mr Farthingay to reconcile himself with the judgment of Heaven;* and therefore leaves his friend to his

---

* We have throughout our narrative hesitated from those *theological* reflexions, which certain of its passages surely invite. Were we to pursue them, we fear the articles of orthodox faith would tremble to the foundations.

copious lamentations, with conventional sentiments of comfort, which, being mere words, and as empty of feeling as is customary on such occasions, we do not trouble to record.

Miss Arabella Farthingay is glad to see him — But cannot say much more, for she is closely chaperoned by her mother, who, having determined that Mr Peach is one of her husband's *tenants* — Directs her daughter elsewhere.

Mr Stokesay Stocks is much occupied, in receiving the congratulations of the company. Nevertheless, he notices the presence of Mr Peach, with warm enthusiasm. — And, further, begs the favour of a word, upon a matter suitable for private discussion between gentlemen. This request he communicates with a curious sort of wink, as though he and Mr Peach were on terms of antient amity and perfect mutual understanding. Mr Peach would much prefer not to be favoured with Mr Stocks's confidence, but he can hardly refuse. — Indeed, refusal is not thought of — Mr Stocks's requests being formally indistinguishable from demands, at least according to the interpretation of Mr Stocks.

— Besides, thinks Mr Peach, Doctor Thorburn is not yet arrived. — I must look for my amusement where I may.

Some minutes later, therefore, Mr Peach is beckoned to a corner of the room, to enjoy the intimate conversation of Miss Farthingay's intended; where he is exceedingly surprized to learn, that the subject upon which the gentleman wishes to be satisfied, is — his maid.

— Nevertheless, reader — Do not think we are so bold as to scorn, what is popularly called Holy Writ. The Testaments, Old and New, command our profoundest respect — No where more, than in this terrible and sublime book of *Job*. We doubt, that all the wisdom of the church fathers, superadded to every ingenious argument of all divines between their time and ours, amounts to one-tenth of the truth, communicated 'from the whirlwind' in the stupendous conclusion to that greatest poem of the Hebrew literature — In which the Creator's answer, to every complaint of injustice, cruelty, and indifference, addressed to him by suffering man, appears to be, thus — Sir — *I* am God — *Thou* art not — And there's an end on't.

— By God, Peach, says Mr Stocks — I was d___d sorry that little piece of yours fled away, before I had the leisure to look her over, in her new dress.

Mr Peach cannot answer — Is fortunate, that no answer is expected.

— D___d sorry indeed, repeats Mr Stocks. — But, hey, sir, what possessed you, to have her cover her head? I'm sure I saw the little pigeon was veiled, before she took flight. D___n me, sir, this is England! — not the court of the Sooltan, ha, ha!

— Sir — says Mr Peach, with a cold formality, worthy of the most austere Puritan of *Cromwell's* day — The young woman must veil her face in public, to prevent her deformity from attracting that vulgar interest, which is so readily kindled in the eye of the idle, the thoughtless, and the unkind.

— What? deformity, do you say?

— You cannot fail to have observed it, on the occasion of your former visit to my house. She is afflicted with a severe discolouration of the lips and mouth.

— Pish, man, I think I should have noticed any thing *severe*. For, you know, she was not much *covered*, when I spoke to her. — Mr Stocks punctuates this observation, by clipping Mr Peach on the arm, and roaring with laughter. — Now I think on it — She might have looked a little bruised about the face — But what of that? — D___n me, she looked well enough, high and low — What — From one *end* to the other, ha! ha! ha!

Mr Peach does not join in the merriment.

— Now I recall it, continues Mr Stocks, she would always look away, when she spoke. Thought it rather becoming, hey? A girl of that class ought to be modest, hey? — Though — Not *too* modest — Don't you agree, Peach? — Not *too* modest?

Mr Peach is in the grip of a *moral* revulsion, which again prevents any reply. — Reader, you may ask, what right a man has to be disgusted, at the behaviour of another, who has but two days earlier arranged the *murder* of one of his fellow men?

We do not dispute it with you. — We leave you, to form your own judgments of the character of Mr Peach — And of Mr Stocks.

— Great Jove! Suppose if she could not speak at all! — she'd then be — The perfect woman!

Mr Stocks is so delighted at this sally, that he must laugh long enough, to draw the eye of the rest of the company. — Who are thus favoured with a *tableau*, that might have been painted by *Reynolds*, and titled, Allegory of Comedy and Tragedy. For there stands Mr Stocks, gaily dressed in velvet coat and striped silk breeches, golden-haired, ruby of cheek, holding the cup of mirth, and laughing as though he had not a care in the world — Which is indeed the case. — While here beside, is Mr Peach — In black — His look, all severity —

We need not belabour our illustration.

— But — says Mr Stocks, when he is recovered — he lowers his voice, to signify that he is come to the heart of the matter he would discuss — What — Will you listen to a proposition, concerning this maid of yours — What was her name — I forget again — Cla—

— Charlotte, says Mr Peach.

— I knew 'twas C— something. Hear me, Mr Peach. — My Bella wants a female attendant, is the nut of it. She has at present a manservant — Negro — a good enough fellow, but, you see, it won't do. He shall be sent off, as soon as we are engaged, and we must procure some girl instead. What say you — shall you spare this Charlotte of yours? There will be no loss for you, sir, I assure you. A suitable consideration — A gentleman need not say more, sir — It will be my pleasure to do every thing. You understand me.

Mr Peach feels a sudden tide of inward joy — Fate has looked kindly on him at last, by presenting him with an opportunity to disoblige Mr Stocks.

— It is not to be thought of, he says. — Charlotte is absolutely disqualified from such a position, by her deformity.

— Nonsense! cries Mr Stocks — but adds no word of explanation or argument. His objection, we think, is not so much to the view proposed, as the mere fact of contradiction.

Mr Peach shakes his head, with all the secret joy of the miser, who refuses the needy petitioner any mitigation of their debt. — Alas, Mr Stocks, the fact is quite unalterable. Charlotte will ever be unsuited to attend a lady of fashion. Besides, I could not possibly entertain the suggestion without consulting the girl's own wishes; which, I am certain, would be opposed to any such proposal.

Mr Stocks regards Mr Peach with unalloyed amazement.

— D'ye say no, then?

— Sir, I do.

— Well!

Mr Stocks looks about — As though to assure himself, that the four corners of the world yet stand where they did, and the entire order of creation has not been set topsy-turvy.

— I should have thought, Mr Peach continues, that Miss Farthingay would be much grieved to be parted from the services of Caspar.

Mr Stocks sets down his cup, and appears to bristle, as though he were a large mastiff, that has taken against a visitor, on some canine whim.

— What d'ye mean by that, Peach? says he.

— Merely that a lady, on the occasion of her marriage, and her removal from the parental home, must find a great deal of comfort in any thing familiar and enduring, amid so many changes in her way of life; and that there must be a peculiar contentment in the continued attentions of a servant, who is intimately familiar with her habits and wants, and may gratify her in a thousand every-day matters, of little significance in themselves, yet together contributing much to her ease, when so much else is new and strange.

The pen, it is said, is mightier than the sword. — Mr Stocks, who had seemed ready to take offence — what construction he put upon Mr Peach's remark, which made him so suddenly jealous of his honour, we shall not guess at — He is, we say, as it were *disarmed*, by this explanation. — Though we think it is not so much the eloquence, nor the sense, of the words, which has served to blunt his indignation, as their *quantity*.

— Hem — says he — Well, you may say so — But for all that, it won't do. A lady of fashion must have a lady's maid, not some proud blackamoor. Your Charlotte — We shall speak of it another time.

Mr Peach bows in acknowledgment.

— We shall look for you again in town. — I should like to look over this, what d'ye call it — Her defect. D___n me if I didn't think her a perfect little miss.

— The prospect is doubtful, I fear, says Mr Peach. — I do not anticipate staying long in Bristol. Besides, the lodgings I have taken are some distance from the town.

A curious light appears in Mr Stocks's eye.

— Lodgings, hey? says he.

Mr Peach assumes, that the inoffensive word has excited some idea in the mind of his interlocutor, and waits to discover what it may be.

— The girl is put up in the same spot, I suppose?

— Indeed. She has no family or other acquaintance in Bristol, where she might otherwise stay.

— And where is it, sir?

Mr Peach thinks the question somewhat extraordinary — But is, for once — *not* surprized.

— A village inn only. You have seen my house, Mr Stocks, and you therefore know I prefer rural retirement to the charms of town. A modest accommodation suits quite well.

Whatever the nature of Mr Stocks's idea, we must think it an happy one, for his good-humour appears perfectly restored. He takes up his cup again.

— Very commendable, very commendable! A village, you say? — I shall make enquiries. By God, you're a decent fellow after all, sir! — your health!

With this amiable remark, the material part of the conversation is ended, and Mr Peach returns to the general intercourse.

We shall not record its every turn and tumble. Much is said — Little attended to — Even less, will be remembered, either by those who talk, or those who listen — And *none* of it need concern us — Until, the arrival of Doctor Thorburn.

The gentleman is, as they say, late to the feast. — A circumstance vexing to Mr Peach, who finds little pleasure in the society, while he awaits the Doctor; and his vexation is compounded, by the announcement to take seats to dine, no sooner than his quarry appears. He is compelled to endure the whole profane liturgy of feasting, and drinking, and addresses, and huzza's, and glees — Rites, to which he has never subscribed with much enjoyment, and, on this night, when he is impatient to proceed to the necessary business, he finds all but insupportable. The only person in all the company, who appears to take as little delight in it, is Miss Farthingay, the intended bride. — Poor soul — says one to another — She is much affected, by the sad accident — The house all blown to pieces, they say! — And it is generally agreed, that her nerves are sensitive, and finely wrought, as befits an interesting young lady.

The hour comes at last, when the gentlemen gather to pipes and cards. Before the tables are made, some brothers of the Anti-Lapsarian Society assemble in conversation. Mr Farthingay stands at the centre — As he must, for a body so extensive, cannot be *peripheral*. Around him are Mr Peach, and Mr Selby White, and Doctor Thorburn, and one or two others, to whom Mr Farthingay again bewails his catastrophe, and, between draughts of excellent brandy, proclaims himself the unluckiest of men.

— In the American States, says Doctor Thorburn, the accident of domestic fire is never heard of.

— Never? cries Mr Selby White.

— Never, says the Doctor, or so rarely, that instances are spoken of as extraordinary events. The atchievement is more remarkable when we consider the universal recourse to timber, as the material for constructing our houses. The supply of timber in the nation of America is so plentiful, that it may with mathematical precision be termed *infinite*.

Says Mr Selby White — Do your American trees not then burn? It must be a great inconvenience, in cold weather.

— On the contrary! cries the Doctor. — There is no wood in the world so well-suited for fuel, as the native woods of the American forest! I myself have seen an entire house, and that of no mean dimensions, kept perfectly warm for a whole winter night, by one single log of New Hampshire maple. No, sir — The reason the houses of America do not suffer by fire, as yours of Europe do, is assuredly not from any deficiency in the flammability of the material! It is entirely owing to the wise measures established in every town, which ensure that the smallest risk of conflagration is instantly advertised, and prevented from becoming dangerous, by the concerted actions of the citizenry, who gather themselves for that purpose, at any hour of the day or night; for there is implanted in them the sacred instinct to serve the common good, without demur or hesitation, by assembling as *brothers*. I have no doubt that when the Continental Congress at New York has concluded its deliberation, these measures, so universally and infallibly effective, will be inscribed among the LAWS of the new nation. — So that the terrible curse of the *house fire*, which over the unawakened remainder of the globe has been so destructive of property and human happiness, will in the American republic be utterly unknown! — and future generations of Americans will marvel at the report of it, as we wonder at the legend of the phoenix.

Mr Farthingay seems not much consoled, by this happy vision. The conversation turns to general matters. — Mr Peach is able to take Doctor Thorburn by the arm, and request a word apart.

— I am commissioned to speak with you, sir, says he, in a low voice, By a friend, who much desires to know you.

Doctor Thorburn's reply is as loud and hearty, as Mr Peach's suggestion was discreet and intimate — Why, then, let him,

Thomas! let him come forth and know me! We have no need of your *I am commissioneds* here. — All shall be free and open! for I despise any servile deference.

— Doctor Thorburn, says Mr Peach, placing his lips very near the gentleman's ear, — The name of my friend, is not to be spoken, where any but a brother in THE CAUSE might hear it. — Mr Peach withdraws his lips, and bestows on the Doctor a look of great significance. — Shall we, he says, take a turn about the room?

Doctor Thorburn appears impressed by Mr Peach's curious information. — In a moment, the two gentlemen have stepped apart.

— My friend sends no letter, murmurs Mr Peach. — Nor any other token, which might be noticed, or *intercepted*. He is hunted by the agents of tyranny — Pray, Doctor Thorburn, do not startle! We may be observed.

— Thomas Peach, says Doctor Thorburn, I do not think I understand you.

— Good — That is good — says Mr Peach — Pretend, you do not understand — Speak so, if we must be heard. Now look aside again — Just so — We are safe. — In this place, I say only that I am instructed to greet you in the name of *Liberty*, by one who holds that name dearer than his own, though his is — Mr Peach again bends his lips to the Doctor's ear — *Jeremiah Sixways*.

Doctor Thorburn is amazed. —

— Look aside, friend! exclaims Mr Peach — a *whispering* exclamation — It must appear that we say nothing not fit for this place. — He raises his voice, and laughs — Ha, ha! A great jest indeed, sir. Ha! ha! — Mr Peach whispers again — Laugh with me.

There is a moment of uncertainty, and then Doctor Thorburn joins in with the pretended jest — Ha, ha, ha!

— Very good — Let us walk on. — You have lately had a communication from citizen Sixways, I know. I regret to say, his letter was certainly intercepted by the lackeys of corruption. He has had no answer, and so sends me in person.

— No answer! — Doctor Thorburn has now caught the whispering habit. — I wrote to the man several days ago.

Mr Peach puts on a rueful look, for which his countenance is well suited. — Then it is as I fear. The hounds of authority are on the scent. Thank the Divine Reason, I am not suspected.

Doctor Thorburn's uncertainty has melted away. He regards Mr Peach with a look of transported affection — Takes his hand — Grasps him, in so vigorous an embrace, as might have attracted notice, were it not that every body in the room is now arrived at that degree of warm conviviality, which is rightly reckoned the chief virtue of wine and tobacco, and passionate expressions of amity are therefore the order of the hour.

— Mr Peach — Citizen — Brother! — I had not known you were *one of us*.

— None must know, says Mr Peach. — The friends of Jeremiah Sixways must be perfectly secret.

— And I would die, my friend, three times over, before I breathed a word of it! — Is there immediate danger? — Doctor Thorburn here casts several glances around the room.

— Not at present. The lap-dogs of oppression have sought citizen Sixways these many years, but he knows their wiles, and frustrates them.

— I am inexpressibly delighted — Thomas, my brother, I am beyond measure pleased to discover there is such a man — Such *men* — Here Doctor Thorburn offers another embrace.

— I may tell you, says Mr Peach, the man we speak of is one, beside whom the fawning slaves of antient illegitimacy are mere flies. Citizen Sixways is a great man — In whom great hopes may be entrusted — The *greatest* hopes. — Mr Peach invests the superlative with emphasis as tremendous as his soft tone will accommodate. — For, he continues, he is readying to atchieve the *greatest* things. — Mr Peach waggles his brows, as though to signify, *YOU, my friend, understand my meaning*.

Doctor Thorburn's blood is excited. — His cheeks are ruddy. — Is there, says he, such a man in this country? — Near at hand?

Mr Peach makes a shew of ascertaining, that they are not over-looked. — There is, he says, *more than one*. — Citizen Sixways has many friends, though he stands at their head. I may not name them — Absolute secrecy —

Doctor Thorburn's eye is moist.

— The day is near, continues Mr Peach, when they will no longer fear the light — But will burst forth, and LIBERTY with them. We want only a little more time — And certain necessi-ties — Above all, the assistance of some far-sighted and devoted man, who has the means to supply those necessities. — But we shall not speak of this here. May I call on you, at your leisure?

My house is yours! cries the Doctor — then recalls where he is, and lowers his voice again. — I will send word to-morrow. Where may I direct a message?

Mr Peach murmurs, that he may be found at the Cow and Welshman, in _____ton.

You shall come to my home, says Doctor Thorburn. — There are *others* — I would have you know them —

— Psssh, says Mr Peach, with another urgent look — Speak no names here.

The Doctor puts his hand to his mouth — leans close — whis-pers, — The watch-word will be, *Philadelphia*.

Mr Peach is about to bow, but recalls that the polite gesture may not be *democratic*. — He nods, instead.

— Now, he says — Let us laugh again — Ha, ha! he cries, in a loud voice — I never heard any thing so amusing!

— Ha, ha! is the echo from the Doctor.

Mr Selby White stands near by. — He begs to hear the jest. Doctor Thorburn is confounded, and turns pale. — Mr Peach is not at all discomposed. — With no more than a moment's hesitation, he begins to relay that anecdote, which proved so inexhaustible a fount of delight, to Mr Stokesay Stocks. — We mean, that poor business of the doormouse and the fish. — You are as tired of it as we, no doubt. Yet the jest comes to Mr Selby White clad in the virgin dress of *origi-nality*, and attended by the effects of sweet wine and brandy, whose

364

alchemy makes witty all that is dull. That gentleman is vastly amused — Repeats the tale, several times, to half the company —

It is time, we think, to make our excuses.

Mr Peach cannot forbear one last duty, before he too makes his exit. He wishes to present his compliments to Miss Farthingay in person. The lady comes out. — Accompanied still, by Mrs Farthingay, all paint and jewels.

— Mr Peach, says Miss Farthingay, giving her hand. — We are very glad to have had your company after all.

— Mr Peach bows. — The honour is mine, he says. — Mr Stocks's invitation has afforded me the opportunity to estimate for myself the happiness which awaits you in your future union, and to offer you my most earnest good wishes for that future.

— What does he say? cries Mrs Farthingay.

Reader — You have seen this character, an hundred times, upon the stage, or met her among the pages of the novel-writer's trash. The old woman must be ugly — vulgar — deaf — Speak all Malaprop — Be vain of her looks, without cause — Ridiculous in her dress, though she dreams herself fashionable — Carping and bitter in her speech — Ever faulting the vices of others, while remaining perfectly blind to her own — &c. &c. The type has grown somewhat tedious. Our authors bring her forward, because every body will laugh at her. It is as easily done, as kicking the cat. — Therefore — though we cannot deny, that Mrs Farthingay may bear some resemblance to the specimen — We shall exclude her from the course of our narrative; along which, at any rate, she has but a very little further to run.

Miss Farthingay is fatigued. — I thank you, sir, for your estimation, she says. — It is doubtless a just one. And also for your wishes, which I know to be sincere.

— I can claim no special merit in the former. Any body may see as well as I, how content you and the fortunate Mr Stocks are to be in your marriage. I am sure you reflect on those prospects yourself, as you anticipate the happy day.

— I think of it often, says Miss Farthingay.

— Then may I offer my hope, that you draw every useful lesson, from those solemn contemplations of your future happiness.

— I shall. Even we that are married have but *one life* to live, after all.

Mr Peach feels the colour rising to his face.

— A life passed in the mutual devotion of a well-matched pair, he says, may well become so rich in joy, that it seems to *outlast death*. But where there is misery in marriage, each day is a kind of extinction.

— You are still the poet, Mr Peach. A moralist, or a satirist, I think. A Juvenal.

— No, Miss Farthingay, the palm is yours. Poetry ought to belong to youth.

— Then I shall surrender them both together. Good-night, Mr Peach. I hope to see you again.

The various interjections of Mrs Farthingay, which we have omitted from our account of the conversation, now become so pressing, as to forbid any further thing of interest from being said. Mr Peach takes his final leave from the house.

He goes out, into the warm night —

Looks up to the sky, still fringed with deepest blue, empty of noise and riot —

We must leave his thoughts unrecorded, or we shall be writing another *Werter*.

He walks home again. Clary is yet awake, despite the lateness of the hour. — She never sleeps, he thinks.

She greets him with several questions, concerning the entertainment he has had. — Where is the house of Mr and Mrs Farthingay? — Of what stile, and dimensions? — Does it adjoin others? — Are there passages behind, as well as at the front? — How do the servants go in and out, and the tradesmen? — Mr Peach is very tired. He cannot imagine, why she wishes to know such things. — Nor can we.

Let us favour him with silence and rest, and so draw this long chapter of *walking* and *talking* to a close.

CHAPTER TWENTY-FOUR

The next morning, Mr Peach receives word from Doctor Thorburn. The message is plain and polite. It expresses no more, than the expectation that he will make one of the party at the Doctor's house, two nights hence. It is tied with a ribbon, and sealed, like a *billet-doux*. — And we doubt any fluttering damsel was ever better pleased to read her lover's invitation, than our sober hero is upon receipt of this.

He commits the few lines to memory, and is about to burn them, when he recalls, that as effective a means of disposing of the paper lies close to hand and one which will save him the trouble of the tinder-box.

He calls for Clary — Who accepts the offer eagerly — We might even say, Greedily — And modestly enquires, whether he might be so good as to procure some *ink*?

— I shall do so. I have need of some myself, though my purpose is the usual one.

— I shall be sure not to consume it all, sir.

Mr Peach regards her, with a *scientific* gaze. —

We do not on the instant recall, whether we have before now remarked on that peculiarity of human nature, by which we frail human creatures may become used to any thing. Place us on an isle of the tropics, like Crusoe, and within a month we should think nothing of drinking rain-water, and eating bread-fruit and the flesh of wild birds, and having no entertainment but watching the waves of the sea. — Or, in the Arctic wilds, and, within the same space of time, behold us, content with seal-skins, and our home in a frozen *ig-loo*. Mr Peach has now for several days had the horrid visage of his maid before his eye, hour by hour. The mysterious and universal law of nature has performed its operation so well, that he has almost ceased to find any thing strange in the sight.

— After all — thinks he — A person's hair may be black, or white, or yellow, or red, and so may their complexion, and we do not shudder at it. Why then may their mouth not be black?

— How does it taste, Clary?

— I know not how to describe it. It tastes like itself. Heavy, and thick.

— It is not unpleasant to you?

— Not at all. I crave it, as I must have craved water, before I was changed.

— I ought to have made arrangements before now. I shall endeavour to prepare better in future.

Clary expresses her sense of obligation, with the affecting simplicity of Miss Clarissa Harlowe herself.

— From her earliest days, thinks Mr Peach, she has been *taught* to speak so — Known no other language, but this discourse of modest and virtuous sincerity. How am I then to determine whether she be sincere indeed? — whether it be the language of the *heart*, or the *book*?

It is a curious puzzle. — More intricate, than it appear at first.

We must leave it, for the present. We have enough to do, without toying with subtleties of philosophy. The unintelligible German Herr *Kant*, we have heard, performed the same outward actions, every day of his life. — Rose and dressed at the same hour — Left the house, and walked the same way through the town, so that the citizens of Koenigsberg set their clocks by his passing — Returned always, at the appointed time. — All this, so the ordinary management of his life might be conducted without *any thought at all*, the better for him to dwell uninterrupted upon his *Vernunft*, and his *Urtheilskraft*, and other syllabic monstrosities. If such are the habits of life, required by philosophy, we shall cheerfully throw it over. — The Germans may have it. — You are heartily welcome, my *Damen* and *Herren.*

Mr Peach continues — I had not given thought to a supply of paper. This was but a single sheet.

— Do not trouble yourself, sir. I have been fortunate to-day.

— How so?

— Did you notice that coarse fellow who came to the inn this morning?

Mr Peach did not.

— He made some enquiries of the hostess. The burden of it was, to deliver a note to me.

— To you! cries Mr Peach.

— Indeed. The sour old witch* did it with poor grace. This is come for you, hussy, she says to me, For I'm to deliver it to Mr Peach's drab, and we're not to speak of it, which I needn't hardly say to you, since you don't say a word.

Clary's imitation of the hostess's voice and manner, approaches perfection. — A veritable *cameleon*! —

— But, says Mr Peach, who knows of your presence here? And what business can any body have with you, to be sending you letters?

— As for the business, it is not worth speaking of. And I cannot think the writer knows me at all, for although the stinking harridan positively insisted his note was to be given to your maid, the salutation is addressed to a *Charlotte.*

The mystery dissolves before Mr Peach's inward eye.

But, he thinks, how could Mr Stocks have discovered the place of our lodging so soon? — I suppose he asked every body, until he had the name of the inn from Doctor Thorburn.

— I care nothing for the substance of his writing, says Clary. — But the substance of the note — It was two sheets of fine paper. So, you see, am I quite satisfied for to-day.

Mr Peach assumes a grave expression.

---

* She refers, we fear, to the hostess of the inn.

— I must inform you, he says, that I know the author of that note, and can guess its contents. You are free, of course, to do as you please. But I should be very sorry to lose you. And I think the position he offers cannot appeal to you.

— Oh! sir, it is no position he offers. — Or, not a position of that sort.

— Is it not? I have good reason to believe that the gentleman in question has thoughts of procuring your service. Permit me to add, what I should blame myself for withholding, that in my judgment he is a shallow senseless man, in whose employ you could not possibly be content, no matter how well rewarded. You yourself called him a coxcomb, with as much justice as impertinence.

— His communication to me was not at all as you have guessed, say she. — But it is no matter. I care as little for either sort of invitation.

Though not certain of her meaning, Mr Peach is nevertheless pleased to see, that she is not minded to leave his service, so soon after entering it. He asks no further. — It would hardly look well in him, to pry into another's correspondence, when he has so recently endured the same intolerable infringement himself, and with such *final* consequences to the spy. — Thus Clary is dismissed. — And Mr Peach goes out, to spend a portion of the very little money in his purse, upon a bottle or two of India ink.

The letter he composes, once supplied with materials, is brief. We shall look over his shoulder again, as he writes.

Reader — we know, it is a very mean thing, to overlook a man's private writing — Or a woman's. — Forgive us — We artists of *necromantic history*, cannot be so nice — For we keep ceaseless vigil on every outward act of a mortal's existence, and indeed do not shrink, from peering into the skull, and observing the bodiless notions that ghost about the brain.

Mr Peach writes, as follows —

DOCTOR THORBURN! — FRIEND! —

By these words you may be certain the bearer has my perfect confidence, and may be entrusted with any thing you wish to return. He shall place this letter directly in your hand.

Much is in readiness. More remains to be done, before success is certain. Mr P___ assures me you are the man I have long sought; the noble hero, of the ONE CAUSE; *the far-seeing man, whose generous deed will kindle the beacon to bring the light of freedom to our darkened state; whose name will be venerated, as the exemplary patron of* LIBERTY.

Destroy this upon receipt. The posts and carriages are not safe. All our correspondence must be by Mr P___'s hand alone.

The time WILL COME!

In brotherly love

To these few lines, Mr Peach appends the signature — *Jeremiah Sixways*.

He looks over the writing, when he is finished. We see no trace of shame, upon his pensive brow. He contemplates the imposture, with equanimity. — Such a mien, we fancy, had the melancholy prince of Denmark, when he forged the letters, that doomed his old school-fellows* to the traitor's axe.

And now, we advance our narrative again.

The evening approaches, when Mr Peach is appointed at the Doctor's house, to put his device into practice.

This same night, some other personages in our drama have likewise their appointments — And their devices —

These you shall not know of, until after the event. But we must record it now. — The solemnity of the occasion requires it. Consider these few sentences of ours, as the tolling of the bell. — Imagine you hear it, out beyond your windows and walls. You know not where the steeple is, whence the slow dull clamour comes repeating — Nor what mournful event it commemorates.

* Rosencrantz and Guildenstern.

Yet, while it strikes, you cannot but listen — The very beat of your heart seems to fall in with its funereal tread — ding — dong —

The day has been still, and sultry. A summer day, when the air is thick, and the sky mired in greenish haze, has its own heaviness, nothing like the grey burdening of November, yet no less oppressive. It seems, by every hour, a storm must break — Yet it does not. The man about town, and the hind in the field, glance perpetually upward, as though awaiting some arrival from the heavens — And hurry about their business, for they hope not to meet the anticipated visitor. The evening is dim and early, though lingering — Neither day nor night, but a protracted twilight.

Mr Peach informs Clary, that he must go to town, and may not return until very late. He finds her brushing her hair — a thing, he has not known her to do — and with a basin of water warming. Her new dress of indigo calico is laid out. — It is a costume in which she looks particularly well.

— Why, Clary, you look as though you mean to receive company.

— No, sir. I shall expect no one here, until your own return.

— Then what are you about, with all this washing and brushing?

— Do you object, Mr Peach?

— I did not know you had a brush. I have not seen it before. Nor the mirror.

— They formerly belonged to the mistress of this house.

She continues occupied with her toilette, while Mr Peach looks on. He is for several moments uncertain, whether he has just heard his house-maid confess to an act of theft, for which, not many years past, she might have been whipped, in the more barbarous corners of the kingdom.

— Her words, he thinks, admit of no other construction. — I must reprove her, and insist she return the trinkets.

He adopts a pose of stern authority. —

And, thinks — She knows me guilty of far worse crimes, by my own free admission. Nay, I know myself guilty of them! — what right have I then, to preach to her, or any body, about what is lawful?

She moves the mirror a little, to observe him, where he stands behind.

Mr Peach sighs. — I shall be glad, says he, when we are able to return home. If my meeting to-night is attended with success, we may leave on the morrow. Pray, do not bring the articles with you. You shall have brush and mirror of your own.

She smiles a little — Exposing the inner part of her lips, like a black scar cut across her face. — She says, Thank you, sir. I wish your enterprize good fortune.

While he rides up to the town, he considers these parting words. He cannot escape a mysterious certainty, that Clary knows the fraud he intends — The dishonesty of his purpose. — It is, he thinks, as though she were my conscience, but an evil one.

He wonders, whether he would be better rid of her.

But, he *cannot* be.

— Is it then true, he thinks, what she insinuates — That she and I are indissoluble, and go under the same fate? — That she is my shadow — Or I hers? —

The mere suspicion of it, has a pinch of horror, which causes him to quicken the gelding's pace, to drown out the noise of his thought by the clipping of hooves. — The horse, suffering no such mental perturbations, knows only, that it is compelled to go faster than it wishes — And nurses its antient resentment.

Mr Peach's meditations would have been calmer, we think, had he chose to *walk*. —

At the Doctor's house, he presents the pass-word of *Philadelphia*. The same varlet at the door, formerly so obdurate in refusing his enquiries, now admits him with all deference, and shews him within.

No announcement is made. Indeed, the house does not appear prepared for his arrival, or any body's. There are no dishes in the hall, nor candles more than the dim evening requires. — But in a moment, Doctor Thorburn himself appears, and greets Mr Peach, with much emotion — And conducts him — *down*-stairs! — Where, in a low bare room at the back of the house, he finds some few furnishings suitable to polite company, concealed beyond the kitchen and the scullery.

— We meet here, says the Doctor, where we cannot possibly be spied on.

The room, Mr Peach observes, has no window but one, and that hardly worthy the name. — A mere aperture, intended to allow the circulation of a little air, for the prevention of sweats and mould — The room having certainly been intended, as a cellar, or larder.

Two others are present. One is a lean man, not yet thirty, of no very clean appearance, his brow very black and his eye very pale. The latter features are a fraction too large for the frame of his face. His length, too, seems excessive. — The proportions all over are exaggerated, or incorrect, so that he has almost the appearance of a figure from a satirical cartoon. He is introduced as Mr Lemuel Clattergate — plain Lem Clattergate, he says. We shall notice him when we must, but no more, for he is an ornament of little significance to our tale — A Rosencrantz, or Guildenstern. — The other guest we must mark with more care.

She is one Madame Denfert, a lady of France, as appears by the accents of her speech — and also, Mr Peach thinks, by her dress, for it accords with no fashion he has seen in England. She wears a white silk shirt, and a black velvet waistcoat, and breeches and boots as for riding; each article corresponding to *masculine* attire. Her natural appearance is likewise not the sort, that bespeaks a native of these islands. Reader, if you have travelled to Muscovy, you may have spied faces of this type. — We think, they have something of the vulpine cast — But with this difference, that the eyes of Madame Denfert are as black as a Persian's. Mr Peach has difficulty in estimating her age. Her complexion is fair and clear, but not youthful, and her whole bearing worldly, with nothing of girlish innocence or reserve. She carries herself like an intelligent and wilful woman of forty, wearing the skin of one twenty years younger.* She greets Mr Peach with a degree of enthusiasm he finds quite alarming, until he reminds himself, that the manners of France lack all knowledge of that decent reserve, which is the foundation and the glory of British society, when it is sober.

— Mr Thomas Peach, says she —

Reader — If you have some acquaintance with the French tongue, you will know, that it shuns the *tch*, which terminates our hero's sirname. Madame Denfert instead pronounces the syllable, with a curiously lengthened noise, recalling the retreat of a wave across a beach of small pebbles — Thus — *peeeesh*.

— I feel I have been attending for the whole of my life, to make your acquaintance.

— *Enchanté*, Madame, replies Mr Peach, with aukward gallantry.†

— We shall be friends for ever hereafter, she says. — We shall be intimates of the soul.

— Indeed, says Mr Peach, wondering whether the woman be mad. — I hope to know you better.

— Ah, but certainly you shall. As I know you already, to here. — Madame accompanies the last words, with a tap of her fingers against the breast-bone of Mr Peach, above his heart.

— I think we have not previously been acquainted, Madame?

---

* To any of our *gentleman* readers, who find this an interesting description — we offer the hint, that they will be very unwise, to conceive an imaginary attachment to *la Denfert*. Sir — you are well warned — Do not forget it.

A judicious friend reminds us — While we are about it, we ought to offer the very same warning, to any *ladies*, by whom it might be required.

† *Gallic* gallantry, we should have said, were it not for the grotesque jingle formed by the attachment of epithet to noun. — Whether the relation of sound between the two words, be mere coincidence, or indicative of the derivation in *etymology* of the latter from the former, we do not know. We suspect the term *gallant* would fall out of use, were its literal meaning discovered to be, *like a Frenchman*.

— To the contrary, Mr Peach. Though to-night I see you for the first time, your name is famous throughout my kingdom.

— Ha, ha! Madam — I think I cannot be of such renown in *France*, when I am hardly recognized three mile from my own door, in *England*.

Doctor Thorburn cries out, — Is it so, Madame Denfert? Is our Tom Peach, who we all thought an inoffensive obscure gentleman, so well know to you and your people? Mr Peach — I find I must apologize. I am not too proud. — Never let it be said, that an American was not the first to recognize true worth, in whatever situation it is found. Had I known, my friend, had I known! — I would not have been so tardy, in bringing you into the confidence of my brothers and sisters in our cause. — But you have been very secret, sir, very secret! — I must commend you for it. — You have hid from us all, in *plain sight*.

— But yes, says Madame Denfert, favouring Doctor Thorburn with such a smile, as Cleopatra might have bestowed on her Antony. — Among my people, we have the very highest hopes of Mr Peach.

Mr Peach would very much like to inform her, that she is mistaken — Has, perhaps, confused him with some other, of the same name. — Or perhaps, he thinks, with that other T___ P___, Esq., the notorious Mr Thomas *Paine*. But he sees at once, that it would not be politic to correct an error, which has made such an impression on the Doctor. His single purpose, he reminds himself, is with his host. — The eccentric Frenchwoman in her mannish attire may be tolerated for an evening, if her delusions serve his project, for he hopes he need never encounter her again, after to-night.

Madame Denfert presses her attentions with such persistence, that Mr Peach has some difficulty extricating himself, in order to speak privately with Doctor Thorburn, and pass him the letter from the supposed Jeremiah Sixways. He is saved at last by Mr Clattergate — That gentleman inquiring of Madame, concerning the present state of political affairs in France, with particular reference to the labouring and manufacturing classes. The lady has little knowledge to impart upon the subject; but becomes excessively animated, when Mr Clattergate further asks to know, whether she can report any instances of machine-breaking, rick-burning, and bread-riots. — These phaenomena are discovered to be Mr Clattergate's chief interests; and, luckily, they engage the attention of Madame Denfert, who, though she can say nothing of events in France, wishes to hear of every act of violence in England, of which Mr Clattergate is able to give report. — And so Mr Peach discovers his opportunity to take the Doctor aside.

— Our *friend*, he says, with a solemn wink, Commands me, to give you this note. You will forgive the discretion. — His most particular instruction was that I should place it in your very hand.

— Am I to read it at once?

— I know nothing of the contents, says Mr Peach — but, when he observes, that Doctor Thorburn may be minded to secrete the letter in his pocket unopened, and return to the conversation of Madame, he adds — However, I heard our *friend* — Mr Peach winks again — Mention, when he gave me the note, that *time is of the essence.*

— I understand you, brother, says the Doctor, and, with a somewhat rueful glance towards Madame, goes to stand by a candle, and breaks the seal.

Mr Peach waits, while the Doctor reads over the letter, the contents of which you were apprized of, at the beginning of this chapter — And reads again, his lips moving silently — And then puts the paper in the flame, where it blazes for a moment.

— FIRE! cries Madame Denfert — not in accents of alarm. — It is nearer the shout of one, who has wagered their whole fortune on an horse at the races, and sees its head pull in front of the others, as the post nears.

— Do not be alarmed, Madame, says Doctor Thorburn.

From which, by the by, we deduce, that the Doctor is no great student, of the various expressive intonations of the human voice.

— A piece of paper burning, says Mr Clattergate, is nothing at all. I have seen the weaving-factory at ____ham blazing so bright that night was like day.

Madame Denfert claps her hands. — Were there many burned alive? she asks — And so she and Mr Clattergate resume their talk, and Mr Peach and the Doctor are again able to speak in confidence.

Doctor Thorburn clasps Mr Peach's arm, with much feeling.

— So, he says — My dear friend — My brother, in *Philadelphian* fraternity — From this day we belong to one another, as all true men shall be joined in equality, under the Constitution of the Confederated States of free America!

Mr Peach hears these sentiments with inward delight, though he takes pains not to expose the emotion. — I must, he thinks, appear to presume his trust; for it is among the curiosities of the human temperament, that we are more inclined to give our confidence, where it is *expected*, than where it is *deserved*. — A truth of great benefit, to all practitioners of fraud.

— You may be assured of my service also, says he. — Particularly so, should you wish to return any token to *our friend*. The good citizen hinted, at our parting, that I might expect to receive some such.

— Well, says Doctor Thorburn, is that so? but tell me, does our brother Sixways —

— Our *friend*, Mr Peach says hastily, and with significant emphasis.

— Naturally — I shall be perfectly discreet — Our *friend* — In this letter, he writes that *every thing is in readiness*.

Mr Peach gives a solemn nod. — So it is, Doctor Thorburn.

— I am aflame with joy, at the news! — Aflame! — Only — the letter tended to brevity. I wonder, to what preparations in particular, our friend refers?

Mr Peach appears to revolve the question with earnest care — And then answers — I must presume, he refers — To *all* of them.

— All?

— All. You cannot be ignorant of the great efforts that have been made, though in the most absolute secrecy. — I am sure I need not enumerate them, in *this* house. — Mr Peach casts a glance towards the window.

— No — No, brother Thomas — Certainly you need not.

— The citizen, continues Mr Peach, stands quite ready, to set every thing in motion. He holds the torch, that will set the first beacon alight. — All the others will follow. There are only certain few necessities — *Expences*, I should rather call them. The procuring of some last essential materials — The compliance of various lesser persons, which can only be secured by *pecuniary* inducements — These are the final obstacles. Paltry matters — Easily resolved — If only our *friend* were a man of means himself, which, alas! he cannot be — Or, if he had the support of some other man. — Here Mr Peach casts an highly significant look towards the Doctor. — Some great man, he says, wholly worthy of so great an action. That hope, I think, is *not* impossible. —

Doctor Thorburn chews his lip.

— But, Mr Peach, he says, our friend also writes, that *success is certain.*

— It cannot be doubted.

— I am in transports, friend! — Transports!

— It is a momentous hour, for all who truly love the cause, and are determined to *give* all they have, for its sake.

— And such a man am I, Thomas, never doubt it! — But — I must ask — This success, of which he writes — In which particular enterprize will it be manifest?

Mr Peach looks to one side — the other — Behind — And, lowers his voice.

— Doctor Thorburn, he says — In *all* of them.

The Doctor looks expectant.

— Not excepting, says Mr Peach — The *greatest* of them — and the *last.*

The Doctor waits a moment longer — And, having determined that Mr Peach will add no more, says — I can only think that you refer to —?

Mr Peach fixes on him the most solemn look imaginable, and, when he has judged the interval sufficient, says —

— I do.

— To — *that*?

— The very thing itself.

— Come, says the Doctor — Come, Thomas, we are all brothers here. Let us not hesitate to name the glorious prospect, in plain speech.

— What single name can be put upon such a thing? says Mr Peach. — Some would call it *triumph* — Though others would call it *treason*. To the minions of corruption, it spells *disaster*. To the selfless heroes of liberty, its name is *hope*. Among such as we are, dear brother, what better word is there, than the one so judiciously selected by the citizen, in his letter — SUCCESS? If you prefer another, speak it. We will not cavil over names, when the time for *deeds* is so nearly upon us.

Doctor Thorburn seems uncertain, whether he is inspired, or confounded.

— Then, he says, it is really true, that our friend has it in his power to encompass — such a thing?

— Doctor — do you doubt it?

— I?

— I had not thought vacillation to be a property of the proud *Americans*. — Those fearless men, who rose up, and grasped their freedom, without shrinking — without lingering — without questioning, whether the time was right —

— And no more it is! — No people on earth are more bold and determined, than we men of the republic!

— I am heartily glad of it, says Mr Peach. — But, if you doubt our friend — If in any corner of your heart, you withhold from him the manly confidence which ought to bind all true brothers together — Say so — And I will return, and advise him of it. He thought, that the spirit of *America* would be the first to lend its *generous* strength, in such a cause; but if he is mistaken — If he must look elsewhere for his friends —

— He shall not! cries the Doctor, in a passion — A son of America will always be the first to answer the call of freedom's bugle!

This last outburst of patriotic fervour is so loud, as to attract the attention of Madame Denfert and Mr Clattergate; to Mr Peach's relief, for he is uncertain how long he could sustain the Doctor's interrogations, were they pursued in earnest. The conversation becomes general, and turns to that very subject best calculated to stimulate Doctor Thorburn's enthusiasm, *viz.* the virtues of the new-born republic. Mr Clattergate is sceptical. — For, he says, the American continent being vast, and fertile, and unpeopled, its colonists must all be a species of *country gentleman*, living on their farms; and so the assembly presently gathered at the Continental Congress, will inevitably produce nothing more than a nation of squires. — The Doctor grows warm in contradiction. Mr Peach takes his part — But also, encourages Mr Clattergate, by offering some hints regarding the favourable climate of Virginia, and the comfortable appearance of Mr Thomas Jefferson's villa, which he has seen in an engraving. Mr Clattergate becomes animated — Is led to declare, that there will be no end to the tyranny of wealth and station, except by the agency of the mechanical classes, who must destroy all the estates and factories of the rich. Doctor Thorburn cries that none are rich, or poor, under the Articles of the Confederated States, for they make all men *equal*. — So it goes on, each party growing more heated, until Madame Denfert laughs, and bids them both be silent.

— Neither your gentlemen farmers of America, says she, nor your hay-burning peasants of England, can compare to the glory soon to be seen, in *France*.

Doctor Thorburn's passion now runs so high, that he cannot withhold a cry of contempt. — France! Will you speak of France?

— But yes, Mister the Doctor, says Madame, I will.

— A nation, sunk in dotage! A people bound in miserable serf-dom, under the yoke of a court and a clergy that vie with each other, which shall be the more venal and extravagant! The world will never learn any thing from France, Madame, but the foppish satires of your *Voltaire*, and the worthless compendiums of your *Diderot*. — Philosophical toys! — Paper sports! — No, Madame, we must look to the *New World*, to shew the *Old* how to rise up in manly vigour, and be free!

— Faugh! — says Madame, with a smile. — I do not call it so very manly. A few gentlemen dispose of some tea, and indulge in a little firing of their muskets, and march themselves about in the woods — And, there! they declare they are done, and go to town, to smoke their pipes, and invent a new government. It is not so very heroic.

— You are grossly mistaken! — The Doctor is scarce able to contain himself. If it is true, that his house is spied upon, then his voice must surely carry to the ears of whichever agents of the ministry stand listening in the street. — When the annals of this age are written, he cries, there will be no greater act recorded, and none remembered with such reverence, as the rising up of the men of America.

— *Bof!* says Madame — A rising, most resembling an old gentleman with the gout, who pushes himself up from his chair.

Doctor Thorburn cannot speak. —

— No, sir — continues the lady — When *France* rises, then there will be something to see.

— France will never rise! exclaims the Doctor. — Sunk in femi-nine torpor — Laughing behind its handkerchief, at a philosophi-cal witticism — A nation of asses — cats — spaniels —

Mr Clattergate interjects — They have no *factories* in France, and therefore the common people remain sunk in agricultural ignorance, and cannot stir themselves.

Madame Denfert appears not the least discomposed, either by the Doctor's insults, or Mr Clattergate's curious political

reasons. Her black eye is bright,* and expressive of amusement. — You are equally mistaken, my dear accomplices, she
says. — When France rises, it will not be a few chests of tea that
suffer, nor a building of brick here, and a spinning-machine
there. In France we shall burn palaces, not factories. We shall
burn whole towns. Every church in the country will burn. Where
the fire will not do, we shall knock down stone walls, onto the
heads of those who hide behind them. We shall not have a few
soldiers shot, or a few farmers a little bloodied by the mob.
There will be countless thousands torn into pieces. We shall
have lakes and oceans of blood. The axes of the wood-cutters
will be sharpened, and used to hew down men, not trees. The
needles of the seamstresses will pick out eyes, not buttons. We
shall not have gibbets enough, and so the priests will hang from
their steeples, and the burghers from their lanterns. There shall
be machines for killing, because the noose is too slow, and those
to be slaughtered are legion. France will have none of your
comfortable Congresses, my good Doctor, and, dear Mr
Clattergate, none of your little nocturnal riots, whose people
are wolves in the night, and in the morning return to be sheep
again. No, no, no — Madame Denfert laughs prettily — We
shall have the earth-quake, that cares not how many it consumes.
And though it begin in France, it will shatter every nation, to the
north and south, to the west and east. We shall make the whole
world our turmoil and our field of annihilation. We shall be the
second arrival of the invisible plague, which four hundred years
ago made the largest slaughter remembered in this corner of the
earth. There will not be many remaining afterwards, to creep
out again, and survey the blasted lands; but those who do, I
think they will say, *This* was the chief catastrophe of the world,
and not your silly little factory-fires, or your musket-men in the
woods. — Do you not also think they will?

---

* Against the objection, that this be senseless contradiction, we again
adduce the example of *Shakespear*. — *vide* the 43rd of his Sonnets.

The silence that greets Madame's question, may perhaps be more easily imagined than described.

— Mr Peach, continues Madame, with a charming nod in his direction. — You do not give your opinion?

— Madame, says Mr Peach — I think you are a visionary.

— Madame Denfert is delighted. — Enchanting! she says — And will you be my devotee, Mr Peach, if I am your Sibyl?

Mr Peach exerts himself, to recall his purpose. — Were I in this company as a private man, he says, and not on behalf of another, I might give another answer. But the *friend* — here Mr Peach directs a significant look towards Doctor Thorburn — The *friend*, at whose behest I am here, will, I believe, incline to the Doctor's part. He is a great admirer of what has been done in America.

The Doctor repays him with an expression of evident gratitude and relief.

Mr Peach thinks — Now is the moment — Now I have him — I must draw him aside, and name the sum —

But Madame Denfert is not so easily shaken off. Her manners, like her attire, have no yielding sweetness.

— I do not care for your friend, wherever he is, says she. — It is your own opinion I desire. What do you say to my visions? Will you be my little baptist? — My prophet?

Mr Peach attempts to be polite. — I fear, he says, it is beyond my poor earthly powers to pronounce on oracles.

— But no, says Madame. — You are Mr Thomas Peach, who makes enquiries of the spirits and ghosts.

— I do not believe I informed you of our Thomas's private interests, cries Doctor Thorburn. — I see you know him more intimately than any of us.

Mr Peach is possessed by nervous agitation. He feels, that the atchievement of his enterprize is very near. The Doctor has been worked upon — roused — flattered — And is ready to be persuaded. The iron is hot, and malleable, and must be struck. — But the persistent attentions of the ridiculous Frenchwoman, threaten to throw all into chaos.

— That is merely an occasional amusement of mine, he says, with a dismissive flourish of his arm. — A curiosity — An hobby-horse — Nothing more.

Mr Clattergate mutters an indistinct remark on *superstitious fiddle-faddle*.

— But I too, says Madame, am most curious, about the speaking with the ghosts and spirits. Tell me, Mr Peach, what you have discovered, upon your *hobby-horse.*

— I shall easily oblige you, Madame, for I have discovered nothing at all.

Again Madame Denfert laughs her pretty laugh. — Perhaps you then conclude, there is nothing to be found? No spirits, or angels, or blessed souls?

— Child's tales, says Mr Clattergate, with a snort, To frighten the people into obedience.

— I cannot say, Madame, says Mr Peach.

— But you must, she says. — A lady requires it of you. I shall be most severe, if you do not tell me all your conclusions.

— Though I dread your severity, I fear I must endure it, for I have nothing to report upon the matter.

— And what of the God? says Madame Denfert. — Do you find Him, or no?

Mr Peach is uneasy in the extreme. — Which, by the by, we think curious, for we have more than once heard him speak quite freely, on the subject of the Deity. But there is in Madame Denfert, something that robs him of all assurance.

— Had I the answer to that question, he says, I would indeed be a person of renown, as you are so kind as to think me.

— Ah, Mr Peach, you are slippery, like the fish! — I shall call you Mr Pêcheur! But, I will catch you — So! — Madame here throws out her hands, as though snatching a trout, and clasps him by the arm.

— Every man of plain sense, says Mr Clattergate, can see that the stories of the Bible are fables.

Madame Denfert turns to him, making her black eyes very great — though she does not release her grasp, on our hero's arm — My friend Lemuel, she says, in mocking astonishment — Will they not burn you alive, for saying such a thing?

— I don't care, says Mr Clattergate. — Every body knows it.

— That the Hebrew testaments are fables, says the Doctor, who has by now recovered the greater portion of his composure, Is not doubted by any educated man. Nevertheless, it is certain that a benign Author of the world oversees His creation, and keeps it in order. It is quite impossible otherwise that we should have implanted in us that natural justice and moral sense, which is the foundation of civil society, and leads us on towards the perfection of the science of government.

Madame Denfert draws herself very close to Mr Peach. — What shall we answer to them? says she. — Shall we agree, or disagree?

Mr Peach retains enough presence of mind, to select an answer he thinks may be pleasing to the patriotic *American*.

— I am persuaded, he says, that these are matters of conscience, which every person ought to answer as they can, without fear of oppression.

— But no! cries Madame — The priests will not allow it! They will come and drag you to the fire, Mr Peach.

— This is not France or Spain, says Mr Clattergate, who is quite out of humour. — We have no public burnings, like your Popish church.

— No? Then do your priests no longer believe in the God?

— Madame Denfert, says Mr Peach — Pray release my arm.

The lady complies, with a pout.

— You are afraid to say that no one believes in the God. In France it will be quite different. There, if any person says they believe in the God, their head will be chopped off at once. If a little child is found at her prayers, she will pulled away by her hair, and her head chopped off, like we do with the little carrot. — *Chop!*

— Doctor Thorburn, says Mr Peach — Another word in private, I beg you.

— I shall have your answer later, says Madame Denfert. — You shall not escape me, Mr Peach, who loves the ghosts.

Mr Peach excuses himself — He has some business with their host, which demands a minute or two — It is absolutely necessary — &c. — And is at last able, to detach himself from the deranged Frenchwoman.

He and the Doctor step apart a little. —

— I am curious, says Mr Peach, to know how you came to be acquainted with Madame Denfert.

The Doctor looks across the room to where she stands, now tormenting Mr Clattergate with her conversation.

— A most remarkable woman, Tom, says he.

Mr Peach restrains himself from remarking, that this is no answer at all. Indeed, he observes that the Doctor seems fascinated by Madame, despite her contemptuous opinion of the American republic, which in any other person he would certainly declare anathema. Mr Peach has difficulty recalling Doctor Thorburn to his original purpose; yet, by degrees, is able to redirect their conversation thither.

You are by now well enough acquainted with its particular savour. — We have no great relish to taste it again. — It will be enough to say, that when Mr Peach judges the moment ripe, he murmurs — That *our friend* wants only some five hundred pounds, to perfect his plans, and bring every thing to fruition; which sum he himself will be honoured to convey in person to *our friend*, in whatever form the Doctor finds most convenient.

Five hundred pounds! —

The annuity, settled on Tho.s Peach by his father's will, stood at one hundred pounds.

Mr Peach's design has brought him to the brink of — We cannot say, *riches* — To the rich, five hundred pounds is not a great deal more than nothing. But to a modest country gentleman, living in retirement, with no child to support, nor any *living* wife — with but two servants, and one of them not requiring to be fed — We can justly say, that the sum represents *comfort* — Perfect security from want — Which, the wise of every age and place have observed, is the only true measure of wealth.

Mr Peach is certain he has done enough to persuade the good Doctor to part with the sum. He waits —

The Doctor looks warmly upon him — His heart filled with visions of LIBERTY —

And then —

Madame Denfert and Mr Clattergate are some six or eight yards distant, to all appearances occupied in talking together. Yet, at the very moment, when the Doctor prepares to put out his hand, to clasp Mr Peach in brotherly affection, and seal his promise — Madame is seen to turn on the heel of her boot — She looks across the room at the Doctor, whose eye has been caught by her motion — She smiles at him — raises a finger, and waggles it, and makes a little pout, as who should say, *Tut, Monsieur, do not think of it* —

Doctor Thorburn's hand is *not* extended —

Mr Peach — he says — in some confusion — Alas — I find at this moment I can do nothing — It is impossible — I wish citizen Sixways every success — The endeavour is glorious, but I cannot support it.

— Doctor Thorburn, begins Mr Peach —

— It is quite impossible, repeats the Doctor — I have placed all my resources, at the service of — *Another* —

He stares at Madame Denfert — Who favours him with a little smile, and a nod — And returns her attention to Mr Clattergate.

The blow falls on Mr Peach as swift, and sharp, and final, as that hideous blade, whose ministrations to the people of France Madame Denfert has lately prophesied.

He begs an explanation — Pictures to Doctor Thorburn, the disappointment with which his *friend* will receive the news — Wonders, whether that reputation for warm-hearted support in the cause of *liberty*, which is popularly attributed to the men of America, be deserved at all — In short — Exercises every means of persuasion, he can imagine.

All unavailing! —

The Doctor cannot be moved. — But only repeats, that it is impossible — That his assistance is promised *elsewhere*. — Mr Peach does not doubt, from the perpetual casting of the Doctor's glance across the room, that the recipient of those promises, is none other than Madame Denfert.

We will do our hero the honour of recording, that he is filled quite suddenly with an excess of disgust — Directed chiefly at *himself*.

This also may be noted, among the interesting arrangements of the human brain. — We have seen Mr Peach pursuing his fraudulent enterprize, without hesitation, or qualm — Entirely untroubled by the least tremble of conscience — For as long as the goal remained in sight. But in the very instant of his failure! the shabbiness of his purpose reveals itself, to his own eyes. For we self-deceiving mortals easily overlook the *means*, so long as we have in clear sight the *end*, where we hope to arrive; but, take away our prospect of that *destination*, and all at once our eyes look down, into the filthy slough where we have directed our steps, in order to reach it; and we observe our boots, all spattered with mud and mire — Observe them, with *revulsion* — Though we chose the path ourselves!

Mr Peach has not even the comfort, of this healthy exercise in the construction of metaphor. — He knows only, that *the game is up* — And now desires no more, than to be away.

It is proverbial, that misery loves company. We ourselves have often found it so. But Tho.s Peach is of a different temper — One of those, who, when assailed by disappointment, or despair, wishes only for solitude, so that the burdens of fate may not be compounded with the demands of society.

He takes his leave of the house more abruptly, than is usually thought polite. — Though, we must note, he has little to fear on that account, for Mr Clattergate disdains the manners of the gentry, and Doctor Thorburn holds that there ought to be no ceremony among *philadelphian* brothers — While Madame

Denfert is not at all put out — But merely says, that she will have an answer from him — As though she were perfectly confident of his walking back into the room, two minutes after he has walked out of it. — A mysterious confidence indeed, for Mr Peach is quite determined never to set eyes on any of them again.

He rides out of the city.

His thoughts, we need not dwell on. — They are dark — hopeless. — His defeat is absolute. —

Observe, now, reader, the *left* side of your book — The great mass of pages, to that side of the division, where the spine lies open. *That* is all the history of Thomas Peach, which you have thus far learned. Measure it, between thumb and forefinger of your left hand. —

It is, we dare say, no small quantity.

Then let us also agree, that you have had a sufficient report of Mr Peach's nature, and his habits of thought and expression, to render it now unnecessary, that we record his reflexions upon every crisis and incident of our tale. We think you know him well enough, to imagine them yourself. The arrangement suits us equally — For we must now be much occupied, with the *external* circumstances of the narrative, and cannot spare the time to paint every colour, and figure, and shadow, of *inward* events.

Mr Peach lets the gelding go as slow as it pleases. — Which is very slow indeed.

He fears no robber — For he has nothing left, to be robbed of.

Once arrived at the inn, he calls for neither ostler nor host, but stables the animal himself — And, having been admitted, makes to his bed without a word.

Of Clary there is no sight nor sound.

Perhaps, she is *asleep*? —

Mr Peach is glad to give no thought to it — To her — To any thing. He is miserable — Crushed. He wishes for nothing, beyond the oblivion of a dreamless torpor.

That wish, at least, we may grant him, by closing our chapter with a stroke of the pen — thus —

CHAPTER TWENTY-FIVE

MURDER! —

The original crime of the world! —

For the first two people born of flesh and blood, were Cain and Abel, and — one slew the other. —

Reader — Confess, that we have made every effort to warn you, in our former chapters. Acknowledge, that you have not been led to the brink of the horrid event, shortly to be revealed, under a false pretence. We hinted our tale would prove gloomy. — Nay — Did we not, in plain language, invite you to put the book aside, if you had no stomach for it?

Perhaps you thought — Pish — Fiddle — This Thomas Peach seems a dull old stick, and his story no worse than a pleasant romp of saucy maids, and eccentric philanthropists, and the like — Silly stuff — The worst of it is a miserly uncle, which is not much. — What have I to fear, from all your *Stygian* hints and mumbles?

But, we beg your pardon. — We know, you are not so trivial in your capacities. It has not escaped your notice, that our narrative is stamped with the *mark of Cain.* —

We have by slow and careful degrees, revealed to you, the history of poor Eliza Peach — MURDERED for the sake of slighted honour — Though the world was led to believe, that she took her own life.

We have hinted, though in delicate and oblique terms, at the REVENGE executed by Mr Thomas Peach. We still fear to pronounce it aloud. — We cannot have you condemn our hero, for mortal sin, and give him up to d___nation — Not *YET* —

We have dared to expose, the approach of the merciless *hash-ishin* — Their judgment as absolute as nature's own law, which decrees death to all that lives — Their execution, as perfect.

We have allowed you into the house, when their sentence fell on the unworthy head of Jenkyn Scrimgeour — whose last words were his own death-knell — *I am Thomas Peach!* —

We confess — we took pains to provide you with a sufficient view of the odious spy, that his unfortunate end might not arouse in you those emotions of *pity* and *fear*, which Aristotle pronounces essential to tragedy.

But, NOW —

Now we can neither veil the dread stain, nor conceal it among the by-ways of our narrative — nor dress it, in an Harlequin costume. For MURDER is done in earnest — And in its most terrible guise.

Here is no clumsy brawl, turned bloody by a drunken sailor's dirk — No senseless affair of honour, where two popinjays take aim at one another, and one is careless enough not to miss. — No — Of all crimes, here is that which strikes us silent with horror — The slaughter of a person, at home — In their own bed.

Nay — *two* persons —

Mr and Mrs Farthingay lie, in their night-caps — In their bed-room — In the very house, where but lately they thought to cele-brate the happy engagement of their child. They lie — NEVER TO RISE AGAIN.

They have been *choked* —

We cannot bear to look close. Let them lie there still, side by side, as they lived. — As for the most part, they lived — Indeed, we think they lived so, tolerably often. — Let us allow them this last comfort.

Mr Peach is on the point of departing the inn, for his journey home to Widdershins Bank, when a note is delivered to him, brought by a messenger in every extreme of haste. It is from the hand of Miss Arabella Farthingay. Her distress of mind, can easily be imagined. — Poor lady! — There are but a few words, thrown off in desperation, imploring Mr Peach to come to her — Instructing him, to prepare himself — No more than that.

— I fear, says Mr Peach to Clary, we must delay our homeward ride a little longer.

— I wonder what is the matter, says Clary.

— You and Miss Farthingay must not see one another, says Mr Peach. — I must go alone.

So the rooms are retained again, and Clary stays at the inn. The keeper is pleased to think, he will have a little more of Mr Peach's money. His wife is displeased — But, enough of them — Who can care for such mean passions as greed, and envy, at such a time? — Neither ourselves, nor you. —

Mr Peach finds Miss Farthingay, at the house of a female friend, among hushed voices, and solemn looks. She is attended to, with tea, which she does not touch, and consolations, which she neither wants nor hears. On the announcement of the visitor she begs all the rest to leave her — sits — And weeps —

— Mr Peach, she says, between outbursts of passion, which pain him to witness — They have taken Caspar — I know not where to turn — Pray, sir — Help me — Mama and Papa are murdered.

Mr Peach stands as though struck by the thunderbolt.

— I have not earned your kindness, says she — But do not forsake me now — Or I shall despair — I shall run mad —

Mr Peach kneels. — I am at your service, madam.

The story is told, in halting fashion. It freezes Mr Peach's blood; yet he retains enough of his senses to remember, that his own horror is as nothing, beside the grief of a child, at the loss of her beloved parents. — He endeavours to be steadfast, and listen. He offers no empty words of comfort, which would accord as little with his sensations, as hers. He does not bid her be calm — the usual plea of the male sex, in the face of female emotion. He only asks, how he may assist her.

— My Caspar is accused, she says — He is arrested.

— What possible cause can there be, to think him guilty of the unspeakable deed?

— None! — None! — Go, Mr Peach, and tell them so!

He assures Miss Farthingay, he will do every thing in his power. He asks, who has care of her meanwhile — Whether her present situation is bearable — He alludes, in the gentlest terms, to the surprizing absence of Mr Stokesay Stocks, at such a time.

— Stokesay is gone to do some thing — I know not what — To speak to some body — I care not. He will not help Caspar — You, Mr Peach, are the one on whom I must rely. — My poor Papa! my poor Mama! &c. —

Mr Peach would stay, and see that she takes at least a little tea, for her phrenzy of grief threatens to bring on a fit, but the lady will not hear of it. She must have him on his way to the magistrate, and the gaol, at once. Every minute of delay increases the violence of her pleas. — He must comply. — And so Mr Peach leaves the house, in the utmost disturbance of mind, and scarcely sensible of what he has promised to do.

Mr Farthingay — whom but two nights past, he saw, and spoke to — Dead! — murdered!

The whole city knows the news. A fog of horror is settled in every street. Each word turns to a whisper. — Even the cries of the knife-grinder and the coal-seller, are muted in solemn respect. Some, with fearful countenances, hurry home, for they think the murderer is *yet abroad*. — Others murmur, he is taken — The negro servant —

It is rumoured the young lady is dead of her grief —

Mr Peach attends the magistrate, presenting himself as a friend and emissary of Miss Farthingay, in which capacity he is admitted with every courtesy, and informed of all the circumstances pertaining to the dreadful event; which are little more than these, that Mr and Mrs Farthingay retired at their usual hour, and the rest of the household after them, and in the morning were discovered by the valet, in their beds, both dead, by obstruction of the passages of breath; and, the house being locked, and there being no evidence of a forced entry, nor any body having heard a disturbance, suspicion must exclusively fall on those persons present within the house during the night, that is, the servants; among whom it is universally agreed, that the negro must be the guilty party, because he is known to have been excessively proud of his station, and reduced to bitter envy in anticipation of the loss of his position, upon Miss Farthingay's marriage.

— Does he confess the crime? asks Mr Peach.

— By no means, sir, says the magistrate. — But he cannot account for himself. He maintains only, that he was asleep all the night above-stairs.

— It would be surprizing, I think, if he gave any other account?

The magistrate is what is called a *worthy* man — Of that sort, whose tomb-stone, when it comes to be erected, by his grieving descendants, will be graved with lengthy encomia on his public virtues, and the good works for which the people of the parish will praise his memory. He murmurs to Mr Peach, that *other considerations* are brought to his attention.

— May I enquire, as a friend of the lady, concerning the nature of these considerations?

The magistrate's look is frank. — As you are *a friend of the lady*, he says, I must be delicate in alluding to them in your presence. It is suggested, that there may be in this dreadful act some element of what the French call a *crime of passion*.

— I do not understand you, sir.

— All will come to light at the assizes. But, sir, as I see you are a gentleman of honour, and concern yourself on behalf of the lady's reputation, it is fit to advise you that Miss Farthingay may be called to the court. I fear there will be witnesses who will testify that the servant Caspar had *particular reasons* to be jealous of his position. — Of, I may say, the *intimacy* of his position.

Excuse us a moment, reader. — We must pause briefly, to recall to your attention some former pages of our tale.

Be reminded, if you please, of the diversion in our narrative which occurred in our twenty-second, when we were flung pell-mell before the ruin of Grandison Hall. — We there overheard some gossiping tongues, which, with the easy malice natural to those who contemplate another's misfortunes, made some remarks upon Miss Farthingay and her devoted servant, tending in the same direction as the hints now offered by our magistrate. — You will recall that Mr Peach was far distant from that scene, and may therefore be presumed innocent of the said gossip. The present conversation, is the first he has heard of it. His sense of the lady's honour is offended — Not so much on account of the rumoured accusation — But in honest revulsion, at the notion that she is the object of such vulgar tittle-tattle, and her name bandied about by those who rejoice in condemning others, for the sins they dream of committing themselves.*

— I trust, sir, says he, that you give no weight to the baseless testimony of envy and petty spite, in the execution of so awful an office as you hold?

The magistrate merely nods. — I assure you, sir, says he, I allude to the circumstance with nothing but the proper regard for the lady's good name. A crime so foul as this can only spring from the most depraved motives. It is in the nature of such a case, that justice must not shrink from enquiring into them, nor fear what it may find, no matter how filthy the nook in which it must shine its light. The lady must prepare herself, sir.

Mr Peach is not such a preening coxcomb, that the mere mention of a lady's honour makes him lose his wits, and go about offering threats, and demanding satisfactions. — He acknowledges the good sense, and the friendly intent, of the magistrate's advice.

— Besides, that worthy says, this crime is unquestionably not the work of any ordinary servant. There is an horrid ingenuity in it, which hardly indicates the act of a footman. There were but four male domestics within the walls of the house last night. The

---

* 'Thou rascal beadle, hold thy bloody hand!
Why dost thou lash that whore? Strip thine own back;
Thou hotly lust'st to use her in that kind
For which thou whipp'st her.' — King Lear.

females may be discounted, on account of the bodily strength required by the deed; and of those others, one is the valet, and two are mere boys, with scarcely the wit to open a book, let alone use it in such a fashion.

— A book? says Mr Peach, with a frown.

— Excuse me — I thought the horrid circumstance was already general knowledge. Mr and Mrs Farthingay were both choked upon pages torn from a book. Their mouths were crammed with the print when they were discovered.

Mr Peach averts his look in his revulsion, and cannot speak.

— The villainy of it is without example, in all my experience, says the magistrate, shaking his head. — But we shall have justice. Miss Farthingay's man Caspar is said by every body, to have been *bookish*. I have inspected the house myself this morning. There is a small library in his room.

Mr Peach sees that the magistrate's opinion is already decided. — He must speak with Caspar himself, if he is to learn any thing of the truth of the matter. — We must here remark, that he is absolutely certain of the servant's innocence, though it is the certainty of *faith*, not *reason* — Nevertheless — Certain he is, and he hastens away, to see what confirmation he may find, of the doctrine he already believes; such being always the method, by which arguments of faith proceed.

Reader — we sincerely hope, that you have never had cause to acquaint yourself, with the inside of a common gaol.

The misery of incarceration — The desperate condition, to which the prisoners are reduced — So destructive of every conceivable purpose, which justice may pretend to ascribe to the sentence of imprisonment, except the mere barbarous urge to *inflict punishment* — As though, in a civilized nation, it were enough to say to the condemned, Lo, we will have nothing to do with you, except to make the passage of your days an earthly Hell — On this subject, abler pens than ours have been exercised. We shall only remark, that in the decades since the time of our narrative, there have been noble efforts at reformation, to the eternal honour of their several authors; which we recall to you, not in order to repeat the praises due to those beacons of humanity, but rather to draw the inference, that the prisons of the year 1785, being as yet unreformed, were places of still more unspeakable and unpardonable degradation, than the prisons of to-day — Enough —

In such a place, is Mr Peach admitted to poor Caspar.

The servant, having only been incarcerated that same morning, retains yet the largest part of his outward humanity. Mr Peach is able to supply the turnkey with several coins, given to him for the purpose by Miss Farthingay, so that the prisoner will not entirely want those comforts, without which he must within days infallibly be reduced to the condition of an *animal*.

— I am very sorry to see you thus, says Mr Peach.

Caspar studies the shackles on his wrists. — My four brothers, says he, in his habitual ponderous and musical tones, Were all taken as slaves.

— Miss Farthingay sends me to assure you, she will spare no effort to liberate you from this unjust confinement. I add my own assurances. — I will do whatever I can.

Caspar raises his arms. — Can you command this iron to break, Mr Thomas Peach?

— I can endeavour to demonstrate your innocence of the horrible crime, if you will help me.

— You are a potent magician, Mr Peach, but that task will be outside your power. My former suggestion is the more plausible.

— Do you not maintain that you are guiltless?

Caspar smiles — Though we think our language ought to have another word, than *smile*, for a gesture expressive of weary and ironical resignation. — I do. — But do those, who are to determine my fate? They do not.

— There is such a thing as justice in this kingdom. You cannot be condemned for an act you have not performed.

— And who will say I have not done it? I? You, my friend? Against all the great number, who will say I have?

— We shall prove it.

— But we cannot. I was asleep all through the night. My grandmother came to me in my dream. She gave me the food I have not tasted since I was a boy. She came to welcome me where she is, among the dead.

Mr Peach shakes his head. — Let us dismiss your dreams, he says, and bend all our efforts towards the elucidation of actual occurrences. — Do you recall no sound at all, in the night? No sign of any thing in the house, where you might not have expected it?

— Mr Peach, says Caspar again, I was asleep.

— Well, then, you were asleep; but some other man has committed the crime, and must have left some trace, and we shall discover them. I am told no window or door was forced, and so only the household is suspected. You must know your fellow-servants. Which of them do you think has done this deed?

— Why, says Caspar, none of them.

— And yet one of them has.

— I say, Mr Peach, that none of them has. You must have a large spirit, to kill a man and a woman. I do not say, a great spirit. But a large spirit. One such as your own, or mine.

Mr Peach is becoming irritable at the man's obstinacy. — But, he remains mindful of his promise to Miss Farthingay, to do whatever he may on Caspar's behalf.

— Sir, he says, you must not say you consider yourself capable of murder. Such language will weigh very heavily against you, in the eyes of the law. You must proclaim your innocence, and insist upon it. Declare only the truth, that you are not guilty of the crime. — That you have no cause to do any such hideous and cruel thing, and nor is it in your nature, as I am sure it is not.

— My nature, says Caspar, very slowly, as though he has not heard of such a thing.

— Miss Farthingay will give her testimony as to your character. I shall be glad to do the same.

— They say, do they not, that I am proud? I am proud.

Mr Peach begins to suspect, that all his efforts are to be in vain.

— They say, continues Caspar, that I am angry? I am greatly angry. My large spirit contains a storm.

Mr Peach sighs. — I have spoken to the magistrate, he says. — I understand that the common talk, is that you became resentful, because you were to lose your place upon Miss Farthingay's marriage to Mr Stocks.

Caspar laughs. — And I visited my resentment upon the old master and mistress? I think I would have done better to strike down Mr Stocks himself.

— Precisely! cries Mr Peach. — This must be our way, to expose the hollowness of their reasons. What cause had you to murder Mr Farthingay? You must press that very point.

— I will tell you the cause, says Caspar. — It will be said, that Mr Farthingay is a tobacco-merchant, whose plantations are worked by negro slaves, and therefore I killed him, because I am an African.

Mr Peach opens his mouth — And closes it again.

— Or it will be said, that Mr Farthingay, and Mrs Farthingay, loved and cared for their beautiful daughter, and therefore I killed them, from jealousy. Or it will be said, that I am a foreign man, and my passions do not run as your nice British feeling does, and I killed them because I am strange and mad, and my soul is not like an human soul. I will be hanged, my friend. It was in my grandmother's face.

— You shall not hang, says Mr Peach. — I will find the one who perpetrated this horror, and shew them to the world. I beg your grandmother's pardon.

Caspar laughs again, with some warmth. — A large soul indeed! I saw it around your house, when I rode by. The air above your roof seemed to shine. When I came the second time, a spirit opened your door, and watched me from within.

Mr Peach is preparing to take his leave, for it is evident to him that Caspar will be of no use. — But he is struck by something, in this last mysterious remark.

— I had not thought my house disturbed by spirits, he says. — Who was this fairy, that answered your knock?

— The old master had a living doll that he used to play with, until he broke it, and sent it away to die. Its spirit came to your house. I saw it as clear as you see me. I think it meant to warn me.

Recall, reader, that incident recorded in our sixteenth — When Caspar came to the house at Widdershins Bank, and Clary opened the door. —

— You are mistaken, sir, says Mr Peach, though he is inwardly a little shaken by Caspar's words. — There are no ghosts in my house.

— Mr Thomas Peach, says Caspar, shaking his head sadly, Mr Thomas Peach, you speak of British justice in one breath, and tell me a lie in the next. You will not be angry that I speak plainly, for I am a dead man, and look beyond the world.

Mr Peach makes one final effort, to resume the subject of Caspar's guiltlessness, and any information which might be obtained, to demonstrate it; but all in vain. — The man appears wholly resigned to his fate, and repeats his surprize, that Mr Peach, of all men, would waste himself in the effort to change a course, which in his mind appears as fixed as the motions of the stars.

— Miss Farthingay will not be comforted by the report I bring of you, says Mr Peach. — It will grieve her deeply to hear you so little inclined to resist an unjust accusation.

— Miss Farthingay, says Caspar, sighing over the name. — Miss Farthingay has already surrendered her comfort in this life.

— I saw her but two hours past. — She was distracted almost to insensibility, by the loss of both her parents, in a single blow, so sudden and full of horror. Yet the one thought which roused her — The *one* prospect, which she looked on with some hope, in the midst of her despair — Was that you, sir, might not also suffer a blow equally undeserved, and equally fatal.

Caspar merely turns up the palms of his hands, as far as the manacles will allow, and says — I cannot help you.

Mr Peach feels he can do no more. Nevertheless, before departing, he assures Caspar, that he will continue to try every thing in his power, to expose the true author of the crime, for Miss Farthingay's sake, if not for the prisoner's.

He returns to the lady with an heavy heart. The only consolation he has to offer her, is the promise secured from the turnkey, that Caspar's stay in the prison will not be absolutely comfortless. — A promise secured, we need hardly add, not by any appeal to the humanity of the gaoler, but with the contents of Miss Farthingay's purse.

Upon his arrival at the house of Miss Farthingay's female friend, he finds Mr Stokesay Stocks present, attending to his distressed lady. Mr Peach has tact enough to know, that Mr Stocks is unlikely to take a sympathetic view of the errand, upon which Miss Farthingay sent him; nor does he think it proper to request a moment of private talk with her, in the circumstances. Mr Stocks is solicitous — Hovers about the poor lady, with butterfly anxiety — Pray, my dearest — Take a little chocolate — Or try the salts — Don't cry — You must not exert yourself — &c. — He whispers to Mr Peach, that not a word must be spoken of the dreadful event, in his dear Bella's hearing. Her nerves are in a state of extreme delicacy, and must be safeguarded against further shocks. — In short, it is quite impossible for Mr Peach to make any report at all. — And Miss Farthingay herself, appears almost stupefied by the attentions of her intended husband, and greets Mr Peach faintly and indistinctly, and as though she has forgotten his earlier visit altogether. He bids her be of good comfort, and promises to call again to-morrow, and places himself at her service, and Mr Stocks's, in any matter where he may be of assistance.

Mr Stocks is grateful, on behalf of both. — But, Peach, he says, as our hero prepares to take his leave — This is a bad business — I shall get my dear Bella away from it all as soon as I can. She must not think of it. A change of air is the thing. We shall go to London to-morrow, or the next day. — They may try the nasty fellow, and hang him, and it will all go off beyond her notice. For she's a dear delicate creature, and I shan't let any thing make her unhappy. — And, with some more remarks of the same sort, Mr Stocks escorts Mr Peach to the door, and sees him away.

Mr Peach's spirits are now sunk so deep, that he almost cares not what he does, or where he goes. The city is all around him — The great press and bustle of a thousand strangers, and the Babel of a thousand voices, and the endless avenues of brick and iron and stone. He feels only, that he has nothing to do with it — That a thousand things are transacted around him, all unknown, all eternally remote — While every thing, that touches him directly, turns to dust. He makes an effort to rouse himself, by recalling again his promise, made both to Miss Farthingay and to Caspar; and so betakes himself to Mr Farthingay's house, in hopes he may discover some further information, pertaining to the horrid events of the night; but the house is locked — The servants, if they are within, will not answer. — And now the day begins to wane.

There is nothing to be done, but return to the inn. — A slow ride, each step of which brings Mr Peach further unhappy reflexions, upon the past and future misfortunes of others, and his own.

Our chapter began, in *horror* — We shall let it conclude, in *gloom*.

CHAPTER TWENTY-SIX

— Well, Clary, says Mr Peach, that same evening — To-morrow we shall go home after all.

— I shall be very glad of it.

— I too will not be sorry to quit the scene of these miserable events.

— Your spirits are low, sir. I think your journey has not been a successful one.

— It has not.

— Perhaps our homeward voyage will raise you again. By reversing your steps, you may restore your ease.

— A gracious thought, child. But, alas, we cannot leave our troubles behind, merely by leaving the place.

— You speak of *our* troubles. — Did you intend a general sentiment?

— No, Clary. You must understand, that my difficulties are now yours as well.

— You do me too much honour, sir.

Mr Peach sighs. — I find you are witty to-night.* I wish you would not be. I do not know how you can bandy words, after the news I have brought.

We ought to inform you, reader, that we have begun this new chapter *in medias res*, in the epic manner. The conversation between master and maid was several minutes old, when we joined

---

* Mr Peach appears to have construed Clary's remark, as a jesting suggestion, that he has hinted at a *marital* union between the pair!

404

it. — It is late in the same day, which witnessed the events of our last; and Mr Peach has informed Clary, of the horrible demise of her god-parents. — Tidings, which she has received quite calmly.

— Your pardon, she says. — I thought only to relieve your solemn spirits a little. I could do more — If you would permit it —

Mr Peach waves his hand, as though her suggestion were a noisome insect. — Have I not repeatedly implored you, never to allude to that subject?

— You have, sir; but I thought I might allow for a weakening of your resolve, at this unhappy time.

Mr Peach sighs again. — Well, Clary, we need no longer cross words about it. You shall have no more imprecations or commands from me, and I, thank Heaven, need endure no more of your coarse impertinence, for within a few days I shall dismiss you.

We have observed before now, that Miss Clarissa Riddle might have served as the living epitome of the sentence of Shakespear, that

> There's no art
> To find the mind's construction in the face.

On this occasion, however, Mr Peach's words produce in her, every mark of visible surprize.

— For what cause?

— For the simplest one, that I can no longer spare even the little wages I give you.

Clary makes a scornful noise — Faugh — Do not think of that, sir. I will work for nothing, if that is all you can pay.

— And what if I cannot even provide you with ink and paper?

— Then I shall provide them for myself.

— By theft, you mean, Clary? By deceit? I cannot condone it. No, child — I must seriously advise you to consider the offer of Mr Stokesay Stocks.

— Ha, ha! — Believe me, I have already *considered* it quite thoroughly.

— That you hesitate to go into the service of Miss Farthingay, or Mrs Stocks, as she shall be, is quite admissible. However, I have good reason to think she retains some kind sentiments towards you, and will not be at all displeased to learn, that the maid her husband has chosen for her is her father's god-child and ward.

— You misunderstand me, Mr Peach. I have told you, the letter I had from Mr Stocks put forward an offer of a very different nature. The ass has taken a fancy to me. If he wants me to wait on his wife, it is only so I may serve him as a mistress. The arrangement would no doubt be very convenient for the gentleman, but I think it would be less to the taste of the lady; and as for myself, I would prefer to hazard my fortune with yours. I am sure, sir, that if you cannot bear to think me a thief, you will hardly advise me to become a rich man's harlot.

Mr Peach, who has been standing, falls into the rude chair beside the window, which admits the pleasant air of a summer night, and allows his head to fall into his hands.

— Is this true?

Clary answers more gently — if gentleness can be imagined, in *that* voice, and *that* mouth — we may perhaps say, there is a fraction less of the iron in her tone — Sir, I had not meant to add to your distresses. — I made a jest of it, because it deserves no more. Why should you be grieved to discover the man a villain as well as a fool? Are not all men much the same, in the heat of lust?

— Poor Miss Farthingay, says Mr Peach, through his hands.

— She will not be *poor*, at least, says Clary.

— Her marriage will bring her ten times as much misery as wealth.

— Will she not now be a rich woman in her own right? — now her parents are dead?

Mr Peach looks up. — I suppose she will, he says.

— Then she may do without the husband.

— I cannot help but observe, Clary, how you speak of the passing of Mr and Mrs Farthingay with perfect indifference. Are you not touched at all by the death of those, who for the greater part of your life must have appeared to you in the character of parents? — By their *murder*?

Clary is silent several moments, before answering. — Mr Farthingay was not good to me. As for Mrs Farthingay, she barely acknowledged me. She despised her husband's experiment. She feared I might supplant her Arabella, in his eye. — Though she need not have. Mr Farthingay would not have used his own daughter, as he used me.

Mr Peach recollects the language used by Caspar, when that gentleman briefly alluded to Mr Farthingay's *living doll*. — He rubs his face with his palms, as we do, when we are weary, and discomfited by the thoughts in our own heads. — I knew Mr Farthingay but slightly, he says, and Mrs Farthingay less. — To respect their memories, is the least duty I owe them, in common humanity. Whatever resentments you harbour — however justified — It is most certain, that some body has inflicted on them a dreadful punishment. Let that be enough for you.

— Is it not yet known who perpetrated the murders?

Mr Peach tells her Caspar is arrested, and will be arraigned. Clary expresses her incredulity; and so he proceeds to explain the various circumstances, which have brought the poor man under suspicion. — You have read these, in our last.

Mr Peach is only now struck by a thought, which may privately have occurred to you, reader, as you perused those pages, *viz.* that there is an horrid *symmetry*, if we may employ the term, between the unnatural appetites of Clary, and the grotesque method used to stop the mouths of the murdered pair. What it signifies — if any thing — he cannot bring himself to contemplate.

The maid herself seems likewise struck by the morbid detail.

— Is it certain, she says, that they were choked on *paper*?

— I cannot think why I should doubt the magistrate's report.

— Of what sort was the paper?

— I understand, says Mr Peach, that you have a particular interest in the question; but it can only be distasteful in the extreme, to indulge the curiosity of your palate, in the circumstances.

— Again, sir, you mistake my meaning. The hour is late, and you are tired. Have you not reflected, that the question of the paper is surely of the greatest significance, for the purpose of discovering the guilty party?

— I do not understand you.

— Was the paper printed?

Mr Peach is about to reply, with some exasperation, that he cannot possibly know whether the poor couple were choked to death on foolscap, or a play-bill, or a mouthful of invitations to the public ball — When he recalls, that the magistrate did indeed make reference to printed pages.

— I believe so, says he.

— Then, says she, they were most likely torn from a book.

— I think the magistrate said as much.

— Why, says she, then surely an effort ought to be made, to discover whether any person in the house possesses a book, from which some pages are torn? Were any such object found, it would appear a strong confirmation of guilt.

Mr Peach rises from the chair. —

He *thinks* a while. —

Alas, the day is too far gone, and has been too crowded with disheartening incident, for his intellectual faculties to rise, and shew their native strength. Nevertheless —

— It is a point to be considered, he says. — Perhaps, if it can be proved that none of Caspar's books have suffered depredation, we may at least weaken the accusation against him.

— I should think, says Clary, all the books in the house ought to be examined. And the house searched. — I suppose the perpetrator might have concealed the volume from which he tore the pages.

— The suggestion has merit.

— It would also seem a simple matter to inspect the pages, with the aim of determining *which* book they are torn from. A man of literary knowledge, such as yourself, sir, might be able to assist the magistrate.

408

Mr Peach draws in the breath of night, scented with the season's luxury of herbage.

— I must consider it.

— We might delay our departure a day or two longer, if necessary, says Clary. — Good-night, Mr Peach.

The conversation has not been long. — Yet we think nevertheless, that it calls for a moment or two of reflexion — That we ought not to proceed immediately, to the busy and surprizing events, of the day following. We shall therefore allow it a chapter of its own, though but a brief one. And we are pleased to say, that Mr Peach is less severely oppressed in spirit, at the end of *this*, than in the sad conclusion of our last. Let him take to his bed —

We shall stand by the window a while — for — Hark! — a nightingale begins to sing —

CHAPTER TWENTY-SEVEN

We had thought to bid our farewells to Bristol — Its squares, and avenues, and alleys — its shops and meeting-houses — proud old temples, and humble Methodist chapels — its ceaseless docks, encroaching on the changeless waters — its stew of *people*, drawn, or compelled, from the farthest corners of the earth — Yet here we are once more, reader! for Mr Peach has awoken, with his promise to Miss Farthingay full in his heart, and the interesting advice of Miss Riddle humming about his brain, and so betaken himself once more to the town, to wait attendance upon the magistrate, and the coroner.

He enquires first, at the house of Miss Farthingay's female friend. The lady and Mr Stocks are not yet departed. There are funerary arrangements to be made — and no one else, to make them. — Mr Peach is pleased to learn that Miss Farthingay will not immediately be removed to London, for he has now some hopes, that the presumption of guilt laid upon poor Caspar, will presently be relieved, and he wishes her to have whatever comfort the news may bring. Indeed, he would have liked to offer his morsel of encouragement in person — But, being informed that Mr Stocks is present within, declines to be announced, and proceeds instead with his pursuit of the several ministers of the king's justice.

We need not describe in minute detail, the delays and obstructions to his chase. They are tiresome enough to Mr Peach, and would be ten times more tedious to you. Nor need we rehearse in full, our hero's interviews with coroner and magistrate. It is enough to say that both worthies are courteous enough to admit him, after

410

the necessary trials of his patience, and to give him hearing, as a gentleman, and friend of the distressed Miss Farthingay. From the coroner he has the unfortunate news, that the pages which were crammed into the mouths of Mr and Mrs Farthingay, have long since been disposed of, being cruel and ugly defacements to the dignity of the deceased. The most he is able to learn, is that they were pages of ordinary print, such as might be found in any common octavo — Not unlike these very pages you turn, reader.

We hope, you do not find the comparison unpalatable. —

Mr Peach, like Bunyan's pilgrim, will brook no discouragement. He returns to the magistrate. — And, in summary, there repeats the ingenious suggestions of Miss Clarissa Riddle, though he is careful not to ascribe them to his house-maid. He rather proposes them, as though they must already have occurred to the mind of the magistrate himself; for, as every body knows, the surest way to persuade a man of any thing, is to let him take it for his own opinion — There being no person in existence, who does not prefer to credit their own ingenuity, above that of another.

The magistrate acknowledges the justice of the notion. — Or rather, confirms to Mr Peach, that he had been just about to put that very proposal to the test — The books in the house shall be examined, says he — I was preparing to go thither, for that very purpose, among one or two others, when you were announced. I doubt any thing will come of it — But we shall see, whether it be material or no — &c.

This promise secured, Mr Peach has attained the limit of his immediate purpose, and can see no better course of action, than to seek the restorative tranquillity of the woods, by taking a lengthy walk along sweet *Avon*, where it bends its way above the town.*

* It may be objected, that a river, by its very nature, cannot be going *above* any place, because it must travel in one direction only, and that *downward*. To such pettifogging pedantry we make no answer. — It deserves none. — My learned sir, if you have stood on the bank of some gentle stream, and observed the effortless and unhurried windings of its passage between yourself and those far-off hills, whence it descends; and

On another day, we should have been tempted to accompany him, and allow our pen the respite of lingering among those Arcadian scenes. To-day, we cannot. — Events press on us, and banish every thought of rustic idleness. Surprizes wait at every turn. — And none, we think, more remarkable, and less to be expected, than the news, that a book is indeed discovered in the house of the late Mr Farthingay, from which several pages have been torn out — And that this highly significant volume, was found among the private possessions of — MR STOKESAY STOCKS.

Mr Stokesay Stocks! — A gentleman of rank, connected to one of the greatest families in the land!

The magistrate is pale, and turns his spectacles in his hands.

— I was given to understand, says Mr Peach, that only the servants were under suspicion.

— Mr Stocks also lay in the house that night, as the guest of Mr and Mrs Farthingay. I had of course excluded the gentleman — It is impossible to conceive — an *Eton* man — A *Cambridge* man —

You will have understood, reader, that Mr Peach is long since returned from his country ramble, and has called on the magistrate again, before returning to the inn.

— Is the defaced volume certainly his?

— I discovered it myself, sir, not three hours ago, in the rooms of the house which had been made over for Mr Stocks's use. It had been thrown out of sight under the bed where he slept. — All the servants confirm it.

Mr Peach is somewhat giddy in his amazement.

— Sir, he says, I think your duty requires you to acknowledge the significance of this circumstance.

---

have never felt the water's seduction, which seems irresistibly to lead you *towards* those sylvan heights! — then, sir, your soul is no better than a dry and shrivelled nut, and we leave you to the satisfactions of your quibbles and cavils. — You shall die, sir, and come to dust, as we shall; but we think *our* existence will have been worth the living. — Good-day, sir.

— It is certainly very significant.

— Can there be any doubt that the hand which tore the pages from the book, is the same hand which executed the horrid murders of Mr and Mrs Farthingay? I think there cannot be.

— I must agree, Mr Peach.

— Then, sir, surely it must now be very uncertain, whether that hand belongs to the servant Caspar.

— I am compelled to acknowledge it. But — a gentleman! —

Mr Peach feels himself warming to his task, as the common saying is. — The truth, sir, he says, bends to no distinction of rank, and no more will justice. Consider the *cui bono*. Caspar has nothing to gain from the foul deed. Though he is to lose his position, when his mistress is married, the deaths of Mr and Mrs Farthingay cannot help him regain it, or serve any other purpose to his advantage. Nor is any supposed rage of pride satisfied by their murder, for the change in his circumstances cannot be *their* fault. — Had he been moved to so monstrous an act, by mere jealousy, or revenge, he would surely have executed it upon the person of Mr Stocks himself — Who also lay in the house that night, and might as easily have been chosen for the victim. Reflect instead upon the case of Mr Stocks. By the death of her parents, Miss Farthingay is made a lady of great fortune. — By her marriage, Mr Stocks becomes possessor of that fortune.

— Horrible! cries the magistrate.

— I think, says Mr Peach, you must at the very least make diligent enquiries concerning the actions of Mr Stocks, during that night. They have not been thought of until now.

— I cannot do otherwise. My duty requires it.

— Shall the servant be returned to liberty? Either myself or Miss Farthingay will stand security for him. It cannot be justice to confine a man in such a state, when his guilt may not safely be presumed.

— There is the testimony of the other servants —

— Hearsay, sir, and from people of little worth, whose resentment of Caspar may easily be ascribed to mere jealousy of his favoured position, and superior atchievements. The evidence of the *book* must carry the weight.

The magistrate is a man of capabilities — and of rectitude — And not without a sense of the worth of his office. Unwilling though he be, to contemplate an accusation of murder — foulest murder — against a gentleman of Mr Stocks's station, he will not shrink from his duty. Mr Peach reminds him, of the title he bears — Holds before him, the sacred imperatives of BRITISH JUSTICE — And, at last — secures the release of Caspar — Which he brings with all haste, to the gaol.

More of Miss Farthingay's coin must be expended, before the turnkey will consent to see him. — But in due course, the prisoner is unshackled, and set at liberty.

Caspar's gratitude is of a curiously solemn sort.

— You are indeed a very great magician, Mr Thomas Peach, says he, as they stand in the street, while the evening begins its slow and misty progression towards twilight.

— It is scarcely the work of an unearthly power, to free a man from confinement for a crime he has not committed.

— So you say, great sir, and therefore I do not say otherwise. But what we know, we know.

Mr Peach enquires, where Caspar will go; for it need not be said, that he cannot return to Miss Farthingay, while she is in the care of her intended. Caspar has friends in the town — In those parts of the town, passed over by the eyes of lords and ladies and gentlemen. — He thanks Mr Peach for his concern, but bids him put his mind at rest. — Do not think of me, he says, I entreat you. To be in the thoughts of a man of power, is very dangerous.

Mr Peach offers him the remaining money, which he had from Miss Farthingay, to procure the servant some comfort in his imprisonment. Caspar is most unwilling to accept it — Says, he cannot be under any obligation to *such a man* — Mr Peach insists — &c. — There is something in a discussion of this nature so very *British*, that we cannot help finding it tedious, because *too familiar* — We shall not record it. — But, having secured the freedom of the amiable servant, which was the purpose of our narrative for these several pages past, we continue without delay to further reversals of fortune, good and ill — For the blind Dam now spins her wheel apace, and our narrative is caught upon it, like Saint Catherine, and cannot rest until it reach its *end*.

We proceed, then, to the morning of the next day.

We find Mr Peach and Clary, at the inn, and once more making preparations for their return to Widdershins Bank. Mr Peach is a little uneasy. — He is not certain, how he will settle the bill of lodging and fare — Has, indeed, passed the hours since his rising, in contemplation of that very puzzle — But — lo! — here is *another* messenger, riding to the humble door of the Cow and Welshman, in _____ton — With *another* note for Mr Peach, bidding him come to town, with all possible haste. He is particularly requested, to bring his female servant with him! — and is urged, to use the utmost discretion — But on no account to delay.

This peremptory note is subscribed —

Stokesay Stocks, Esq.!

— What business, thinks Mr Peach, can the odious fellow possibly have with me now?

— The language of the note, he says to himself, proceeding with his contemplations, Suggests a matter of importance; yet he gives not the slightest hint as to its nature.

— Am I then to dance attendance upon Mr Stokesay Stocks, merely because he wishes me to? It will require me to ride again to town, and will detain me there for I know not how long. — I shall have to go another night at the inn, at further expence.

— Yet — Mr Peach's meditations here take a less gloomy turn — I may perhaps also consider, that a postponement of our departure, resolves the difficulty in settling my bill TO-DAY.

He says to Clary — I think we ought to oblige the gentleman. His note is quite insistent.

— As you please, sir, says she. — Only, I shall not want to be in the presence of Miss Farthingay. She would know me even in my new cloaths and veil.

Any precaution, however, proves unnecessary. For Mr Stocks's business with Mr Peach, is not of the sort that may be transacted in the presence of his intended. — As you shall learn, in a moment.

The familiar journey passes slowly, for either Clary must walk while Mr Peach rides, or *vice versa* — He being unwilling to allow her to mount the saddle in front of him, before the eyes of the town — And the gelding being still more unwilling, to be burdened with a double cargo, when that animal considers *one* rider, to be an imposition barely tolerable.

Mr Peach is particularly doubtful concerning that part of Mr Stocks's instructions, which requires that Clary accompany him. He can only presume, that the gentleman intends to press upon Clary the offer of employment, which he has formerly proposed in general terms. An unwelcome prospect! — yet Mr Peach draws some inward comfort, from the maid's evident inclination to refuse any such proposal.

Upon arrival in town, he is met by a lackey bearing another message from Mr Stocks, which directs him to a fashionable coffee-house, in the elegant quarter. Mr Stocks has taken a small private room in the establishment. — And there it is, that he greets Mr Peach — Clary having been requested to wait beyond, until called for.

Mr Stocks is pale, and — we should have said, in a state of *agitation*, except that the term denotes a restlessness of motion, entirely unknown to the gentleman, whose deportment is at all times indolent and careless. — Let us say, he is *distracted*.

— My dear Peach — he says, taking our hero by the hand — Much obliged — It's the most confounded delicate thing. You are a gentleman, and we shall understand one another — I love the good old honest frankness — Don't you? — I'm sure, sir, I may rely on you, in a matter of honour.

Mr Peach can distinguish head nor tail in this chimaerical manner of speaking, and begs to be made acquainted with the matter, upon which Mr Stocks has requested to see him.

— Quite so — One ought to explain the d___d thing first. But your discretion — Entire discretion — I need not doubt it?

Mr Peach assures Mr Stocks, that he cannot imagine any thing could pass between them, which would not be spoken in confidence.

— It's only my Bella. — Such a fine creature, and her nerves — She ought never to know of it, you see. It must all go off quietly, between ourselves and the d___d magistrate fellow. Dear Bella need never hear a word. She is such a delicate thing — A flower, Mr Peach! a lily, or rose, or what have you. We must shield her, you see, or she may — Wilt — Her petals fall off —

Mr Peach expresses his surprize, at Mr Stocks's allusion to the magistrate.

— A bothersome dunce! d___n him! — He comes to me, d'ye hear, and pesters my people, and now he says, that I shall have questions to answer, regarding the nasty affair of the old fellow and his wife. — *Shall!* — *questions!* — Indeed! — I don't wonder you look astonished, Peach. — I told the varlet, my cousin, Sir Nigylle Stocks, *shall* hear of this.

Mr Stocks blusters a little further in this vein, before Mr Peach is able to intrude upon his indignation, with the reasonable enquiry, as to why the magistrate's behaviour has caused Mr Stocks to send for *him*, and his house-maid?

— Ah — now — Here's the rub, as the fellow says in the play — here's the rub of it, Peach — Rub-a-dub-dub — You may assist me, by bringing that little maid of yours before the magistrate. — Hey? — A very little matter — A few words, and it will all go off, and the whole d___d nonsense is finished, and forgotten. — Most particularly, *forgotten* — You understand me, sir.

Mr Peach confesses, that he does not.

— I must be frank — For, you know, I hate your snivelling dodging fellows — I must tell you, Peach, that I encountered your pretty piece, upon an affair of gallantry, on the night in question. — You are a gentleman, sir — You know the fashion in such things. Upon my honour, all was done, just as it ought to be — In every point according to the chivalry of it. Only, now I require that the little baggage come before this pestering ass of a magistrate, and give her oath of her part in the affair. You see how it stands. — The fellow must be compelled to give up his ridiculous notion, that I *shall answer questions*, when he learns I was not in the house in the night. There is some tom-foolery of evidence — some book they all speak of — Pish and trash, Peach. — But ten words from your Charlotte to the magistrate, and it is done — Never spoken of again. My Bella is such a dear sweet innocent thing, she need not trouble herself with a gentleman's chivalry. — You agree, I know. — Let's shake hands on it.

Mr Peach's successive sensations of amazement, confusion, and disgust, as he hears this *patched* explanation, may be imagined.

— I recall, he thinks, with mounting revulsion, that I did not see Clary at the inn, when I returned from my disappointing evening at Doctor Thorburn's house; which was the night when the horrid murder was done, and for which this jackanapes now requires his loathsome *alibi*. — Yet how could I have imagined, that she had willingly gone out, to prostitute herself to the whim of a shameless rake?

Mr Stocks interprets Mr Peach's silent contemplation, as a form of consent. — A presumption, which would hardly occur to any other mortal; but, as we have observed formerly, Mr Stocks is so perfectly accustomed to having his way, that he takes all the world to be in accord with his wishes, unless the world be very determined in its insistence to the contrary — And sometimes even in the latter case.

— Excellent! — he says, with more of his usual good cheer, for, having explained to Mr Peach what is required, he has no doubt every body will do as he expects, and the rest of the business will take care of itself. — Then there's no time to lose — Will you be so good as to go to the magistrate at once? It's only next-door. — Come, let's fetch your Charlotte — 'Pon my soul, Peach, the piece is quite the little wench — Hey? — But all was done most properly, have no fear. I think I know, how a gentleman is to behave in these affairs — &c. — Now, Charlotte, he says to Clary, when they are in the street, Here are your master and I, going to take you to see the magistrate, which is a name for an important fellow in the law. You shall have nothing to fear. — I will speak of some things, which you will remember, and you have no more to do but tell this magistrate fellow the truth of them. He shall perhaps ask you to swear it on a Bible. You shan't mind that, I hope, Charlotte? — and there's a guinea for you before, and you shall have another after. — Here is the first.

Mr Peach is glad, that the face of his maid is veiled. — He knows he will see no shame there, at the exposure of her miserable transaction, and he fears her indifference would fill him with unbearable disgust. He is likewise not at all displeased, that there is no possibility of addressing her, while Mr Stocks continues his blandishments. — For, in truth, he has not the least idea what he would say. He feels by instinct, that he has no right to express his revulsion. — She has acknowledged herself a wicked and depraved creature — *And so has he* — Yet he is revolted nonetheless.

To receive the inducements, of a man such as Stokesay Stocks! and to *accept* them! — a man, engaged to be wed, to one whom Clary ought to view in the light of a childhood friend! —

But none of his indignation can be spoken aloud. — Only, Mr Peach finds he cannot restrain himself, when he sees the coin held up in Mr Stocks's well-formed hand, but must coldly remark, that if the gentleman intends the maid to give her affidavit on his behalf, it is quite improper for him to offer her money, for the principles of justice demand that a witness speak without fear or favour. He fixes his look on Clary — or rather, on the shadow of her, visible behind the veil — And adds, that no *more* payment must pass between them — Adding to this hint, a look as cold as his language.

Mr Stocks withdraws the guinea. — Very true, he says — All must be done properly — I see you are the very fellow for it, Peach — &c. — And more in this vein, all exactly as though Mr

Peach were his greatest friend in the world, and the two of them on terms of the most affable mutual understanding.

So they come to the magistrate's house. — Here Mr Peach addresses Clary at last.

— Well, child, he says — Are you prepared to stand before the officer of the law, and declare your part in this?

Clary bows her head — and answers —

Mr Peach is utterly astonished, to hear her accents changed to those of a shy simpering country Jill!

— I am, sir, says this altered voice — Though I'm terribly fearful, and you must say to the master, about my blemish, or I'm sure I'll be too frightened to speak a thing.

— Fear nothing! cries Mr Stocks. — When the old fellow hears you speak so pretty and modest, Charlotte, he shan't care at all that your mouth is black. Come within — Remember, I shall protect you. No harm will come to you — A gentleman's word is his honour, you know.

They are admitted to the presence of the magistrate without delay. — For Mr Stocks, though called to answer questions concerning a capital offence, is nevertheless to be accommodated in every thing, on his way to the court-room, and, if necessary, to the gallows. 'The law's delay,' which Prince Hamlet so justly enumerates among the reasonable arguments, in support of suicide, is not for such as he. — The magistrate greets him humbly — Greets Mr Peach, in more familiar terms — Gazes with severe disdain, at Clary — And so, to the business.

— Here's the young lady I spoke of, says Mr Stocks, with a flourish of his cane. — She shall confirm every thing. Lift up your veil, now, Charlotte, there's a good girl — Don't be afraid.

— Must I? says Clary to Mr Peach, in a frighted whisper.

— This person, says the magistrate to Mr Peach, is in your employ, I understand, in the character of house-maid?

— She is, says he, very stern. — She shall answer every thing you put to her.

Clary emits a little cry of feminine terror. — Oh!

— Why is she brought before me with her face concealed?

— She suffers from a discolouration of the mouth, which makes her shy of exposing it to public view.

The magistrate addresses her. — You shall not pretend to be *shy*, child, if what this gentleman alleges be true, as, alas, I do not doubt it is. Lift your veil. We will not judge your mouth by its outward appearance, but by the confession proceeding from it.

Clary puts the veil up over her bonnet, and stands with head bowed, to all appearances a witless country girl, awed and confounded before the gravity of the law.

— What is your name, child? says the magistrate.

— Charlotte Puzzle, your worship, she murmurs.

— You must look at me, when you speak.

— Yes, sir.

Mr Peach sees a look of horror descend on the magistrate, at his first sight of the ink-blackened organ.

— I am called Puzzle, she says, because no one knows the proper name, for I'm an orphan, with no mother nor father, and no better than a beggar till kind Mr Peach took me on. I think Charlotte be my own name, though.

Mr Peach has not before the present occasion given much thought, to Clary's declared conviction, that she exists under the influence and ministry of the prince of all malign powers. — It is not a proposition of the sort to invite serious contemplation, even for a man such as Mr Peach — were there another such man — Which we think there cannot be.

Yet he wonders now, whether her black mouth might not indeed be a fleshly temple, dedicated to the FATHER OF LIES.

— Very good, Charlotte, says the magistrate, though visibly discomposed at the sight before him. — Very good — Now you must swear to answer truly every question I may put to you, and so we shall make what is called your affidavit, which means that you declare the truth of your testimony, on peril of the penalty of the law, and of your immortal soul.

421

— I do swear it, says Clary. — Mr Peach always taught me not to lie.

— I wish, says the magistrate, recovering his august severity, That you had also learned from your good master, the *whole* of what it is, to be an *honest* girl.

Clary whimpers, and bows her head, and mumbles, that the gentleman swore she did no wrong.

— Well — says the magistrate — We are not here to judge or condemn you. Your master may do so, hereafter. It is not for me to say, what consequences you will suffer from your folly. My concern is only that you answer every question here, and do so wholly and honestly.

Clary trembles a little, and nods, and murmurs her assent.

The clerk prepares his pen and paper.

The magistrate sits.

— Now, Charlotte Puzzle, he says, I shall ask you about the events which occurred three nights past, that is, on Tuesday last, the __th day of this month. It is the night when this gentleman Mr Stocks declares you came to him, at an house in ____-street, upon an assignation, previously suggested by the gentleman, and agreed to by yourself. I suppose you remember it?

— I do, sir.

— And did you come to that house?

— It wasn't proper of me to refuse a gentleman, says Clary.

The magistrate raises his brows. — I did not ask you the *why* of it, Charlotte, he says. — You need not waste your breath with justifications. You are only to answer to the facts. I say again, did you come to that house, upon Mr Stocks's invitation?

— Don't be afraid, Charlotte, interjects Mr Stocks, in an encouraging tone. — No harm will come to you.

The magistrate turns his severity on Mr Stocks, advising him in the most emphatic language, that he must not interfere with the girl's affidavit. Mr Stocks is somewhat indignant, at the appearance of correction, but merely nods, in the manner of one who politely consents to a request — As though he says, *Well, old fellow, I shall on this occasion condescend to comply with the requirements of justice.*

— I did, your worship, says Clary.

— And you were received at the house, by Mr Stocks, in person, as he has declared?

— Oh, yes, sir. Every thing was very fine.

— Mr Stocks's account is that he received you a little before dark, around the hour of nine o'clock. Will you swear to that?

— I do seem to recall the night coming on. The evening was all a-mizzle, I remember, with no shadows to see the length of.

— Well, but will you give it as your sworn affidavit, that you were admitted to the house, around the hour of nine o'clock?

— Very well, your worship.

The magistrate sighs. — It is so recorded. Now, all that remains, is to declare that from that hour, until the dawn of the next day, you were in the company of Mr Stocks, within that same house. I do not require you to say any thing of what passed between you. That is for your own conscience, and for your master, if he will continue your master. Do you swear only to the fact of it?

— Which is it I must swear to, your worship?

— Bless me! — To what I have just now said — That from nine o'clock, when you were received by Mr Stocks at the house in _____-street, until five o'clock in the morning, you remained in that same house, and Mr Stocks with you throughout.

Clary looks about her, as though uncertain. — Why, no, your worship, she says.

— Hey? says Mr Stocks.

The magistrate also frowns a little. — You do not swear to that, Charlotte?

— I'm not to swear, unless it be true, I'm sure.

— Come now, Charlotte, says Mr Stocks. — Don't be a silly girl.

The magistrate once more demands Mr Stocks's silence. — As for our Mr Peach — he begins to be overcome by the sensation, that the scene unfolding before his eyes is a species of *masque*, or a satyr-play — Some curious ingenious performance, given in a language he barely knows — Acted by phantoms — At the behest of a madman.

— Be careful now to speak the exact truth, Charlotte, says the magistrate. — Will you now say, that you did *not* pass that entire night in the company of Mr Stocks, within the house?

— Not so much time, your worship, for it was only two or three hour, and then the gentleman got up and bad me go home. I was surprized at it, for it was all pitchy black abroad, and the middle of the night.

— Now, Charlotte, says Mr Stocks, what's this? This won't do.

— Sir, says the magistrate, I shall require you no more to disturb the proceedings, or you shall leave the room.

— Require me! will you?

— Indeed I will, sir, and do.

— The gentleman has a dreadful temper, your worship, says Clary — Pray don't arouse him.

— What, says Mr Stocks, raising his cane, Will you speak of my character, baggage?

The magistrate stands. — He is very pale, but all determination. — We shall have no threats here, he says. — Mr Peach, you are witness. I shall call for the beadle.

— Peach — says Mr Stocks — and now there are signs in him of rising passion — A thing unprecedented, from his first appearance in our narrative — Peach, he says, bring your b___h to heel — Tell her she'll be whipped for lying.

— The girl shall give her affidavit, says the magistrate. — Fetch Mr Clarke — Request that he bring his men.

An attendant goes out, to find the beadle. Mr Stocks cannot help notice it. — He attempts to resume a careless air — Well, he says, never mind your beadle, or the rest of them — Devil take 'em. — He fences a stroke or two in the air with his cane, and sits again.

The magistrate draws a long breath — And returns his attention to Clary.

— Miss Puzzle, says he, I must urge you to consider what you say, and be exact in your recollection. Will you swear, that you left that house in _____-street about the middle of the night, and did not return to it, and that you have no knowledge of the whereabouts or the doings of Mr Stocks after that hour?

— For the hour, your worship, now I think of it, it was just before the mid-night he sent me away, for I heard the old church tell twelve as I went over the bridge. I thought of ghosts being abroad, and crossed myself three time, and said the Lord's prayer twice together.

— That is a circumstance, Mr Ussher, says the magistrate to the clerk. — Let it be recorded.

— It's a d___d lie, says Mr Stocks.

— Sir —

— You shan't instruct me to listen, while this piece of flesh tells her d___d w___e lies. I am the cousin of Sir Nigylle Stocks.

— He would talk so, your worship, says Clary, in a trembling voice, While he treated with me. He promised to be a gentleman, and make me rich, for he said he'd soon be rich as old king Midas, but he was all *w___es* and *d___ns*.

— Did he say he would soon be rich? cries the magistrate.

Mr Stocks leaps from his chair. — D___d filthy b___h, he says — D___n your filthy lying mouth — Feel my cane!

Mr Peach steps in his way — Entreats him, to be calm — to remember, who he is, and where he is. The magistrate shouts aloud for Mr Clarke the beadle. — For several moments, all is tumult — And worse is threatened. — Luckily, the intervention of Mr Peach is sufficient to restrain Mr Stocks from any act of violence. Mr Stocks has certain conditions which must be met, before he can strike a gentleman out of his way — as, for example, if he has been drinking with his fellow bucks; or, if the gentleman has given him direct insult, or made a contemptuous remark on the king, or the ministry, or the antient university of Cambridge, or the college of Eton; or if the gentleman wears blue and buff, or is a foreigner; among several others, which we need not enumerate. — Mr Peach meets none of the requirements, in the present instance, and Mr Stocks must therefore withdraw.

The magistrate addresses Clary again. — Mr Stocks, he says, has given as his affidavit, that he entertained your company for some two hours, within the house, and then fell asleep, in your presence, and that you were still in his company when he awoke several hours later, near day-break. Do you mean to say you will contradict his sworn word? Remember, child, it is a grievous offence against God, as well as the king, to swear what is not true, and the punishment for bearing false witness is most severe.

Clary bursts into tears — A sight, which produces in Mr Peach no less an extreme of amazement, than if she had sprouted an unicorn horn from her forehead — Must you rail so, she says, when I only say what happened, as it was, and nothing more! He swore in his note he'd be a perfect gentleman, and now he calls me w___e and b___h and is as like to kill me — I did hear him say, he was never afraid to do what must be done, to have his way.

— Brazen hussy! cries Mr Stocks.

Clary hides her weeping face in her hands — Let him be taken out, your worship — I fear for my life —

— You shall fear me, Mr Stocks exclaims, gesticulating his rage, the left hand with his cane and the right with a fist — D___n your eyes! d___n your w___e's mouth! I shall throw your d___d lies down your throat!

— Oh! shrieks Clary, listen to him! — He told me, he do love nothing so much as to cram a person's mouth shut with *words*!

— Did he say so? cries the magistrate — Mr Ussher — Record it in the affidavit! —

The clerk is a picture of terror — But bends over the paper, and writes.

— Do you give this ugly black-mouth baggage an hearing, against the word of a gentleman? — I will have you all whipped for it — You are ruined, sir — My cousin shall know all — You shall beg pardon at the end of my boot, before the week is out — &c. — Mr Stocks continues to threaten and rail, and is kept from a rash act only by the stubborn immobility of Mr Peach, until the arrival of several handy fellows, led by the beadle; in whose presence Mr Stocks becomes once more conscious of his superiority, and makes his own way from the room, before they can threaten his dignity further, by compelling his departure.

Clary sobs a little more, and hides her face still, and mumbles her gratitude to the magistrate, for protecting her from the gentleman's fury, which she fears might have made him do any thing, for, she says, she heard him boast many times, that a great gentleman such as he might *do whatever he pleased, and fear no punishment.* — The magistrate casts a glance at Mr Peach. — Mr Peach looks at the magistrate. — Mr Ussher writes again.

— Come, come, girl, says the magistrate, addressing Clary with less severity than he has used hitherto, You have doubtless been a very silly child, and I trust you are very sorry for it, but you must not cry. Be brave, and tell the truth. — No one shall complain of you for doing that.

— I am a poor foolish wretch, cries Clary, to be ruined by the fine promises of a villain! — And, in spite of the urgings of the law's appointed officer, she weeps again, more copiously than ever.

Mr Peach wonders whether he be dreaming. — Or whether, by some incomprehensible accident, the Clarissa Riddle whom he knows, is presently standing in the street outside, and her place taken within the magistrate's house by this Charlotte Puzzle, who, though identical in every feature, is a different person altogether. — A fiction — a concoction of words —

The magistrate's heart is not so hard, as to remain untouched by the lamentations of a simple girl, seduced by the careless gallantry of a rake. His revulsion at the hideous stain on her face, is quite overcome. He speaks to her ever more gently — Leads her, by careful prompts, through her affidavit — And by such degrees, educes the whole of her testimony, which is in all important points just as you have heard, to wit; that she entered the house, chosen by Mr Stocks for his wicked assignation, at about nine o'clock, and left it before mid-night; that she passed the intervening time in the company of the gentleman, but knows nothing of his whereabouts for the remainder of the night, except that she heard him say, *he had some business to attend to*, in a manner she did not like; that she found his character peremptory, irascible, and violent; and that he boasted of expecting soon to become very rich. In short, she utterly contradicts Mr Stocks's account, that he fell asleep in the house, in the early part of the night, and awoke many hours later, still in her company, and did not return to Mr Farthingay's house until after dawn; and, moreover, she paints his character in colours conforming to the display of offended rage, which the magistrate himself has just witnessed; and describes every circumstance, in terms which must appear to cast the gravest suspicion upon Mr Stocks himself.

— On one point, says the magistrate, I must be very particular. — Is it your exact recollection, that Mr Stocks threatened to choke you, or any body, with *words*?

Clary makes a great shew, of exerting her brain — Eyes squeezed shut — Brow furrowed as a winter field — Not me, sir, she says, unless you mean just now, when he was threatening I know not what, but I do remember he said, he loved to cram a mouth shut on words. — Why do you ask it, your worship? — It was but one small thing he said, among all his great swearing and swaggering.

The magistrate looks again towards Mr Peach, with a significant expression. — Never mind, Charlotte, he says — It is a matter for the law — You need not concern yourself with it. It shall be recorded in your affidavit. — Let it be noted exactly, Mr Ussher. — Now, when Mr Ussher is finished, you shall read over the whole affidavit, and put your name to it, to swear its truth in every particular. You can read and write, I know.

— Yes, your worship, says Clary, my good master taught me.

— Mr Peach, says the magistrate, drawing himself straight — I must require you, as a gentleman, and her employer, to give the girl's character. Her testimony stands in direct contradiction to

the word of Mr Stocks. It is no small matter. — Do you swear on
your honour, that you have always known the girl honest, and of
virtuous and godly habits? We may set aside her foolishness in
this particular matter, as owing much to the inducements and
protestations of the gentleman.

Clary turns herself, to look at Mr Peach. —

Every eye is upon him.

Reader — We are curious, whether you have in your own person
ever known that peculiar inward condition, which we may call a
divided mind?

We do not speak of any thing so common-place, as mere
doubt — That ordinary affliction, which comes upon us at any
time, when a choice of actions presents itself to us, and we are not
in the instant certain which way to proceed. *Doubt*, is nothing —
The mind approaches it with a little trepidation, perhaps, but no
great difficulty, for we have within us, the machinery to overcome
it — our reason, judgment, and our will. We consider the choice —
weigh it — Decide — Act — All this, a thousand times an hour. It
might be said with some justice, that life itself consists in this
perpetual selection, between the possibilities before us, from one
moment to the next.

No — The condition of which we now speak, is of a different
species altogether.

A *divided mind*, is that state in which there occur within us,
two utterly distinct and opposed conceptions, at the same time. —
Conceptions, of what we do — of who we are — of where we
stand, and what lies ahead of us — Each of the two, as clear, and
whole, and reasonable, as the other; and yet it appears impossible,
that both should appear simultaneously, within a single brain.*
Much might be written, of this remarkable phaenomenon. Our
philosophers, and our natural scientists, ought, we humbly
suggest, to make it the object of their investigations. — We cannot

* odi et amo — quare id faciam, fortasse requiris? nescio, sed fieri sentio
et excrucior. — Catullus.

at present do their work for them — Indeed, we who labour in the field of *necromantic history*, have quite enough of our own to be doing. We only remark upon it now, because our Mr Tho.s Peach, at this very moment of our tale, finds himself as perfectly *divided* in his mind, as though he had been cleft in twain by an invisible surgeon.

His case stands thus. —

On the one side, is a consciousness of the situation in which he finds himself, and a vision of what he must do next, which are wholly reasonable, consistent in their parts, and coherent in the whole, and which accord with the truth of the world, as it presents itself before him. On *this* side, his answer to the magistrate will take some such form, as follows: — That the young woman, who has just given her account of the events of the night, in which Mr and Mrs Farthingay met their horrid doom, is to his knowledge named not Charlotte Puzzle, but Clarissa Riddle; that he first met her, only some few weeks previous; that he ought not to give her character with authority, upon so short an acquaintance, but that in general he has found her secret, strange, wilfully dismissive of common notions of virtue and moral justice, and eminently capable of untruth; that although he has become fond of her, he suspects it would be better for him, if he had not; that there are grounds to suppose, that she is not entirely a natural human creature; and that by her own confession, she believes herself to be possessed by the Devil, or otherwise under the immediate influence of that gentleman, what or wheresoever he may be.

Mr Peach can see this whole explanation, laid out before his mind's eye, like a Dutch landskip; perfectly rendered, complete in all its details, and vivid with life. It is, he thinks, the TRUTH. — It represents, what *is*. — There will not be slightest difficulty, in presenting it to the magistrate, or to any body. No hesitation attaches to it. — He will know just what he says, and why he says it.

Let us term this, the *day-light* side.

On the *other* side of his mind, there is — Some other thing.

This, is not so easily rendered in propositions and predicates. This, is the *nocturnal* side. — No homely Dutch scene, but the dismal and turbulent composition, of a *Salvator Rosa*, or one of those dream-prisons imagined in the tormenting visions of *Piranesi*. — It speaks to Thomas Peach, in the voice of his dear Eliza, who is dead two years and more, but comes at his call. It grows from the plot of fresh-dug earth, behind the house at Widdershins Bank, where Jenkyn Scrimgeour rests for all eternity. It is written in words assembled by the chance motions of a blind finger, as it passes over the chaotic lexicon of the demon Azroë. — It is every thing in his own history, and his knowledge, which is dark, and strange, and unspeakable; yet it *is* history — knowledge — Not madness, nor fairy delusion. It touches on many things, which are to Mr Peach as certain and substantial as his own head. As, for example — it contains the freedom of Caspar, from an unjust accusation — The future happiness of Miss Farthingay — The simple thought, that Mr Peach and Clary might within two minutes walk out of the magistrate's house, and return to the Cow and Welshman in _____ton, and then go home.

Most eminently, this *other* thing, whatever it be, includes within it the absolute impossibility, of speaking aloud the words, *This young woman here before you, sir, is an agent of Satan.* — A declaration, which is just as evidently beyond the limits of speech, as, on the day-light side of Mr Peach's mind, it is plainly true.

If we were compelled to reduce his rupture to one line, we would say — That Mr Tho.s Peach stands before the magistrate, with every eye upon him, knowing the *truth*, and knowing also, that he will say, *instead of* the truth — Another thing.

— Sir, he says, I have always known Charlotte an honest and sensible girl. Her character is blameless. — I vouch for it. If she has fallen prey to the specious chivalry of a seducer, it is no worse than many an honest serving girl has done. There is a note sent to her from the villain, declaring his intentions honourable, and promising to do only what was proper. — I might shew it to you, if it were required. That she was foolish enough to credit such declarations, may justly be ascribed to her youth and inexperience, and reflects no worse on her, than that her poor head was turned by a fine gentleman's flattery.

The magistrate removes his spectacles, and taps them against his waistcoat buttons, while assuming a posture of serious contemplation.

— I am obliged to you, Mr Peach. — Your word is sufficient.

Clary turns away from Mr Peach, and bows her head.

— These are heavy matters, says the magistrate, in an unhappy tone. — There will be a scandal, before there is a trial.

— You have done no less than your duty, says Mr Peach.

There are some further mutual assurances and compliments — And the execution of the required formalities. — With them, this interesting scene concludes; and Mr Tho.s Peach, and Miss Clarissa Riddle, go out of the magistrate's house, and into the street, and on through the thoroughfares of the city, and then beyond it, for the last time.

The day is not yet so far advanced, to prevent them pausing only a short while at the inn, where Mr Peach promises he will settle his bill *to-morrow*; whence, despite that promise, they continue onwards, out into the fields and hills, ever farther from the noise and confusion of the town; until, under the last of the late twilight, they arrive, somewhat foot- and saddle-weary, at the house at Widdershins Bank, where so much of our narrative has passed. — And through the whole course of all those miles, and hours, Mr Peach exchanges with Miss Riddle, not a single word.

CHAPTER TWENTY-EIGHT

TWENTY-EIGHT! a substantial number, for a chapter, in a book!

To you, reader — You, who have accompanied us the length and breadth of more than *two dozen* chapters — We must express our sincerest thanks. We fear, we have not always been the most amiable of travelling-companions. But of *your* behaviour, no one shall complain a jot. — Sir — Madam — You are a paragon.

You find us, you observe, in a valedictory humour. — We feel, in our pen, that this twenty-eighth chapter, shall be our *last*. —

Of the whole history of Tho.s Peach, Esq., once of Somersetshire, we have given you, scarce two months! — It is difficult to credit, that such an heap of pages should be necessary, to contain so minuscule a proportion of a man's three score years and ten. — That more might be told, we need hardly say. It cannot be otherwise. — You will never be persuaded, that such a man — and, we dare say, such a woman — if woman she be — Would retire to the country, after this adventure of Bristol, and live out their days in unexceptional peace, without further troubling the historian.

But we must make a stop *somewhere*. — We would not have you tire of our company.

Recall, then, our original view of Thomas Peach, in our chapter the second. Be pleased to remember, he had in that moment just received the news, that the annuity settled on him, under the will of his father, was terminated, by his uncle's malice.

From that event, all the rest has sprung. — For had Mr Peach not suddenly found himself facing the prospect, of being unable to quit his rent, he would not have been compelled to seek out poor Mr Farthingay, at the meeting of the Anti-Lapsarian Society; and, therefore, would not have been invited to interview Miss Riddle, on her way to her intended confinement in the asylum; nor been subsequently required, to attend Mr Farthingay at Grandison Hall; thus, would never have enjoyed his accidental meeting with the poetical Miss Farthingay, and her amanuensis; &c. &c.

We may therefore consider the abrupt and malicious impoverishment of Mr Peach, to be the *beginning* of our tale, and all that followed therefrom, its *middle*; which only now requires us, to make an *end*, in the manner of a nursery-tale — or, if you prefer, of Homer, in his Odyssey — By restoring our hero, to prosperity.*

In order to arrive at this satisfactory conclusion, we must briefly narrate some of the consequences, which follow from the events depicted in the foregoing chapters; and then present you, with one final scene, in the house at Widdershins Bank.

We assure you, there will be no *murder* — no *horror* — no mad prophecy, nor fraudulent enterprize, nor false witness. Our last Act, we dare say, is all mid-summer.

Or — *Nearly* all —

But first, the *consequences*. —

It will easily be imagined, that the shadow of suspicion cast upon Mr Stokesay Stocks, by the discovery of the book with its pages torn out, grew all the darker, after the affidavit of Charlotte Puzzle. A man of rank is protected by his station, from very

---

* We need hardly say, we allude to the opinion of Aristotle, that a story ought to have a beginning, a middle, and an end. — We confess, we are not deeply read in that old Greek gentleman's Poetics. In strictest truth, we are not read in them *at all*, and ought to hesitate in criticism. — But we declare nevertheless, that we think this antient and oft-repeated rule, to be exactly as profound and instructive, as if its author had pronounced, that every day the sun *ought to* have a rising in the east, and a passage across the zenith, and a westerly descent.

many of the indignities and sufferings, which other mortals must endure, but there is no place in the world high enough, nor any name so great, that it is proof against the assault of *scandal*. Fine walls and windows will keep out the rain, and a rich and pleasant estate, may banish the disease of poverty; an heavy purse will fee the doctor and lawyer, to ward against the inconveniences respective to their professions; but there is no remedy against rumour! — for its thousand tongues are as elusive as ubiquitous, and, like the heads of Hydra, only grow in more profusion, if one be lopped off. When a whisper of *murder*, gathers over a man such as Mr Stocks, it cannot manacle him, and commit him to gaol, to await the course of justice, as though he were a mere *Caspar*. It must lay other bonds on him — Invisible, airy — yet strong nevertheless, for they fall upon his *reputation* — And what is rank, but reputation? Indeed, it might be observed, that not only are the great *equally as* exposed to the depredations of scandal, as the low, but that this is the one evil, among all the vicissitudes of mortal life, which the wealthy and mighty suffer *more* acutely than the poor and humble. For there is not much to interest the public, in the affairs of Wat the tinker, or Joseph the horse-boiler — But if rumour should attach itself, to the name of — George the *king*! — Then all the world, will talk of nothing else.

A storm-cloud gathers over the head, of Mr Stokesay Stocks. He may defy it, and curse it, and summon every lawyer in the land, to drive it off — He might just as well direct his threats at a natural cloud, as at this metaphor of ours — You may order the weather to accommodate you, sir, but we think, you had still best not forget your umbrella.

In the circumstances, an engagement is not to be thought of.

Miss Farthingay remains at the house of her female friend. — Mr Stocks repairs to London. He writes her several letters, to proclaim his enduring passion. The sentiments are trite — Lacking grace in the expression — Miss Farthingay has a poet's ear, and finds them displeasing.

435

It is perhaps equally significant, that she will now have the command of her father's estate.

We shall not dispute, which of the two reasons weighs more in the balance of Miss Farthingay's judgment. — It need only be said, that taken together, they are quite heavy enough, to determine her against any renewal of Mr Stocks's proposals. In short — She will not now consent, to become Mrs Stokesay Stocks.

Huzzah! —

When he is not composing his ineffectual letters to Miss Farthingay, Mr Stocks devotes much of his time in London, to soliciting the influence of his relation, Sir Nigylle.

Of this man we do not wish to say much. He was very great, in his day, when his party was *in*, and his faction was *up*. His name is now forgotten — As is the fate of all those, whose fame rests entirely upon the machinations of politics, flattery, and favour. For these are foundations of sand, which slip, and subside, at a whim, or with the changing of the tide. Sir Nigylle built a colossal mansion, upon this base, which, not long after the events of our narrative, swallowed it entire, and him with it. Let him rest for ever, in the obscurity his atchievements merit. — Nevertheless — in the summer of the year 1785, his reach is very long — His finger, in every pudding — His transitory empire of patronage and bribery is at its greatest extent, like that of Rome, under the mad Caesars.

No scandal can therefore be permitted to attach to the name of *Stocks*.

The inquest sits, to examine the deaths of Mr and Mrs Farthingay. After much deliberation, and careful investigation into every circumstance of the tragedy, the coroner records his verdict, of *death by misadventure*.

There has been no murder. — There will be no trial.

The curious and morbid detail, that the deceased were discovered with their mouths crammed full of printed pages, is dismissed, as a fanciful elaboration of the valet's. For the pages cannot be produced. — And the valet himself, confesses he had been drunk, and his recollection may be at fault. The magistrate, who laboured so tirelessly, to discover the events of the fateful night, is by great misfortune taken very ill before the inquest, and compelled to retire to a remote corner of Scotland, for his health — Whence he supplies a written account of his findings, which, curious to say, makes no mention at all of the hastily concealed book, or its torn pages, or the affidavit of Miss Charlotte Puzzle.

The said affidavit is not presented. Mr Ussher, the clerk, appears to have forgotten he ever recorded such a thing. — Perhaps he cannot spare time to consider it, for he has lately come by a sinecure, as Comptroller of Lock-gates, for the county of Worcestershire. — Fortunate man!

Mr Stocks's affair of gallantry, is never alluded to. — Indeed, no such affair can ever have occurred at all, for Mr Stocks makes his sworn declaration, that he passed the whole night asleep in the house of Mr Farthingay. The coroner therefore has no reason to seek out the mysterious Miss Charlotte Puzzle. That no such person exists, would come as a mighty relief to him, had he done so. — But he does not. — It is monstrous to think, that a man such as Mr Stocks would interest himself in a serving-maid, at the time of his intended engagement!

Poor Mr and Mrs Farthingay are adjudged to have choked together, upon the stones of some ripe fruits, which it was their custom to take, with some wine, before bed. A doctor has examined the corpses — And finds this explanation consistent, with the evidence of anatomy.

We shall not enquire too closely after this doctor. He has hopes of preferment — They are realized. — That is the whole of his story.

Thus it is, that no Angel of Truth pursues Mr Thomas Peach, nor indeed Miss Clarissa Riddle, to their place of rustic retirement, and no Sword of Justice is left hanging above the house at Widdershins Bank. The air of that pleasant steep-sided valley remains quite untroubled by allegorical objects of any sort — And is made busy only by those mundane presences, which have filled it every June since the house was raised, and will gather there again every future June, until Britain herself turn to ash and dust; — the glittering flies, and the swallows, and the flotsam shed from the sweet poplar.

Mr Peach had thought, upon his return home, to pare the oeconomy of his household still further, by parting with Jem the stable-lad, whose pittance he regrets he can no longer afford. But the complaints of the boy, upon receiving his notice, are so piteous, that Mr Peach's resolve is cruelly tested. Jem cries that he has no other home to go to — That his family despise him — That he can get no other place, because of the halt on his tongue — That life is a pageant of despair — Human existence, a dream concealing an Abyss — That if he is to be cast on the bosom of the unfeeling world, he will take his own life — For the only thing, which gives beauty and worth to creation, is — Here Jem stammers excessively, and casts several aching glances towards Clary, who observes the performance with a composed smile — Is, says Jem — to be found *here* — *Here*, he says, is comfort — All beyond, is winter snows, and the blasted heath! He swears, he will forgo his wages, and live like the birds, or the forest creatures. — Mr Peach thinks, There is no forest in Somerset-shire. — Jem will drink from the pure crystal that descends from the mountains, and gather the nuts from the trees, and whatever else nature freely supplies. — These hills, thinks Mr Peach, scarcely deserve the name of *mountains*; and the streams hereabouts are somewhat rusty in colour. — Jem does not ask to be paid at all — only, let him not be *expelled from Paradise*! In short — he is quite romantic — For which Mr Peach can only blame himself — Would to Heaven, he thinks, I had never given him that accursed Werter!

Clary begs to suggest a solution. — Might you not sell the horse?

It is a brilliant stroke. It severs two knots, in one blow — For not only does it supply a ready method, of raising a sum of money, sufficient to defray the modest expences of the household, for no little time — But also, it relieves Jem from the consequences of his rash promise, to work without reward; for the labours of a stable-boy can hardly be required, where there is no animal to be stabled. Thus Jem may be allowed to continue his occupation of the hay-loft, at no inconvenience nor cost to Mr Peach.

We might add, that the proposal has a *third* advantage, which is, it accords very well with the inclinations of the horse. —

To be compelled to walk, instead of ride, is certainly some inconvenience. Yet, it also promises some pleasure. — For, after these late checks, and disappointments, and tragic events, Mr Peach's heartiest wish, is to surrender all such schemes as his Bristol adventure, and devote his days, to wandering the country, in the sweet melancholy of contemplation.

It is decided. The horse departs. — Jem remains. His happiness is restored. — Though Mr Peach on occasion seems to hear, as he lies a-bed, some sounds of distress, emanating from the stable-loft, in the night — Curious muffled moans — Poor boy, he thinks — No doubt he is at his *Goethe*.

Thus Mr Peach atchieves an interval of tranquillity, which is, at present, the best he can hope for. The strange and ghastly business of Bristol is left behind entirely, and his peace restored. — *Almost* entirely, we ought to say; for he is one after-noon surprized, at the arrival of a letter, which proves to have been sent from the town.

He is relieved to learn, upon perusal, that the letter threatens no visitor — Demands no reply. It may be folded away and forgotten, as soon as read.

It is written in a large and ornamental hand, upon good paper, which has been scented, after the manner of a *billet-doux*. Except, the scent is not violet-water, nor attar of rose, nor any thing sweetly entrancing. It is something Mr Peach cannot quite fix in his mind. — An odour, almost smokey — somewhat bitter, with an hint of pitch — Not altogether unlike the Scottish *usquebaugh*. There are merely a few lines.

DEAR Monsieur Pêche — or, Pêcheur!

I rejoice, that you are delivered from want, and all your
SUPPLICATIONS for ASSISTANCE, have been
ANSWERED!

   You shall have each thing, that you desire! It is my decree!

   I embrace you eternally! We shall be the FRIENDS OF THE
SOUL.

   Until we meet again —
   Your servante [sic]
   LUCE DENFERT

The lady, thinks Mr Peach, is most decidedly eccentric, even for a
Frenchwoman.

As he puts the letter by, his eye lingers, for an idle and passing
moment, upon that common-place *envoi,* 'until we meet again' —
au revoir, as the French say — And he wonders at Madame
Denfert's allusion to so unlikely an event. — But it does not
signify. Shall we ourselves, reader – we, or you – take note of this
new prophecy of *la Denfert*? Her former visions were not much to
our taste. — But nor, we must confess, were they entirely fantastical. Can it be, that she and our hero are destined to meet once
more? —

Was that a cloud, that for an instant dimmed the summer brilliance of our closing scene?

A passing shadow merely — And already gone. The caprices
of a mad Madame seem as far-off as France herself, from that
secluded retreat where Mr Peach is once more embowered. —
Most particularly so, in blithe and verdant June, when the day
seems all but endless, and the profusion of nature, infinite and
eternal.

— It is very good to hear you so content, says Mrs Peach.

The shutters under the eaves, kept closed through the long
hours of light, lie open, now that all the world is quiet. — We
note in passing, that the room is never troubled by bats, or flies,
or spiders — Nor any other part of the house, by any vermin.

440

The animal creation, it is often said, fears unnatural presences. We once thought it a silly superstition. — As, perhaps, reader, did you.

— I shall always be content, so long as you are with me, says Mr Peach.

The night is clear, and the heavens shed their radiant influence within. — By which we see Mr Peach, lying in his bed, alone.

— But you are sometimes glum, she says. — Even though I am always with you. I think you spoke a mere sentiment.

— We have had our troubles these past several weeks, I confess, my dear. I would not have cared for them at all, except I feared they might drive us from this house.

— Then we must certainly stay.

— I hope we shall. The estate must now belong to Miss Farthingay. She has a good heart, and will not see me thrown onto the parish.

— She won't marry that fine gentleman now, I suppose?

Reader — You may again understand, that we have omitted much of what has already passed between husband and wife. Let us presume Mrs Peach to be fully apprised, of all that has occurred. — All, save certain details, concerning the behaviour and character of Clary the maid, of whom Mr Peach is strangely unwilling to speak, while talking with his wife.

— I rejoice to say she will not. Though she won't lack for other suitors. She is witty, and handsome, and will be very rich.

— Why, then she is the ideal of womanhood. She has every necessary virtue.

— The last-named will certainly raise her very high in many a man's estimation.

— Every thing would be resolved, if only you would marry her yourself. The house would come to you, and you need never fear leaving it.

— But, my dear, Miss Farthingay would not wish to dwell with her husband in a low country cottage, I think.

— Ah! so she is a proud lady. I thought she must have *one* flaw. You speak of her as though she had none.

— I'm sure she has many. Her selection of epithets in poetry is not always just, I have observed. No doubt her other failings will easily be discovered, if I look into it further. No, Liza, I have only ever known one woman to be altogether perfect.

— Gracious! who is it? You can't mean me.

— Indeed I can, and do. You are the best of your sex.

— But, Tom, I am dead, am I not?

Mr Peach sighs a little. It is often difficult for him to know, whether Mrs Peach be merry or serious. — The dead, he supposes, may more readily be both together, or neither, than mortal beings, whose passions are enmeshed in time and circumstance, and must rise and fall with them.

— You are, my dear, says he.

— I think it is a great disadvantage in a wife, to be dead.

— Many married men would not agree.

Mrs Peach laughs.

The mirth of a ghost, is a thing not often imagined, by our fanciful writers of Gothick tales, or in the fire-side stories, passed from grandmother to child. In such tales the ghosts do not laugh, unless it be in an evil or cruel humour. But our narrative is not of this sort. — We are an *historian*. — And we tell you, that Mrs Peach laughs, gaily and free, as she did in life.

— I suppose you must be right, she says. — Poor Miss Farthingay! to be outshone, in your estimation, by a dead woman!

— Miss Farthingay is too sensible to care for my estimation, Liza. Besides, she knows I revere your memory.

— Ah — I recall — She is acquainted with Sophy, I think you once said?

Mr Peach has in fact repeated that part of Miss Farthingay's history, not an hour ago, but he is accustomed to Mrs Peach's uncertainty, over every thing connected with the sequence of time.*

---

* We are reminded of the beautiful prayer of Doctor Donne, in which he begs the lord God to lead us at our last awakening into *that house, where there shall be no ends or beginnings, but an equal eternity.* — We are

— Indeed, my dear. She has had the history of our romance from Sophonisba. I think she was quite moved.

— I should hope she was, if she aspire to write poems. I would not like to imagine any poet a dull blockish soul.

— Nor I. Yet she was ready to wed herself to Mr Stocks.

— There! My opinion of her is now reversed. You have discovered her deepest flaw. You may not marry such a person, after all.

— I am glad to hear you forbid it. I hope you know, Liza, that we speak only in jest? I shall always remain yours.

— Even if I am dead?

— Even so.

— Tom, my dear?

— What is the matter, Liza?

— How does it happen, that — I am not at rest?

Mr Peach settles himself into a more upright posture.

It is not uncommon for Mrs Peach to put this question. The conversation that follows, always conforms to one pattern, for which he now prepares himself.

— I cannot say, my love. I know only so much as you have told me yourself. What do you feel, when you reflect on it?

— Why — I suppose — I am *left behind*, am I not?

— It may be. But, who do you think has left you behind?

— I recall now. — I think, I recall — There was to have been a Judge. I remember as much, Tom. We were to be judged, whether deserving of rest — Or of bliss — There was to be a judgment.

Mr Peach listens silently.

There is a long interval, in which no word is spoken, in the room under the eaves.

— But, says Mrs Peach, the Judge had departed. — Or died. I do not exactly recall — Only, that it was to have happened — But

---

pleased that the ingenious Doctor is these two hundred years at rest, and did not live to hear our tale of Thomas Peach. — We fear his eloquent hopes, might have been a little dashed.

did not. That is the truth of it, I think, Tom? That the Judge has left His seat — Is absent, and will not return. —

— So you have often told me, Liza.

— Have I? I am not quite certain I recall — Yet I think I do —

— Do not trouble yourself, dear. Here you are, and we are content. No more needs answering.

— You were always philosophical.

— It is an easy philosophy, since it requires nothing from us, except to be happy where we are.

— As soon as you say so, my dear, I feel it's true. — All I am, is that I love you.

— And I likewise, says Mr Peach. — Let us then have no more talk of Miss Farthingay and her charms.

Which request Mrs Peach may grant — or she may not — We rather suspect, the latter — But we shall not care. Let the couple — if couple they be, for, we say again, there is not the smallest doubt, that Mr Peach sits *alone* in his bed — Let them converse, on whatever subject they please.

We, however, defy the instruction. — We must have but a little more of Miss Farthingay, whether Mr Peach wills it or no, for she is to appear in the concluding scene of our narrative. — Though whether accompanied by her *charms*, we do not think it proper to decide.

It is the feast-day of the Baptist, at the very height of summer. Some weeks are passed by, since the events of our former chapters, during which nothing has occurred, worthy the note. — But now — once again — Visitors come riding, between the flourishing hedge-rows, into the valley of Widdershins Bank.

We need not be alarmed, at the risk of any disturbance in that tranquil retreat, for the riders are familiar. We dare even say, they are welcome, to Mr Peach at least. — Less so, to Miss Riddle, but we shall not be so nice in respecting *her* opinion. — They are, Caspar, soberly dressed, and Miss Farthingay, in her mourning weeds.

Jem is lying on the stable roof, picking his teeth with a length of straw, and looking up at the azure empyrean — Which not three months past he would have termed, the *sky*, and never thought to study. Now it appears to him an infinite depth, full of mystery, and correspondent to somewhat within his soul. — The approaching riders rouse him from his reverie. When he sees, that they intend to stop at the house, he leaps down in great excitement, for it has been many days, since he last had any opportunity to play the stable-boy.

Miss Farthingay requests to be announced. Jem, who would once have been struck with awe at the sight of a negro gentleman, and an handsome lady all in black, and fallen helpless prey to the catch on his tongue, now makes a courteous greeting — his expressions polished to a smoothness, unthinkable in the days before his acquaintance with the language of Goethe — And promises to fetch the master. He further advises them, that if they go in-doors, they must speak ever so quietly, and tread gently, for the mistress is very sickly in the room above, and can't be disturbed, begging their pardons.

Clary is no where to be seen. — We presume she has instantly absented herself, upon observing the approach of *this* particular company.

Mr Peach is very glad to see them. — Welcomes them within — Is about to call for Clary, to bring some tea, when he likewise remembers, that neither Caspar nor Miss Farthingay ought to encounter his maid — And so once more prepares the tea himself.

He has noted the lady's mourning habit, and renews his sincere condolences upon the tragedy, adding one or two recollections, of the late Mr Farthingay's amiable and convivial nature. He wonders, when the funerary rites are to be conducted? for he wishes to reverence the memory of his friend, and respect the grief of Miss Farthingay, by his attendance.

— Then I am sorry to disappoint you, says Miss Farthingay, for Mama and Papa are already committed to their place of rest. It was this last Sunday. I hope you will not be offended. No invitations were issued. It was my wish to bid them farewell, without pomp and ostentation. The eyes of the world have been too much on the Farthingays.

Mr Peach begs her have no thought of it.

— I shall continue in my black a while longer, she says.

— It is to your credit, madam. The honour done to the memory of such dear relations is much greater, in the shew of private grief, than in funerary ceremonies.

— I agree with you perfectly, Mr Peach. Although I must also confess, I find the colour to my taste.

— You look well in it.

— How gracious you are to offer a compliment, when you must be inwardly appalled at my vanity. To admire my own looks, in mourning! — No, sir, you shall not protest at my teazing. Besides, it is not merely a fondness for black, nor even satisfaction with my appearance, that persuades me in its favour. I have discovered it is very convenient to wear these cloaths, when one is female, and three-and-twenty, and possessed of a fortune.

— I believe I understand you, madam.

— Men are remarkable creatures! — They think nothing of vexing a woman to distraction with their advances, no matter how unwelcome, nor how many times she begs them desist; and yet will become perfectly reserved and polite, merely because she has changed the colour of her dress.

— It is, says Caspar, a kind of *black magic*. — He intones this witticism, for so we must suppose it to be, in a manner so serious, that Mr Peach has not the least inclination to smile, or applaud — Is sensible, indeed, that neither his amusement, nor his applause, is looked for — And thus a silence follows the remark.

— You do not intend to marry, then? he says, at last.

— I do not, she says, unless you, Mr Peach, were to offer yourself, in which case I should certainly consider it. However, your boy reminds me, that your wife is in the house above-stairs, which leads me to think I shall not expect a proposal.

There will be some, who find such raillery unbecoming, in any young lady that aspires to modesty and politeness, and still more

446

so, when the young lady is by outward shew in mourning. But you, our reader! — we think, you have a better understanding of the character of Arabella Farthingay. — Indeed, we do not think you judge, as the common herd judges. — If you did — You would have closed this book, long ago.

Mr Peach declares, she does him too much honour.

— On the contrary, I have not done you enough, and have come here with the very purpose of making good the deficiency. But we shall speak of that in a moment. — Indeed, Mr Peach, I find I have no need of an husband at all. Though I have tormented my brains with the question, I cannot now discover any reason why I should want one. Is that not strange?

Mr Peach merely observes, that he is pleased to see her follow her own free choice, upon a subject so important to her happiness in life.

— I have been considering, she says, whether I might *always* wear black. It might become the fashion. The veil I shall dispense with, in time, but the rest of the habit is as serviceable as cloth of any other colour. I might even say, it is *more* to my preference.

Miss Farthingay concludes the remark with a smiling glance at Caspar. — Which he returns.

Mr Peach thinks he will turn the conversation to other matters.

— May I hope, he says, that in breaking off your engagement, you have also rescinded the opinion you once gave me, that you must *live in prose*? The loves of Clorinda are not to be thought of, I know, in this time of grief, but perhaps the day may come when you will readmit the muse to your company.

— Poor Clorinda! says Miss Farthingay. — She has been sacrificed in the flames, like the Joan of Arc. — Or I should rather say, like many another garlanded *heifer*, for she did not deserve comparison with the Joan. She made but an insipid martyr. I have burned the silly girl and all her musings.

— I am sorry to hear it.

— Do not be. It was the enlargement, not the defeat, of my poetic ambitions, which condemned her. I have determined to take aim at an higher sphere than hers. I shall no longer turn my pen to simpering love-sonnets. It shames me that I ever aspired to it.

— Will you now write in the *epic* stile?

— I cannot think, Mr Peach, why we moderns ought to observe those antient ranks in the empire of poetry. Seventeen hundred years have gone by, since the Aeneid of Vergil. Why must only that verse be allowed the highest dignity, which imitates the epic of Rome? No — I feel, there is another way — And I shall find it, not by improving my Latin, nor copying any other model, but by following my own heart. I am not Clorinda. I am Arabella Farthingay. — It is the latter's sensations and reflexions I must attempt to cast in verse, and not the former's. Else what will I produce, but hollow maxims, and insincere sentiment?

Mr Peach suggests, somewhat diffidently, that it would be a curious thing, if poets were only permitted to write about *themselves.*

— I shall not argue with you, says Miss Farthingay. — I do not pretend to make the laws of poetry. Only I feel I have found what *I* must do, and must not do. You shall see it, when it is done, and then you may be as severe in your judgment as you please.

— I beg your pardon, Miss Farthingay. I must not be such an hypocrite, as to praise you for following your inclinations in the matter of matrimony, only to condemn the same policy, in the higher sphere of Art.

Caspar claps his hands twice, in approval, we must suppose.

— But you, Mr Peach, says Miss Farthingay — What will you do now? I hope you will not surrender to an humble existence in prose, when you recommend the higher course to another.

Mr Peach merely says, that he is content in his modest retirement.

— That will not do, says Miss Farthingay. — Do you not agree, Caspar?

— Most certainly it will not, says Caspar.

— Caspar, Miss Farthingay says, insists that you are a very great man.

— Not great, says Caspar, as the Duke of Marlborough was great, or as Hector was. Mr Peach will not bear the burden of renown, or be commemorated in the epics of the age. But he is great, as an oak is great, or the ocean.

Mr Peach acknowledges the compliment, but dismisses it, as perfectly fanciful.

— Caspar's judgment, says Miss Farthingay, is swayed by the conviction that he owes you his liberty. — Please, Mr Peach — You shall hear me speak — I now forbid your interruption, as is my female right. My own sense of obligation is as deep as his, for you came to me when I was in such distress as I hardly dare recall, and performed the one service I asked of you, which no one else in the world would have undertaken. Had you not exerted yourself at once, without question, on my behalf and his, I have no doubt Caspar would have been lost. — And I myself lost as well, after a different fashion, for the union I had persuaded myself to accept, would certainly have been as destructive to my spirit, as the hangman's noose to his. You may protest all you wish, that you did no such thing, but I remain persuaded that you saved us each from a mortal sentence. — Not a word, Mr Peach. — Caspar says that to owe a man one's life is a fearful obligation, which must be repaid with the utmost haste and diligence. I have therefore decided upon your reward, for my own part at least. You shall have the use of this house in perpetuity, now it is mine to dispose of. There will be no talk of rent. The place is yours. If it is really your only wish, to continue in seclusion here, then you may do so, without fear, for as long as you live.

Mr Peach's emotions compel him to his feet. Tears threaten to spring from his eyes. — He is, perhaps, thinking of his wife.

— Furthermore, says Miss Farthingay, it is my wish that an annuity be bestowed on you, so that you may enjoy the use of this modest corner of my estate, entirely free from want or anxiety.

— Miss Farthingay, says Mr Peach — I know not what to say — I cannot accept.

— You are quite mistaken. You cannot refuse. Your permission is not required, nor sought. I am perfectly decided.

— Whatever service I may have done you, was no more than any friend would have done. I cannot possibly think myself worthy of such generosity.

— Mr Peach. Do you know the source of all my poor Papa's riches, which are now mine? You cannot be ignorant, that he made himself wealthy in the tobacco trade.

The *association of ideas*, is a mysterious law indeed. For, in this moment of happy crisis, the thought which comes immediately to Mr Peach's brain is — *fumous Farthingay!* — And he at last understands the epithet, which Miss Farthingay applied *extempore* to her late father.

— I am to be a woman of ease and leisure, she continues, upon the backs of enslaved men.

Mr Peach cannot help but steal a glance at Caspar — Who sits, quite composed, as he has throughout the greater part of the conversation.

— I do not altogether know what I shall do, to reconcile myself to the odious knowledge. Perhaps I shall teach myself not to think of it, as we do when we demand the sugar for our tea. But at present I find I must make some effort towards acts of generosity. Though they may be no more than a luxurious salve to my conscience, it appears I cannot do without them. It will therefore do you no good at all to protest you are under no obligation to me. I do not care. You shall have your house, and your annuity, whether you deserve them, or no. It is all for my own sake.

Mr Peach can only stammer his gratitude.

— Besides, says Miss Farthingay, Caspar insists that you must be placated.

Mr Peach feels, he ought to be serious — Ought even to resent, being made the object of her teazing — And yet knows, there could be nothing more absurd, in this extraordinary moment, when all his troubles have been banished at a stroke, than a grave answer — A protest — An old man's reproof.

Miss Farthingay continues — He holds fast to some African superstitions, I fear. I have often commanded him to put them out of his head, but my commands are ineffectual, and I have no hopes of beating him into submission. There is nothing to be done with him. You are an ocean, or tree, or some such splendid figure, and require our reverence and awe. He informs me also that the spirits of the dead come at your call, and do your bidding. You are a very Prospero, it seems, and we are not to risk your displeasure, in any thing. Since I have no *dukedom* to offer, I must hope you are satisfied to be made master of *this bare island*.* — Miss Farthingay here gestures, to indicate the house, and its plot of land.

— I must not contradict you, madam, says Mr Peach, placing his hand upon his breast. — Your goodness overwhelms me. If I may be permitted to dispute with the gentleman, I will say, that I am not at all a great man, nor even a good one. — Yet if I am honoured above the rest in any thing, it is that I shall for ever have the privilege of naming Miss Arabella Farthingay my benefactress.

The lady rises. — Then we are sealed, she says. — I have done my first worthy deed. There will be others. — I think I should like to do something for those who raise their voices against the Atlantic trade. I have been contemplating a poem on the plight of the slaves, in blank verse.

Mr Peach agrees that the subject is eminently worthy.

— And I hope, continues Miss Farthingay — I most earnestly hope — That you will consider me not in the character of a bene-factress, despite your noble sentiment — nor as the lady of the manor — But, as your friend. If I am indeed to remain in mourn-ing, and continue a spinster, I shall require some occasional company to enliven my single state. You must visit, when your devotions to Mrs Peach permit any leisure.

---

* The poetical lady here alludes to some phrases of the epilogue spoken by Prospero, in concluding Shakespear's Tempest.

Mr Peach is honoured by the invitation, and asks, whether Miss Farthingay intends to reside at Grandison Hall?

She is all at once serious. — No, no, she says — I have no wish to see it restored, nor to return. What would I do, with a ball-room, and three cooks? Poor Papa was never entirely happy, since he took that house. And though Mama had it all made to her taste, she would always return from a visit to Bath, complaining that the mansions of her friends were more *a la mode*. — Mr Peach — Do you think it is very sinful in me, that I sometimes find myself a little glad they are both at rest? Papa's heart was of late almost broke by the failure of a favourite project of his, while Mama suffered agonies for many years, because her daughter grew into a poet.

— Madam, says Mr Peach, you spoke some moments ago, of the virtue of sincerity. I am entirely convinced that we shew the departed more honour, when we mix our affectionate remembrances with candour, than in eulogies and paeans pronounced without true feeling.

— A very just opinion, says Caspar.

— You are kind, says Miss Farthingay. — It has been a great comfort to me, to learn that poor Papa and Mama met their deaths by accident. You have heard the verdict of the inquest, I hope?

Mr Peach has. — The news-papers are read in all the village taverns.

— That dreadful talk of *murder* — I can scarce think of it, even now.

— It is very natural, says Mr Peach, that you should not wish to.

— Was it not said, that Stokesay was suspected of such a crime? — That he was guilty, because of a *book*? It cannot be. — Stokesay would no more read a novel, than do murder. He has not the wit for either.

— Pray, my lady, says Caspar, do not think of it.

— No — I shall not. Though I have cause to be grateful, that I recalled his lack of wits before succumbing to his proposal.

Caspar makes no further comment.

— You warned me I should not marry him, says Miss Farthingay, addressing Mr Peach still.

— If I presumed to advise, says he, it was only out of a concern for your future prospects.

— Mama and Papa were so delighted at the proposal. I believe it was the first thing to make them happy, in a year.

— I do not doubt their natural fondness for their child would have outweighed their selfish pleasure in the connexion, had you opened your heart to them, and confessed your reluctance.

— Perhaps, says Miss Farthingay, with a sigh. — I shall comfort myself with that hope, when I think of them. Shall I admit to another unworthy thought? I almost think Papa and Mama's accident was their last kindness to me. For I was about to sacrifice my pleasure in life, for their sake, when fate decreed instead that they should surrender theirs, so I might be free.

— It cannot be unworthy, says Mr Peach, to be sincerely thankful, for any blessing your parents have bequeathed.

— How *implacably* generous you are. I think I might confess to any wicked thought at all, and you would instantly persuade me it was perfectly virtuous. Do you calm your own conscience so easily, Mr Peach? — But forgive me — your conscience needs no soothing, I know. You live here, in this delightful retirement — Far from temptation, strife, and evil. — You have done nothing you regret, nor have any thoughts you wish away. You dwell in the Arcadia, dreamt of by Horace, in his odes and epistles.

Caspar intones — *Et in Arcadia ego.*

— Very true, says Miss Farthingay. — I am in your paradise, and ought to leave it. It was the woman made Adam fall. I would not have the like sin laid to my account. — Farewell, dear sir.

With further assurances of friendship on her side, and gratitude on his, Miss Farthingay takes her leave of Mr Peach.

And thus our scene is concluded — and our chapter — And, our book also.

For, by the lady's generous act, Mr Peach is secure for ever in possession of the house, where he may commune with his beloved Eliza — And is, moreover, assured of a comfortable living, sufficient to banish every mundane trouble from his door. Miss Farthingay has served us as *dea ex machina*, descending on our stage, to dissolve every obstruction, that stands in the way of an happy end. In the language of Madame Denfert, our hero indeed appears to be *delivered from want* —

But had we not resolved, to cast the deranged Frenchwoman from our thoughts? — *Vade retro, Satana!* —

— Pray, sir, says Caspar. — A word in private.

Forgive us, reader. — It seems we are not quite finished with you. —

The lady has stepped out, and is exchanging a polite word or two with Jem, while the lad fumbles over the horses.

Caspar and Mr Peach remain a moment longer within.

— Sir, says Caspar, in a grave murmur — we would assign his part to the *basso* voice, and mark it *mezzo-piano* — Sir, says he, on my life I swear, I will never speak your secret aloud. — And he confirms this unexpected declaration, by the gesture of sliding his finger across his mouth.

— I do not understand you, says Mr Peach, with some impatience. — You have mistaken me entirely. I am not what you think me. I am no magician, nor command spirits. I am only Thomas Peach, Esquire, of no importance, nor significance, to any person in all the world. I shall be grateful to you, sir, if you will cease to imagine otherwise, and still more so, for refraining from any further hints of your erroneous opinion.

Caspar is silent for several breaths. — And then assumes an oratorical pose.

— I did not attend the inquest, he says. — My face was not welcome. They did not wish to remember, that such a man as I had ever been. But, because I was not there, I had no part in all their forgetting. They have not washed out the truth from my mind. I remember, how the man of law found that book, whose pages had been ripped away, and forced down the old master and mistress's throats. Now, the men will all swear, There was no book, and no pages. Your spell is complete, great sir, and has done its work, and your secret is gone clean from every brain but mine. Therefore I must tell you, and swear it on my three souls, that I will say no word of it again; for otherwise you may send your vengeful spirit to stop my mouth. Here is my promise. It cannot be broken.

Mr Peach requires several seconds of astonished silence, before he is confident of having penetrated the meaning of this extraordinary speech.

— Am I to understand, sir, that you hold *me* responsible, for the deaths of my old friend Mr Farthingay, and his wife?

— I am no body, and hold no opinion at all. I know only these two things, and this is the last I shall speak of either. The first of them, I have mentioned in your presence before. It is, that I saw the spirit who serves you, with these very eyes. — Caspar indicates the orbs in question, by directing two fingers of his right hand towards his face.

Once more, reader, we bid you remember, that momentary exchange of looks, recorded in our sixteenth, between Caspar by the road, and Clary, shadowed and silent, within the door of the house.

— The other thing I know, Caspar continues, which goes also into oblivion, the instant I walk out of your house, is that I learned from which book the pages were torn, that ended the lives of the old master and mistress.

— You are perfectly mysterious, sir, says Mr Peach, in some exasperation at this strange performance. — What possible concern is it of yours, or mine, or any body's, whether it was one book or another?

— No concern at all, says Caspar. — Within this next minute it will be eternally forgotten, that the book was the third volume of the Clarissa, by Master Samuel Richardson.

In the interval that follows, Caspar once more makes the gesture across his mouth, to figure the sealing of his lips, and then, with a bow, turns, and leaves the house.

The visitors ride away.

Mr Peach stands, quite still —

By mere coincidence, he is by the window, in the end-room, exactly as we first saw him.

We wondered then — WHO IS THOMAS PEACH? Reader — You have your answer – Or, part of it. Should you desire the rest, our necromantic pen may perhaps oblige you, at some future date. — Though we invite you to reflect, whether the desire be altogether wise.

Quickly now — we hear Clary's step —

For pity's sake, let us be gone before the maid returns! —

You too must follow us away, reader — you, our old companion and friend. — For behold! There is *no more to read* —